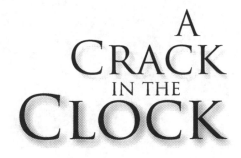

A
CRACK
IN THE
CLOCK

A CRACK IN THE CLOCK

THREE GIRLS, THREE WATCHES, AND THE ADVENTURE OF A LIFETIME

BRITTANY HARRIS
AND
MORGAN PAIRO

authorHOUSE®

AuthorHouse™
1663 Liberty Drive
Bloomington, IN 47403
www.authorhouse.com
Phone: 1-800-839-8640

Published by AuthorHouse   01/18/2013

ISBN: 978-1-4817-0522-6 (sc)
ISBN: 978-1-4817-0523-3 (e)

Library of Congress Control Number: 2013900288

"**Y**OAKE!" came Kyoki's cheerful voice, rousing the other from her sleep.

"Mmm." Yoake moaned, turning over.

"Come on, Yoake, it's time to get up."

"I don't care."

"You have to get up, or else you'll be late for your first day."

Yoake looked maliciously at the purple-haired third year who stood over her with a big grin on her face. "Fine." The second year transfer groaned getting out of bed. Her legs felt heavy and her head was reeling.

"So, were you having a good dream?" Kyoki asked as Yoake got dressed.

"No."

"Really? You were whispering in your sleep."

"Huh?" Yoake looked at her senpai confusedly from under her shirt. "I've never heard that before."

"Oh . . . well you were saying some really weird stuff . . . and people call me crazy." Kyoki said, smiling. "Anyway, Hana is waiting for us, so you need to hurry up!"

"I'm coming, I'm coming." Yoake said. "Go tell her that I'm still changing and I'm almost done. Okay?"

"Right." With that, Kyoki bounded out of the room.

"*She's insane.*" Yoake sighed as she continued pulling on her uniform. When she finally finished, she noticed something on her pillow. It was a pocket watch, golden in color, but obviously not made of gold. Instead, it was a darker, steam age, rustic gold. The cover was detailed with waves around the edge that had rungs stretching out from the center with little outward-pointed spades in between each of them. As a finishing touch, someone had placed a golden chain through the top, almost like the string of a necklace. "What is this?" She said as she picked it up and examined it. On the back was the word 'Aurora' surrounded by what looked like streams of light. "That's weird, is there an Aurora at this school? I'd better tell her she lost her watch." With that, she put the little watch around her neck, grabbed her school bag, and headed out.

Outside the girls' dorm, Hana and Kyoki were waiting for her. "There you are." Hana said, rolling her eyes.

"Yeah sorry, I slept in." Yoake apologized, scratching the back of her head in embarrassment.

"Cool watch." Kyoki commented.

"Oh, it's not mine. There's a name on the back so I'm going to give it back to its owner." She flipped it over and showed it to them.

"'Aurora?'" Hana wondered.

"Pretty." Kyoki said.

"There's no Aurora here."

"Are you sure?" Yoake asked.

"Positive."

"Well it has to belong to someone, so I'll just put it in the lost and found."

"Fine. Now come on, we don't want to be late."

"Right." With that the three of them headed to class. But Yoake couldn't forget about the watch. The name on the back obviously meant something, but she couldn't figure out what.

As the girls walked on, Kyoki suddenly stopped. "Do you guys feel something weird?" she asked.

"No," Hana answered, "What do you mean?"

"Nothing, I guess. It just felt like someone was watching us . . ."

"It's just your imagination." Hana said, grabbing Kyoki's arm and dragging her off, "Damn it! Between Yoake getting up late and you stopping for every chilly feeling, we'll never get to school. Now let's GO!" As Kyoki was dragged off, she took one last look behind her but saw nothing except a few old trash cans and an alley.

Just as the girls rounded the corner at the end of the block, a boy who looked about seventeen let out a deep sigh of relief. "Holy crap," he said to himself, "They almost saw me. If I get caught now, he'll have my head." He stood up quickly, attempted to smooth out his scruffy black hair, and dusted off his uniform.

"I better get going," he muttered, "If I'm late . . ." He shuddered; he really didn't want to think about that scenario, and walked to school.

Ding, ding, ding went the school bell as Yoake walked into the classroom. "Thank goodness. I made it on time." she sighed.

"I assume you are our new student." the teacher said from behind the desk at the front of the room.

"Huh? Uh yes." Yoake blushed, looking over at her teacher. He was young, not much more than 25, with blond hair pulled into a low ponytail that hung halfway down his back. Two black eyes stared at her with intrigue from behind clear, thin-framed glasses.

"Well, are you going to take your seat or just stand there staring?"

"Oh yes, sorry, sir."

"Don't apologize, just go sit down." he scoffed as Yoake sat in the only empty desk at the very front of the class.

Well that was uncomfortable. she thought.

"Alright class, quiet down so I can take attendance," he called, then immediatly began listing the names of each student in the class to be answered with a call of 'here', 'present', or just a silent raised hand. "Yoake Hikari."

"Here." Yoake answered.

"Yami Kurai."

Silence. "Yami Kurai." Again there was no answer. "Why that little . . ." Yoake heard him hiss under his breath. "Alright, that's every—"

"Sorry I'm late." said a shaggy-haired boy—who Yoake assumed was Yami—as he walked in.

"It's about time." the teacher said. "Unfortunately, there are no more desks for you to sit in, so you'll have to stand for today."

"Yes, sir." the boy said sadly as he moved to stand against the back wall, the teacher watching him the whole time, clearly annoyed.

"Alright, now that we have everyone, let me introduce myself." the teacher announced. "My name is Mr. Satoru, and I am your new teacher." The rest of class proceeded normally but Yoake couldn't shake the strange feeling in the pit of her stomach. Something about Yami seemed off. Sure lots of students came late and teachers often got annoyed with them, but something about the way he had looked at Mr. Satoru with a combination of apologetic sadness and outright fear concerned her. Students shouldn't be afraid of their teachers and on top of that Mr. Satoru was new, what could he have possibly done to warrant fear? Yoake shook her head; she had to be imagining things.

"No, Miss Hikari?" Mr. Satoru said, making the girl jump. The whole class was staring at her and she could feel heat rising in her cheeks.

"If you think I'm wrong," Mr. Satoru continued, "feel free to come up here and correct me." He pointed to the board where he had been explaining the principles of factoring to the class.

"No I—uh-um-I'm sorry, sir," Yoake said, hanging her head. Mr. Satoru simply grunted and turned back to the board.

"Kindly refrain from daydreaming in my class, Miss Hikari." Yoake nodded and spent the remainder of class trying her best to pay attention.

Fifteen minutes later the lunch bell rang, Yoake nearly jumping out of her seat in her haste to get to the cafeteria. Just as she left the room, she heard Mr. Satoru call Yami to his desk, but left too fast to hear anything else.

Once she reached the lunch room, Yoake quickly found Kyoki and Hana and sat down, pulling out her lunch.

"So how was class?" Hana asked, biting into her sandwich.

"Fine I guess," Yoake answered, "the new teacher is a bit scary though."

"So you guys got the new one?" Kyoki asked, "I heard some second years say he's really cute, is that true?"

Yoake stared, confused, at her friend and shook her head. "I don't see it," she said, "he seems kind of touchy. He got really ticked off at a student who came in late."

"Who's touchy?" the sudden voice from behind nearly made Yoake jump. Quickly, she turned around, coming face to face with Mr. Satoru.

"I do hope you won't be daydreaming in my class anymore, Miss Hikari," he continued, staring down at her. Yoake shook her head furiously as Mr. Satoru simply chuckled, "Have a nice lunch, girls." With that, he walked off.

"Okay," Hana said. "That's creepy."

"I know." Yoake nodded. "I hope he doesn't make a habit of sneaking up on people."

"That would give you a heart attack." Kyoki giggled at an annoyed Yoake.

After school, Yoake strode back to the dorm alone. She had fallen asleep during her afternoon class so had to stay behind for detention. As she walked, she swore she could feel someone behind her, but every time she turned around, no one was there. Frightened by her own paranoia, she ducked into a nearby alley to sit down, take a few deep breaths, and calm herself.

Suddenly, a voice sounded from above her. "Finally," it hissed, "I very well couldn't do this in the middle of the street; all those other pathetic humans would only get in the way." Yoake looked up to see a humanoid creature jump down from the roof of the building she was leaning against, landing directly in front of her.

"Who—?" she started, but the pale, black eyed creature placed a hand on her cheek, slowly drawing his black claws down her jaw while she stared back at him, wide eyed.

"Shh . . ." he said, "I just came to get something from you." His hand trailed down her neck, to her shoulders, and still lower.

Yoake suddenly screamed, punching him and jumping away. "Don't touch me!" she yelled. The midnight haired creature just giggled, barely phased by the blow to his cheek. Just then Yoake noticed the tail swishing back and forth behind him. "Who are you?!" she screamed, "What do you want?"

The monster laughed, slowly walking toward her. "Me?" he asked, "my name is irrelevant but if you must call me something, the name 'Yeldi' works. As for your second inquiry, it's not what I want, it's what my master wants, namely that lovely pocket watch you've got on your neck." Suddenly, he lashed out, reaching for Yoake's neck. She screamed and tried to duck but the wall behind her prevented it. Yeldi's fingers wrapped around the watch and he pulled, trying to break the chain.

"No!" Yoake yelled, pulling the watch back toward her, "I won't let you have it!" Just then, a light burst from the watch as it fell open, all colors of the rainbow pouring from the little piece. "What the—?" Yoake said as the colors began to wrap around her. Yeldi jumped back, away from the light, trying to shield his eyes as Yoake rose into the air, the colors swirling and surrounding her. She saw the light melt with her skin, hair, clothes, her whole body. Suddenly, her uniform skirt puffed outward, layers of colored lace appearing from nowhere, and shortened. Her top did the same, plate armor forming on the shoulders and sides. Gloves appeared on her hands, white like the glowing light around her, with small jewels circling the wrists. Her hair grew longer, curls and waves forming as a jeweled circlet appeared on her forehead. On her feet, her school shoes grew into knee high dark purple boots. The watch melted into the plate armor on her chest, fusing with the metal and leaving only the clock face visible. As a finishing touch, a shining silver bow appeared in her hand along with a quiver full of bright arrows.

She came to the ground, a new fire burning in her eyes as she stared at Yeldi. "I don't know what you and your 'master' want with my watch, but I won't let you have it!" She pulled one of the arrows from her back, a bright yellow one, and strung her bow. "Now get out of here. AURORA BEAM!" The arrow flew straight at Yeldi, creating an enourmous explosion.

The humanoid easily jumped out of the way of the blast and landed on the roof he had jumped from, growling at Yoake, "So you woke up, did you? Well, no matter, I'm still gonna take that watch from you!" He charged at her, so fast she didn't have time to draw another arrow. By instinct, she used the sharpened edge of the bow to block and swipe at him. Bringing her arm across the front of her body, she whipped it back and a blast of light shot out of the bow that hit him square in the chest, throwing him against the wall. He fell to the ground, panting, and looked up at her in fury. "Alright. Now I'm really mad." Once again, he charged and, fast as lightening, he threw punch after kick after claw, but she was equally as fast, dodging, blocking, and countering his attacks.

"This has gone on long enough." Yoake said, using her bow to push him back a couple meters. "I think it's time to end it." Drawing a blue arrow and stringing it she cried, "AURORA TYPHOON!" She shot the arrow and, as it travelled, it spun like a football before breaking up into a dozen other arrows of the same size that spiraled toward Yeldi.

He was able to jump out of the way just in time to avoid the barrage, but not without receiving a serious burn from one of the arrows as he barely dodged the attack. "This isn't over!" Yeldi shouted from his landing point on the same roof he had jumped down from twice before, "You may have awoken but my master *will* have that watch!" With that, he turned and raced away, clutching his wounded arm.

"Get back here!" Yoake yelled, trying to run after him, but the power suddenly left her, the watch falling closed against her chest and her uniform returning to normal. "The hell . . . ?" she panted. Slowly, she stood, still panting, and made her way toward the dorm.

When she got back, she was immediately pounced on by Kyoki. "Where ya been?" she asked.

"Uh . . ." she tried to think of an answer, telling Kyoki straight out would make her sound insane. "I took a new way back. I thought maybe it would be faster but it wasn't."

"Oh, okay." Kyoki smiled and let go of Yoake.

"How was detention?" asked Hana, who was on her bed reading.

"It was detention."

"Hmm, true."

Yoake sat down on her bed, holding the pocket watch up to inspect it. The thing seemed like a normal device but after what had just happened . . . She shook her head. This whole day was just too weird. Kicking off her shoes, Yoake lay down and stared at the ceiling.

"So I'm guessing you didn't find the owner of that watch?" Hana said, not looking up from her book. Yoake shook her head.

"Well then," Kyoki said, "finders keepers. It's nice; just hang on to it. I'm going to take a shower. I'll be right back." With that, Kyoki grabbed her bag and walked down the hall. Yoake ignored her friend, and continued her staring contest with the ceiling. A yawn escaped her as she glanced at the time on her watch. It was already getting late. Slowly, she pushed herself off the bed and changed into her night clothes.

"Good night," she called to Hana, who still hadn't put her book down.

"Night," Hana replied.

The next morning Yaoke woke up to the light shining on her eyes. Sitting up and stretching, she said, "Man that was a weird dream."

"Must've been." Hana said as she pushed off her covers. "You were talking in your sleep again."

"Yeah." Kyoki added. "And you were tossing and turning and making the damnedest faces."

"Oh sorry, did it keep you guys up?" Yoake asked sheepishly.

"Nah, we just went to bed later than you."

"You should probably get some help to stop that." Hana suggested. "Now hurry up and get dressed so we aren't late again."

"Okay, okay. I'm coming." Yoake said as she got out of her bed. *'It really must have been just a dream. Huh, so there's no watch or Yeldi, or powers.'* But as she thought, she looked down at her bedside table and saw the little watch. *'Or not.'*

Just then, Yoake turned as Kyoki yelped happily, "Look what I found!" she said, holding up a pocket watch. It was the same size as Yoake's, but it was black instead of gold. There was no necklace chain, just one designed to hold the watch onto a belt loop or pant waist. The front panel was cut out in bits, trapezoid-like holes over each of the twelve Roman numerals and one large one in the center so the gears were visible. On the back was another large, glass filled hole and around that was a swirling pattern, almost like spirits traveling around the circular surface. Finally instead of 'aurora,' the word 'Faust' was carved into the back in jagged, strange letters.

"Cool," Kyoki said as she read it, "I love that story. I'm totally keeping this; screw the original owner."

Hana rolled her eyes at Kyoki's overly excited state and proceeded to pack her bag. "If I wasn't here," she said with a sigh, "I don't think you two would ever make it to school."

Yoake giggled. "You're probably right."

Morning lessons quickly came and went and soon Yoake found herself gathering her books and heading out of the classroom. However before she could leave, she heard Mr. Satoru's velvety voice say, "That's an interesting necklace you've got there."

Yoake froze in her tracks and, turning around reluctantly with a forced smile, said, "Oh thank you, sir."

"Where did you get it?" he asked as he sipped his coffee.

'What does he want now?' Yoake thought but continued to smile and answered, "Oh it was a gift."

"Who from?"

"Uh . . . my mom, for my birthday."

"May I see it?"

"I'd rather you didn't. See it's really special to me and I don't like letting other people handle it, cause they might handle it wrong or too rough and break it, and I have to get to lunch so—"

"I understand. I will see you after lunch, Miss Hikari."

"Yes, sir. Uh good bye." With that Yoake hurried out of the classroom as fast as she could, with Mr. Satoru watching her every step.

Finally she was able to sit down beside Kyoki and Hana at the lunch table. "Where've you been?" Kyoki asked.

"Mr Satoru stopped me and asked about my watch." Yoake answered.

"What did he want?" Hana asked, suspicious.

"Oh nothing. He just asked where I got it and what not." Yoake said. "But I told him that I got it from my mom."

"You lied?"

"Well if I had told him that I found it on my pillow yesterday morning he might have thought I stole it from someone."

"Hmm, good point."

"I think you have a crush on your teacher." Kyoki teased.

"I do not!" Yoake shouted, her cheeks turning bright red.

"So why are you blushing?"

"Well, because he creeps me out! Why would I have a crush on a total creep?"

"Okay, whatever you say, Juliet."

"Kyo—"

"Would you two knock it off." Hana interrupted.

"She started it." Yoake murmured.

"Well I'm finishing it."

Kyoki huffed in disappointment. "Party pooper."

Yoake sighed in relief as she took out her lunch. Before she started eating, something caught her eye. Across the cafeteria, she could see Yami sitting alone. "I'll be right back," she said, standing. She walked over to where the boy was seated and sat down.

"Hi," she greeted cheerfully causing Yami to nearly jump out of his seat. "My name's Yoake Hikari. I'm in your class with Mr. Satoru."

"Uh-h-hi, I'm Yami Kurai." he said, looking down. He seemed nervous about having Yoake near him and his eyes kept glancing form side to side as if he was looking for someone.

"Why are you here all alone?" Yoake asked.

Yami shrugged. "I just don't want to disturb anyone." he said quietly.

Yoake shook her head and grabbed his hand. "Sitting alone just won't do," she laughed, "come on. You can sit with me and my friends."

Yami blinked, clearly confused. "I uh . . . okay." he stammered and grabbed his food, following Yoake back to her seat. "Guys," Yoake said as soon as they made it back, "This is Yami; he's in Mr. Satoru's class with me." Kyoki and Hana waved cheerfully to Yami who sat down, albeit nervously.

"Hi." Kyoki greeted.

"Uh, hi."

"Yami, these are my friends." Yoake introduced. "The crazy looking one is Kyoki—" Kyoki stuck her tounge out at Yoake for calling her crazy, "and the calm one is Hana."

"Th-those are nice names." Yami said nervously.

"Thanks." Kyoki said. "Yours isn't too bad either."

"Th-thank you."

"Why are you so nervous?" Yoake giggled.

"Uh . . . I'm not that good at talking to girls."

"It's okay, you're with friends here."

"Huh?" Yami looked at Yoake who had a big smile on her face and a strange twinkle in her eye that he had never seen before. Looking across the table he saw that, although they didn't have the same smiles as Yoake, Hana's and Kyoki's eyes were filled with the same sparkle as their friend. "Th-thanks, you guys. That makes me feel a little better."

"Glad to help," Yoake said. "You can sit with us from now on if you want."

Yami looked up at her and a smile slowly crossed his face. "I'd like that."

The rest of lunch proceeded without any major incidents and after a quick farewell to Hana and Kyoki, Yoake and Yami walked back to class. As soon as they walked through the door, Yami froze. Yoake turned to see what was wrong and out of the corner of her eye, she thought she saw Mr. Satoru staring at Yami. However, when she turned to face her teacher, he was looking at his desk, grading the quizzes they had taken before lunch. She shrugged, pulled Yami to his desk, and sat down.

That night, the girls sat in their dorm, doing homework and talking. Suddenly, Kyoki threw her textbook across the room, "This is impossible!" she yelled, glaring daggers at the discarded calculus book.

"What's wrong now?" Hana asked, only half listening to her frustrated friend.

"That nonsense is impossible!" Kyoki answered, "I don't know how that jerk of a teacher expects us to do it when he spends half of class talking about his grandchildren!" Hana rolled her eyes as Kyoki continued to rant about the evils of all mathematics, Yoake looking up from her reading assignment just in time to deflect a pencil aimed at her head.

"Hey!" she yelped, "Watch where you throw things!" Kyoki turned and immediately apologized. Soon they were done with their assignments, or in the case of Kyoki, done cursing them to the lowest circles of hell, and went to sleep.

Hana, as usual, was the first to wake up the next morning. Rolling over, she stretched and felt her hand knock against something. Quickly, she leaned over and looked over the side of her bed to see where whatever it was had landed. To her utter surprise, a bronze pocket watch stared back at her. Slowly, she picked it up and inspected it. The metal had a dull shine to it, the front cover was cut with circular flower-like designs, leaving the numbers visible through the metal. Curious, she flipped it over and searched it, half expecting to find a word carved into it. Soon she found it, the word *Roseus* carved onto the back in a very floral print. "Well, I'll be damned . . ." she muttered, pulling the bronze necklace chain over her head.

Just then, Kyoki stirred and rolled over. "Morning," she said, rubbing her eyes.

"Morning," Hana answered. Suddenly, Kyoki ran over to Hana's bed, nearly tripping as he foot got caught in her own sheets.

She fell to the ground with a loud thump that instantly woke Yoake. "What's going on?" she asked.

"Nothing . . ." Kyoki answered, rubbing the side of her head, "but . . ." she turned to stare at Hana again, "Miss Grumpy-gills over here just found her own mystery watch!"

Yoake immediately jumped out of bed and dashed over to Hana, Kyoki right behind her. Hana tried to scoot away from the two with little success.

"So yours says *Roseus*." Kyoki said, pulling that watch up and flipping it.

"Yes, now let go! You're hurting my neck!" Hana yelped, trying to adjust the chain so she could breathe.

"I think it's pretty" Yoake said, looking over Kyoki's shoulder.

"Yeah I guess so," Kyoki said, dropping the watch, "but mine is so much more badass!" She held up her own pocket watch proudly.

Hana sighed "Next thing you know, the whole school is going to have pocket watches. Come on, we better get to class."

The day started normally, but Mr. Satoru didn't say anything to her. When the bell for lunch rang, Yoake gathered her things and waited for Yami but he was caught by Mr. Satoru. "It's good that you're making friends." he said.

"Yes, sir. Thank you." Yami said nervously, as if waiting to be reprimanded.

"I hope these new companions won't stop you from completing your . . . other duties."

Yami shook his head furiously, "No, sir, of course not."

"Good. Now go on, there's someone waiting for you."

The two looked out to the hallway where Yoake was waiting. She saw them looking and waved, to receive a sheepish wave back from Yami. Mr. Satoru smiled at her and nudged Yami toward the door, "Have a nice lunch, children," he said as the door closed behind them.

As they walked to the lunch room, Yoake couldn't help thinking about what she had overheard. What did Mr. Satoru mean 'other duties?' Was Yami behind on homework? No, that couldn't be it, they had only begun their friendship yesterday. Maybe Yami had some kind of part time job and Mr. Satoru didn't want him getting fired. *Well,* Yoake thought, *I guess it's nice that Mr. Satoru is looking out for him.*

"So I saw Mr. Satoru talking to you." Yoake said, making Yami cringe. "I think it's great that he's looking out for you."

"Huh? Uh . . . yeah." Yami responded holding his books closer to his chest. Yoake laughed at his nervousness, confusing him. "What did I say?"

"Oh . . . nothing." Yoake giggled. "I just think it's funny that we're the same age, yet I find you so adorable."

"Adorable?" Yami looked at her confusedly.

"Yeah, adorable." She smiled wider at the flustered boy. "Now come on, the others will be waiting for us."

"Uh . . . yeah."

Yami trailed behind Yoake into the cafeteria, smiling nervously to Hana and Kyoki as he sat down. It was then that he noticed Hana's new watch. "That's, um, that's very pretty . . ." he said, turning a slight shade of pink.

"Oh thanks," Hana said, glancing down at the watch hanging from her neck.

"Come on," Kyoki groaned, rolling her eyes, "there's no way that flowery trinket is as good as mine!" She held her own watch up to Yami who sputtered in reply.

"My watch is much cooler, right?" Kyoki asked, waving it in Yami's face.

"Um-I-uh—" he said as he waved his hands frantically. Just then, Yoake put her arm around Yami, pulling him away from Kyoki.

"Stop scaring him!" she chided, "Eat your lunch." Kyoki huffed but complied, biting into her sandwich.

"Don't worry," Yoake continued, turning to Yami, "She's really harmless; no need to be scared." Yami nodded and smiled slightly.

"My God, you're adorable!" Yoake said, nearly crushing Yami in a hug.

After lunch the two walked back to class and sat down. Yoake nearly dozed off during afternoon lessons; chemistry was *not* her favorite subject. When the final bell rang, Yoake stood, collected her things, and waited by the door for Yami. Sadly, he was stopped by Mr. Satoru.

"Go on ahead," Yami called to Yoake, "I'll see you tomorrow."

"Are you sure?" Yoake asked, "I could wait for you if you want." Yami shook his head.

"No, it's O.K., just go."

"Alright, if you're sure," Yoake said, nodding slowly, and left. She caught up with Kyoki and Hana outside and the three walked back toward their dorm together. As they made their way back, they decided to stop in a park to do their homework outside. The day was comfortable and they hadn't had the chance to sit outside together in a long time. Soon they were laying in the grass happily, all thoughts of homework forgotten until suddenly a voice called to them, "Long time no see."

Yoake turned and sat up, coming face to face with Yeldi who sat atop the flagpole about twenty feet away. She glared at him as he jumped down and slowly walked over to the girls.

"Who is that?" Hana asked, staring at Yeldi.

Yoake looked from the creature walking toward them to her friends and back again. "Get out of here!" she said, trying to push the other two girls away, "It's not safe."

"And leave you alone with what ever the hell that is?" Kyoki said, "I don't think so."

"No, you don't understand I—" Yoake tried to explain but Yeldi was getting closer. She watched in horror as he raised his hand, a green and blue swirling sphere appearing just above his palm. Smirking, the monster sent the sphere toward Kyoki and Hana.

"No!" Yoake yelled. Quickly, she opened her pocket watch, the lights immediately coating her body just as they had the day before. Kyoki and Hana starred in a mix of wonder and horror as their friend transformed. When the light died down, a very changed Yoake stood before them, bow poised and ready. Instantly, she pulled a purple arrow from her quiver and let it loose. The arrow collided with Yeldi's sphere in a huge explosion that sent all four of them flying backwards. The girls landed with a hard thump, Yoake recovering first. Just as she was about to load another arrow, Kyoki grabbed onto her arm.

"I don't know what's going on," she said, "but I want to help if I can. I'm not letting you fight that thing alone, got it?" Yoake looked at her friend, about to say that the best thing for Kyoki and Hana to do would be to run, but suddenly an idea hit her.

"Open your pocket watch," she said, making Kyoki raise one eyebrow quizzically, "It worked for me so just try!"

Still slightly skeptical, Kyoki nodded and opened the watch. What happened next removed all traces of skepticism from her mind.

Black light poured from her open watch, lifting her into the air. Skull-like clouds swirled around her as her skirt shortened, leaving a black and red pleated one in it's place. A black, laced corset with red ribbon holding the back together tied itself around her. Shoulder guards appeared from the swirling clouds around her, with red straps crossing her chest to hold them up. Thigh high black and red striped stockings flew up her leg, metal plated combat boots appearing on her feet. Studded fingerless gloves encased her hands as the clouds melted into her skin. Her hair was run through with red streaks, growing longer and longer until it rested next to her tailbone in one ponytail off to one side of her head. A black circlet similar to Yoake's appeared on her forehead and as the clouds began to dissipate, her weapon appeared. A long scythe with an obsidian blade appeared in her hand, the top adorned with three tassels, each with a silver skull on the end. Her pocket watch melted into her headband, leaving only the front visible. As she landed, she swung the scythe as if to test it.

"Holy crap!" Kyoki yelped happily, "This is sweet! I like! I like!"

Hana stood up and said, "Okay, now it's my turn." She opened her watch and a stream of flowers and pink light poured, surrounding her and lifting her in the air. Her skirt shortened just like the others, and her hair also lengthened, both turning pink. A thick, green, braided belt circled her waist as pink leg warmers and tennis shoes appeared on her legs. Long pink gloves covered her arms and hands, brown and green lace on the ends. Her own watch fused with her right glove, just above her hand. On her neck, a floral choker appeared along with two leaf shaped earrings on each ear. Her own circlet then flowed from the stream of pink still surrounding her, a line of flowers running around it. As a finishing touch, two long, thin swords appeared in her hands, each with a green hilt and strong pink blade. She landed next to Yoake and instantly began looking herself over, "This is a little much, don't you think?"

"I think you look cute," Kyoki said, "but we have bigger problems right now!" She pointed to Yeldi who had by now recovered from the blast and was glaring at them.

"So what?" he snapped, "I'll just take all three!"

"Think again!" Kyoki yelled, "SOUL STORM!" She swung her scythe toward Yeldi as hundreds of ghosts issued from the blade, all flying at lightning speed toward the monster. He tried to jump away but suddenly Kyoki appeared from the center of the cloud of spirits.

"Got'cha!" she laughed, smirking. Quickly, she slashed at him, but he twisted, kicking her away before she could slice him in half but not before his shirt was cut clean through.

"My turn," Hana said, swirling her swords, "Let's see what these babies can do!" She launched toward Yeldi as he fell, swinging her left sword and slashing his tail. The monster screamed in pain and tried to swipe at her. Hana blocked with her right blade and jumped out of the way. Suddenly, he screamed again as another one of Yoake's arrows hit him square in the chest, sending him crashing into a tree trunk. Slowly, shakily, he stood and glared at the three girls surrounding him.

"Alright, you ass," Kyoki hissed, pointing her scythe at Yeldi, "start talking." Yeldi's eyes darted back and forth between the three, and he smirked. "What's so funny?" Kyoki demanded.

"Calm down." Yoake said.

"Master will not be pleased." he said, still smiling—it was as though he was happy about it.

"Shut up!" Kyoki pressed her scythe against his throat.

"Kyoki." Hana said.

"I'll have to be punished, Master will make sure I am."

"You don't seem too broken up about it." Kyoki snapped.

"What's the point of getting upset?" Yeldi laughed, "I can't change it. Master doesn't like failures and that is what I am so I will be punished for it." He sat down and leaned against the tree, staring at the sky as a joyless chuckle escaped his throat.

"You don't have to go back." Yoake said.

"Huh?" Yeldi glared up at her, his laughter suddenly coming to a grinding halt. "I don't?"

"That's right. You don't have to follow your master. What reason do you have anyway?"

"You don't understand, human. This is what I chose, and I can't turn back."

"That's not true."

"Like I said, you don't understand." Yeldi chuckled. "It was my choice, my choice."

"So you're going to throw your life away to this 'master' because you chose to?" Hana inquired.

"More or less." he said with mischief in his eyes. "I don't expect you to get it, you're just a pathetic human."

"Who are you calling pathetic?" Kyoki raged.

"Knock it off." Yoake said.

"So what should we do with him?" Hana asked. "He chose this life. Should we give him his just reward?"

"Go ahead, you'll be doing me a favor." Yeldi said, smirking. He tilted his head back as if to offer it to Kyoki's blade.

"Gladly." Kyoki pressed her scythe closer, but stopped when Yoake put a hand on the pole. "What?"

Yoake pulled the scythe from Yeldi's throat much to his and the other two girls' surprise. "Go on, get out of here." she said. "We don't want to kill you."

"We don't?" Kyoki asked.

"No, we don't."

Yeldi chuckled. "Of course. The good guy sense of honor, right?"

"No, the human sense of compassion." Yoake said. "You wouldn't get it." She stepped back, pushing the other two back with her. "Now get out of here, and tell your master that he will *never* get these watches."

Yeldi stepped forward. "Alright. This just got interesting. But don't forget, that little 'compassion' of yours might get you killed some day, and when that day comes, Master will be there to take your power from your cold dead hands."

"Okay, that's enough." said a voice. They all turned to see a man in his early 20's, with shaggy dirty-blond hair and green eyes standing a few feet away. "I think you've done enough damage for one day, Yeldi."

"What the hell are *you* doing here?" Yeldi growled.

"Who are you?" Yoake demanded, aiming an arrow at him.

"Don't shoot, I'm a friend. My name is Tybalt, I'm here to help." he said and, reaching into his pocket, he pulled out a watch. "See, I have a watch, just like you, so please, lower your weapons." Yoake did, but cautiously, unaware that Yeldi was taking advantage of the distraction to sneak away. Tybalt, however, saw him. "Don't go anywhere!" he shouted. Yeldi froze and turned around as Tybalt raised his pocket watch and opened it. Suddenly, out of the little device came a shower of ghost-like animals that swirled in a tornado as Tybalt cried out, "Canis!" and the tornado formed into a large black-furred dog with red eyes. "Stop him."

The dog growled and ran after Yeldi, quickly catching up and clamping its jaws around the creatures's already injured tail. He screamed in pain and fell to the ground, only to be dragged back by the dog. "What do you want?" Yeldi snapped as soon as the dog stopped pulling on him.

"The same thing I always want," Tybalt replied, "come home."

Yeldi shook his head furiously. "No," he snapped, "now call off this mutt and let me go!"

"All I want is for yo—"

"I've told you over and over and over that I can't come back and you know very well why so just stop! O.K? Just stop!"

"Fine then!" Tybalt shouted, signaling for his dog to release Yeldi, "Go back to Saekrin and see where that gets you. Go on, get!" Yeldi growled at the older man and stormed off. Tybalt sighed, looking sad and angry. He closed his watch and as the dog disappeared, turned to face the girls who were staring, confused, at the previous shouting match.

"What was that about?" Kyoki asked. Tybalt waved his hand dismissively but offered no explanation.

"You said you were here to help us," Hana said, stepping forward, "What exactly did you mean?"

Tybalt held up his watch, "What I meant is I'm here to explain these and why you three have them."

"Finally," Yoake said, "I was wondering what was going on. So . . . who is Yeldi? Who is this 'master' guy he keeps talking about? You mentioned Yeldi going back to someone named Saekrin, is it him? Why are they after our watches? How do the watches work? What—"

"Whoa, whoa, whoa, slow down." Tybalt said, raising his hands, "I'll answer all your questions but not here. It's too dangerous, follow me." He turned and led the way into the woods, the girls following curiously behind him. They weren't sure weather or not they could really trust Tybalt so kept their weapons up just in case.

After about five minutes of walking, the group stopped at the bank of a small river. "What the hell is this?" Kyoki asked, "We gonna go swimming or something?"

"No," Tybalt said, shaking his head, "You see, there are certain points at which a holder of the watches can—for lack of a better term—jump from one world to another. This river is one of them and I am going to take you to my world, the world that your watches came from." The girls stared at Tybalt, expressions of confusion, incredulity, and shock etched onto their faces. He held up his watch, hovering it over the water. Suddenly, the river below started to swirl, all colors mixing together and melting around what looked like a whirlpool of light. Tybalt turned to the girls again, beckoning them over. Slowly, they complied, coming to stand right next to him at the very edge of the river. "Jump," he said.

"What?" Kyoki yelped, "You're nuts!"

"I'll be right behind you, just go." Tybalt answered.

Hana and Kyoki looked at him skeptically, but Yoake moved forward, "I'll go." she said.

"Are you crazy?" Kyoki exclaimed, "We don't know where that thing leads!"

"It could be a trap." Hana added.

"It could, but I have a feeling it isn't." Yoake said. She looked at the portal and, after looking back at Tybalt, who nodded, walked in. Colors around her swirled like a rainbow soup. Before she could process everything, they disappeared and revealed another world. Yoake stared in amazement at the spectacle around her. It was a beautiful room filled with white stone that seemed to shine, but Yoake couldn't find any real source of light. On the sides, stood huge stone statues of beautiful creatures the likes of which she had never seen. Each one was carved of the same stone as the room, each different and regal, looking as though she could reach forward, touch them, and have thier carved skin feel warm under her hands. Between each statue stood a six foot podium with ornate swirling designs carved into them and velvet purple cloths draped across. As she walked forward, staring in awe at the decoration of the room, Yoake suddenly noticed the ceiling. Above her, the colors of the life-like mural moved in sync, forming the image of a giant clock, but the numbers were different than the ones she was used to seeing. Yoake turned suddenly as her companions arrived.

"Holy crap!" Kyoke said, spinning so she could take in the room, "This place is amazing!"

"Yes," Hana agreed as she landed next to Kyoki, "It looks like some sort of temple."

"That's because it is." Tybalt said. He suddenly appeared next to Yoake, gesturing to the whole of the room.

"Welcome, friends," a soft voice said from the far end of the hall, "I'm very glad to see that you have finally arrived." Yoake turned to see a beautiful woman watching them. She was dressed in a white, Grecian style robe, and had two white feathered wings on her back. Her deep blue, pupilless eyes stared back at Yoake, radiating gentleness and calm. Long hair fell down her back, shining blues and greens around the white ribbons running through it, all connected to an ivory circlet resting on her forehead.

Tybalt bowed, motioning for the girls to do the same. "Rise," the woman said and the four obeyed.

"Who is that?" Kyoki whispered as they stood.

"She is the high priestess of our world," Tybalt answered, "Lady Alia."

"Tybalt," Alia said, "you have done very well, bringing the humans here." Tybalt bowed again, "but I am sure they have many questions," she continued, "Please follow me." Alia turned and led the group to the very front of the room where a glowing white, gold, and silver box stood. It was large, nearly five feet tall and seven wide, with carved figures running around its sides and top. Yoake recognized them as the statues that surrounded the room. Alia held up her hand and the lid of the box began to slowly rise into the air. Gently, she moved her hand, letting the lid fall softly onto the purple pillow behind the box. Inside, were dozens of white shelves with circular holes cut in them, each about two to two and a half inches in diameter. They were all empty except for the very last one, tucked away in the bottom corner. Resting inside that hole was a small, copper pocket watch with ruby stones circling the rim.

"What, what is this?" Yoake asked, staring in wonder at the watch.

"This is our most scared shrine and within this box is the home of all of the magical watches of our world. Each one has its own unique power. When a soldier finishes their training, they come here and swear to uphold the virtues of honor, courage, and integrity and to protect the peace of this world. They are then presented with their own watch to be used only in the service of others, to help them, to protect them, but something has gone very wrong." She closed the box sadly, turning her face to the ceiling above, "One of our own has begun to steal the watches in the hopes of attaining great power for himself. I sent the remaining watches to many different worlds in the hopes that he would not be able to get to them, but all was in vain. He tracked them down and has already acquired many. You three have the final active watches and must protect them from him."

"Excuse me," Yoake said, nervously, "What do you mean by 'active watches'?"

"And who is this 'he'? Kyoki added.

"And how are we supposed to stop him?" Hana finished.

Alia smiled at them. "Active watches are those that have been unlocked by their destined user. Every watch has one except the one that remains in the box. That poor boy was never able to claim his. You three were chosen by those pieces to be their wielders. As for who 'he' is—"

"May I take this one, my lady?" Tybalt asked suddenly. Alia nodded and Tybalt bowed in thanks then continued. "The person we're talking about is called Saekrin. He was once a great soldier for our world, very respected and admired among his comrades and the people, but their praise soon became dull for him and he began to seek out greater challenges and fights to test his power. But that too soon became too easy, too boring. He became restless, constantly trying to push the limits of his watch in the hopes of attaining greater and greater power, even going so far as to talk of challenging the gods themselves. He was one of my closest friends, and it pains me now to think of what he has become, how consumed he is by foolish pride. One day, I confronted him while he was working and tried to talk to him, to make him see that the path he was traveling along had no finish line, the cup he wanted to fill no bottom, but he laughed, saying I was too simple-minded to understand the plans he was dreaming of. The next day, he and Yeldi broke into the temple—how he managed to rope my baby brother into his schemes I will never know—and stole four watches. Lady Alia and I were there at the time and were able to force him out and send the remaining watches away, but not before he took Lady Alia's. That watch is our most treasured for it is said to have been a gift from the gods to the very first high priest.

"After that, I chased him through world after world, trying to get to the watches before he did, but always he was one step ahead of me. I finally tracked him to your world and tried to find the watches. When I saw that they had chosen you to be the bearers of their power, I was overjoyed to finally have allies to help me. Sadly, I have still not been able to locate him. I hope that together we will be able to either bring Saekrin back to his former, gentle, brave, relaxed, compassionate self, or destroy him."

"So are you here to take away our watches?" Yoake asked.

Tybalt shook his head. "No, I'm only supposed to protect you from Saekrin, so he doesn't get those watches. We're supposed to work together."

"So you're our babysitter." Kyoki concluded.

"No!" Tybalt yelled, obviously annoyed. "I was given this position in order to keep you girls out of danger."

"Like a babysitter." Kyoki said, irritating him further.

"Kyoki." Hana sighed, and Yoake put her head in her hands, exasperation written on her face.

Alia chuckled, grabbing their attention. "I can see why these watches chose you three. Your hearts are full of love and compassion, especially for each other. You will indeed make a great team."

"Even with such different watches." Tybalt added.

"They all compliment each other." Alia shrugged.

"Yes we do." Yoake said.

"So are you willing to accept the burden?" Alia asked the three.

"These watches chose us. I don't think we have much of a choice." Yoake said.

"You do have a choice." Alia said. "I can take your watches from you now and you can forget everything that has happened, or you can keep them and face the rough times ahead."

"I'm keeping mine." Kyoki said.

"If Kyoki is then I am." Hana said, then added, "Some one's got to keep her out of trouble."

"I guess it's settled then." Yoake said. "We keep them."

"Very well." Alia looked at Tybalt. "Tybalt, I am trusting you to keep them safe. Don't let Saekrin harm these girls, that is your first priority."

"Yes, my lady." Tybalt bowed.

"Now that that's settled I think it's time you returned to your own world."

"I agree." Yoake nodded.

"Aw, can't we stay here a little longer?" Kyoki whined.

"We have school in the morning." Hana said. Kyoki huffed in disappointment, making Alia giggle.

"They remind me of you and your friends, Tybalt."

"Yes, I was thinking the same thing." Tybalt said, smiling for the first time since the girls met him. "Alright, ladies, let's get you back." He held up his watch and the portal opened again.

Three of them walked through it, but Yoake stopped.

"Something wrong? Tybalt asked, confused.

"I was just wondering," Yoake said, "How will we be able to find you once we get back?"

"Don't worry," Tybalt replied, "I'll be watching you always. I'm sure Saekrin will be near you as well if he has found the location of the watches, which I'm fairly sure he has. Besides, I'm your guardian, right? It's my job to watch out for you girls." He smiled at her and Yoake nodded, finally jumping through the portal.

She landed next to Kyoki and Hana back beside the river. They looked at each other for a few minutes, trying to figure out if what had just happened was real, but then a voice called to them.

"It's getting late, girls." Tybalt called from the tree he was sitting in, "You better get back to your dorm." They nodded and set off through the woods, picking up their abandoned homework as they went.

Once they arrived home, they quickly showered and change, too tired from the day's events to talk, and were asleep as soon as they lay down.

The next afternoon, Yoake looked around her classroom, bored out of her mind. Mr. Satoru was talking about some chemistry formulas again and she really didn't care. Her eyes drifted out the window and for a second she thought she saw Tybalt sitting in the tree across the street, but when she looked again, he was gone. With a sigh, she looked at her watch, 2:55. She had been in school for almost seven hours but it felt like seven years. Just as she was about to doze off, Mr. Satoru finished his lecture.

"That's it for today, class," he said, "but tomorrow we will be joining the other second year classes and the third years for a trip to the national zoo, so check the weather reports and dress appropriety. We will meet here at eight o'clock tomorrow morning and then set out. Do not be late, understood?" The class nodded. "Good," he said just as the bell rang, "Alright, you are all dismissed."

"I'm so excited!" Kyoki yelled as they walked back to their dorm. She bounced up and down in front of her friends, trying to get them as excited as she was.

"Calm down, Kyoki," Hana said, smiling, "I'm excited to but that's no reason to—"

"I bet there'll be tigers, and bats, and snakes, and lemurs, and . . ." Kyoki continued to list various animals as they sat down in their room.

"Enough!" Hana yelled, "We get it! There's going to be lots of animals; so please stop and just be quiet." She glared at Kyoki who started laughing.

"What's so funny?" Yoake said, pulling out her algebra homework.

"I just wanted to see which would happen first: would I run out of animals or would one of you blow your top?"

"Moron," Hana snapped. Yoake sighed as a small argument ensued. She walked to the window to let in some fresh air in the hopes that it might calm her companions. Instead, it just made them unleash their anger on her.

"Close that!" They both screamed and Yoake practically ran over to the window to comply.

"Trouble girls?" The three turned to see Tybalt sitting on the sill. He watched them curiously for a moment then stepped into the room. "What's going on?"

"Nothing." Hana snapped then sighed, "Kyoki's just being her normal weird self." In response, the other third year stuck out her tongue.

"See," Yoake said, rubbing the back of her head sheepishly, "It's all fine, but umm . . . uhh . . ." she fumbled for a few seconds, trying to come up with a new topic, ". . . Do you have any ideas as to where Saekrin might be?"

"A few," Tybalt answered as he sat down in the chair beside the desk, "but I'm still looking. This city of yours is very crowded."

"Are you going to come with us to the zoo?" Hana asked as she pulled out her literature book.

"Of course he is," Kyoki giggled, "he is our *babysitter* after all." She cast a sly grin at Tybalt who glared back, snarling.

"I. Am. Not. Your. Babysitter." he hissed through clenched teeth.

"Kyoki, don't start that." Yoake sighed. "It pisses him off."

"She knows, that's why she does it." Hana said from behind her book.

"Well I would rather not have him mad at us—well at her—only one day after having met us."

"Hmm, good point."

"Hey! I'm still here, you know!" Kyoki yelled.

"Yes we know." the other two said in unison, which amused Tybalt.

"You three are something else." he laughed. "I've never seen the same bond that you girls share. It really is amazing."

"What about you and your friends." Yoake said. "Alia said we remind her of you guys."

"Maybe, but our bond wasn't nearly as strong."

"You call making fun of me a bond?" Kyoki protested.

"That's part of the package." he shrugged.

"And you make fun of us all the time." Hana pointed out.

Kyoki stuck out her tongue but laughed. "I'm going out for a bit," she said, "see you guys later." With that, she walked out, closing the door behind her.

"Wonder where she's going . . ." Yoake said sarcastically.

"The roof." Hana said.

"Well duh."

Sighing, Tybalt stood and walked to the door. "I'm going to follow her," he said, "just to make sure nothing happens." Yoake and Hana nodded in farewell then went back to their homework.

The next day, Yoake jumped off the bus that took her and her classmates to the zoo. Looking up at the sky, she glanced back at Yami who was slinking off the bus in his normal fashion. "Looks like it's gonna rain." she said.

"Great." he mumbled.

"What's wrong?"

"I'm not very comfortable around animals." he said. "So where are the others?"

"Here!" Kyoki beamed, making Yami jump.

"Why do you feel the need to do that?" Yoake scolded.

"What?"

"Nevermind." she sighed, Hana giggling.

"Is that everyone?" came Mr. Satoru's voice as he scanned the small crowd of students in front of him. "Good. Now everyone pick a group of no more than four."

"Well, this works out." Hana said.

"What are we, five?" Kyoki mumbled.

"Oh don't complain, we would've gone together anyway." Yoake said and turned to Yami. "Are you going to be in our group?"

"I don't really know anyone else, so I guess." he shrugged.

"You guess?" Kyoki said, feigning hurt, and jumped over to him, grabbing his arm. "Come on, wall flower, let's go find those tigers."

"Wait I—" But it was too late for him to protest as she began dragging him toward the lion pit.

"We'd better go save him." Yoake sighed, Hana nodding in agreement.

"Before you go," said Mr. Satoru, surprising them, "Take a map. There's a check-in at noon at the gazebo in the center of the zoo. Don't be late."

"Yes, sir." they said quickly and bolted off. Soon they stood outside the pit, looking down at the lions. Two females lay half asleep in the shade of one of the trees while a male paced, looking up at the staring people every few minutes as if to make sure they hadn't gotten any closer to his territory. Kyoki stared at them all, happy as a clam, while Yami looked anywhere but at the large animals.

"Kyoki," Hana said once she and Yoake had caught up, "don't run off like that. We're supposed to stay in a group remember?" Kyoki waved her hand dismissively and went back to watching the lions.

"You O.K., Yami?" Yoake asked when she noticed that the boy looked rather uncomfortable.

"Me?" he asked, jumping slightly in surprise, "yeah, I'm fine I just, I just need to go to the bathroom. I'll be right back." Quickly, he scurried off, leaving Hana and Yoake rather confused.

"I wonder what's wrong?" Hana asked.

"You heard him," Kyoki answered, still focused on the lions, "When you gotta go, you gotta go." Yoake sighed but looked into the pit to see what was holding Kyoki's normally short attention span. Nothing interesting seemed to be happening until Yoake looked to the left of the cage where a zoo employee was piling some disgusting looking meat for the lions. The male was the first to approach and from the way Kyoki was eyeing the lion and worker, it looked like she hoped one would get eaten. Once the meat was dished out and the worker left the pit unscathed, Kyoki turned away, leaning against the wall.

"I hope Yami gets back soon," she said.

"Hey." came Yami's voice. The three looked over to see him walking back to them, with Mr. Satoru alongside him.

"I see you kids are having fun." the teacher observed.

"Yes, sir." Yami said, trying to avoid his eyes.

"Well then, if you are having so much fun with your group, please stay with them." he said, both endearingly and sharply at the same time, and walked away.

"Feeling better?" Yoake asked Yami.

"Hm?" Yami looked up at her and smiled sheepishly. "Uh, yeah, thanks."

"You are so cute!" Kyoki exclaimed squeezing him with a hug.

"Well now that we're all together again, let's go see the other animals," Hana said, pulling out the map. They scanned the paper for a few minutes, making a list of all the animals they wanted to see before they had to meet up for lunch, and set off. First, they went to the elephants were Hana was nearly sprayed by a mother elephant trying to clean off her baby. Next, Yoake had suggested the monkey house because she wanted to see the lemurs. Kyoki hated monkeys so stood at the exit and waited for them.

"Where do you want to go, Yami?" Hana asked. She sat on a bench outside the monkey house between Yoake and Yami, Kyoki standing behind and looking over her shoulder.

"Umm . . . ," Yami muttered as he looked at all the exhibits, "I like birds."

"O.K. then," Yoake said, standing, "Then let's hurry to the birds. We've got about an hour before we have to go to the gazebo." Hana and Kyoki nodded and they set off again. An hour and five incidents of dodged bird poop later, they walked toward the gazebo. They could see the rest of their class already waiting, along with Mr. Satoru.

"Looks like you kids made it back just in time," he said, smiling. Yami looked down, shaking slightly. Suddenly, a scream rose into the air as a crowd ran toward them.

"Run!" yelled a man as he dashed past them, "They're loose!" Immediately, the class began to panic, running in every direction to get away from the stampede of escaped animals. Yoake, Kyoki, and Hana tried to stick together in the crowd but soon lost sight of Yami.

"Where is he?" Kyoki asked, obviously worried and scared.

"I don't know," Hana replied, "but we have to find him." Just then Yoake gasped. "What is it?" Hana asked.

"I think we might have bigger problems," Yoake said. She pointed to the top of the gazebo where Yeldi sat, looking down at the girls and laughing.

"Yeldi!" Yoake shouted, "We should have known this was your doing!" The creature just continued to laugh.

"My master has graciously given me another chance to take those from you," he said, pointing to their watches, "and I intend not to disappoint him."

"As if, you jackass!" Kyoki shouted.

Yeldi smirked and jumped down from his perch. "Did you have fun with my brother?"

"What's that supposed to mean!" She tried to charge at him, but Hana and Yoake grabbed her collar.

"Calm down." the younger girl hissed.

"Whatever." Kyoki huffed and took hold of her watch. "Let's smoke this bastard!" She opened her watch and the dark skull clouds immediately began to pour from it, surrounding her and lifting her into the air. Hana and Yoake watched her as her clothing transformed and the scythe appeared in her hand. When she landed, Kyoki glared back at the other girls. "Are you just going to stand there? Transform and let's destroy this bastard!" The other two looked at each other for a moment, then nodded, opening their own watches. Blinding light filled the space around the gazebo as their own magic took over. They landed just behind Kyoki, who smirked. "Finally." she said.

"Let's just concentrate on getting the animals back." Yoake said, looking around. All of the people had run out of the zoo long ago but the animals remained.

"Look!" Hana yelled. She pointed to the animals and the girls saw that they were running in circles around them, only concentrating on them.

"What's going on?" Yoake asked, scared.

"My master's power has granted us control over these beasts," Yeldi laughed from his perch. He stood and pointed to the circling animals, "Attack!"

A tiger charged at them, running at full speed toward Hana. Quickly, she jumped out of the way, deflecting the tiger's claws with one of her swords. As Hana tried to fight off the tiger, Yoake ran as fast as she could from the jaguar chasing after her.

"Nice kitty!" she yelled, jumping onto a fence. She pulled a red arrow out of her quiver and, as the jaguar drew closer, strung her bow. Just as the large cat was about to pounce, Yoake fired. The arrow sped toward its target, hitting the jaguar in the chest and sending it into the animal pit on the other side of the gazebo.

"Little help here!" Hana called, as the tiger pounced again. Yoake and Kyoki ran over to help her but it wasn't needed. Hana pulled her swords to her, slashing the air in an X shape.

"FLORA SLASH!" she screamed as a large, pink X flew toward the tiger, crashing into it and sending it flying into the sky. The girl's looked around for the other animals, but many were gone and in their place stood Tybalt in a tree overlooking the battle. He saluted to them as Yeldi growled fiercely.

"Nice!" Kyoki called as she tried to fend off the lion slashing at her. The lion pounded at her scythe again and again. Suddenly, it's other paw came up, scratching against her stomach. Kyoki yelped in pain and jumped back. "That's it!" she yelled, "SOUL STORM!" Ghosts instantly appeared in the air around her. Kyoki swung her scythe, sending the crowd of spirits toward the lion. It tried to dodge but there were too many, and soon they had it pinned down. Yeldi growled as the lion was thrown way. "Come on! Get down here, coward!" Kyoki yelled at him but he just smirked.

"Kyoki, don't be so rash!" Yoake said to her friend. "You're hurt, you need to rest."

"No, I'm—Ah!" she cringed in pain, blood coming out of her mouth as she coughed.

"Kyoki!" the other two cried.

"I'm coming!" Yoake said and ran over to Kyoki.

"Right." Hana nodded, then gasped. "Guys, look out!" she called. The two looked up to see that the three creatures had recovered and were readying for another attack. By nature those were animals that stalked injured prey first, so they had their eyes on Kyoki.

Yeldi smirked again. "Lunch time."

"I got it!" Tybalt said, jumping from his spot in the tree. Opening his watch, he summoned an elephant, a hippopotamus, and a giraffe in order to fend off the beasts.

Hana nodded at Tybalt and ran to her friends. "How's it look?" she asked.

"Bad."

"Hana, use your watch!" Tybalt called as one of the predators finished off one of the creatures. "Ah!" he cringed as the spirit returned to his watch.

"Tybalt!" the three cried.

"Don't worry, this happens often."

"Right." Yoake nodded.

"What did he mean use my watch? To heal?"

"That's my guess."

"Well you'd better guess faster!" Kyoki said through the blood.

"So do I just . . ." Hana held the hand her watch fused with over Kyoki's wound. "Please let this work." Her glove glowed and the gash closed up.

"Alright!" Kyoki said, abruptly jumping back to her feet as soon as the wound closed. Looking at Yeldi with a dark expression, she picked up her scythe. "Okay, now I'm mad." Twirling the weapon over her head she shouted, "SOUL HURRICANE!" The spirits swirled around and around, making a large cloud that started to block out the sun.

"What the—" Yoake said, puzzled.

"How is she doing that?" Hana added.

Tybalt narrowed his eyes.

"TAKE THIS!" Kyoki cried and slammed the end of her scythe on the ground, sending the giant cloud down onto the hypnotized animals and Yeldi.

But they weren't the only ones effected by the storm. Yoake and Hana cried out in pain as they too were hit by the barrage. "Guys!" Kyoki cried and tried to stop, but the attack had already reached its full power and had taken control.

Suddenly the cloud dissolved, going back into the scythe. It was thanks to Tybalt that it stopped. He grabbed hold of the scythe and got it under control, the black mass slowly beginning to fade. Once the clouds had completely disappeared, they could see the enormous amount of damage the attack had caused. Kyoki collapsed from the amount of energy the attack had used, Tybalt catching her as she fell. Holding the unconscious girl in his arms, he looked up at the scene around him. The other two were also unconscious, and the gazebo had been ripped in half, but thankfully that was the worst of the damage. His gaze then caught sight of a robed figure as it smirked at him and walked away. He knew exactly who it was and would have chased after him, but his first priority was the girls. Frustrated, he sighed and gently put Kyoki down. He then put his hands on the ground and a blinding light came from him that repaired everything around them.

❧❦❧

"You useless bastard!" Saekrin snarled at Yeldi, "I lend you some of *my* power and you still manage to fail!" Yeldi sat kneeling in front of the older creature, eyes downcast out of respect and fear.

"I'm sorry, Master." he said softly. His body tensed as he heard Saekrin snarl from somewhere above him.

"I don't want your damn apologies," Saekrin snapped, "Shirt. Off. Now." Yeldi gasped, but the sharp look in his master's eyes coupled with his own growing fear made him obey. Soon he was topless, still kneeling in front of Saekrin. He tried to keep his eyes down, but when nothing happened for a few minutes, dangerous curiosity got the better of him and he raised his gaze slightly. As soon as his eyes landed on the weapon his master had chosen for his punishment, Yeldi wished he had kept his focus on the ground. Resting in Saekrin's hands was a long, nine tailed whip with sharp pieces of dirty glass and rusted metal tied to the end of each strand. Yeldi shifted nervously, wishing he could melt into the floor right then and there.

"Stop squirming, boy," Saekrin growled and Yeldi stopped immediately. He closed his eyes, trying to brace himself for the pain, but no amount of concentration could prepare him for the first blow. A scream tore through the room as Saekrin brought the whip down onto his servant's back, metal and glass digging into Yeldi's flesh. The boy gasped as he tried to hold back tears. After who knew how many years with his master, Yeldi knew he should be used to the pain, considering the number of scars, burns, and bruises that covered his body. Another gasp echoed out as Saekrin crashed the whip down again. Blood ran down Yeldi's back, pooling around his legs, as more and more blows found their place on the young creature.

"Look at me, boy." Saekrin said, suddenly pausing in his work. Yeldi turned slowly and brought his eyes up so they locked with his master's.

"Tell me," Saekrin continued, gently coiling his whip, "why do you constantly fail?" Yeldi looked down; he knew the words he was supposed to say, but for some reason they wouldn't come out.

"Well?" Saekrin yelled. He brought his hand up, smacking his servant and sending the boy crashing to the ground, "Answer me, you worthless piece of shit." Yeldi tried to stand but suddenly Saekrin's foot collided with his side, the force slamming him into the hard wall. He could hear footsteps coming toward him and even though his most basic survival instinct told him to stand and run, he just sighed and allowed his master to continue to hit him, kick him, scream at him. What was the point of resisting? Saekrin was his master and he had failed. He deserved this; he always deserved it. Just as he began to cough up blood, Saekrin stopped, squatting down in front of his slave. He tilted Yeldi's head up with the butt of his whip, forcing his servant to look him in the eye.

"Now," Saekrin said, smiling sadistically, "why don't you answer my question, boy."

"I f-fail because I'm weak, Master" Yeldi said, panting and coughing up more blood, "I'm worthless and weak and I don't deserve to live."

Saekrin's sadistic smirk grew as he stood, giving Yeldi one last smack in the face for good measure.

"Don't fail me again, boy," he chuckled darkly as he left, "or next time I won't be so nice."

When Yoake woke up, she felt sore all over her body. Slowly, she opened her eyes and saw a bright, white light above her. For a moment, she thought it was *the* light but her eyes soon adjusted and she saw that she was in what looked like a hospital room. She looked left and right, hoping to find Hana and Kyoki. After a few seconds, she found them in the two beds next to hers, Hana reading a magazine and Kyoki humming a nonsensical tune.

"Morning," Kyoki said once she noticed that her friend was awake.

"Where are we?" Yoake asked. The older girl shrugged.

"Some hospital. The doctor said that the police found us unconscious at the zoo and brought us here. Don't ask me where Tybalt went, I don't know." Just then, a brown haired doctor who looked to be about forty years old walked in.

"Hello, girls," he said, "I'm glad to see you're all awake. You have some minor scrapes but nothing serious. I'd say you are incredibly lucky. The police are outside and would like to talk to you about what happened." Yoake was about to protest, but the doctor had already left. She slumped against the pillow behind her and sighed. They obviously couldn't tell the police what had really happened; they would sound crazy.

"Let's just say we fainted or tripped or got trampled." Hana said, still reading. Kyoki looked over at her and stuck out her tongue.

"That's silly," she said, "we all fainted in the same spot? Who would believe that?"

"Well, I don't see you coming up with any ideas." Hana snapped back.

Yoake sighed. "What if we say that we tried to climb onto the gazebo to get away from the animals but fell off and hit our heads?" she said, looking at her friends hopefully. Hana and Kyoki thought for a moment then nodded just as an officer walked in.

"I need you girls to tell me what happened inside the zoo," he said, "did you see anything that you think would help us figure out how the animals got loose?"

"No," Kyoki said, "we were talking to our teacher and then a huge crowd showed up and yelled at us to start running. That's when we saw the animals coming."

"We tried to run," Hana continued, "but then we saw that our friend Yami was gone so we went back to try to find him."

"Yami?" the officer asked, "does he have black scruffy hair, kind of shy?"

"Yes!" Yoake exclaimed, "Is he O.K.? Wait, how do you know him?"

"I'm just guessing," the officer answered, "there was a boy who kept running around and asking where his friends were. He was the one who actually told us there might still be people in the zoo. Don't worry, he and the rest of your class are fine." The girls let out simoltaneous sighs of relief at the news. "Now, if you would please continue,"

"Yes," Yoake said, "We went back to find Yami but instead found the animals. They chased us and we tried to climb the gazebo to get away. The animals left after awhile but when we tried to come down, we slipped. The next thing I remember is waking up in here." The officer nodded as he finished writing in his notepad.

"I believe you will be discharged soon," he said, "We may need to contact you again, but for now thank you."

"You're welcome, sir." Yoake replied.

"Guys!" cried Yami as he ran into the hospital room. "Will they be okay, officer?"

"According to the doctor, yes. Now, come on, I think your friends need to get some sleep."

"No, it's okay." Yoake said. "We're just glad to see that you're alright, Yami."

"I think I'll leave you kids alone. Take care." With that, the officer walked out.

"I think we owe you a big thanks." Yoake said to the shaggy-haired boy. "If it hadn't been for you, I don't think the police would have found us."

"Yeah thanks, so much." Kyoki said, smiling, and Hana nodded.

"I see you girls are recovering nicely," Mr. Satoru said as he walked into the room, Yami immediately tensing. The teacher moved to stand next to Yami at the foot of Yoake's bed. "I'm glad the animals didn't hurt you." For a moment, it seemed as though he was talking to himself, but the girls ignored it. After a few moments of strained silence, the teacher spoke again. "We should go and let them rest, don't you think so?" Mr. Satoru continued, turning to Yami. The boy looked up and nodded quickly, following the teacher out of the room.

"Well that was awkward . . ." Kyoki said, rolling over, "I'm going to sleep. All that fighting made me tired."

"Me too," Hana said as she set her magazine down, "Night, guys." Yoake bid both of them good night and soon decided to follow their lead and get some sleep.

The next day, an officer walked them back to their dorms to get their clothes. After he left, they changed, but just as they were about to leave for class, Tybalt walked in.

"Don't ever do that again!" he snapped, looking pointedly at Kyoki.

"What'd I do?" she yelled back, "We won, didn't we?"

"It's no good if you try to use an attack you don't have the stamina for! You were injured! What the hell were you thinking?"

"I just did it!" Kyoki snapped, "I wasn't-

"No, you weren't thinking, were you?"

"Shut up!" Kyoki yelled, "If you did your damn job, we wouldn't have gotten hurt!" She lunged at him, raising her fist. Tybalt didn't move to dodge, instead, he caught her hand and held it tightly.

"Let me go!" Kyoki shouted, struggling to free her arm. Tybalt shook his head.

"Listen," he said flatly, "You cannot use that kind of attack again, not until you train more. Right now your body doesn't have enough stamina to sustain it. If you try to do that again, the power will overload your system and you could die." Kyoki suddenly stopped her struggle and stood still, looking at the ground. Slowly, Tybalt released her hand, which fell limply against the girl's side.

"I'm sorry," Kyoki said softly, "I just—I wanted so much to stop him." She walked over to her bed and lay down, pulling the blankets over herself. The room was silent for about five minutes before Yoake spoke. "I think we should hurry up and get to class . . ."

"You're right," Hana said, nodding, "Come on, Kyoki."

"Not until he," her hand shot out from under the clovers and pointed straight at Tybalt, "leaves." Sighing, the blonde left. As soon as the door closed behind him, Kyoki stood and pulled on her bag. "Let's go." she grouched, walking toward the door.

"You know we're not angry at you, right?" Hana said as they made their way to class, "we just don't want that to happen again."

"Hana's right," Yoake continued, "We're just concerned and besides, we didn't completely know how the watches worked and—"

"So now I'm your guinea pig?" Kyoki snapped, glaring at Yoake.

"No, no, no," she said, "That's not what I meant. It's just that I think we should learn more about the watches before any of us try to use large attacks like that again." Kyoki nodded although she was still glaring and turned, following Hana to their classroom.

"Yoake!" Yami called happily as soon as the girl walked in, "I'm so glad you're alright! I didn't think you'd be in school today."

"Yes, Miss Hikari," Mr. Satoru said from behind his desk, "so glad the animals didn't harm you." he smiled at her, but for some reason the expression made shivers go up and down Yoake's spine. Class went by quickly for Yoake, so engrossed as she was in her thoughts of Kyoki and the argument in the dorm. When the bell rang for lunch, she didn't move and it wasn't until Yami tapped her shoulder that she stood and walked to the cafeteria.

"Hey, Hana," Yoake said as she sat down next to her friend. Hana nodded in reply and took another bite of her sandwich. A few seconds later, Kyoki walked in and angrily plopped herself down beside Yoake. She, Yami, and Hana watched nervously as Kyoki took out her lunch and began to eat, all the while glaring at the space in front of her.

"Look," Hana said, setting her sandwich down, "We're not mad at you about what happened. No one is angry. We're just concerned and we don't want you or any of us to get hurt." Kyoki ignored her and instead continued to glare.

"Hana's right!" Yoake added, "Please just talk to us!" Once again, Kyoki ignored them.

"Fine!" Hana snapped, "If you want to grouch and ignore us go right ahead. Are you even listening?" she paused and began to wave her hand in front of Kyoki's face, "Hello in there! Is anyone home?" Suddenly, Kyoki looked up, all signs of anger gone.

"Did you say something?" she asked, turning to Hana. Yoake stared in absolute confusion at Kyoki.

"You're not angry?" she asked. Kyoki shook her head.

"About what?" Kyoki replied, raising one eyebrow in confusion.

"What happened this morning!" Hana said.

"Oh that," Kyoki said, smiling, "I forgot about that nonsense like two hours ago."

"Then why were you upset?" Yoake asked. Sometimes Kyoki's idiosyncarcies went too fast for her to keep up.

"Math is the worst subject on the planet and the damn teacher won't teach us anything. Whoever invented calculus needs to be shot. Shame on him, shame on his wife, shame on his kids." Kyoki stuck out her tongue at no one in particular then went back to devouring her burger. Yami smiled at the girls; if nothing else they were funny.

"So how's your life?" Kyoki asked suddenly, turning to Yami. The boy looked up at her, surprised, and immediately turned a very healthy shade of red.

"It's umm . . . it's fine." He said, "Nothing really interesting, just normal stuff I guess."

"Okay then . . . ."

Three hours later, Kyoki, Hana, and Yoake walked back to their dorm to get started with their weekend homework, but suddenly Tybalt appeared, looking very good in some Earth clothes he'd managed to find, and led them away.

"Where are we going now?" Kyoki whined as they trudged through the same forest he had taken them through when they had first met.

"The fight at the zoo made me think. You girls need training, so I'm going to take you back to my world where you can get some practice."

"Yay!" Yoake cheered.

"So cool," Kyoki added, pulling out her watch, "I can't wait to see what this thing can do." As soon as she said that, Tybalt twitched nervously, he didn't like how Kyoki's words sounded, but the girls were too excited to notice.

"Here we are," he said, stopping at the banks of the river. With a quick nod to the girls, he brought up his watch and opened the portal, the river instantly beginning to swirl. Quickly, Yoake moved to the edge and jumped in, Kyoki and Hana soon following behind. The colors of the portal swirled around them as they passed into Tybalt's world. All to soon, they landed inside the white temple with a soft thud.

"Hello, girls," Alia said as she walked in, "I was wondering who was coming. Is there something wrong?"

"No, my lady," Tybalt said, landing next to Hana, "I felt that the girls to could do with some training and since they are out of school for a couple of days, I thought this would be a good opportunity."

Alia nodded, giggling slightly. "I was wondering when you would realize that."

Tybalt moved to respond but couldn't find the words. It was obvious she was right. "I'm sorry, my lady," he said, "I know I should have thought of training them sooner."

"There's no need to apologize," Alia said, "You're here now and that's what's important. Why don't you show them around since their visit was so short—lived last time."

"Yes, Lady Alia." Tybalt bowed. "This way girls." He led them out of the temple and into what looked like a large forum. The girls stared in awe at the buildings around them. They were tall, with domed roofs, almost like those they had seen in Russian history books. The high columns of the buildings looked like they were made of the same white stone as the temple and as they walked through the paved streets, they could see that the doors were covered in ornate carvings. People pushed against them on all sides as they made their was through the crowd.

"Come on," Tybalt said, grabbing onto Yoake's hand, "It's easy to get lost around here if you don't know the way." He led them through winding streets until they reached the outskirts of the town.

"Here we are," he said, motioning to the building behind him. Yoake, Kyoki, and Hana gasped at the sheer size of the complex. It was a large black citadel, with spires on either side, guard posts jutting out of the ground, and a large field where they could see soldiers sparring with each other. Tybalt led the girls to the front gate where they were stopped by one of the guards. He was slightly shorter than Tybalt, with shoulder length dark green hair and wearing a white tunic, loose dark blue pants, combat boots, and a breastplate.

"Hey, Tybalt." the man said. "It's been a long time since we last saw each other."

"Alkest, how are you, my friend?" The two shook hands like old comrades, much to the confusion of the girls. Seeing their faces, Tybalt chuckled and said, "Girls, this is an old friend of mine: Alkest." The shorter of the two soldiers reached out and shook each of the girls' hands.

"How'd you get stuck with guard duty?" Tybalt asked, punching his friend playfully in the shoulder.

"How'd you get stuck as a babysitter?" Alkest countered.

"I am not their babysitter!" Tybalt shouted, making the girls laugh.

"He's kinda sensitive about that." Yoake said.

"Yep." Kyoki added. "I would know."

"Anyway." Hana interrupted. "We came to learn more about the watches."

"Well then I might as well come with you," Alkest said, "I haven't seen this guy in ages." He wrapped his arm around Tybalt as the small group set off. Soon, however, his arm was back at his side and he began pointing out different buildings to the girls.

"Over there is the barracks," he said, pointing to a four story square shaped building, "and over there is the mess hall. I wouldn't go in there if I were you, not unless you like waking up at three in the morning to puke."

"I missed you," Tybalt said, laughing.

"Yeah, same here," Alkest said then suddenly he became very serious, "So have you had any luck finding him?"

"Not unless you count finding the right world." Tybalt answered, "He's insane but he's still damn smart. It's not like he's going to make it easy for me to find him, especially since he already knows all to well that I've been tailing him."

"Excuse me," Yoake said, tapping lightly on Alkest's shoulder, "Did you know Saekrin?"

"I did," he answered, "and if you girls are going up against him, you're in for one hell of a fight. I remember when he was still around, he was the shyest guy I'd ever met when he first showed up, but by the end of his training, he could kick the entire regiment's ass by himself."

"Yeah and it wasn't pretty." Tybalt added, "When Yeldi got assigned to have Saekrin as his mentor, part of me was happy because I knew my baby brother would be learning from the best, but somewhere in my head I could tell that something was very wrong."

"That kid used to follow Saekrin around like a puppy." Alkest added, "It was kind of funny, actually. Saekrin drove the kid pretty hard, but everyone does that to the trainees. Sadly, somewhere it crossed the line. I don't know. All of a sudden Yeldi just stopped being himself. He stopped going to the regiment parties, didn't even want to leave the barracks unless Saekrin was going too. Both of them started acting really weird. I remember this one time a bunch of us were going to go into the forest over there," Alkest motioned to a large expanse of trees to the west of the compound, "so we tried to get Saekrin to come along. He used to like going in there and he'd been so reclusive lately we'd wanted to get him to do something, spar, have some fun, but he refused."

"That's weird." Hana said.

"That kind of reminds me of . . ." Yoake stopped.

"Of what?" Tybalt asked.

"Never mind. It's not important." she said shaking her head, "I'm sorry I interrupted, please continue."

"Well there's not much more to tell," Alkest said, "Since Saekrin wouldn't come, we started walking out and ran into Yeldi. I tried to get him to come along but he said that he was busy and dashed off back toward Saekrin's room. Nothing happened for a few seconds, but then I heard this smacking sound. I turned around to see what it was and for a split second I thought I saw Yeldi holding his cheek, but he stopped so fast I couldn't tell if he'd actually done it."

"Are you telling me you thought Saekrin was abusing my brother and didn't say anything?" Tybalt snapped, glaring at Alkest.

"N-no, no," Alkest answered, raising his hands defensively, "I just—I didn't have any proof and I didn't really see anything and if I did see something I only saw it that one time." Tybalt stopped glaring at his friend but still looked incredibly irritated for the rest of the walk.

"Here we are," Alkest said after another few awkward minutes of walking, "the training field is just over there." He pointed to a large open space about ten meters away where several soldiers were fighting. Yoake could see about half of them training with watches while the others worked on hand to hand combat.

"In case their watches don't work or get taken." Tybalt said when he noticed the slightly quizzical look on Yoake's face.

"There are so many people . . ." Kyoki said, shuffling slightly so she stood behind Hana.

"Ever since Saekrin became a traitor, we have been training a lot more," Alkest said, "in case he ever comes back, which he probably will."

"Makes sense," Hana said, nodding.

Suddenly, Kyoki grabbed Hana and Yoake by their wrists and started dragging them toward the field. "Let's get going!" she yelled, excitement shining in her eyes. Tybalt sighed and followed the girls toward the sparring soldiers.

"Alright," he said once they stood in the far corner of the area, "First, you girls are going to have to transform." Kyoki nodded and immediately opened her watch. Black light poured out, surrounding her and lifting her into the air. Yoake and Hana soon followed, rainbow lights and flowers flowing from their respective watches. Soon they all stood, transformed and ready for battle.

"Let's get this show on the road!" Kyoki cheered, swinging her scythe.

Suddenly, all of the other people who had been training began to wander over to where the girls were standing, all the while whispering "Is that them?" "The humans? Yes I think so" and the like.

"Um . . . why are they all staring at us?" Yoake asked uncomfortably.

Tybalt laughed. "Don't worry it's not hostility, it's simply curiosity. You see we're not used to newcomers. So anyway," Tybalt continued, turning to the crowd and beckoning two of them over, "Hey, guys these are the ones I was telling you about."

"These are the ones the watches chose . . ." said one of the people who moved forward. He was tall with a very serious expression on his face that seemed to criticize their every movement, "They're too young."

"Hey!" Kyoki yelled, "Young nothing. I could kick your ass in ten seconds flat!"

Hana sighed, holding Kyoki by the back of her shirt. "Don't start. We don't want to alienate everyone on our first visit." Yoake quickly nodded in agreement.

"O.K, girls," Tybalt said, "these guys are going to be your trainers. This," he pointed to the serious one, "is Erasure. He will be Kyoki's teacher."

"Great," Kyoki mumbled, "I get the stick in the mud . . ."

Having heard her mumble, he responded, "The scythe is a symbol of death, which is not to be taken lightly. You will learn to use it properly." She responded by huffing indignantly.

"Moving on . . ." Tybalt interrupted, "This is Sakura and she will be your teacher, Hana, so be respectful."

"I am honored," Hana said, bowing to her new teacher.

Yoake looked around for a third person. "So where's my trainer?" she asked.

Tybalt grinned. "You're looking at him."

Somehow, Yoake wasn't shocked, but she was slightly confused. "But I've seen your power; you're not an archer."

"True, but Saekrin killed our last archer master and archery is a basic art needed to pass training as a soldier, so I've know the general idea." Smirking slightly, he added, "After all, I did graduate at the top of my class."

Suddenly, from the other side of the field, Alkest's voice rang out, "Yeah, show off to your new student, why don'tcha!"

Unfazed by the comment, Tybalt continued, "Right, so now you three are going to spar so we can get an idea of your powers. Sound good?"

"Oh yeah! You guys are going down." Kyoki cheered, making the other two smile as if to say 'yeah right.'

The girls stood in a triangle, staring each other down as the crowd moved to form a circle around them. Suddenly, Kyoki charged, swinging her scythe toward Yoake who dodged easily. Kyoki ran after her, still trying to slash her in half.

"What are you doing?" Hana asked, quickly jumping between Kyoki and Yoake, "We're supposed to be sparring not fighting."

"I am fighting," Kyoki responded, swinging the butt of her scythe toward Hana's stomach, "so get out of the way!"

Yoake took advantage of Kyoki's distraction to push her away with her bow. "Calm down. It's just practice." She then grabbed an arrow and aimed. "But if you want to play that way, I'm game." She fired it hitting her opponent in the shoulder. Kyoki hissed in pain, glaring at Yoake. Just then Hana jumped in, slashing at Yoake who dodged and aimed an arrow at her. Hana swung her sword at the arrow, deflecting it. The two jumped apart, allowing Yoake to restring her bow. A green arrow flew toward Hana, nearly hitting her in her leg.

"Watch it!" Hana yelled, "We just got finished telling Kyoki not to take it to far."

"Sorry!" Yoake called.

"Pay attention," Kyoki hissed from behind Yoake. It was then that she noticed that Kyoki's scythe was positioned around her waist, "I win." She swung her scythe backward, tripping Yoake and sending her to the ground. Kyoki stood over her friend, an almost murderous glint shining in her eyes, "You're mine now." she hissed.

"What are you doing?" Hana yelled, staring in horror at her two friends. Kyoki ignored her. Instead she raised her weapon and swung it down toward Yoake.

"NO!" Hana yelled.

"Enough!" The girls turned to see Erasure holding the pole of Kyoki's scythe, just below the blade, "that's enough." Kyoki glared at him, then looked down at Yoake, then back at Erasure. Suddenly, realization dawned on her, eyes widening and she let go of her scythe.

"I-I'm so, I'm so sorry." she said, shaking and dropping to her knees, "I-I'm sorry, guys."

"I'm fine," Yoake said, standing.

"You need to stop being so crazy!" Hana yelled, "Think about what you're doing once in a while!"

"I said I was sorry!" Kyoki snapped back, "What more do you want from me?"

"A little more than half a second of thought would be nice!" Growling, Kyoki raised her fist with every intention of punching Hana in the jaw but Erasure stopped her.

"I said that's enough." he stated flatly, "Come with me." With that, he took Kyoki's arm and dragged her across the training field, the confused stares of Hana, Yoake, Tybalt, and the rest of the crowd following behind them.

"I never thought that she could get like that." Yoake said still staring.

"I was afraid something like this would happen, but I never thought it actually would." Tybalt said.

"Why?" Yoake asked.

"She just reminds me too much of . . ." he trailed off, shaking his head, "never mind."

"Come with me please, Hana," Sakura said, leading the girl to the opposite side of the field from Kyoki and Erasure, which left Yoake and Tybalt alone.

Alright everybody," Tybalt said, turning to the crowd, "show's over. Go on, get!" Laughing, the crowd of soldiers dispersed, going back to their own training.

"O.K. Let's get started," Tybalt said, looking back at Yoake, "string your bow for me." Yoake did, pulling out an orange arrow.

"Good, now you see that target over there." Tybalt pointed to a black and white target about twenty meters away, "I want you to see if you can hit that." Yoake nodded and let her arrow loose. It flew straight toward its target, only to miss my a full three feet. Blushing, Yoake looked at the ground.

"What are you so embarrassed about?" Tybalt asked, "pull out another and let's keep going." For the next three hours, Tybalt watched Yoake shoot her arrows, giving her a few pointers here and there. Her aim slowly grew better and better and after she missed the target only by a few centimeters, Tybalt called for a break.

Yoake smiled, panting, and, after asking her tutor where to find the water, walked off to get a drink. As she made her way back, she saw Tybalt and Erasure around a corner, talking.

". . . is too similar to him." Erasure said as Yoake jumped back, pressing her back against the wall behind her.

"I know," Tybalt said, "but she is the strongest in terms of power."

"You saw the look in her eyes when she stood over Yoake, can you honestly tell me that you're not worried?" Tybalt shook his head.

"Kyoki is strong," Erasure continued, "I can see that, but so was Saekrin. I remember him very well. Oh, the potential I saw in that boy," he sighed, then continued, "He was the best I ever trained, strong, brave, hard working. Honestly, I should have payed attention to the signs, the reclusive behavior, the paranoia, but I ignored them all in favor of helping him realize his dreams of greatness. Saekrin would watch you all train, you know, and he would study your moves, finding the strengths and weaknesses in all of your techniques." At that, Tybalt's eyes widended. "He seemed so eager-shy but eager—and, well, emotionally and socially normal when I first met him. I guess that may have been why I ignored my instincts. You and he were so close and I thought that he was just over excited, but I was wrong. After he left, I was assigned to the investigation squad and found some of his old things," Erasure said, "It was just some notebooks but it was all there: names, dates, weapons, every last piece of information he had gathered about everyone he had ever served with, along with some journal entries. As I read them, I could see his descent. It was all there, on every page, his thoughts and suddenly everything became clear to me. I now understood all the extra training he had put in, all those nights he had worked himself to exhaustion trying to master new techniques, but most of all I could see all the instability within him and, most shocking of all, the contempt he held for the rest of the unit. He has become a pure psychopath. I don't want to make the same mistakes with her as I did with him. I can see it in her eyes, the desire to become the best, to become the most powerful and it scares me. We cannot afford to have another Saekrin. Keep her close, Tybalt, and watch her."

"I understand," Tybalt said, "and I won't let what happened to my old friend happen to her." Erasure nodded to Tybalt and the two walked back to the training field.

"So Erasure trained Saekrin too?" Yoake thought out loud.

"So you heard us did you?" said the older man's voice, startling her.

"Oh, I'm sorry, sir. I didn't mean to hear I just—"

"It's alright, Yoake." he said. "Fate wanted you to hear that for a reason, and we must not question her judgment."

"Um okay." Yoake said nervously, then added, "Well I'm sure Tybalt is waiting for me." With that, she dashed back off to the field. Once she arrived, Tybalt immediately put her to work again. "Alright, now we'll work on hand-to-hand combat." he said

"With my bow?" Yoake asked.

"Yep." he nodded and tossed her a practice bow. "This way you don't accidentally kill me."

She caught it and nearly dropped the object it was so heavy. "What the—"

"It's a common training technique." he explained. "Train with something heavier than your real weapon, so that in battle the weapon is lighter and easier to use. Erasure is doing the same with Kyoki, if I'm not mistaken. It would make sense, considering he came up with the idea." He got into a fighting stance. "Now attack me."

"Are you ready?" Yoake asked.

"Have at me." he said.

"Okay." Yoake nodded and without getting into a fighting stance, charged at him. She swung her bow at him a few times, but he easily dodged them, and landed a blow to her stomach that knocked her to the ground a few meters away. "You weren't ready to attack." he said walking up to her and helping her stand. "I was, and because of that I easily knocked you down. That's also why Kyoki so easily beat you earlier. You need to take a moment to physically and mentally prepare for battle. Get in a fighting stance."

"Um okay." Yoake wasn't sure how she should stand since she hadn't had proper fighting training, so she got in the first position that can to her mind. She stood up strait, with her knees locked and heels together. For some reason Tybalt found that funny. "What?" she asked confused as to why he was laughing at her. He lightly pushed on her back, causing her to nearly lose her balance and fall over. "What was that for?" she demanded.

"You're not getting ready for a ballet." he said. "First of all, you need to stand with your feet shoulder-width apart, with one foot slightly in front of the other. Like this." He demonstrated the position and Yoake followed. After a quick inspection, he kicked one of her feet farther forward. "There you go. Now bend your knees." She obeyed. "Good. Make sure you do that, because your upper body has more weight than you lower body, making you naturally top-heavy. Bending your knees and standing with your feet like that provides a good anchor. Now if I push you again," He did, but this time her stance was rock solid and she didn't fall, "you won't fall over. See how that works?"

"Yeah. Okay now I'm ready." she said.

"Not quite." he said. "You're too stiff, you lack balance.

"But isn't that what a good stance provides?"

"No. Tell me something, what happens when you hit a rock?"

"Nothing."

"Not the first time. But if you hit that rock on the same place multiple times, then what will happen?"

"Well I guess eventually it will crack."

"Right, and it will never be the same rock again, but what happens when you hit water?"

"It gives way."

"And?"

"And . . ." She searched for an answer, and suddenly realized what her was getting at. "it reforms when the pressure is gone."

"Exactly. A hard stance is only good until someone with a harder stance comes along and breaks you. So you have to be ready, and give way when you know you can't stand up to an attack. Then reform to give a counter attack, just like water. So say I push you again," He did, but much harder, "and you can't hold me back. What do you do?"

Struggling against the pressure he had put on her arm she answered, "This?" She gave way, surprising him, and took a few steps forward to regain her footing.

"Yes very good. Now counter-attack."

She did and swung the bow at him again, this time, when he hit her stomach, she was able to stay standing and attack again. This continued for the rest of the day, but soon, the world's two suns had set and the girls were taken into the barracks for some dinner and a place to sleep.

"So how do you guys like your teachers?" Yoake asked, settling onto her temporary bed.

Kyoki scowled, "Erasure is a strict, mean, grumpy old man. He took away my scythe and made me work with some heavy metal one. It was so annoying, but when he finally did give it back, mine felt way lighter and I could swing it faster, so I guess he knows what he's doing."

"You'll get very strong if you keep training with him," Yoake said, "after all he—" she suddenly stopped herself, deciding it was best not to tell Kyoki and Hana what she had heard earlier.

"After all he what?" Hana asked as she pulled her blankets over herself.

Yoake shook her head, "Never mind. Tybalt did that with me, too." she said. "He told me that it was 'a common training technique' that Erasure himself came up with"

"That sounds like something he'd think of." Kyoki muttered.

Yoake rolled her eyes and looked at Hana. "How is your teacher?"

"She's wonderful," Hana replied, "I can tell she knows exactly what she's doing and she taught me so many new ways to fight. I can't wait to test them out in battle. But she also taught me a lot of other things, like how to calm yourself before a fight so you don't make rash decision and how to improve my healing ability through meditation."

"Cool," Yoake said.

"Pfft," Kyoki laughed, "how is that nonsense going to help you win in a battle? Power is what you need, not calmness. Well whatever works." With that, she tucked herself into bed and was soon asleep.

The next morning was spent in training but after lunch, Tybalt sent the girls back to their own world because they still had obligations there, specifically homework. Considering the training they had just gone through, all three found their normal routine to be rather boring and spent the evening watching old movies before going to sleep.

When she woke up, Yoake quickly got dressed and met Hana and Kyoki, who had already woken up half an hour ago, outside. They walked to class and met up with Yami on the way.

"Hey, Yami!" Kyoki said, wrapping her arm around his shoulder, "how was your weekend?"

"F-fine," Yami replied, "What about you? I went by the girls' dorm to find you but one of the other girls said you guys were gone. Did you go somewhere?"

"Sort of," Yoake said, "We um . . . we went to—"

"To see my grandparents!" Hana chimed in, "Grandma invited me and the girls to her house for the weekend."

"Oh, I hope you all had fun . . ." Yami said, trailing off slightly.

"I'm really sorry we didn't invite you," Hana said, trying to comfort him, "but my grandparents are kind of old fashioned and don't like the idea of unrelated teenage boys and girls sleeping in the same room."

"I-I understand." Yami said, smiling slightly.

"I've got an idea!" Yoake exclaimed excitedly, "Why don't we all do something together next weekend?" Kyoki and Hana nodded happily, Yami once again smiling. Yami and Yoake bid the other two farewell as they walked into their class.

"Good morning, children," Mr. Satoru said when they walked in. Yoake waved in response.

"G-good morning, sir," Yami replied.

"Did you kids have a good weekend?"

"Yes, sir." Yoake said.

"I'm glad, now take your seats." Yoake nodded and moved to her seat, Yami in tow.

"Hi, Wynona," Yoake said, sitting down and turning around to face the girl behind her. She looked back at Yoake, brushing some strands of brown hair out her face.

"Hey, how's life?" she asked. Yoake shrugged.

"Can't complain. Did you understand the math homework?"

"Girls, please quiet down," Mr. Satoru said, "Miss Hikaru, turn around and pay attention, you might better understand the material" he smiled the same way that sent shivers down her spine.

"Sorry, sir," she said, blushing slightly. Mr. Satoru nodded then turned back to the board and began explaining their newest lesson. What felt like years but was actually only seven hours later, the final bell rang and the class left.

"Miss Derim," Mr. Satoru called, "could you please wait for a moment?" Wynona stopped and walked back to the teacher's desk as Yoake walked out of the classroom.

"I'll see you tomorrow, Yami." Yoake called, waving to him as she turned toward her dorm.

On the way back, Kyoki stopped. "Guys, I'm getting that feeling again."

"Just let us get back to the dorm then you can go." Hana said.

"NOT THAT FEELING!" Kyoki shouted. "I mean the feeling that we're being followed." A week ago the other two would have brushed it off as another one of her crazy paranoia, but considering the events of the past few days, they paid attention. "There." She pointed to an alley and they all ran to it to investigate.

Not surprisingly, Yeldi was there waiting for them. "Hello, ladies." he said in his usual smugly sarcastic manner.

"Oh, you're in trouble now." Kyoki said.

"And why's that?"

"We've had training." Yoake said. "Ready?"

"Ready." The other two nodded, and the three of them opened their watched, transforming.

"Ah ah ah . . ." Yeldi chuckled, wagging his finger at them, "I'm not the one you're fighting today. She is." He pointed the back of the alley where the girls could see a figure walking toward them. As it drew closer they could see it was . . .

"Wynona!" Yoake yelled, shocked. Yeldi laughed as the girl came to stand beside him.

"You like?" he asked, wrapping one arm around Wynona's shoulders.

"What did you do to her?" Yoake demanded. She could see that something was very wrong. The girl's normally bright eyes now held only a dull, glazed over, unfocused look and her nails had lengthened into long, fierce looking claws.

"Me?" Yeldi asked, feigning surprise, "I haven't done a thing. However . . ."

"'However' what, you bastard?" Kyoki snapped.

"Well . . . ," Yeldi mused, then began laughing, "why don't I let your former friend tell you." Gently, he pushed Wynona forward, "tell them, girlie, go on, tell your friends exactly what's going on."

Yoake, Kyoki, and Hana stared in horror as Wynona slowly walked closer and closer to them, her movements erratic and twitchy like a movie zombie.

"I am here," Wynona said, "to take your watches . . . for my master."

"What?" Kyoki yelled, "Damn it, Yeldi!" The monster-boy simply laughed again.

"As I said," he chuckled, "I have done nothing, but my master thought it might be a good idea to use his power on one of you humans. I think the experiment went rather well, don't you?"

Yoake opened her mouth to respond but was cut off when Wynona suddenly lunged for her. She jumped out of the way, landing about two meters back from where she had been. Glaring, at Yeldi, she tried to think of a plan.

"We can't just stand here!" Kyoki growled. She jumped forward, swinging her scythe toward Yeldi, but before she could hit him, Wynona moved between them. The girl held up her clawed hand to block the attack, but Kyoki continued to swing.

"No!" Yoake yelled. Quickly, she strung her bow and launched a violet arrow toward Kyoki. The arrow collided with Kyoki's scythe, forcing the girl backward.

"What the hell!" Kyoki snarled, "Why'd you do that?"

"We can't hurt Wynona," Hana answered.

"Then what do you suggest we do?" Kyoki asked.

"There has to be a way to get her back to normal." Hana said. She closed her eyes, thinking for a moment. "I've got it!" She beckoned the other two girls over to her. "Yoake, Kyoki, I need you to get Yeldi away from her, then I can use my healing ability to wake up Wynona."

"You think that will work?" Yoake asked. Hana nodded.

"Well, it's worth a shot." Kyoki said, turning back to the fight and smirking at Yeldi, "Besides I want to try out the stuff I learned this weekend."

"What are you mumbling about?" Yeldi snapped impatiently, then turned to Wynona, "It doesn't matter. Get them!"

Wynona obeyed, moving at lightning speed toward the three friends. Swinging her scythe, Kyoki blocked the attack, jumping onto Wynona's back. She pushed off the girl and quickly made her way toward Yeldi. Yoake strung her bow again, pulling a red arrow from her quiver.

"How dare you use my friend!" she yelled and sent the arrow flying. Instantly, Wynona turned and tried to run back to protect Yeldi, just as she had before, but Hana's swords at her throat stopped her.

"I'm sorry about this." Hana said, pulling her captive closer. Suddenly, she kicked Wynona in the back of her knees, forcing the girl to the ground, "but this has to be done." With one hand holding a sword against Wynona's throat, Hana moved her other hand over the girl's head. A soft light began to glow between her hand and Wynona's forehead, just as it had over Kyoki's wound, and slowly the shine returned to the girl's eyes as her claws receded. Soon, the Wynona they knew lay unconscious on the ground.

"What now?" Kyoki said, smirking at Yeldi who glared back, snarling. She held her scythe up as dark clouds began to swirl around it, forming a black, floating sheath around the blade. Suddenly, she lept into the air, aiming straight for Yeldi's throat. "REAPER SLASH!" she yelled, bringing her weapon down toward its target. Yeldi growled and dodged, but not before the scythe grazed his arm. He landed on top of a nearby building, still glaring at the girls.

"Fine," he spat, "take your friend." With that, he turned to leave.

"That's right!" Kyoki yelled, "Run! Run back to Saekrin and tell him you failed again!" Yoake watched as Kyoki yelled and for a second, she thought she saw him tense, but he was gone too soon for her to tell.

"Guys!" Hana called, immediately gaining the attention of the two other girls. They ran over and saw that Wynona was waking up.

"What are we gonna do?" Kyoki asked, "We can't let her see us like this."

"Quick," Yoake answered, "close your watch." Hana and Kyoki nodded and as soon as their watches closed, their clothes returned to normal.

"Where am I?" Wynona said as she slowly opened her eyes, "What happened? Yoake, what are you doing here?"

"We were going home from school and you suddenly collapsed." Yoake answered quickly, "Kyoki and Hana saw us and came over to help. You really should get more sleep; you look exhausted." Wynona nodded slowly and stood.

"Thank you for staying with me," she said, "I think I should go home now."

"You okay by yourself?" Kyoki asked. Wynona nodded and with a wave, walked off.

Yeldi sat bowed before Saekrin; he had just finished explaining to his master what had happened that day and was waiting for a beating, but it never came. Shocked, he looked up slowly when the only sound he heard from the older creature was laughter, cold, cruel laughter.

"Don't look so sad, boy," Saekrin chuckled. Yeldi watched his master closely, unsure of what was happening, "We now know more about our adversaries in this world," Saekrin continued, "Friends are obviously a very important concept to humans, but . . ." he trailed off for a moment, making Yeldi tense in fear, ". . . I would bet that family is even more important to them." Yeldi's eyes widened; he knew the pain of having to fight one's own family. "Leave me, boy." Saekrin hissed, his mood suddenly angry. Quickly, Yeldi obeyed, standing, and walked out of the room, his masters sadistic laughter echoing down the hall.

❧

"We need to kick Yeldi's ass once and for all!" Kyoki snapped once they got back to the dorm, "This can't keep going on! Who knows what he and his bastard of a master are going to do next?!"

Hana nodded. "You're right," she said, "but we need for form some kind of attack plan. We've been on the defensive since the beginning."

"We're not ready." Yoake commented. "We still need more training."

"Screw training!" Kyoki said. "We've got the power, let's use it!"

"But what's the point of using power if we don't know *how*?" Yoake snapped back, making Kyoki close her mouth angrily. "Training helps us experiment and grow stronger. We can learn our weaknesses and the things we can't control."

"Fine." Kyoki said realizing that she was talking about the incident at the zoo.

"Look, Kyoki, don't be so mad about it." Hana said. "She's right, and you tend to be really rash and make really quick decisions without thinking about them."

"Fine then," Kyoki said, "Oo! I've got an idea for something we can do while we wait for the weekend!"

"What?" Hana asked, curious. Kyoki wasn't the type to be particularly rational.

"We should talk to Tybalt and see what he knows about Saekrin. We already know he was one of that bastard's comrades, so he must know something about him."

"That's actually a good idea!" Hana said happily.

Kyoki scowled. "Don't look so surprised." she snapped, then sighed, "but how are we going to get in touch with him?"

Yoake shrugged. "We'll have to figure it out somehow." she said, walking to the window and opening it, "I guess we could just yell out the—" she stopped suddenly as Tybalt appeared on the window sill.

"Did you girls need something?" he asked, stepping into the room.

"We need you to tell us everything you know about Saekrin," Kyoki said, "absolutely everything. We can't sit back and let him dictate how this goes any longer." Tybalt nodded.

"I understand," he said, "but you I've already told you girls just about everything I know."

"Please," Hana said, "There's got to be something."

"Alright," Tybalt responded after a few moments of thought, "I'll tell you everything I can think of. First off, I met him during basic training. He was eager, shy, didn't talk to many people and generally tried to stay out of the way, but I guess that's not important right now. I'm sure you guys want to know about his power." The girls nodded.

"Alright," he continued, "Saekrin is a hypnotist; his watch allows him to take control of the mind of any living creature he wants. Because of this, he is very dangerous in battle, not so much for offensive moves although he did learn how to force some incredibly powerful techiniques out of his watch, which is air based, but I digress. Hypnotists are generally spies. They get behind enemy lines and take control of the generals. That's why I've been having such a hard time finding him; he knows very well how to cover his tracks. The other thing you should know about him is that he controls two watches. He's the only one to have that ability in two thousand years."

"When Alia and Erasure found out, they were so happy because Saekrin would be such a powerful fighter, a great soldier, but now that joy has turned to tears. His second watch is very special. It changes to suit his whims, to be specific it changes to suit the situation."

"What the hell!" Kyoki yelled, "Then how the hell are we supposed to beat him?" Tybalt shrugged.

"If I knew that, I would've caught him by now."

"Good lord, you're no help." Kyoki yelled, picking up a pillow and throwing it at Tybalt, "get lost!"

"Kyoki!" Hana said, "What are you doing?"

"Talking is getting us nowhere!" she snapped back, "We need action and he," she pointed at Tybalt, "isn't helping us a bit."

"He's training us." Yoake retorted. Kyoki opened her mouth to reply but Tybalt beat her to it.

"I think I should just go," he said, "You girls have school in the morning and still have homework. We wouldn't want your grades to start slipping, would we? See you." With that, he jumped out the window and disappeared.

"Nice going," Hana growled, "you've managed to alienate the one person on this planet who is helping us." Kyoki scowled back at her friend, picked up her biology book, and got to work.

The walk to school the next day was tense and awkward. Kyoki and Hana had decided they weren't going to speak to each other anymore and Yoake was very worried. How were they supposed to fight together if they were angry at each other?

"Hi," Yami said as Yoake walked into the classroom, "what's wrong? You look upset."

"It's nothing," she answered, "really, I'm fine." Yami nodded slowly, obviously unconvinced but decided to drop the subject.

"Did you understand the algebra homework?" he asked. Yoake shook her head and he sighed.

"Good morning, class," Mr. Satoru said, taking his place in front of the blackboard, "Today we will be reviewing for your test on Thursday so I suggest you all pay close attention. Now . . ." Yoake tried her best to pay attention but all she could think about was her two friends. Hana and Kyoki had know each other before Yoake even came into the mix. They'd always been friend, they fought like two dogs over an old bone, but still maintain a very close relationship. Kyoki was the one who introduced Yoake to Hana, and she'd always had been the one that broke up their fighting, keeping them together as a group. Lately however, Yoake felt her ability to do so fading away. Kyoki and Hana were fighting a lot more often ever since they got the watches, and she couldn't help but feel that the objects in question and the events that accompanied were driving a wedge between them.

Kyoki in particular she was worried about, especially after hearing Erasure's talk with Tybalt. Kyoki was strong, there was no doubt about that, but she was rash and didn't think, apparently a lot like Saekrin. She couldn't help the feeling that Kyoki might feel restricted by the slow pace they were going at, and was worried her purple-haired friend might do something she'll regret, again. She sighed.

Suddenly, a hand on her shoulder jerked her out of her thoughts.

"It's lunch time . . ." Yami said nervously, abruptly pulling his hand away.

"Thanks," Yoake said, looking down at her notebook. Another sigh escaped her when she realized that she hadn't taken any notes because of her musings. Nonetheless, she grabbed her lunch box and walked out of the room, Yami in tow, to the cafeteria. When she arrived, she saw Hana sitting alone.

"Where's Kyoki?" Yoake asked worriedly as she sat down.

Hana shrugged. "Don't know, don't care." she said flatly, popping a strawberry into her mouth.

"Di-did something happen?" Yami asked, looking back and forth between Yoake and Hana, "What happened to Kyoki?" Just then, Kyoki walked into the cafeteria. She glanced over at Yoake, glared at Hana, then walked off and sat with a group of third years at the back of the room.

Yoake sighed; this couldn't go on much longer. They had to concentrate on what was important: finding and defeating Saekrin. *"If Kyoki can't get past a tiny argument . . ."* She didn't want to think of the consequences of that.

Soon, lunch was over and Yoake and Yami made their way back to class. Another three hours of review later, the bell rang, signaling the end of the day. Yoake waved good bye to Yami and dashed off to meet her roommates. She soon spotted Kyoki waiting for her, but Hana was nowhere to be seen.

"Where's Hana?" Yoake asked once she reached Kyoki. The older girl scowled.

"Last I saw it—her—she was helping clean up after a physics experiment. Let's just get going." Yoake opened her mouth to protest but suddenly Kyoki grabbed her sleeve and forced her to follow along. When they arrived back at the dorm, Kyoki tossed her bag onto her bed angrily and pulled out a textbook. Yoake followed suit, glancing at the door every so often in the hopes that Hana would arrive soon. Yoake's concern increased as the hours went by and still Hana did not return.

The day was special for the three of them, as it was their "Friendship Anniversary". Eleven years ago, tomorrow Kyoki first introduced Yoake and Hana, thus the friendship between them had started. *"But if Hana and Kyoki can't forgive each other—"* Suddenly, a scream rang out through the room.

"What the hell was that?" Kyoki jumped to her feet.

"Get back!" the voice said again.

"Hana!" the other two girls cried in surprise.

"Guys? Is that you?" Hana asked.

"Hana, where are you?" Yoake asked.

"The supermarket. I went to get some stuff for dinner tomorrow and Yeldi attacked."

Kyoki was a bit confused. "But our meals are provid—"

"I don't think that's an issue right now!" Yoake interrupted.

"Why don't you just transform and fight him?" Kyoki asked.

"There are people around. I can't let them see me."

"Hang tight, Hana, we're on our way. Try to get out of the store. We'll find you." Yoake said. "Come on, Kyoki."

"Yeah, yeah I'm coming."

"Well hurry up. He's destroying to store trying to find me." Hana said.

"Ok," Yoake said, "We're on our way just hang on a little longer." With that, she grabbed Kyoki and dragged her out of the dorm. They ran as fast as they could, past block after block of houses and shops until they reached the store. People were running out, screaming and trying to trample each other in their haste to get away. Kyoki and Yoake tried to push through the crowd but it was like trying to go upstream in white water rapids.

"Don't go in there!" one of the people dashing past them yelled, but they ignored him, instead forcing their way through the automatic doors. Inside, they saw Yeldi standing on top of one of the tall aisle shelves. All around him, the stands had fallen over like dominoes, food spilling everywhere. He looked left and right, scanning the store in an attempt to find Hana.

"Where are you, love?" Yeldi said mockingly in a very bad imitation of a British accent. He chuckled to himself before jumping onto another one of the few shelves still standing knocking over the shelf he had been standing on in the process. Quickly, Kyoki and Yoake moved to hide under one of the fallen shelves, hoping to avoid being seen.

"I wonder where she is . . ." Yoake said as they crawled through the debris.

"Like I care," Kyoki snapped back, but Yoake could hear the faintest traces of worry in her friend's voice.

Suddenly, a voice called to them. "Guys! Over here!" Hana said, waving them over.

"Hana!" Yoake said as she and Kyoki crawled over to their friend.

"Boy, am I glad to see your faces." Hana said. Suddenly, there was a tiny squeak from behind her. Moving aside, Hana revealed a small girl that was using her as a shield. "Oh guys, this is Kimi." The small blond girl tried to wave but a sudden crash made her whimper and cower ever further behind Hana. Yoake and Kyoki looked around for the source but found none, quickly concluding that Yeldi was searching for them under the debris.

"We need to transform." Kyoki whispered to Yoake. She nodded.

"But what about . . . ?" she asked, pointing to Kimi.

"I've got an idea," Kyoki answered, turning to the frightened girl, "We're going to see if we can find a way out of here without that big scary thing finding us, okay?" She started to crawl away with the two other high school girl but suddenly Hana stopped.

"What's wrong?" Yoake asked. Hana shifted so the girls could see what had stopped her; Kimi had grabbed hold of her shirt.

"We'll be back soon," Hana said, trying to comfort her, "but we need you to stay here. Stay hidden and we'll come back and get you as soon as it's safe." Kimi nodded and reluctantly let go of Hana's sleeve. With a quick nod to the other girls, Hana set off crawling again. Soon the three were out from under the fallen shelf.

"Ready?" Yoake asked. Hana and Kyoki nodded and all three opened their watches. Light burst forth, filling the entire store and nearly blinding the crowd that had gathered outside. Seconds later, the girls stood, transformed and ready for battle.

"Heh, so you finally decided to show up," Yeldi chuckled from his seat atop pile of fallen shelves.

"What the hell is wrong with you?" Kyoki yelled, "How could you attack when so many innocent people are around? They could have gotten seriously hurt thanks to you!"

Yeldi shrugged. "Acceptable losses," he said flatly, "mere expendable creatures. We are all expendable in the end, really, so it doesn't matter."

"Bastard!"

"Kyoki, stop," Hana said, glaring at Yeldi, "arguing with him isn't going to get us anywhere. Let's focus on getting him out of here and then we can worry about other people."

"Wow! You guys are so cool!" said a voice suddenly. The girls turned to see Kimi sitting under the shelf they had crawled out from under and smiling brightly at them.

"We told you to stay put," Hana sighed.

"But I was lonely and scared . . ." Kimi said softly, "I didn't want to be alone."

"So that's what you meant by hurting other people," Yeldi laughed.

"Leave her out of this!" Yoake yelled.

Yeldi simply continued to laugh. "Maybe I will; maybe I won't," he said as he jumped off his perch, landing right behind a terrified Kimi and putting one of his clawed finger to her throat "It all depends on you. Give me your watches and I'll let her walk out of here alive."

"Kimi, duck!" Yoake shouted as she loosed an arrow straight at Yeldi. He easily dodged it, taking Kimi with him.

"That's it!" Kyoki snarled, "Today you die! REAPER'S BLADE!" She held her scythe high in the air, dark clouds swirling around it. They fused to the blade, creating spikes made of pure black energy. Kyoki lept forward, bringing her weapon down toward Yeldi, but missed as he suddenly leaped out of the way separating himself from the little girl he was holding hostage.

"My turn!" Hana yelled. She ran over to the pile of shelves he had been sitting on and used them as a springboard, propelling herself into the air after the creature.

"VINE WEB!" she yelled, slicing her air with her swords. Each time she brought one of the blades down, a new, green vine appeared in the air. They moved as one around Yeldi, binding him high above the ground.

"You're finished!" Yoake said, stringing her bow with a bright violet arrow, "ROYAL BLAST!" The arrow flew straight toward their captive but suddenly, just as it was about to collide with Yeldi, it disappeared.

"What the—?" Kyoki gasped, stunned.

"Girls!" the group turned to see Tybalt running toward them.

"What are you doing here?" Hana asked.

"Lady Alia called me back this morning and when I returned I couldn't find you. Then I heard some people talking about a strange creature trashing the local supermarket. It didn't take a genius to put two and two together and as I was running over here I thought I saw—"

"You seem to have gotten yourself into a bit of trouble, Yeldi," hissed a cold, velvety voice, a sadistic chuckle playing on the words.

"Master!" Yeldi exclaimed, looking over at the source of the voice. The group quickly spun around to see a figure walking toward them, its smirk revealing a pair of sharp fangs.

"Is that?" Yoake gasped. Tybalt nodded. The girls stared at the creature walking closer and closer. He had long, snow white hair pulled into a low ponytail at the base of his neck, black claws like Yeldi's only slightly longer, a pair of thick soled black boots, grey pants, a tunic-like shirt, and a long dark purple coat with plate armor on the sides and shoulders and golden embroidery on the hem.

"Saekrin," Tybalt snarled.

"It's been a long time, old friend," Saekrin hissed mockingly. He brought his hand up, slashing the closest vine and sending Yeldi crashing to the ground beside him. Yeldi immediately bowed at his master's feet, waiting patiently for orders.

"Good day, ladies," Saekrin said, cold grey eyes scanning each of them slowly, "I'm so glad we finally have this chance to talk in person. You've done quite a bit of damage to my boy here." Yeldi jerked his head up slightly at Saekrin's words.

"I'm sorry, Master, I—" he began, but a harsh glare from Saekrin silenced him instantly.

Turning back to the girls, he continued, "I apologize that we have to meet on such unfriendly terms."

"Any time we meet you will be unfriendly." Yoake said.

"Oh that's too bad, I was hoping we could all be friends." he said as he walked over to Kimi and leaned down to her eye level. "What do you think, my dear? Do you think you could be my friend?" Kimi stared at him, mesmerized by the strange man standing in front of her. Slowly, he brought his clawed hand to her rosy cheek.

"Stay away from her!" Hana shouted.

"Oh calm down." He stood, Kimi collapsing as he moved. "I just erased her memory of today's events. You don't want your secret getting out, do you?"

"Why would it matter? You know who we are, it's not like we have superhero names." Yoake said.

"I suppose not," Saekrin mused, "but it's more fun for me this way." He turned and started to walk away, obviously finished talking, "Come, Yeldi." The boy immediately stood and followed his master toward the door.

"Get back here, you bastard!" Kyoki yelled, suddenly lunging at Saekrin. She swung her scythe with every intention of cutting him in half. Yeldi watched in horror, too late to stop it from colliding with his master, but he wasn't needed. A loud crash sounded through the store as Saekrin brought his hand up, swatting Kyoki away as if she were nothing more than an annoying insect.

"Kyoki!" the other two girls yelled, running over to their fallen friend.

"You know, you girls are rather cute," Saekrin chuckled mockingly, "I almost feel bad about having to kill you . . . almost."

"Saekrin," Tybalt growled at the smirking creature before him.

"Yes? . . ." he replied, chuckling darkly, "What is it, friend? Have you finally come to take your baby brother away from me? You say I'm such a bad influence on him." As if to make his point, Saekrin turned to Yeldi and smacked him, sending the boy to the ground hard. Yeldi slowly picked himself up and settled onto his hands and knees, hoping not to draw any more of his master's attention. Tybalt growled at the sight of his little brother's abuse, making Saekrin chuckle. "What's the matter, Tybalt? This was the boy's choice, and this is the price he has to pay. It's a small price considering . . ."

"Considering what?" Tybalt snapped, but Saekrin only chuckled in response and, motioning for Yeldi to follow, left. For a second, Tybalt debated running after him but when he turned to the girls, he saw that Kyoki's foot was sticking out at an odd angle and was most likely broken. He sighed, it was just like the zoo, so he closed his watch and went to help the injured girl. "How's she doing?" he asked.

"It's probably broken." Hana said.

"Can't you heal it?" Yoake asked. Hana shook her head.

"Sakura told me that healing bones is very difficult because if you do it wrong it can cause permanent damage. I haven't learned how to do it yet and I think if I tried I might only make it worse."

"Then I guess it's straight to the hospital for you," Tybalt said, pulling Kyoki up so she could lean on him.

"I'm fine. I'm fine," she snapped, trying to push him away. For a second she stood on her own, but with a loud yelp of pain, came crashing to the floor.

"No, you're obviously not," Hana said, exasperated, "So just let us help you." Slowly, Kyoki nodded and put her arm around Hana and Yoake, sending a pointed glare toward Tybalt. He reached forward and gently closed each of their watches, returning the girls to normal.

"I'll meet you girls later," he said then glanced at Kyoki, "I don't think I'm wanted here."

Later that day, Hana and Yoake stood beside Kyoki as a doctor bandaged her ankle. Thankfully, it had not been broken, just badly sprained. Once he finished, the doctor looked up at Kyoki.

"You're going to have to use crutches for a few days." he said. Kyoki jerked her head up suddenly, eyes wide.

"No way!" she yelped, "I can't! I have to—" she stopped abruptly. She had almost revealed the watches.

"You don't have a choice," the doctor continued, "If you try to walk on that ankle by itself, then it will only get worse. Just use the crutches for a little while and your ankle will heal in no time." Kyoki sighed and nodded.

"Good, I'll be right back, just stay here." With that, the doctor walked off to get a pair of crutches for her.

"What did I tell you about acting rashly?" Hana asked pointedly, turning to the injured girl.

"Umm . . . no?" she answered sarcastically.

"You always do this!" Hana continued, "If you'd just think things through before you do them, then you wouldn't get hurt so much."

"Guys, guys," Yoake said, "let's not fight, okay? All this day taught us is that we need to train more and get stronger so we can beat Saekrin, and get the watches back, and save Yeldi—"

"What?!" Hana and Kyoki yelled.

"What do you mean 'save Yeldi'?" Kyoki asked, "You heard him; he chose to follow that bastard. It's not our problem or responsibility to help him at all." She folded her arms across her chest pointedly.

"Yeah," Hana continued, "we're supposed to beat him not save him."

"I-I know," Yoake said, rubbing her arm awkwardly, "it's just . . . well . . . you saw how Saekrin treats him. It's like Yeldi isn't even human—"

"He's not." Kyoki snapped.

"You know what I mean," Yoake said, "and anyway, no matter what he's done, no one deserves to be treated like nothing but a slave, a tool, something to be used however the other person wants."

Kyoki opened her mouth to respond but the sound of the door made her stop. The doctor handed her the crutches, quickly made sure she knew how to use them, and then let her go. As the girls walked back to their dorm, or in the case of Kyoki, hobbled back, they were silent.

"I-I'm sorry I charged in like that," Kyoki said suddenly, looking down as a blush coated her cheeks.

"What did you say?" Hana asked, "Speak up." Kyoki mumbled something, still keeping her eyes locked on the ground.

"Huh?" Yoake said, leaning over a bit.

"I said I'm sorry!" Kyoki yelled. The other two looked at her in shock for a moment, then Yoake put an arm around her friend's shoulder.

"It's okay," she said, "let's just move on and concentrate on getting the job done."

"Right!" Hana chimed in, smiling. Kyoki looked up at her friends and grinned.

The next morning, the girls woke and, while Hana helped Kyoki stand, Yoake walked to the window to let Tybalt in. "Hey, girls." he said as he climbed through the window. "How's the ankle, Kyoki?" She just huffed at him. "As stubborn as ever I see."

"So that guy we saw," Yoake said, "that was Saekrin?"

"Yes." Tybalt nodded.

"So that *thing* is what we're up against?" Hana asked.

"I'm afraid so." he replied.

"Damn it!" Kyoki yelled. "How are we supposed to fight him? He's indestructible!"

"Not really, just very powerful." Tybalt corrected, "which means you are all going to have to train a lot more."

"But you've been training with him since before he became a psychopathic bastard," Kyoki said, "How come you haven't beaten him?"

"As I said," Tybalt answered, "He's very powerful. My power alone isn't enough to defeat him, but you three have the potential to do it."

"I see . . ." Hana mused, "I think what we should do now would be recon. We can assume that he knows who we are and that if it really is our watches he wants, then it seems logical that he would want to stay close to us and watch for an opening."

"Right!" Yoake said, "If he hasn't found us yet, then we can be extra careful, and if he has all we have to do is look for new people in our lives and that's probably him."

"Or Yeldi," Kyoki interjected, "We can't discount the fact that he probably has his little ass of a slave on the job too." She looked at Tybalt for a moment before remembering who Yeldi was, "sorry."

"It's alright," Tybalt sighed, "I know what my brother has done to you and you have every right to be angry with him."

"Alright then!" Kyoki said, pushing herself up and onto her crutches, "Let's get this show on the road." With that, she wobbled to the door, verbally dragging Hana and Yoake after her. Tybalt waved them off before jumping out the window.

"So where do you think we should start?" Yoake asked.

"When we get to class," Hana began, "we should look for any new students or faculty and tail them as best we can. Kyoki, I think you might have to sit this one out." At that, the third year scowled but nodded; she wasn't going to be much use in a possible fight in her current state.

"Got it." Yoake said happily, turning to go into class, "See you guys later." Quickly, she walked into the room and sat down, but a sudden voice made her jump.

"H-hi, Yoake," Yami said softly, standing in front of her and rubbing his arm awkwardly.

"Hey, Yami," she answered, "What's new?" It was then Yoake noticed a large bruise just above Yami's wrist and, as his sleeve moved with the rubbing of his hand, she could see more going up his arm. "You okay?" she asked slowly, concerned.

"Y-yeah," Yami replied, shaking a bit, "I just, I just got hurt in a fight but—"

"Who were you fighting?" Yoake yelled, standing, "Tell me who hurt you. I'll kick their ass!" Yami flinched at the sudden volume and frantically shook his head.

"No," he said, "It-it wasn't a fight like that. I-I-I got hurt during a . . . a sparring match. I take k-karate lessons and it was a practice fight and we got carried away and, and, it's alright. I-I'm alright. You, you don't have to hurt anyone." Yoake stared at Yami with an expression that read clearly "oh."

"Class," Mr. Satoru's voice said from the front of the room, "Please take your seats. There is someone I would like you all to meet." Yoake looked over to find a boy standing next to her teacher. He was tall, with short dark brown hair and black eyes. As his eyes scanned the class, they paused on Yoake, glaring like he already hated her.

"This is Akira Kotobushi, our newest student," Mr. Satoru continued, indictating the boy beside him, "Now," he turned to Akira, "please take a seat." Yoake looked around and sadly found that the only empty desk was the one right beside her. The boy sat down, shooting Yoake another glare as he did so. For her part, Yoake turned to look out the window, trying very hard to ignore the piercing stare. She stayed in that position for the rest of class, concentrating so much on tuning out the boy beside her that she didn't hear a word of her teacher's lecture. Suddenly, a low voice hissed in her ear.

"I'm *so* glad that you're my partner." Akira said, instantly making Yoake jump.

"What are you talking about?" She asked then heard Mr. Satoru sigh.

"As I just finished explaining," he said, "I have paired you all up so that you can do a project on some aspect of the history of biology, specifically the medical field. You and Mr. Kotobushi will be researching the medical technology of the western middle ages." Yoake opened her mouth to protest but the lunch bell interrupted.

"See you after lunch . . ." Akira said, smirking. Yoake nodded dumbly as she stood, walking out of the room with Yami toward the cafeteria.

"Hey, Yoake," Kyoki said as the other girl sat down, "You too, Yami. How's it going?" Yami smiled nervously as Yoake shrugged.

"Not bad," she said, "but . . ."

"But what?" Hana asked.

"I think Yeldi might be in my class," Yoake blurted. Kyoki's eyes immediately snapped up.

"Who? Where? I'll kick that little bastard's ass!" she snarled, brandishing one of her crutches as viciously as she could.

"I think it's—"

"Hello, partner," Akira said suddenly, sitting next to Yoake. Kyoki and Hana glanced back and forth between the two, obviously wating for an explanation.

"Uh . . . hi," Yoake said, "Guys, this is Akira Kotobushi. He just joined my class and we're supposed to work together on a history project." The two girls nodded, introduced themselves, and settled into a rather awkward silence.

"So . . ." Akira said, "What kinds of things do you do around this school?"

"Well there are lots of clubs and sports," Hana replied, concentrating more on her sandwich than the conversation.

"And, um, sometimes there are games to watch . . ." Yami said. As soon as Akira's eyes fell on him, the boy turned very red and began to stare at the table. Another silence descended on them, broken only by the children's chewing.

"Boys," Mr. Satoru said, suddenly appearing behind Yoake and making her jump, "I need some help getting the projector set up for the next lesson. Could you assist me?" Yoake twitched nervously; the way her teacher had asked sounded more like a order than a question.

"Sure," Akira said, standing. Yami simply nodded and followed the two other males out of the cafeteria.

"Good lord, he's scary," Yoake said once they were gone.

"Which one?" Kyoki asked, "Your teacher is a plain and simple creeper but the new kid is just—how should I put this—a super creeper."

"Is he the one you think might be Yeldi?" Hana asked. Yoake nodded.

"Yeah," she said, "I mean, he came into class and glared at me, then he kept looking at me like he wanted to eat me, and now he just came over here like he was stalking me or something." She shivered at the thought and went back to her soup.

"Well, if he is Yeldi," Kyoki reasoned, "I think you should stay as close to him as possible and after school we'll talk to Tybalt about what to do next."

"I'm proud of you, Kyoki," Hana said, smiling.

"Huh?"

"You're thinking strategically instead of acting rashly." she continued. Kyoki scowled and stuck her tongue out.

"Don't patronize me." she snapped. Yoake sighed; even when their common enemy was somewhere among them, her two friends couldn't seem to stop fighting.

After school, as the three were walking home, they took a short cut through the park when they heard a voice say to them, "I was wondering when you'd show up." They turned around to see a boy leaning against a tree.

"Akira?" Yoake said.

"Maybe, maybe not." he said. "That's for you to decide."

"Enough chit-chat!" Kyoki interrupted. "Let's smoke this guy!"

She moved to open her watch but Yoake stopped her. "Wait, we don't know for sure if it's Yeldi. So maybe we should call this one off."

"But—"

"Kyoki."

"Ok. Fine."

"You're giving up? I feel insulted." Suddenly Akira's eyes became cloudy, distant and a figure seemed to walk out of him as he collapsed to the ground.

The girls gasped when they saw who it was. "Yeldi?" Hana said, puzzled.

"What the hell!" Kyoki yelled.

"It took a lot of Master's power to get me into that kid's body and now you're just going to walk away from the fight? That's both cowardly and insulting." Yeldi said crossing his arms.

"Why you! Come here and say that to my face!" Kyoki tried to run at him but Hana caught her by the collar.

"Down girl." she said.

"Call us cowards but we will do what we want." Yoake said. With that she turned and started away, the other two following behind.

Yeldi growled and shouted, "Fine walk away! See if I care!"

"Keep walking." Yoake whispered to her friends.

"What are you—" Hana started.

"Just keep going." She stopped walking, letting the other two walk away before she turned around and looked Yeldi strait in the eye.

"What?" Yeldi snapped.

"My offer still stands."

"Will you stop with that!" Yeldi said. "I told you—"

"I know what you told me, and I don't care that you think there's no hope." Yoake walked up to him and looked up, finally getting a good look at his face. His eyes were full of despair, not evil. Somehow, she was able to see the good in him, although chained and repressed by fear. When she saw that, she made a vow. "I will *not* give up on you, not ever."

He gasped. What was she thinking? There really was no hope for him, so why was she being so stubborn? In an effort to dissuade her, her pushed her back and shouted, "Why the hell do you care? What happens to me is none of your business, so just stop!"

"No." she answered calmly staring him down.

"Stop looking at me like that!" He charged at her, but when she narrowed her eyes even further, he stopped and sank to his knees, tears streaming out of his eyes as he sobbed, "Please just look away. You remind me of *her*."

"Who?" she asked.

His only response was an enraged cry. "You damn bitch!" he shrieked as he slashed at her face, but she easily dodged him. "Look away, damn it! Stop! Why can't you just give up? Why do you have to be the hero?"

"I'm just trying to help."

"Why? What is possessing you to try and help me?"

"Nothing is possessing me, I'm doing it out of my own free will."

"But why?"

"Because I want to!" she snapped. "Why do I need a reason to help people?"

Suddenly the fury and confusion left his eyes and he broke out into mirthless laughter. "So you're telling me that you don't have a reason to help me? You're not looking for personal gain at all? HA! How naive. You think that's how the world works? Well you're wrong. You have to give something in order to receive. So what do you want from me?"

She sighed and said, "Fine, if you insist, all I want from you is cooperation."

"Even if I did cooperate there is no hope for me."

"Why do you keep insisting on that?"

"Because it's true. I practically gave Master my soul, so I can't defy him, even if I wanted to."

"What do you mean?"

"Ask my brother. I have to go; it looks like 'Sleeping Beauty' is waking up." He pointed at Akira, who was stirring back to consciousness. "See you 'round." With that he ran off.

"Yeldi wait!" she tried to call after him, but he was already gone "And he says I'm stubborn."

A groan from Akira reminded her that he was there and she ran over to him as he sat up. "What happened?" he said weakly and looked up at Yoake. "Oh, hey partner."

"You feeling okay?" she asked.

"I feel like I've been kicked by a horse."

"I can imagine."

"What?"

"Nothing. What's the last thing you remember?"

"Uh . . . Yami and I were helping Mr. Satoru with the projector, then it's all a blank." he said rubbing his head.

"Okay, then. Well, do you want me to help you to the dorms?"

"Yeah sure." He let her help him stand up. "So there will definitely be curious people, what do we tell them?"

"I guess it works out that we are partners on the history, so we can tell people we were working on it."

"Okay." he nodded.

When they got back to the dorms they said their good-byes and Akira went toward his dorm. Before he walked in however, he turned around and said, "By the way, give Tybalt my best."

Yoake looked at him in shock, but he had already disappeared through the door. She walked up to her room and walked in to be nearly tackled by her roommates. "Are you okay?" Hana asked.

"Did you kick his ass?" Kyoki said.

"No and I'm fine." Yoake answered.

With that, she went and sat down on her bed and Hana said, "Hey, Yoake." Yoake looked up at her friend to feel Hana's hand strike her cheek.

"What was—"

"You idiot!" Hana yelled. "Did you even think about what you were doing? You left yourself vulnerable, he could have killed you!"

"But he didn't."

"That's not the point!"

"Yeah!" Kyoki snapped, "What gives you the right to just go off on your own and leave us out of it. What happened? Tell us. Now." She glared hard at Yoake who averted her eyes, trying not to look at her friends. "Well?" Still Yoake said nothing. Suddenly, Kyoki lunged forward and tried to grab her, but without her crutches she fell, tackling Yoake in the process. "TELL US WHAT HAPPENED!" She yelled, shaking Yoake's shoulders, "TELL US NOW OR I SWEAR I'LL—"

"All I did was try to talking to him!" Yoake yelled.

She looked up at Kyoki who stared in shock at her. "Wh-what?" she said as Hana helped her back onto her bed.

"I tried to get him to join us . . ." Yoake answered, standing, "I thought that if we had him on our side, it would be easier to beat Saekrin."

"Well, what did he say?" Hana asked.

"He said he had 'practically sold his soul' to Saekrin and to ask Tybalt what he meant. I don't know what to do."

"I understand you wanting to help him," Hana said, "but I also think that you should have discussed it with us first, or at least told us what you were going to do. We're supposed to be a team and that means we have to trust each other. Don't you trust us?"

"Of course I—"

"Then why didn't you tell us what you were planning?" Kyoki yelled.

"I don't know," Yoake answered, "I-I-I don't know what I was thinking. I guess I just want to get him out of there. You saw how Saekrin treats him; no one deserves that and I firmly believe there is good in him. We just need to dig it out!"

Hana sighed. "I understand your desire to help others, but please . . . just include us in your plans." Yoake nodded.

"I'm sorry," she said, "oh and do either of you know where Tybalt is?"

"It's cool," Kyoki smiled, "but no I don't. He usually comes in the morning, so just wait til then. What do you need him for?"

"I just want to ask him some questions about Yeldi." Yoake said. Kyoki shrugged and rolled over.

"Night all," she said. Hana and Yoake each bid her good night and soon fell asleep.

The next morning as the girls began their normal routine, Tybalt climbed through the window. "Good morning, ladies." he said cheerfully.

"You seem to be in a good mood." Hana observed as she made her bed.

"Do I? I guess I am in a pretty good mood today."

"Get a good night's sleep?" Yoake asked as she tried to pull Kyoki's covers off of the sleeping teen, only to receive a groan in response.

"Yes, but I also talked to a friend last night." Tybalt said. "Anyway, you kids seem to be doing well, all things considered."

"Yeah, except *someone* decided to try and get Yeldi onto our side without telling us about it first." Hana said looking at Yoake.

"I said I was sorry, okay? Just drop it." Yoake retorted, continuing to struggle with Kyoki. "Come on Kyoki, if you don't get up, you'll miss breakfast." At that, Kyoki shot out of her bed and into the bathroom to get ready without a word. Yoake chuckled. "Works everytime. Tybalt there's something I want to ask you."

"Ask away." he shrugged.

"Does the name Akira mean anything to you?"

Tybalt looked at her in surprise. "I think that's the name one of my previous students . . . well *one of* his names."

"What do you mean by that?"

71

"His real name is Artan. He's a shapeshifter and he often takes on an alias in order to maintain his disguise."

"How do you know him?"

"He was supposed to be Saekrin's student, but when Saekrin betrayed us, I was chosen as his teacher. Why?"

"I think he might be in my class." Yoake said, much to the surprise to the others in the room.

"Wait, Akira is your creepy project partner, isn't he?" Hana said and banged on the bathroom door. "Kyoki, hurry up!"

"Yeah." Yoake said. "I was walking back with him after Yeldi ran off and as he left he turned around and said 'Give Tybalt my best.' I assumed he meant you." She looked at him. "But he walked away before I could ask anything else."

Tybalt smiled and laughed. "Yeah that sounds like him, and yes I did know he was here. He was the one I talked to last night, but I had no idea that he was hiding out in your class."

"Well, if he was your student how did you not know he was here?" Hana asked.

"He ran away just after Saekrin left our world. I hadn't seen him until I ran into him last night."

"Why?" Yoake asked.

Tybalt sighed and was silent for a moment. As he opened his mouth to answer Kyoki walked out of the bathroom. "All yours, Flower Power." she said.

"Hang on a second." Hana said.

Kyoki looked at her, then at Yoake, finally at Tybalt before she said, "Did I miss something?"

"Yes" Hana said. "I'll fill you in later."

"You were about to say . . . ?" Yoake said to Tybalt.

"Right," Tybalt nodded. "Well, Artan left to follow Saekrin on his own without any explanation, but his intentions were obvious. His father died in the battle against Saekrin and they were very close so it wasn't hard to figure out that—"

"He was out for revenge." Yoake finished.

Tybalt nodded again. "Yes. I'm guessing that's why he's here, because Saekrin is. Why he's at your school, I'm guessing is because he knows that you girls have the watches."

"Well, it would have been nice for him to tell us." Kyoki said.

"I don't think he had the chance." Hana said.

"He did when he was with Yoake."

Tybalt sighed, "I'm sure he had a reason for not telling you." Kyoki grunted and hobbled over to Tybalt, trying to push him out.

"What are you doing?" Hana asked.

"Isn't it obvious?" Kyoki answered, continuing to shove, "We need to get changed; he can't be here." Tybalt laughed and nodded.

"Alright, alright," he said, moving toward the window, "It's Friday so I'll meet you here after school and then we'll head out for more training." The girls nodded and, as soon as he was gone, shut the window.

"Hey, Yami," Yoake said as she sat down. For a moment, she looked around for any sign of Akira and found him talking to a group of boys from the soccer club in the back of the room. Yami nodded in response before going back to his notes.

"What'cha doing?" Yoake asked.

"I heard w-we were going to have a pop quiz today so I thought I'd study," he said. Yoake's eyes widened at the news and she frantically began searching through her notes. Just as she found her notes from the day before, the bell rang.

"Class," Mr. Satoru began, instantly gaining the students' attention, "I've been hearing some rumors that say I'm giving a pop quiz today. However, these are false. I was planning on having it tomorrow." This revelation was followed by sighs of relief from around the room, "however," the teacher continued, "since you all have decided to study today, we'll just have to have our quiz now." He smiled at them, making Yoake sigh. She looked over at Yami, who seemed very pleased with himself for studying, and put her head down; so much for a good day.

"Urgh, that was torture," Yoake complained, sitting down next to Yami in the cafeteria.

"What was?" Kyoki asked as she tried to pull out all the carrots in her soup.

"Mr. Satoru gave us a quiz today that was supposed to be tomorrow." she answered sadly.

"Ouch," Hana said, "How do you think you guys did?" Yoake simply shook her head, but Yami smiled.

"I think I did okay," he said, "there was a rumor he was going to give the quiz today so I studied." The rest of lunch proceeded quickly, Kyoki and Hana arguing over who was the best new band and Yoake and Yami simply laughing at the ridiculous insults and reasoning being thrown back and forth.

As Yoake walked back to class, Hana suddenly stopped her, "We need to talk to Akira." Yoake nodded.

"Why don't we catch him after school?" she said, "I know where his dorm is." Hana nodded and walked off.

Once the final bell rang, Yoake quickly waved good bye to Yami and ran off in hopes of catching up with her friends and, more importantly, with Akira.

"Hey where's the fire?" Kyoki asked playfully as Yoake ran past her and Hana. Instantly, Yoake stopped and turned around.

"Whoops, sorry," she said, "You ready?"

"Have been since yesterday." Kyoki answered, smiling.

"Me too," Hana added and the three set off to find Akira.

"So . . ." Kyoki said as they walked, "which dorm is he in?"

"West boy's dorm." Yoake answered quickly, "We're almost there." Just as they walked up to the entrance, Akira came strolling by.

"Hey!" Yoake called, beckoning him over. He waved and complied, coming to stand in front of the girls.

"What's up, partner?" he asked, "How do you think that quiz went?" It was then he noticed the serious look on her face, "What's wrong?"

"We need to talk," Yoake said, "Come on." Akira shrugged and followed the girls into the small park that stood between the girls' and boys' dorms. Once the group was situated on one of the benches, Yoake spoke.

"We need you to tell us the truth," she began. Akria looked at her with confusion written across his face.

"About what?"

"Tell us who you really are," Kyoki snapped, "Artan." The boy's eyes widened for a moment, but then he smiled.

"I knew I shouldn't have said that." he muttered, "so I guess Tybalt told you everything." Hana nodded.

"Well, he told us a lot but we have some questions for you." she said. Artan sighed.

74

"Ask away."

"First off," Kyoki snapped, picking up one of her crutches, "if you're trying to stop Saekrin why the hell didn't you tell us you were here?!" she brought her crutch down onto the boy's head, earning a pained yelp.

"Ow! I wanted to take down the bastard myself!" he answered, "if you talked to Tybalt you already know what he did to my family. I have to avenge my father!" Hana sighed.

"But we could help each other," she said, "don't you think it would be easier to defeat him with friends rather than just by yourself?" Artan looked at the ground and reluctantly nodded.

"I'm glad to see you all have finally had a proper introduction." came a voice from overhead making them all jump. They looked up to see Tybalt sitting in a tree that overlooked the bench.

"You know you really have to stop doing that." Yoake said. "You're as bad as my teacher."

"I am your teacher."

"My *school* teacher." Yoake corrected.

"Mr. Satoru does that too?" Artan said and chuckled. "Saekrin was another one. I guess it must be a teacher thing. So . . . they say you told them everything, Sir."

"Well, I gave them my side," Tybalt said as he jumped from his branch, "but I think you should tell them yours."

"Right, well long story short I was supposed to be Saekrin's student, but he went insane and what—not, so Tybalt became my teacher."

"Did you ever meet him?" Hana asked, "Saekrin, I mean."

"Nope, the only time I ever saw his face was when I watched him kill my father."

"Oh, that makes more sense." Yoake said.

"What?"

"Why you want revenge." she answered. "You watched your father die in front of you. It must have been an awful experience."

"Yes, and an ocean is a bit damp." he returned sarcastically. Kyoki laughed in an attempt to lighten the mood.

"Anyway . . ." she said, "now that we know about each other, we should get to working together." Tybalt nodded.

"Artan," he said, "You should come back and train with us. If you all are going be a team now, you should get used to working together, learn to play up each other's strengths and compensate for each other's weaknesses."

"Right!" Hana agreed.

"Well then," Kyoki giggled, standing, "Let's get moving. It's Friday, we have the whole weekend to learn more!" Tybalt sighed, amused by the girl's enthusiasm and the fact that she seemed to have forgotten that she was still on crutches.

"Alright, but you girls should grab some clothes for the weekend. You too, Artan. Don't worry, I'll be right here when you're ready."

"Right!" they all said happily and ran off to pack.

"Do you think I should bring my Ipod?" Kyoki asked, holding up the device. Yoake laughed and continued to pack. Soon, all four children once again stood in the park, waiting excitedly for Tybalt to open a portal. With a smile, he opened his watch, golden light spilling out and separating into all colors of the rainbow. The lights swirled around them, finally crashing into the ground and opening the familiar portal. One by one, they jumped through, quickly landing at the entrance to the training ground.

"Damn, I'm glad to be back," Artan said.

"Why is tha—" Yoake began but stopped abruptly as her eyes fell on him. He stood just behind them but looked very different. His skin had darkened to a light tan and his eyes had turned a brilliant blue. Long dark green hair cascaded down his back with long pointed ears poking through the strands. His clothing had also changed. No longer was he wearing the school uniform but instead, he wore a white tunic, silver belt, dark pants, and metal plated shoes. Metal guards covered his arms and shoulders like armor, with red accents adorning the edges.

"You clean up nice," Kyoki chuckled.

"Yeah," Hana agreed. Artan blushed at the comment, looking at the ground so she wouldn't see.

"Alright!" Kyoki said, "Let's get this party started!" She opened her watch and transformed in a sea of black light. In her excitement, she tried to run over to the rack of weapons in the middle of the field, but without her crutches, she fell after only a few feet.

"What happened?" Erasure asked. He had run over as soon as the girls had landed and now stood looking down at his student.

"She was hurt in a fight with Saekrin." Tybalt explained simply. Erasure grunted and waved Sakura over.

"Can you heal her?" he asked, pointing to Kyoki. The woman nodded and sat down on her knees beside the girl. Hana and Yoake watched as a soft green light began to glow around Sakura's hands.

"Hana," she said, "Come down here. You should know how to do this." Nodding, Hana moved so she sat opposite her teacher.

"For wounds like this," Sakura continued, "You need to first find the exact problem; this is obviously a bad sprain. Next, concentrate your power on one area, usually the area where the most damage is, except in the case of broken bones which I'll teach you about later." Hana nodded again, leaning in a bit so she could get a better look at what her teacher was doing. Soon, the glow faded and Kyoki sprang up.

"Thanks," she said happily, jumping up and down to test her fixed ankle.

"If you're feeling better," Erasure stated, "Come with me." Kyoki giggled and immediately followed the man to the weapons she had been going toward earlier.

"We should get started as well," Sakura said, standing.

"Right," Hana replied, opening her watch and transforming just as Kyoki had.

"Wait for me!" Yoake giggled, also transforming. She followed Tybalt onto the field and the day began.

Just as dinner time was approaching, Tybalt called to the other two groups, signalling for them to come over. Yoake had spent the last few hours learning about each type of arrow and what kinds of damage they could do.

"I think we should have a small sparring match before dinner," Tybalt said. Kyoki nodded excitedly, already twirling her scythe in anticipation.

"I'm in!" she laughed, "So which one of you wants to be taken down?" Erasure rolled his eyes at the comment and made a mental note to talk to Kyoki about overconfidence later. Hana stepped forward, pointing one of her swords at her friend.

"I'll play," she said, "but I promise you, I won't lose." With that, the others moved away from the match, giving the girls enough space to practice their attacks. Kyoki had traded her training scythe for her own and stood ready for battle. Hana smirked back, hoping to bring her cocky friend down a peg.

Suddenly, Kyoki sprang forward, bringing her weapon down toward Hana's head. Hana quickly held up one of her swords to block, swinging the second up. Kyoki leaped back, landing a few feet away, and smiled. Before she could mount another assault, Hana rushed forward, driving one sword up and the other down. Kyoki spun her scythe, catching the swords and deflecting the attack, but Hana had seen it coming. She let go of one of her weapons, using the second as leverage and forcing Kyoki's scythe into the air.

"Damn it," Kyoki yelled. She jumped up to avoid being cut and caught her weapon mid-flight, landing smoothly on the ground behind Hana. The other third year quickly spun, picking up her discarded sword in the process.

"SPORE DANCE!" She cried. Kyoki watched her curiously, keeping her scythe close in case she had to defend herself quickly. Hana's swords glowed with a yellow light, shining against the metal. She held one up, spinning it between her fingers, while the other slashed the air. Both sent out a thick cloud of yellow dust that shot straight for Kyoki.

"Hana what are you—" Yoake yelled from the sideline, moving to run in and stop the fight, but Sakure placed a hand on her shoulder.

"That attack won't hurt Kyoki," she said reassuringly, "It's a confusion style attack meant to make the opponent lose their focus and let their guard down." Yoake nodded slowly, glad that Hana wasn't going to hurt her friend.

Kyoki stared into the cloud that now surrounded her, unable to see any more than two feet in front of her. Growling, she tried in vain to find her opponent.

"Where are you?" she hissed. Suddenly, she spun left, hearing a giggle, but then it stopped and reappeared on her right, then front, left, back, right.

"That's it!" Kyoki yelled. She held up her scythe and began to spin it above her head, creating a small cyclone and scattering the spores. As the cloud disappeared, she saw Hana standing about ten feet to her right and chuckled.

"You're mine now," she laughed, "SOUL HURRICANE!" Her spinning scythe instantly picked up speed as black clouds began to form overhead.

"Not again!" Tybalt growled. Kyoki laughed at the fear in Hana's eyes and continued to build power. Ghoulish spirits danced around them, forming a wall and separating them from the others.

"Kyoki what are—?" Hana gasped, but stopped as Kyoki's sycthe came down, sending the entire host of ghosts toward her. Twisted laughter filled the air as Erasure and Tybalt tried to get through the barrier. Suddenly, a scream rang out across the training field just as Erasure broke through. He grabbed Kyoki's scythe, instantly stopping the attack. Yoake ran forward to where Hana sat on the ground, frozen in shock and fear. Small cuts dotted her body from where the ghosts had begun to attack her. Slowly, Kyoki brought her weapon down and dropped it.

"Hana, I—" she began, reach forward to help.

"STAY AWAY FROM ME!" Hana yelled, "What is wrong with you? This was just a sparring match and you went too far AGAIN!"

"I'm sorry I—"

"Well 'sorry' isn't good enough. Don't you get it? You could have killed me! What were you thinking?" Kyoki stared at Hana, all remorse instantly evaporating.

"I was thinking that I could get stronger!" she yelled back, "If we're going to beat Saekrin, we need all the power we can get!"

"That doesn't mean you can use lethal force on your friend!"

"I wasn't! You overreacted, you coward!"

"I overreacted?" Hana shouted, holding out her bleeding arm, "I overreacted? You tried to use a super attack on your friend. What do you expect to do with that power?"

"Protect people!" Kyoki answered, "and beat that bastard Saekrin!"

"'Protect people,'" Hana laughed mirthlessly, standing, "How can you expect to protect anyone? You couldn't even protect your own BROTHER!"

Both girls froze.

"Kyoki," Hana said slowly, "I-I didn't mean to say—" Without a word, Kyoki turned and slowly walked off the field.

"Wait!" Yoake yelled, standing, but Tybalt stopped her.

"You saw her face," he said softly, "Nothing you can say will reach her right now." The group stood in silence, tense and strained, until Artan finally spoke.

"I don't understand," he said, "why is she so upset?" Hana sat on the ground, healing her wounds and crying silently. Yoake sighed.

"I shouldn't have said that . . ." Hana muttered, "I shouldn't have said that." Yoake turned to Artan who was still waiting for an answer.

"Kyoki's little brother died in a car accident seven years ago." she said slowly, "They were outside playing and Kyoki's mother had always told her that it was her job to watch out for her brother and make sure he didn't get hurt. She was teaching him to ride a skateboard and she gave him a push to get him started, but he couldn't stop. He rolled onto the road just as a car came speeding through the neighborhood. She tried to run into the street, to push him out of the way, but she was too late. He died in her arms."

Artan stared at Yoake, shocked, "Oh Mother Fate . . ." he breathed. Yoake nodded. For another half hour, they waited for Kyoki to return but she never did. Erasure went off to search for her but when he returned said she was refusing to come out of her room.

"I didn't mean to hurt her this much . . ." Hana said sadly, "Maybe I should go talk to her."

Tybalt shook his head. "There are times when apologies only make things worse," he said, "I think I should take you girls back to your own world." With that, he walked off to go get Kyoki. Five minutes later he returned with the girl. Yoake opened her mouth to speak but the dead look in Kyoki's eyes made her stop.

"I'm sorry, Kyoki," Hana said desperately, but she was ignored. Quietly, Yoake and Hana picked up their bags and followed Tybalt away from the field. Once they stepped off the base, Tybalt opened a portal and the girls jumped through.

"Let's go get something to eat." Yoake suggested, helplessly trying to lighten the mood. They made their way up to their dorm and set their bags down, all but Kyoki. She moved to the closet and began to put more into her bag, even pulling out a suitcase and stuffing everything else into it.

"What are you doing?" Hana asked, concerned. Again, she was ignored. Without a word, Kyoki walked to the door and left.

"Damn them!" Kyoki snapped as she stormed down the sidewalk, pulling her suitcase along behind her, "I said I was sorry but if they really want to kick that bastard's ass, they should start training as hard as I do!" She growled and flopped down onto a nearby bench, "It's getting late," she continued, "maybe I should go back . . . I mean, well, NO! Let them stew for a while. They deserve it. After all, Hana and her stupid stupidity, why did she have to talk about my brother? It's not like I didn't try to save—" She put her head into her hands and wept quietly, thinking about her deceased family and the friends she had just walked out on.

"Bad day?" asked a voice from beside her. She looked up to see none other than Yeldi sitting by her side, watching her with a smirk on his lips.

"Go away!" She snapped, "I'm not in the mood to kick your ass right now." Yeldi chuckled.

"Who said I was here to fight you?" he asked, "Can't I enjoy the sights of this world?"

"So your 'master' is giving you some free time?" Kyoki laughed bitterly, "He doesn't seem like the type to let you slack off." Yeldi flinched slightly at the comment, hand instinctively moving to defend himself. She was right and he knew it. Saekrin would never let him just wander around.

"Alright," he said, "You caught me. I'm here to talk to you." Kyoki looked up at him, confused and skeptical but interested.

"What?"

"Well," Yeldi continued, "it's obvious that you and your teammates don't get along. They don't understand you. What you want is power, is that so bad?" Kyoki tentatively shook her head.

"Right! And you want to protect people with that power, correct?" She nodded.

"Then you should come with me." He held his hand out to her but she slapped it away.

"There is no way in hell that I would ever work with you!" she hissed. Yeldi pulled his hand back, looking hurt.

"But they want to stifle your power," he said, "I know that you and Hana are always fighting. She wants you to hold back but why should you? If you are stronger, you should show it." Kyoki tried to stare at the gravel on the ground and ignore him, but couldn't help feeling that he was making sense.

"And besides," he continued, "all you want is to protect those you love, to make sure that they are safe. Your friends should be grateful that someone as strong as you would chose to work with them. My master knows just how you feel."

"He does?" Kyoki asked, looking up at Yeldi.

"Of course," the creature said, "Master Saekrin wanted power too. He wanted to protect our world, but the rest of them, they got scared of his power. That's what your friends are, scared. They are scared of you and that's why they don't want you to get stronger. If you stay weak, they can control you. Come with me. We can show them why they should have listened to you." He held his hand out to her again. Kyoki stared at it for a few moments, debating whether or not to take it. At first, she hesitated. She loved her friends and didn't want to hurt them, but they had hurt her. Why should she stay behind with them when it was obvious she was stronger? Slowly, she reached up and took Yeldi's hand.

Yoake walked into class the next day with Artan, her mind in a fog. She was looking forward to seeing Yami, but when she looked around the classroom for him she saw that he wasn't there. To her surprise, neither was Mr. Satoru. "Is everyone disappearing?"

"Looks like it." said a voice behind them.

Yoake turned around to see Tybalt standing in the doorway. "What are you—"

"I'm subbing for your normal teacher." he explained.

"Oh . . . wait what?"

"He's been covering as a permanent sub at the school to keep an eye on you three. Couldn't you tell?" Artan said.

"No."

"Yep." Tybalt said. "So you'd better start calling me Mr. Tsumasi."

"Yes, sir." Yoake giggled, but she was still worried about Yami and Kyoki, "Have you seen Kyoki?" she asked hopefully. Sadly, both males shook their heads.

"Sorry," Artan said, "I started tailing her after you guys left, but she disappeared."

"I hope she's okay . . ." Yoake mused.

"She's a tough girl," Tybalt said, trying to comfort her, "I bet she's fine." Yoake nodded slowly, hoping to convince herself that he was right. Just then the bell rang, signaling for Yoake and Artan to take their seats. Once morning's announcements were complete, Tybalt stood and addressed the students.

"Good morning, class," he said, smiling, "as you can see your teacher is absent today so I will be filling in. My name is Kata Tsumasi. Now, I understand that you all had some projects due." Yoake looked over at Artan who put his head in his hands. With all the stress of Kyoki's disappearance and training, they had forgotten about their school work.

"Alright," Tybalt continued, "we'll do this alphabetically so . . ." he picked up his attendance sheet and scanned the list of names, "Miss Arikawa and her partner, please come up and begin." Yoake sighed in relief; now she and Artan had some time to work, maybe even another day. Suddenly, she felt a small jab on her elbow. Looking down, she saw Artan poking her with a small piece of paper. She took it and began to read the note.

"I can't believe we forgot." it said. She sighed and pulled out a pen.

"Me neither," she wrote, "but at least Tybalt decided to go alphabetical. We might not have to go today; my last name begins with an H." Once she finished, she handed the paper back to Artan. Faintly, she could hear the two girls at the front talking about modern medicine but was too worried about other things to really listen. When she looked at her desk again, she saw that Artan had passed the note back.

"That should buy us time. My 'last name' starts with K." it said.

"Wonderful! But what are we going to do about it? I mean, we're going to have to present eventually." she watched as Artan read her reply and sighed, then scribbled something and handed it back.

"Let's spend lunch in the library. We can work then." Yoake looked up from the note and nodded to Artan, hiding it in her bag. For the rest of class, the two waited impatiently for the bell, hoping it would ring before "Mr. Tsumasi" reached H.

"Okay, everyone!" Tybalt said, as the third group finished, "the bell is about to ring so we'll pick up with Mr. Fukiji and his partner after lunch." The class nodded and soon the familiar ding of the bell set them free.

"I'll meet you there," Yoake called as Artan headed toward the library, "I just need to get my lunch." Turning, she hurried toward the cafeteria. Kyoki hadn't come back that night and she and Hana hadn't seen her on the walk to school. She was starting to get very worried about her friend. What if she was lost or got kidnapped or killed or—Yoake shook her head; she couldn't afford to think like that. Once she reached the cafeteria, she spotted Hana sitting in their usual place.

"Hey," Hana greeted sadly. Yoake walked over and stood next to her friend.

"Have you seen Kyoki?" she asked. Hana shook her head.

"Alright then . . ." Yoake replied. She hadn't expected Kyoki to suddenly show up; the girl had never liked school very much anyway so why would she just walk in now?

"Well, I've gotta go help Art-Akira with our project so I'll see you later." Hana waved as Yoake walked off and went back to slowly eating her lunch.

Once Yoake reached the library, she looked around for Artan, quickly finding him seated at one of the computers.

"Where's your lunch?" he asked as he opened the internet.

"Oh uh . . ." Yoake muttered, "I forgot it . . ." Artan looked at her skeptically.

"You went down to see if Hana had seen Kyoki, right?" he asked. Yoake looked up at him in shock.

"How did you know?"

"You would make a terrible poker player," he answered, "It's written all over your face. You're worried out of your mind."

"Yeah, I guess you're right," Yoake said, "but aren't you? I mean, what if something happens to her?" Artan shrugged.

"There's not much we can do and we can't make the situation any better by wasting energy worrying. Tybalt was just like you are now when Saekrin left and—"

"Don't you dare compare Kyoki to that bastard!" Yoake shouted, suddenly standing. The rest of the people in the library stared at her in confusion, "sorry," she muttered and sat down again. Artan looked at her, concerned, but decided to drop the subject.

"Let's get back to work," he said, "Then maybe Tybalt, I mean 'Mr. Tsumasi,' will give us an A." He smiled at her and began to search the internet. For the rest of lunch, the two worked diligently and by the end, they were finished.

"I think we're done," Artan said, stretching, "It's not great but at least it's something." Yoake nodded and stood.

"Let's get back to class," she said, "If we're late, we'll definitely get in trouble." Artan nodded.

"Glad you kids made it back," Tybalt said just as the bell rang.

"Yeah." Yoake panted.

"Remind me to have you do some endurance exercises." Tybalt commented at her long breaths.

Yoake looked up and glared playfully at him. "And you say Saekrin is evil."

"Oh come on, it won't be that bad."

Yoake grunted and walked to her seat, Artan sitting next to her. She looked up as Tybalt glanced at the attendance sheet again, trying to figure out who was next. A sigh of relief escaped her when her name wasn't called.

"I think we're safe for the rest of the day." Artan whispered.

"Please don't talk while others are giving their presentations, Mr . . . ," Tybalt said, pretending to look down at the attendance sheet, "Kotobushi." Artan muttered a small apology and went back to watching the presentation. Only a few more groups were able to go before the bell rang because the last group of the day had a small meltdown. They had tried to do a demonstration involving a van der graaf generator. Sadly, one of the students had dropped the cellphone they weren't supposed to have onto the large ball at the top and the whole device had exploded.

"Hey!" Hana called as the school stood outside. The resulting explosion had set off the fire alarms and sent the entire school out the doors, "What happened?"

Yoake sighed, "You don't want to know. The short answer is science class is more dangerous than you'd think." Hana looked at Yoake and Artan quizzically but didn't press the issue.

"Well," she said, "I've got to deliver this attendence sheet to the vice principal so I'll see you later." Yoake waved as Hana ran off.

"We are definitely not going today." Artan giggled as they walked back into the building. It had taken almost forty-five minutes, but the fire department had finally determined that it was safe and allowed the students back in to get their things.

"No, I suppose you aren't," Tybalt said from behind them, "but with an attitude like that, I think the two of you should go first tomorrow." Yoake sighed, but she was grateful that they had some time to perfect their project.

"Well, I guess I'll see you tomorrow." Tybalt said as he waved them off. Yoake nodded and left to meet Hana just outside the school.

"Nice day?" she asked. Hana simply nodded.

"Tests?"

"No." The girls sighed as one; small talk was useless.

Artan looked back and forth between the two for a moment. "Well . . . this is uncomfortable." he commented as he followed them up to their room.

"Where do you think she is?" Hana asked after a few minutes, speaking the question that had been on both girls' minds all day.

"I don't know . . ." Yoake answered as they walked into their dorm. She stared at Kyoki's empty bed. For just a moment, in her mind's eye, Yoake saw Kyoki sitting there once again, complaining about some piece of homework or humming along with her Ipod, but all too quickly the vision faded and a deserted bed stared back at her.

"I miss her too," Hana said, gently letting her bag hit the floor. She sat down her her bed and kicked her shoes off.

"I'm sure we'll find her." Artan said putting a comforting hand on her shoulder as he sat next to her. She looked up at him in surprise to see a twinkle in his eyes that made her turn away as her face turned red.

Just then, here was a knock on the window. Yoake turned to see Tybalt sitting just outside. Sighing, she opened it and let him in.

"Girls," he said solemnly, "I have some bad news." Instantly, Yoake and Hana ran to him, pressing him against the wall in their haste.

"What is it?" Hana demanded, "Is it about Kyoki?"

"Do you know where she is?" Yoake asked hopefully. Tybalt shook his head.

"I'm sorry but no."

"Then what's the problem?" Yoake asked, already losing patience.

"Hana," Tybalt said, turning to the girl, "I'm afraid your sister has disappeared."

For a moment, the room was silent, so silent that the ticking of the clock sounded as loud as thunder, as Hana stared into space. Then suddenly, she ran for the door. Yoake tried to call after her but her friend was already too far away. Quickly, she ran after her, still shouting for her to come back, with Tybalt following close behind. Hana dashed into the street, looking in every place she passed, alleys, doors, trash cans, anywhere an eight year old could hide.

"Kumi!" she yelled as she ran, "Kumi, where are you?" Hana sprinted from place to place, Yoake and Tybalt trying to stop her. The male member of their group had changed into the form he used as a teacher so didn't draw any more attention to the group than Hana already was. Faster and faster, becoming increasingly frantic with every step she took and every failed location she tried, Hana ran, tears stinging the corners of her eyes. As she dashed into the large field at the north end of town, Yoake finally caught up to her.

"Hana, stop!" she cried, grabbing onto her friend's shoulders and shaking her, "This isn't going to help find her!"

"But-but-but . . ." Hana stuttered, but her words were lost as she descended into tears. Yoake pulled her close and slowly lowered them both to the ground just as Tybalt walked over.

"Where, where did you last see her?" Hana asked between sobs.

"She was following someone. I couldn't see who and I'm sorry to say I lost them both." he answered.

"Tybalt," Yoake said as she tried to comfort her crying friend, "can you go look around again? I'll stay here and we'll meet you back at the dorm later." Tybalt nodded and walked off, leaving the two girls alone.

Suddenly, Hana shot up, shoving Yoake away. "I know who did it," she hissed, hand forming fists so tight her knuckles began to turn white, "I know who did this! YOU BASTARD!" she screamed, clawing at the air in front of her, "YELDI!"

"Did someone call my name?"

The girls turned to see the young creature sitting on top of a tree about fifty feet away.

"GIVE MY SISTER BACK!" Hana yelled. She started to charge at him but Yoake held her back.

"What sister?" Yeldi asked, "Damn, you girls can't keep track of anything, can you? I see the loud, annoying member of your trio has disappeared as well." Yoake glared at him.

"We can still beat you!" she shouted. Hana nodded and both girls pulled out their watches, instantly transforming.

"Oh, this is going to be fun . . ." Yeldi chuckled, pulling out a watch of his own. It was silver with a ring of rubies running around the front.

"Where did you get that?" Hana said.

"Are you finally going to fight us with your own watch?" Yoake asked, readying her bow.

"This?" Yeldi said, feigning surprise as he glanced at the watch in his hand, "Oh no, this isn't mine. It's a gift from my master; something to help me finally kill you girls." Slowly, he drew his hand over the watch as he spoke, "You see, normally a watch will only respond to the person who is destined to wield it and sadly, I do not have one of my own." He pressed his hand against the front and a bright red light began to glow from between the two, "However, Master has discovered a way to separate the watches' power from the item itself." Gently, he drew his fingers back and, to the girls' utter shock, a long, flaming katana formed, pulling itself from inside the watch. Yeldi smirked as he wrapped his hand around the hilt. The katana shook, fighting him, almost as if it were trying to resist the intrusion, but Yeldi continued and with one swift, graceful movement, he removed it completely.

"Now," he smirked, pointing the blade at the girls, "now we can have some fun".

"Not good." Hana said as Yeldi sent a fireball hurtling toward them.

"I got it." Yoake said and Hana nodded, jumping out of the way. Yoake drew an arrow and fired it at the attack but it was swallowed up but the flames. "Crap!" she said, quickly dodging as it hit the ground where they had been standing and exploded. The force of the blast knocked her quiver over her head as she was thrown face-first onto the ground. She had jumped out of the way just in time to avoid being burned alive, but not without receiving a serious burn on her back from the outburst of flames. "Ah!" she cried, pain shooting through her body.

"Now where have I seen that before?" Yeldi asked in mock contemplation. "Oh yeah! That's payback from our first meeting."

"Damn you." Yoake shouted.

"Oh! It looks like the 'calm collected leader' is getting angry." he chuckled as he sauntered up to the pain stricken girl on the ground. "That's good, it means I have the the upper hand."

"Stay away from her!" Hana yelled, running to attack, but Yeldi created a wall of flames around them, shutting her out. It was large enough around so as not to hurt them and just high enough that Hana couldn't jump over.

Standing over his captive, he smirked sadistically. "Ready to die?" he asked. When she did not answer, he made the flames disappear from the sword and gently lifted her head with the tip of the dull edge. "You know you look kinda cute lying on the ground like that, all helpless and weak. You can't do anything, not without hurting yourself even further and making this," he touched the blade to her burned back, making her cringe, "any worse. So, do you want me to put you out of your misery—I promise it'll be nice and quick—or do you want to keep fighting and force me to put you in more pain?" He lifted the sword from her back, flicking it slightly so it drew blood, but still she didn't answer. "Come on, Yoake, just answer the question: do you want to die quickly and painlessly, or do you want me to put you in so much pain you'll be begging me to kill you."

"Like hell I'd do that!" Yoake hissed. She tried to get up but her injured back prevented her from moving. "Damn it."

Yeldi shook his head. "So much determination, so much fire and it's all being wasted. Why don't you just admit that you're nothing without a 'full team.'" he said as he knelt down and grabbed her face. There were tears in her eyes and on her cheeks. "Aww don't cry." He brushed away a tear. "You're going to make me feel bad and pity you. I'm sure she's alright, wherever she is. You should be crying for yourself and how your death is so near you can taste it." He pulled her forward and licked the blood along the incision he had made on her back. A sadistic grin cracked his face as he felt her body tense up, a combination gasp and whimper escaping the girl. He sat her up—probably putting her in more pain by the look on her face—and leaned in close to her, their faces only centimeters apart. "Oh I get it, you're crying because of the pain, not because you're worried about your friend or the little girl. How selfish."

"You call this pain?" she said, surprising him. Both intrigued and angry that she wouldn't give in, he dropped her and stood. From the ground, she continued, "This is nothing, not compared to what I've felt before; what *they* felt."

"They?"

"You think I'm crying because I'm in pain. Maybe I am a little, but I've felt worse, *much* worse." she said as she weakly stood up, her head still hanging from her shoulders. "I'm crying because of a memory, a memory that has burned itself into my mind for more than ten years. It's that memory that keeps me going, that keeps my faith, even in you, and it's because of that memory," She lifted her head, wildfire blazing behind the tears, "that I will *never* give up!" He was startled by her gaze, and the sheer forcefulness made him stumble backwards. He was not aware, however, that it was taking all her effort and willpower not to scream in pain.

"Look at you," Yeldi chuckled, quickly regaining his composure, "You're barely standing. How can you hope to win?"

Yoake shook her head; she could hear Hana calling to her, trying to break through the flames. "I don't," she said, "I just hope that I can save the people I care about." She glared at him, pulling an arrow from the quiver that hung off her arm, the charred strap barely holding it on, and strung her bow. Her head pounded as she drew the string back, screaming in pain, and she swayed dangerously.

Yeldi laughed, watching her try to aim, and held up his blade again. "You sure about this?" he asked, smirking, "Because I'm going to enjoy tearing you apart." Suddenly, just as he was about to advance on her, the world spun and she collapsed. She could hear him laughing above her and tried to stand, but her body refused to obey. "Looks like I win," Yeldi laughed, squatting down to her level, "and as a souvenir, I think I'll take this." He reached forward and wrapped his hands around her watch.

"N-no!" she gasped, reaching up to try and take it back, but her body still wouldn't let her.

He chuckled and let her watch go. "But my master will want something to show for my work . . ." He looked at the wall of fire and smiled, "So maybe, I'll take hers instead." Yoake growled and once again tried to stand, but all she could do was shake uselessly. "Don't try to move," Yeldi said, almost sounding concerned. He leaned down to her ear and whispered quietly, "I'm sure you'll see your friend soon." With that, he stood and turned, slowly walking to the edge of the ring. Quickly, without looking back, he jumped over the flames and disappeared. The last thing Yoake saw was the disappearance of the fire and Hana running to her before she descended into unconsciousness.

❧

"No!" Yoake screamed as she woke, instantly sitting up and reaching desperately in front of her. Slowly, reality set in and she looked around. The room was small, white, and sterile-looking, but she could instantly tell that she wasn't in a hospital. Gently, she placed a hand on her stomach and found bandages winding around her body; someone had taken care of her burns.

"Yoake!" she looked up to see Hana running toward her, followed closely by Tybalt and Aria, "I'm so glad you're awake! How are you feeling?"

"Where . . . am I?" Yoake asked, looking around again.

Tybalt sat down on the bed and placed a hand on her shoulder, gently easing her back down. "Don't worry," he said, "You're in a hospital at the barracks. Hana called me and tried to heal you herself, but the wounds were too much for her, so we brought you here. Also, you should know that—"

"Yeldi got away . . ." she finished sadly, "I'm sorry . . ."

"What are you apologizing for?" Hana asked incredulously, "If anything . . ." she trailed off, staring at the ground, "I should be saying sorry to you."

"Why?"

"He took my watch." she growled, "After he took away the fire wall, he came after me. He was so fast I couldn't keep up and he hit me from behind. When I woke up, you were unconscious and he was gone, along with my watch."

Yoake looked at her friend sympathetically, but noticed another emotion in her face. "There's something else, isn't there?" Hana nodded silently, tears trickling out of her eyes. "What?"

"I was right, that son-of-a—"

"Ahem." Tybalt interrupted.

"Sorry. Yeldi left something for me after he disappeared." She held out her hand to reveal a little dollar-store locket that Yoake immediately recognized. "He has my sister."

"Oh no!" Yoake gasped and tried to sit up, but her wounds wouldn't let her.

"I sent out a search party and I'm pretty sure Artan went looking on his own." Tybalt explained.

"Oh . . . he . . . he did." Hana said, blushing. "You didn't tell me that."

"Well, he wasn't in his room when we got back to the dorm. I asked his roommates where he was and they told me he just said that he had something he needed to do and walked out."

"He could be looking for Kyoki." Yoake suggested.

"Maybe," Tybalt looked at a blushing Hana. "but I doubt it."

Suddenly voices came from the hallway. "Sir, I can't let you—"

"I'm going in there damn it. Now go away!" Artan burst in the room, a nurse behind him. He was panting and looked pretty badly beaten up.

"Artan!" Hana cheered.

"We were just talking about you." Tybalt said as Hana ran up to him. He cringed as she tried to hug him, receiving an apology from her. "Where the hell have you been?"

"Where the hell do you think?" he snapped as Hana sat him in a nearby chair. "I was looking for the little girl. I guessed maybe your little brother," he glanced at Tybalt, "kidnapped her and by the looks on your faces I'd say I'm right."

"We ran into Yeldi in the park." Yoake answered, "and as you can see it didn't go well."

"Yeah, looks like it."

"He beat me to a pulp, and took Hana's watch." she continued.

"But haven't you guys kicked his ass before?"

"Apparently, Saekrin has the ability to take control of other watches. Yeldi demonstrated that today, with painful results."

"So he told you that he has your sister, or did he hypnotise her like he did to me?"

"Neither, though I'd prefer the latter because at least I'd know if she was okay." Hana said and held out her hand. "He left this. It's my sister's."

"Oh." he said. "May I?" She nodded. He took the little locket from her and examined it.

"She got that after getting a shot at the doctor's office." Hana said smiling. "It's her most prized possession."

"Can it be opened?"

She took the little piece back and opened it. Inside was a picture of Hana, Kyoki, and Yoake all standing around the little girl. "She always called Yoake and Kyoki 'big sisters', the same way she did me." Hana said.

"Yeah." Yoake sighed. "She kind of filled a void that both Kyoki and I shared, so we went along with it, treating her like she really was our little sister."

"What do you mean that you and Kyoki 'shared.'" Alia asked.

"Well Kumi filled it, so it's not really there anymore."

"No, no. I understand why you put it in past tense, Yoake. I am asking what put it there in the first place?"

"Oh . . . well I . . . I guess you guys should know." Yoake slumped back, not quite laying down, not quite sitting up and started, "This pain in my back is nothing compared to the pain I felt on a day that will live in my heart and mind forever."

"Now why can't she write her school papers like that?" Tybalt said, trying to lighten the mood.

"Tybalt, please." Alia scolded, silencing him.

"No, it's okay." Hana said, surprising everyone. "You're going to need a little humor after hearing this."

"Right. I was about five years old when it happened. I lived in a Tokyo suburb, but I don't really remember my address. Anyway, I lived with my parents and my, at the time, three-year-old brother. My dad was a smoker and for some reason insisted that we keep the lawn mower in front of the porch. It was a nice house, a great family, and an incredible life."

"Get on with it." Artan said.

Hana elbowed him in the ribs. "Relax. It's a hard memory for her to bring up. Can you blame her for trying to stall?"

"Sorry." he said, directing his apology to both of them.

"Go on." Alia said.

"Yes . . . well, one day I was playing in the backyard in my pink play tent with my dolls and such when I smelled smoke. At first I thought it was just my dad, but then I actually saw the smoke. I ran into the house and saw through the front windows that our porch had been set ablaze. My mom was standing by the front door, on the phone with the fire department and my brother was ogling the flames, and my dad was trying to put them out." She paused for a moment and, with a sigh, continued, "Then I watched in horror as the fire reached the lawn mower and it exploded. It knocked me backward and forced me into a space where I was safe from the flames, but also caught not only the rest of the house on fire . . . but also . . ." She trailed off as tears began streaming down her face.

Tybalt gasped, Alia said a silent prayer, and Artan just stared at her with his jaw hanging down to his chest. None of them needed her to tell them what she was about to say. Hana just stared at the floor. She had heard the story before; more times than she cared to recall. Yoake fought against the tears as she continued, "I was stuck there with no way to get out, so I was forced to watch as my family burned to death. My parents were screaming at me to get out and save myself, and my brother was screaming for help. I can still hear them, as if it was happening in front of me again. That was also the day I got this." She pointed to a mark on her neck that was darker than the rest of her skin.

"I thought it was a birthmark." Artan said.

Yoake shook her head. "No. It's a constant reminder of that day. I don't know how I got it. All I remember is the emergency team treating it when they finally showed up." She smiled a bit, but it was a tragic, ironic smile. "It's kind of funny. They found my family's charred remains before they found me. They searched the soggy charcoal that was my house after the fire was out and I just stayed where I was. I didn't want 'the strange people dressed like aliens' to find me, so I curled up tighter. That's also when I discovered the burn on my neck. The pain was unbearable and I cried out. That's when they found me. I was taken to a hospital and treated for minor burns, except my scar."

"Well it's a good thing you got that thing then." Tybalt said

"After that, the hospital sent me to a therapist, and that's where I met Kyoki." Yoake said. "We became friends instantly and her family adopted me. Then she introduced me to Hana and that's where it all started."

"So Kyoki isn't just *like* a sister to you." Artan observed. "She *is* your sister."

"Legally speaking yes." Yoake nodded, and laughed a little. "It confused the hell out of Kumi."

"Yeah, I remember that discussion." Hana said.

"Kumi, I'm guessing, is your sister." Tybalt said.

"So the therapy obviously helped seeing as you're not afraid of fire." Artan commented.

"Well . . . when I saw Hana trying to get over the wall of flames that Yeldi made, it reminded me of it. That's why I tried to stand up. So I could prevent it from happening again."

"That's unbelievable." Alia said.

"What is?"

"That you, not only survived such an event, but also have taken it and used it to make you stronger."

"Well, there is a saying in our world: 'what doesn't kill you can only makes you stronger.'" Yoake said.

"Do you ever wonder what would have happened if that never did?" Tybalt asked.

"All the time, and you know what? I'm okay with it. If it didn't happen, I never would have met Kyoki, or Hana, or Kumi. All the stuff that's been happening recently would be happening to another group of girls, I think." Yoake smiled at them; a truly happy smile. "I may have lost my family that day, but I gained a new one, and even though I miss them, I wouldn't trade this new one for the world."

Despite her smile, Hana sighed wistfully. "If only the *whole* family was here."

Artan put his arm around her comfortingly. "Hey, don't worry, we'll find her; we'll find them both." Hana didn't say anything, but buried her face against his chest and she cried.

"Well, I think we should let you rest." Tybalt said as he stood up. "My lady . . ." he said to Alia, gesturing to the door. Artan also stood, taking the crying Hana with him. "Take it easy, okay? Just rest and don't strain yourself." Tybalt said as he reached the door.

"Is that an order from my teacher?" Yoake said raising her eyebrow and smiling.

Tybalt smiled back. He found it amazing that she could smile after telling them about such an awful memory. He looked at her and said, "What do you think?" and walked out, closing the door behind him.

Yoake giggled, laid down, and fell asleep.

Over the next few days, Yoake stayed in that hospital room. Tybalt, Hana, and Artan returned to Earth because all of them still had to attend school, but they visited everyday, Artan bringing that day's homework for her to do.

"What have you been telling the school about where I am?" Yoake asked him after the fourth day. He smiled.

"Hana said you had the flu so Kyoki's mother came and got you. She's a good student so no one suspected anything. Don't worry, okay? You just concentrate on getting better as fast as you can. It's so boring in 'Mr. Tsumasi's' class without you."

"Well maybe it wouldn't be so boring if you tried paying attention instead of staring out the window." Tybalt said, placing a hand on Artan's shoulder. The boy yelped, jumping nearly five feet in the air, as Yoake laughed.

"Lady Alia told me that you should be able to go home tomorrow." Tybalt said turning to Yoake. She smiled happily; she missed going to school, not that she would ever admit it outloud.

"But for now," Tybalt continued, "go to sleep." Yoake nodded and lay down, soon drifting off.

"Hey, welcome back!" Artan said, waving Yoake over. She ran to her desk and sat down.

"Good morning, Yoake," said a soft voice from in front of her. Quickly, she turned to see Yami standing there.

"Hey!" she said, happily jumping up and hugging him, "Are you okay? Where were you? How've you been?" Yami shook as she continued to squeeze him.

"I-I'm fine," he answered, "I was just about to ask you the same thing. When I got back, you weren't here. Artan said you had the flu. I'm glad you're feeling better." Yoake giggled and pulled back, pumping her fists in the air.

"You bet I am!"

The rest of the morning proceeded as normal, Tybalt having Yoake and Artan present now that both partners were in class again. When lunch rolled around, Yoake ran down to the cafeteria and sat beside Hana.

"What's wrong?" she asked, instantly reading the look on her friend's face. Hana said nothing, just continued eating her lunch.

"Hana, please . . ." Yoake said, but still she received no answer. She continued to try to get her friend to talk for the next half hour but it was all in vain. When the first bell rang, signalling for everyone to head back to class, Hana simply stood, threw her leftovers away, and left.

"I wonder what's wrong . . ." Yoake muttered as she sat down beside Artan.

"What's wrong with who?" he asked.

"Hana," she answered, "she looks like something is bothering her and she won't tell me what."

"I noticed that too," Artan said, "She started acting strange after the last fight. I hope she's okay . . ." Yoake nodded and did her best to pay attention to Tybalt but it was hard. As soon as the final bell rang, she dashed out of the classroom and nearly slammed into Hana who had already started walking back to the dorm.

"Hey, wait up!" Yoake said, but Hana once again ignored her, "What's going on with you? You're not talking to me and Artan said you've been acting strangely since the last fight. I know you're worried about your sister but we'll get her back and I'm sure that Kyoki is fine wherever she is." Yoake continued talking for the entire walk; Hana just staring at the ground, "Please just tell me what's wrong . . ."

"'What's wrong!'" Hana yelled suddenly, throwing her bag onto her bed, "'What's wrong!' I'll tell you what's wrong: everyone we love is leaving and it's all because of those stupid watches! Why did we have to get them? Since when did it become our problem to stop some alien nutbag?" Yoake stared at Hana, shocked at the sudden outburst.

"What do you mean?" she asked, "Even if you don't care about what Saekrin is doing, we still have to protect the people."

"No, we don't! We didn't have to get involved in this at all!"

"But we're involved now, aren't we?" Yoake countered, "and we have to see it though!"

"Can't you see that all those damned watches have brought us is trouble? Kyoki is gone! My sister is gone! And now I can't even fight to get them back because that bastard took my watch! Well I'm done!"

"But Hana—" Yoake began.

"But nothing! I can't take this anymore. How can you stand there and keep going when you're the one who's been hurt the most? That burn on your back didn't just magically appear. He was going to kill you! If we keep going like this, we'll die!"

"No we won't!"

Hana laughed bitterly, "and what makes you so sure about that? Huh? Yeldi nearly killed you and what do you think will happen when we eventually have to fight Saekrin himself? You saw what he did to Kyoki and he didn't even have to try; he just waved her away like she was some insect!"

"But—"

"I don't like to admit it, but no matter how much of a reckless spaz she was, Kyoki was the strongest of us, we couldn't beat him with her, how are we going to do it without her?"

"I—"

"Stop," Hana snapped, "I'm done. I can't do this anymore. I won't let them hurt anyone else. The only reason they took Kumi was to get to me!" she stared for a moment at the ground, "maybe if I stop fighting they'll give her back. If I'm not a threat to them, then they would have no reason to keep her."

"Hana, you can't be serious!" Yoake cried. "Your solution is to just give up! You think they'll just give her back? No! We have to fight them no matter what!"

"You're wrong!" Hana yelled, shaking her head furiously, "Our fighting is what caused this. Think about it, we can't be the first native resistance Saekrin has faced on his demented quest, right? What do you think happened to those people? Their families? It's obvious he doesn't think like normal people! He doesn't care who he has to step on, whose lives he has to tear apart! Do you really think we stand a chance against someone like that?"

"I do!"

"Then you're a fool," Hana said softly, moving to grab her bag, "I wish I could be as foolishly certain as you are, but I'm not and I think that, in a fight, I would only be a burden to you like this. I couldn't help you in the last fight and I'm no better now. So consider this my resignation," She picked up her bag and walked to the door, "good bye, Yoake."

"No! Hana! Wait!" Yoake screamed, but she was already gone. "Hana, please don't go . . ."

❦

Back at the school, Tybalt had just finished proctoring detention and was walking back to the office he had been temporarily assigned, looking at a student file. The name read Yami Kurai. He knew he had seen that face before but couldn't quite put his finger on it. Sadly, he was so involved in the file that he accidentally bumped into someone. "Oops. I'm sorry, Mr . . . ?"

"Satoru," the other man smiled, "and it was my fault. Tell me, are you the one who has been subbing for me?"

Tybalt nodded and kept staring. Something about that teacher seemed . . . familiar. "Yes, I heard you were sick; feeling better?"

"I am thank you." Satoru answered. "Well, I've got homework to grade, and I don't want the little darlings to wait too long." He moved past Tybalt toward the classroom, but as he brushed against him, Satoru leaned over and whispered, "Nice to see you again, old friend . . ." With that, he was gone.

Tybalt stood frozen in place. The other man's voice had suddenly dropped to a low velvety whisper as he walked by. It was a voice Tybalt has known for years, the voice to whom he entrusted his younger brother, and a voice he would never forget. Abruptly, he turned around to see Satoru smirking at him as he walked into his classroom.

"Saekrin . . ."

Tybalt ran back to the dorm and jumped in the already open window. There he found Yoake sitting on her bed, a very disheartened look on her face. "Where's Hana?" he asked.

"She . . . She went home." Yoake answered.

"She what?"

"She went home, in other words, she left."

"Oh . . . it's just you and Kyoki—"

"No, just me." she snapped. "Or have you forgotten that Kyoki's disappeared."

"Yoake, please calm down—"

"How can I calm down when everyone I care about has disappeared?" she said standing.

"Yoake!" He put his hands on her shoulders and sat her back down. "You have to stay calm. What happened to 'not giving up'?"

"Well, maybe I have to stop being so stubborn? Maybe if I want to actually protect those I care about I should just . . ."

"Just what? Just give up? Yoake, it's too late to turn back. Even if you follow Hana, Saekrin will follow you. He knows who you are and will pursue you until you are no longer a factor. Do you understand? Even if you left, you wouldn't be safe." He looked over at her bureau where her watch was laying. She had resorted to staring at the ground to avoid looking at him, but he knelt down and lifted her chin as he put the little piece in her hands. "Hey, it's going to be okay. Alright?" Slowly, she nodded and he stood up. "That's a girl."

"So, um, what did you come in for?" Yoake asked once she had composed herself. Tybalt gave her a quizzical look for a moment.

"Oh, right," he said, "I have some bad news—"

"More?" Yoake asked, laughing bitterly, "It seems like every time you come in here something's wrong."

"Yoake this is serious," Tybalt said, "Your teacher, Mr. Satoru,"

"What about him?"

"He's Saekrin."

Yoake stared at her mentor for a moment; her face blank as if she had gone into shock. "Saekrin is, is," was all she could manage before she descended into nonsense. Suddenly, her head shot up and she ran out the door.

"Where are you going?" Tybalt said, quickly catching up to her.

"I have to find Hana," Yoake said, "she has to know, even if she doesn't want to fight anymore, this is important." Tybalt nodded.

"I'll go search to the north," he said, "you go south."

"Right." With that the two split up and began running all over town.

"Hana, where are you?" Yoake muttered to herself. The first place she had checked was Hana's home. She dialed Hana's house on her cellphone. "Hello? Yeah, it's Yoake. Is Hana there? No, okay, thank you." Then she went to the park, the mall, the bookstore, any place she could think of that her friend would be. Just as the sun was beginning to dip behind the horizon, she sat down on a bench, panting and even more worried than ever.

"Where did she go?"

"Looking for someone?" chuckled a sarcastic, mocking voice from in front of her. She looked up to see Yeldi slowly walking toward the bench.

"What do you want?" she growled, glaring daggers at him.

"Shouldn't it be obvious?" he answered, "I want that pretty little watch of yours, however—"

"'However' what?" Yoake snapped, "I don't care what's happened, I'm not going to let you take this from me. Besides," she stood and opened her watch, instantly transforming, "You're all alone. I beat you once by myself and I can do it again."

Yeldi laughed, "that's where you're wrong," he giggled, "you may be alone, but I'm not . . ." He turned to look behind him and smirked. Yoake tilted so she could see what he was looking at and nearly dropped her bow, sauntering over to stand beside Yeldi was none other than-

"Kyoki,"

"Hello, Yoake," she said, leaning on her scythe, "Long time no see, how'ya been? Where's Hana? Don't tell me that pathetic excuse for a fighter finally quit."

Yoake starred in shock at the girl who had once been her friend. "Kyoki . . . why? How?"

"Oh, it's simple really," Kyoki said, twirling her scythe lazily between her fingers, "You see, you girls were the problem, not me. You wanted me to stay weak so I wouldn't be a threat to you. You're the leader, right Yoake? I mean, you got your watch first. But I'm stronger and you know what, Saekrin understands how I feel better than you ever have."

Yoake felt her legs shake underneath her. No, no, no, of all the places Kyoki could have been, why was she with Yeldi?

"K-kyoki . . ." she said stunned, "are, are you going to take my watch?" Smirking, the older girl shook her head.

"As I was saying," Yeldi cut in, "We weren't ordered to take your watch," he turned to Kyoki who suddenly disappeared.

Yoake looked around frantically for her and seconds later found herself on the ground, Kyoki's scythe pointed directly at her throat, "we were told to kill you."

Yoake's eyes widened as she stared into Kyoki's. How could this be happening? Quickly, she shoved the curved blade away with her bow and jumped away. "How could you, Kyoki, we're sisters!" she yelled.

Kyoki humphed. "You were never my family," she chuckled cruelly, "and that's what makes this so easy." Suddenly, Kyoki lunged for her, swinging her scythe down. Yoake blocked and again jumped away, stringing her bow.

"I don't want to do this!" she yelled, pointing the green arrow at her friend, "but I will."

"No you won't," Kyoki laughed. She ran at Yoake, challenging her to fire, but all Yoake could do was shake. Kyoki slashed at her, sending her flying backward into wall. Coughing up blood, Yoake stood and strung her bow again.

"To slow," Kyoki laughed, instantly appearing in front of her and sending her fist into Yoake's stomach. More blood forced its way out of Yoake's mouth as more and more blows found a place on her body. Smirking, Kyoki delivered one last kick and sent Yoake flying away from the wall and into the empty street. Laughing like a sadistic madman, Kyoki stalked over to her.

"You know you really are weak," she said, twirling her scythe again. Yoake pushed herself up by her elbows and tried to scoot away but to no avail. Tears stung the corners of her eyes as Kyoki pressed the blade of her scythe against her throat.

"P-please, Kyoki," she begged.

"Please what?" Kyoki asked sacrastically, "please kill you quickly or please make it slow or please don't do it? I really need you to be specific."

"Don't!" Kyoki stopped for a moment, pretending to think it over.

"No, I don't think I will spare you. Good bye, my friend." Slowly, she raised her weapon as Yoake closed her tear filled eyes waiting for the blow to come, but it didn't. Cautiously, Yoake opened her eyes and saw Kyoki staring down at her, eyes wide and looking torn. Suddenly, she dropped her scythe and backed away.

"I-I can't." she mumbled.

"Why not?" Yeldi demanded from behind her.

"I just, I just, she's my friend."

"Not anymore."

"But she used to be!" Kyoki cried, spinning around to face Yeldi, "she was more than that; she was my sister. Look at her, she barely has any will to fight, she's not a threat to him, can't we just leave her alone?" Yoake watched in shock as Kyoki pleaded for her life with Yeldi, what was happening?

"Fine," Yeldi said, eyes downcast, but Yoake could swear she saw tears shining in the corners of his eyes, "but, but you're going to have to explain to Master why she's still alive. He's not going to be happy."

"I can handle it," Kyoki said happily, then turned to Yoake, "don't misconstrue this as some kind of friendship thing, I just don't feel like killing anyone today." With that, she turned away and walked over to Yeldi. As they jumped over a nearby building, Yoake swore she heard Yeldi mutter, "I hope you're right," under his breath, a single tear rolling off his chin.

"WHAT?" Saekrin roared. Kyoki and Yeldi had just finished explaining what had happened and it was obvious that their leader was furious, "Why did you leave her alive?"

"W-well," Kyoki said, but Yeldi cut her off.

"She is no longer a threat, Master," he said quickly, "she has no more allies and her power is next to nothing. There was no reason to kill her."

Saekrin snorted. "I wasn't asking you, boy," he said, turning back to Kyoki, "now tell me, Kyoki my dear, what possessed you to leave her alive?" He reached down and tilted her head up so she could stare directly into his sadistic grey eyes, "Could it be that you still consider her your friend?" Kyoki tried to answer but all she could do was shake, for the first time since she had come to Saekrin, she was afraid, terrified. Suddenly, he pulled away and she came to her senses, shaking her head furiously.

"No, sir," she said, "Yoake means nothing to me."

"Then why," Saekrin sighed, "isn't she DEAD?" He turned sharply and smacked her, sending her crashing to the ground. Yeldi leaped up to go help her, but the glare Saekrin sent his way made him kneel down again.

Slowly, Kyoki tried to stand, but Saekrin swung his foot at her and sent her flying into the wall. Kyoki could hear her heart thumping in her chest, growing louder and louder as Saekrin walked over to her.

"Yeldi," he said, "get those for me." She couldn't see what he was referring to but a gasp from Yeldi made tears spring to her eyes. Suddenly, she felt herself being pulled up, coming face to face with Saekrin.

"Now, my dear," he said, "you will see what happens to disobedient dogs." Gently, he took her hands and pulled them above her head. Kyoki cried out as a short 'click' sounded throughout the room. Quickly, she looked up and found that she had been handcuffed to a notch in the wall. She tried to pull the cuffs out but all in vain. Shaking, she tried to twist around. Sadly, all she did was get herself stuck facing the cold grey wall; the color eerily similar to the eyes of the creature standing behind her.

"Now," Saekrin said, sadistic joy dripping off his words, "I want you to learn this lesson and learn well." Kyoki's breathing was erratic, growing more and more frantic as the seconds ticked by and nothing happened. Longer and longer the silence stretched until she thought she would go crazy if something didn't happen soon. Suddenly-

"AH!" she cried out in pain as a whip slammed against her back, instantly ripping her shirt and breaking the skin. More and more blows connected with her back, sending blood running down and staining the fabric.

"Please," she begged desperately, "please sto-AH!" She could hear Saekrin chuckling from above her as he continued slamming his weapon down. Her vision blurred as blood began to pool around her legs and she coughed, resting her head against the wall. Just as she was about to pass out, Saekrin stopped.

"You've taken your punishment very well," he said, gently running his clawed fingers through her hair. She flinched at the contact, "but there's one more thing I need to do. Yeldi, give me that rod."

Kyoki tried to turn and get even a glimpse of what Yeldi had handed his master. She could feel Saekrin bringing something closer and closer to her skin, heat radiating off the object.

"AAAHH!" A piercing scream echoed through the room as he brought the fire poker down onto her back and began running it down the torn flesh. She lost count of how many times he slashed the hot metal across her back before she was overcome by pain and passed out.

"Now you'll never forget who you belong to, human," Saekrin chuckled. He dropped the poker and walked to the door, "Bandage her, Yeldi," he said as he left, "she may still be useful."

"Yes, Master," the younger creature said softly, sadly. Once Saekrin was gone, he pulled out the first aid kit from the medicine cabinet and walked over to Kyoki. She was still unconscious, but he began anyway. As he worked, he could see the markings Saekrin had made in her flesh, the word was written in his own language so the girl wouldn't be able to read it if she tried, but to Yeldi it was clear as the scars that covered his body. Saekrin had burned his name into the girl's pale, broken body.

Tybalt found Yoake sitting, shaking on the ground, a few minutes after Yeldi left. Slowly, he reached forward and tried to help her up, but she didn't react.

"Yoake . . ." he said slowly, "are you alright?" Gently, he picked her up and leaped onto a nearby roof. Still the girl didn't react.

"Yoake," he said again once they were safely out of sight, "Please, I need you to tell me what happened. Did Yeldi hurt you? How did you get those cuts?"

Yoake looked up at him, eyes wide and staring at him like he couldn't see him, "I-I . . ." She trailed off, eyes darting to the ground, "I know where Kyoki is . . ."

"Really?" Tybalt exclaimed as he pulled some bandages out of one of his pockets and began dressing Yoake's wounds, "I'm sorry, but I can't say the same about Hana but where did you find her?"

"She-she-she—" Yoake tried to answer but quickly descended into choking sobs. Tybalt patiently waited for her to finish, pulling her a bit closer in an attempt to comfort her.

Slowly, she calmed and, taking several deep breaths, told Tybalt what she had seen. "Kyoki is with Saekrin now." she muttered as she whipped some final tears from her eyes.

"WHAT?" yelled a voice from above them. They looked up to see Artan land in front of Yoake, "Are you seriously telling me that she betrayed us?" Yoake nodded slowly. "Argh!" Artan screamed, kicking a nearby air conditioning vent, "You can't be serious!" She nodded again, tears stinging the corners of her eyes.

"Come on," Tybalt said, standing and picking Yoake up with him, "I'll take you back home." He closed her watch and jumped from roof to roof, heading for her dorm with Artan in tow. All through the trip, Yoake was silent. Everything was falling apart around her. Friends were disappearing, siblings were betraying her. As her fingers closed around her watch, she could feel her anger rising. It was all because of these that this was all happening.

"Stay here and rest," Tybalt said as he set her down onto her bed, "Artan and I will keep looking for Hana and if we see Kyoki, we will bring her back."

Artan nodded, determination shining in his eyes. "I'm not going to let anything happen to Hana!" he said. Both Tybalt and Yoake looked at him, confused. Yelping, Artan waved his hands frantically, his face turning as red as a tomato. "What I mean is, I'm gonna find her . . . and Kyoki."

Tybalt laughed a bit, amused by Artan's sad attempt to hide his growing crush. "Don't worry, it's nothing to be ashamed of."

"Ashamed of what?" Artan asked defensively.

"You know what." Tybalt smiled at his former protégé, mischief sparkling in his eyes.

The two walked out, Artan's voice continuing to deny any feelings he possibly had for a certain Earth girl. Yoake sat in her bed, still shaken up from the day's events. She barely noticed the bandages that Tybalt had wrapped around her wounds; though to be honest she barely noticed the wounds themselves. There was a much deeper pain in her that couldn't be seen. It wasn't from a physical weapon, it was pain from the sting of betrayal. It cut deeper than any blade ever could. Her eyes started bleeding tears and her hands shook in anger, pain, and sadness. "Why?" she sobbed. "Why, God? Why? Why have you let this happen?" she screamed.

Her screams echoed through the girls' dorm, alerting her classmates. A group of girls from her school, lead by Wynona, burst into her room. "Yoake, are you—" she stopped when she saw Yoake sitting on her bed sobbing into her knees. She went over to her friend, sat down on the bed, and wrapped her arms comfortingly around the crying girl.

The next day she walked to school alone. Artan was still out searching for Hana, and she didn't see Yami. As she walked into her classroom, she prayed to God that Tybalt was teaching her class, or that he was wrong about Mr. Satoru. But when she looked over at the teacher's desk she saw the familiar figure of Mr. Satoru sitting there. As she looked at him, she definitely saw Saekrin in the young teacher's face; how could she have missed it? She kicked herself for not noticing the similarity before. She tried to slip silently to her desk but he caught her.

"Good morning, Miss Hikari." he greeted.

"Uh . . . g-good morning, sir." she said, avoiding his eyes.

"I noticed that Mr. Kotobushi isn't with you this morning."

"Um, yeah, he's sick today."

"Oh, what a shame. Ah well."

"Um, sir, could I talk to you before lunch, today, or after school, which ever's better."

"That would be fine."

"Thank you." Nervously, Yoake waited for the final bell to ring, having already decided to talk to her teacher after school. There would be no students in the building so if Saekrin decided he wanted a fight, no one would get hurt. As soon as the bell rang, Yoake began to shake. She had only met Saekrin face to face once and that had been with her friends, but now she was alone and he would have no trouble (and no guilt for that matter) killing her. Slowly, she stood and walked over to the desk, keeping her eyes locked on the ground as her teacher finished grading the paper in his hand.

"Now," he said, putting the paper down, "What is it you wanted to talk about?"

Yoake shifted from foot to foot nervously, still unsure of what to say. Slowly, she took a deep breath and spoke. "Where is my friend?" she asked, hoping she sounded a lot more confident than she actually was.

"Yes . . ." Mr. Satoru mused, "She hasn't been in school for a while has she? Her teacher is quite worried, but I assure you I don't know."

"Are you sure?" Yoake asked, trying her best to imitate the interrogations she had seen on television and failing miserably.

"As I said," Mr. Satoru answered, "I don't know where the girl is, but I'm sure she's just fine."

He smirked slightly at her and at that Yoake exploded. "Stop it!" she yelled.

"Stop what?" he asked, concerned. Slowly, he stood and moved to her, but Yoake backed away.

"Don't come near me!" she screamed, "I know who you are! Tybalt told us everything, Saekrin! Now GIVE BACK MY FRIEND!" She glared at him but all he did was chuckle, a dark, evil sound that soon filled the room, bouncing off the walls. Each sound seemed to mock her.

"Well, it was fun while it lasted," Saekrin muttered, still laughing. He leaned against the desk as he spoke, staring at the ceiling, "but I suppose now it's over." As he spoke, he slowly began to change. His hair grew longer and lightened until it was stark white, pale skin became even paler, and long black claws sprouted from his hands. Yoake shook as she stared at him, eyes wide as he continued to change. Soon, the true Saekrin stood before her, smiling maliciously. Gently, he pushed himself off the desk and came toward her. Yoake tried to run but her legs wouldn't obey and she soon found he was only inches away. "Poor girl," he chuckled, running a clawed hand through her hair, "you look so frightened, what's wrong? Surely it's not me; you were so confident during our last meeting . . ." His other hand moved down her neck to grasp the watch that hung there, "This little trinket has caused you so much grief hasn't it. Hana has quit and Kyoki, well . . ."

"W-What have you done to her?" Yoake asked, internally cursing herself for letting her fear show.

Saekrin smirked and pulled away. "She is such an independent girl," he sighed, sounding exasperated, "I had to show her who is in charge." He moved his hand across his neck, motioning a small slice.

Yoake gasped. "No!" she screamed.

"Calm down," Saekrin said, moving close to her again, "she will live. I just arranged it so she will never forget me." Slowly, he placed his hand on her cheek, "And you know what—"

"Saekrin!" both turned to see Tybalt standing in the doorway, watch out and ready for battle, "Get away from her!"

The white haired man stood and sighed. "Must you always spoil my fun?" he asked, feigning hurt.

"I said, get away from her." Tybalt repeated.

"Oh, come now, I was only just getting to know her." Saekrin grabbed Yoake's chin and, much to her horror, wrapped his arm around her waist, pulling her close to him.

"Let me go!" she shrieked, trying to push him away.

"Now, now, princess, don't struggle." He squeezed her waist. "It will only get worse." Despite his warning, she continued to push, but in vain. "Oh, I see that you insist on being difficult, so I will just take what I want and leave." He reached for her watch, but before he could get it, she opened the little piece and transformed, forcing him to let go.

"I won't let you have it!" she cried.

He shook his head in disappointment. "Pity. I was going to let you live if you had only just cooperated with me, but now I see that the only way I will get what I want is if I pry it out of your cold, dead hands."

"You're damn right!" she said.

He just chuckled. "Tell Artan's father I said hello." He moved to attack, but Tybalt was faster.

He opened his watch and summoned a bear that clawed at Saekrin before the cobra-like man could make a move. "I told you to stay away from my student!"

"Your *student*." Saekrin sneered. "Well I must say, old friend, that your standards for a protege have gone down since I last saw you."

"Yoake is the best student I've trained, and I won't let you degrade her." The bear took another swing at Saekrin, who lept out of the way and landed on the windowsill.

"Well, it's been fun and all, but I think I've had enough for now. I'll see you around." With that, he jumped out the window and disappeared.

Yoake and Tybalt ran over to the window in an effort to chase after him, but he was already gone. "Are you okay?" he asked and reached for the little cut on Yoake's neck.

"I'm fine." She said, slapping his hand away.

"Still depressed, huh?"

"He said he beat Kyoki!" she yelled at him, making him step back in surprise. It wasn't like her to suddenly explode like that.

"What?" he asked, cautiously moving a bit closer to her.

"He said he 'showed her who is in charge,'" She answered, "and then he moved his hand like, like this." Slowly, she moved her hand the same way Saekrin had his, miming a slicing motion.

"Calm down," Tybalt said slowly.

"Calm down!" Yoake yelled, "He's hurting my friend and I can't find her and I can't do anything about it! How could he-!" She was cut off by her own tears as she descended into sobs, knees buckling under her. Tybalt quickly moved forward and pulled her close, trying his best to comfort her. He sighed; Saekrin was obviously getting crueller. He remembered him playfully punching new recruits but that behavior had definitely escalated to pure, simple sadism. Gently, he lifted Yoake to her feet, closed her watch, and helped her back to her dorm.

"We'll find her," he whispered, "Don't worry. We'll find her."

The next morning Yoake woke with a start. She quickly scanned the room but all she found were two empty beds and her backpack. Sighing sadly, she stood and proceeded to get dressed, picking up her bag as she walked out the door.

"What's wrong?" a voice asked suddenly as she walked to class. She turned instantly and came face to face with Yami.

"Oh it's, it's nothing." She answered, trying to sound much more confident than she felt. Yami stared at her for a moment as if he wasn't sure whether or not to believe her, but finally nodded slowly.

"Alright," he said, "but if something's wrong, you know you can tell me, right?" Yoake smiled at him and he gave her a half grin back. Suddenly, she reached forward and wrapped her arms around him.

"You're adorable!" she giggled, letting go, "and thank you." Yami smiled back at her and they walked into their room. Yoake looked over at the teacher's desk as they entered, hoping to see Tybalt sitting there, but to her horror, Mr. Satoru, or as she now knew him, Saekrin, grinned back at her.

"Good morning," he said. Yoake shook as his eyes bored into hers, images of their last encounter flashing through her mind.

"Yoake," Yami said, "are you okay?" Quickly, she shook her head and turned to him, nodding.

"Yeah," she answered, "Sorry. I guess I kind of spaced out for a moment there." Yami nodded slowly and walked with her to her seat.

"Bastard," Artan growled once Yoake sat down. She looked over to see him glaring daggers at Saekrin who continued to sort papers as if nothing was out of the ordinary, "How can he just sit there and pretend to be a nice teacher."

"He was never a nice teacher," Yoake countered, smiling slightly at her attempted joke.

"I guess so." Artan answered. He glared at Saekrin as the man stood and began to read off the attendence.

"The substitute told me that you all got a lot done," he said, "so I think the best thing to do would be to have a quiz—" The whole room groaned, interrupting him, "now, now," he continued, "you should all be prepared and for that matter, this is why they are called 'pop' quizzes. So, if you would all be so kind, pencils out, eyes on your own paper, and absolutely no cheating." Yoake shivered as he finished. When other teachers said that, it sounded like they were reading from a script, but when Saekrin said it, there was a thinly veiled threat behind the words. With a sigh, she waited for Saekrin to hand her a paper. She could see Yami shaking like a leaf as their teacher walked ever closer. *Poor guy* she thought. As Saekrin walked by, he placed a hand on Yami's shoulder.

"Don't worry," he said, "It's just a short quiz. I'm sure you'll do fine." Yami tensed immediately, nodding frantically, and looked down at his paper. Yoake glared as Saekrin handed her the quiz.

"Oh, don't look at me like that," he whispered, "You and," his eyes flicked to the desk next to Yoake, "Artan, have nothing to worry about and," he leaned in closer, "you might want to know that the little one is safe with me."

Both Artan's and Yoake's eyes shot up, looking, shocked, at one another. As Yoake looked down at her quiz, she couldn't concentrate. How did Saekrin know about Artan? Who was the 'little one' he was talking about? Was it Hana's little sister? Question after question piled into Yoake's brain, making it impossible for her to concentrate on the quiz. By the time Saekrin had called for everyone to stop, about fifteen minutes later, she hadn't answered a single problem. Melancholically, she passed her blank paper forward to Yami who handed it to Saekrin.

"So how do you think you did?" Artan whispered. Yoake shook her head sadly, ripping a small piece of paper from her note book.

"I didn't answer any of them," she wrote, "I was thinking about what he said. How did he know about you and do you think he has Kumi?" She quickly slid the note to the edge of her desk, allowing Artan to snatch it up. After about a minute, she felt something poking her and took the paper back.

"I don't know," it said, "but I think we should find out ASAP. Maybe Yeldi saw me transform or something. If he does have Kumi . . ." Yoake's thoat tightened at the thought of the girl being anywhere near Saekrin. She had a pretty good idea of what he did to Yeldi and after hearing him talk about Kyoki, she was sure that anyone close to him was no doubt covered in bruises and scars.

"If he does have Kumi," she wrote, hoping her words sounded much more determined than they did in her head, "then we have to find her and get her back before he—" she paused, trying to come up with a way to finish her sentence without crying, "does something." Weak and she knew it but it was the best she could come up with. As she pushed the paper back toward Artan, it was suddenly snatched away.

"What's this?" Saekrin asked, standing between the two desks. He unfolded the note and began to read, a small smirk forming on his lips. Yoake could feel the class starring at her and Artan, obviously hoping that their teacher would read the note out loud.

"While this is rather nice," he said, still smirking, "I would prefer that you refrain from writing love letters in my class."

Yoake's cheeks turned a deep scarlet as the rest of the students began to laugh loudly. Quickly, she glanced over at Artan to see him glaring at Saekrin. Once the laughter died down, Yoake put her head on her desk in an attempt to tune out the rest of the day. Thankfully, it worked and soon she and Artan were heading back to the dorms.

"That bastard!" Artan yelled, punching the air in front of him as if it were Saekrin, "What the hell is wrong with him—I mean aside from the obvious—but what the hell?" Yoake said nothing as the two continued up to her dorm. She sat down on her bed while Artan leaned against the wall beside the window.

"Urgh!" he growled.

"What happened?" called a voice from outside. Both turned to see Tybalt sitting on the window sill on the other side of the glass. Artan quickly opened the window and let him in.

"You know this place does have a door." the boy grunted. Tybalt shrugged and sat down next to Yoake.

"So what happened?" he asked. Before Yoake could answer, Artan jumped in, obviously ready to blow off a large amount of steam.

"That ass!" he snarled, "Not only did he give us a pop quiz the day he gets back, but when he caught Yoake and I passing notes—"

"You were passing notes in class?" Tybalt asked jokingly, "such bad children."

"Oh shut up!" Artan snapped, "and you know what he did after that? You'd think he'd read out what we wrote but noooo. He tells everyone we were passing love notes. LOVE NOTES! How much of an ass can he be? I wouldn't even be passing love notes to Yoake. I'd give them to Ha—" He stopped abruptly at what he had been about to say but Tybalt caught it and laughed.

"Don't laugh at me." Artan mumbled. Yoake smiled sadly; even the half mention of Hana made her nearly cry.

"I think I'll take a walk," she said, standing, "Have fun guys." With that, she walked out, leaving Tybalt and Artan worriedly watching her go.

Once she was outside, Yoake stretched her arms above her head and stepped onto the stone path that led from the dorms to a small park on the other side of campus. The trees blew gently in the evening breeze, giving her a welcome sense of calm and peace, but, just as she stepped into the park, a voice destroyed it.

"Yoake?"

She looked up and saw Yami sitting on a bench beside the path. "Oh, hi, Yami." she said solemnly.

"Something wrong?"

"Um . . . no I'm just moping about the test Mr. Satoru gave us today."

"That bad huh?"

"Yeah." Yoake laughed slightly as to assure him that nothing was wrong.

"You want to sit with me?"

"Sure thanks."

"No problem." Yami smiled at her as she sat down.

"I can't believe Ar—Akira and I got caught passing notes. We were sure he was going to read them outloud but instead he told the class that they were love notes. Love notes! Can you believe that?"

"Were they?"

Yoake chuckled, "No."

"Then what did they actually say?"

"Nothing much just asking how we did"

"What else?"

"Um . . . well uh." Yoake sighed. "I guess you can know."

"Know what?" Yami looked at her curiously.

"Yami," she looked back at him with a serious yet pleading look on her face, "can you keep a secret?"

"I keep a lot of secrets, Yoake. One more isn't going to make much of a difference."

"Okay, but try not to make a scene." Yami nodded and Yoake opened her watch.

The boy watched in wonder as the light surrounded her, transforming her clothes and hair, and stared in shock at the girl in front of him when it finished. "Wow." he said.

"I know, it's pretty cool, huh?" Yoake said. "but this came with a curse. Mr. Satoru is actually—" She stopped when she heard a chuckle escaping him. "What?"

"Nothing, nothing. I just didn't think you'd get *this* desperate."

"What do you mean?" Yoake took a step back as he stood up.

"You mean you haven't figured it out yet? You are so *blind!*"

"Stop stalling and tell me what's so funny!" she yelled impatiently.

"Maybe I should show you." the boy chuckled. Yoake stared in horror as his hair lengthened and became more scraggly, his ears, teeth, and fingernails elongated, and a tail sprouted from him back. "Now do you recognize me?"

"Yeldi!" Yoake readied herself to fight but a voice interrupted them.

"No!" Yoake spun to see Kyoki standing less than six feet in front of them. "She's mine."

"Fine then," Yeldi shrugged, "I'll leave her to you. Don't mess up this time or you know what'll happen." With that, he was gone.

Kyoki looked at her sister in remorse. "Why did you have to come outside tonight?" she said. She was already transformed and under the corset, Yoake could see the marks of fading cuts, bruises, and even a burn scar.

Slowly, she reached forward to her friend. "What happened?" she asked, moving closer.

Kyoki looked down and sidestepped her, trying in vain to pull her corset up to hide the marks. "N-nothing," she said, "It's none of your business."

"He did that to you, didn't he," Yoake said, tears already stinging the corners of her eyes, "Kyoki, if he's hurting you, come back to us, please."

The older girl just shook her head. "I can't. If I try to leave, he'll kill her." Yoake was about to ask who "her" was but realization suddenly dawned on her.

"He said he'd kill Kumi?" she yelled, "Kyoki, just take her with you. Come ba—"

"I can't!" Kyoki was crying now, "You don't know, Yoake. You don't know what he's like. He's crazy. He'll do anything, ANYTHING to get what he wants." Yoake stared, dumbstruck, at her friend, unsure of what to say. "Yoake, I'm sorry." Suddenly, she found herself on the ground, held down by swirling black ghosts. Kyoki stood above her, a sad, desperate look in her eyes.

"What are you doing?" Yoake asked, terrified.

Kyoki looked at the ground, at a spot just to the left of her captive's head. "He wants you dead." she whispered, "and if I don't kill you, he said he'll punish Kumi. I can't let that happen. I just—" she tried to look at Yoake but was only able to hold her gaze for a second before tears clouded her vision. Yoake could feel her own eyes watering at the sight of the broken girl. "I-I don't want to kill you," Kyoki sobbed, "but, but," she pressed her blade close to Yoake's throat, drawing the cold metal slowly across the pale flesh.

Yoake closed her eyes, bracing herself for the pain that was to come, but none came. Slowly, cautiously, she opened her eyes to see Kyoki stepping away from her. A flash of light drew Yoake's attention and she glanced over. In Kyoki's left hand she held Yoake's faux diamond bracelet, a gift from her late mother. "Run." Kyoki mumbled, turning.

"W-what?" Yoake asked as she stood slowly, "Why did you take tha—"

"RUN! And don't go to school; he'll know. I need this. I'm sorry. He told me to take your watch, but you have to stop him, you and Hana. I'll—I'll tell him you didn't have it." she turned around slightly, holding up the bracelet, "this will prove you're dead. You love this; I know it. I'll use it to prove you're dead. NOW JUST GO!"

Yoake stared for a moment at Kyoki, then the older girl ran off, leaving Yoake alone once more.

"I've done as you ordered, Master," Kyoki said, kneeling before Saekrin. He smiled as he gently ran his clawed fingers through Kumi's hair. The girl tried to curl away from him, but he held her tight, forcing her to stay in his lap. For a moment, she looked to Kyoki, desperately pleading for the older girl to help, but that thought soon died. Saekrin chuckled darkly and continued to tease Kumi's hair. She wondered absently where the other strange creature, the nice, quiet one, had gone, but quickly turned her attention back to Kyoki as the monster holding her spoke.

"Do you have it?" he asked, a hint of amusement in his voice.

Kyoki shook violently, terror wracking her body. "N-no, Master," she said softly, eyes firmly locked on the ground. She tensed instantly, hearing Saekrin snarl from above her. "But, but she is dead." she continued, silently praying that he wouldn't hurt Kumi, "I brought this as proof," slowly, she produced Yoake's bracelet from her pocket and handed it to Saekrin, "It was a gift from her mother; she never took it off." Tension filled the room as Saekrin studied the piece. Kyoki shifted nervously.

"Wh-who's dead?" Kumi asked, scared. Saekrin grinned at her, crushing the bracelet in his hand.

"A final obstacle," he answered, "Yoake is dead."

Outside the room, Yeldi's heart clenched and he slid down the wall, tears spilling from his eyes.

❧

Yoake walked around the park, unsure of what to do. She couldn't go back to school, Seakrin would know Kyoki was lying about her being dead. On top of that Yami was Yeldi, or rather the other way around. Wandering aimlessly through the city, she found herself going back to the places where recent events had taken place, starting with where she had first found out that Kyoki had joined Saekrin, and working backward in time from there, even going back to the grocery store and the alley where she had first met Yeldi.

It was hard for her to process everything: Kyoki, Kumi, Yeldi, everyone. A cold wind chilled her to the core, her uniform barely enough to protect her from the November weather. She looked up and saw three little girls playing with a ball in front of a house. Yoake stopped and watched the little girls play. It was almost like she was seeing herself playing with Kyoki and Hana when they were little. Suddenly the ball rolled into the middle of the street, pursued by one of the little girls. Unknown to her, a car was coming up the street. Yoake dashed for the girl and managed to get her out of the way, but got hit herself instead. Luckily, the car hadn't been going very fast and didn't do much except knock her to the ground.

"Are you okay?" the little girl asked.

"Yeah, I'm fine." Yoake stood up. "See?"

"Okay. Thanks." the child then went back to her friends.

The driver of the car got out and began apologizing, but Yoake assured him there was nothing wrong and they went their separate ways. Yoake did stay to watch the girls some more, but after awhile she had to walk away. They were too much like Yoake, Hana, and Kyoki, and she just couldn't bare to watch anymore.

Suddenly, Yoake found herself on a small stone bridge. To any other person, it was just a simple bridge, but for Yoake, it was so much more. It was the very bridge where Kyoki had first introduced her to Hana when they were little. Yoake walked to the stone rail and looked at the water. So many times they had played on that bridge and looked at that same water. For a moment, she thought she saw Kyoki's reflection in the water, smiling at her. Suddenly, Hana joined the Yoake in the river, giggling at something. Yoake's head shot up, looking from side to side frantically, hoping and praying that the vision had been real. Sadly, it was nothing but cruel imagination. Hana wasn't with her; she was off at home somewhere, worrying about Kumi and hoping that, in her absence, Saekrin would give her back. With a sigh, she thought about the madman they had been fighting. How could Kyoki have gone with him? Tears began to obscure her vision as she thought about her friend, her sister, beaten and suffering and Yami had known! No, *Yeldi* had known. She looked up to the sky as the tears slipped down her cheeks. Yami had been her friend, at least she'd thought so. He was so quiet and sweet, but now everything made sense: his stuttering whenever their teacher had been around, how he'd tensed up when Satoru had—Saekrin had put his hand on his shoulder, everything. How could she have been so stupid?

Again she looked down at the constantly moving water, endlessly flowing and flowing without a care, just like the world. The world didn't care if Kyoki was beaten, there were plenty of children who were abused. The world didn't care if Kumi was gone or if Hana was worried sick. There were plenty of missing children and worried families and the world wouldn't care if—She stared at the water, going and going off to nowhere, just like it would carry her if she-

"What's the point?" she asked herself, leaning a bit farther over the rail. "If I die I couldn't . . . maybe I could. If I die, Kyoki might come back. And with me out of the way, Saekrin—of course he already thinks I'm dead—but still! Yes, I'll do it." She took a deep breath and climbed over the rail. She looked down at the water and prepared herself for the jump, but then a voice startled her.

"Looks like Kyoki was lying." it said. Yoake turned and saw Yeldi standing behind her wearing his signature smirk on his face. "Then again, she may not be after all."

"What do *you* want?" Yoake hissed. She was in no mood to deal with him.

"Nothing really." he said. "So you gonna do it or what?"

"Yes I'm going to—" She looked down at the water and froze with fear.

To make matters worse, Yeldi jumped onto the rail and looked with her, saying, "It's pretty deep, you'd definitely drown and even if you don't the rocks will do you in." He sat down and sighed. "You know, I thought about this a couple times, once I even tried, but Master was there to catch me, and give me a thorough beating for it." He flinched at the memory and Yoake could see how much it pained him. Leaning closer, he whispered in her ear. "Think about it, you jump off with this crazy thought that everything will be better, but, you realize how wrong you are and you regret even thinking about it. Then SPLASH!" Yoake gasped. "It's too late and you're nothing more than a ripple in the water."

She didn't respond, shaking and gripping the rail.

"Now you're scared." he observed. When she continued to remain silent, he decided to test her fear. He gently put his hand on her back, as if to comfort her, and she looked at him confusedly. But comfort wasn't his intention. To her horror, he gave a rough push, and laughed when she grasped the rail even tighter.

"What was that for?" she shrieked.

"You really are terrified." he responded

That was it; he had crossed the line. Yoake swung her arm around in an effort to punch him, but he easily dodged her fist, causing her to lose her balance. As she fell, she braced herself for the impact. She could feel the cool water run past her skin with an icy grip of death. Her head hit the rocks and cracked open, turning the water warm with the thick red liquid. She lay at the bottom of the stream, not quite dead, but getting very close to death as her life flowed away with the blood leacking out of her skull. Images flashed in her mind. She thought of Hana, and who would be there for her if she died? Kyoki, to whom she begged to come back. Kumi she told to stay strong. Tybalt and everyone else she was letting down she quietly thought *"I'm sorry"* as her life finally slipped away

Then suddenly, her head snapped backward, and she was back on the bridge, but barely. She opened her eyes and, looking up, she saw Yeldi holding her by her shirt collar, a sadistic look in his eyes. "What are you waiting for?" she shouted defiantly. "You want me dead don't you? So just get it over with!"

He smirked. "Sure." To her surprise, instead of letting go of her shirt, allowing her to fall into the river, he pulled her back up, her cheeks turning red as he wrapped his arms around her. With her in his arms, he held her close and whispered quietly in her ear, "Dying won't help anything. It won't bring them back, and it won't stop Saekrin."

"What are you—"

"You're the only hope," he said as he placed something in her hand, "for both our worlds." Without letting go, he jumped back onto the bridge, taking her with him. Then he unwrapped his arms and stepped back. "Take my advice and forget this even happened." With that, he disappeared, leaving her shocked and confused.

"What did he—" Yoake said and looked down at the thing he put in her hand. "No way." she breathed when she saw it. "Hana's watch." She looked up for Yeldi to ask him why he gave it back to her, but he was gone. "Yeldi, what are you trying to tell me?"

Suddenly a barking dog interrupted her thoughts, followed by Tybalt's voice crying out, "Yoake!"

"I'm here." she responded. She was approached by a black bloodhound with red eyes, Tybalt and Artan following close behind. "Hey, guys." she greeted.

"Oh thank the gods." Tybalt nearly tackled her with a hug.

"Tybalt," Yoake choked, "I can't breathe."

"Sorry." he said, letting her go.

"Can you blame him?" Artan commented. "You've been gone for hours. We got really worried and came to look for you."

"Thanks guys, but I'm fine."

"The dog picked up Yeldi's and Kyoki's scents earlier and Yeldi's here. Did something happen?" Tybalt asked.

Yoake smiled slightly. "Something happened alright. Look what Yeldi gave me." She held out Hana's watch.

"He *gave* that to you?" Artan said, puzzled and mildly incredulous. "But didn't he take it in the first place?"

"Yes, I was confused too, but I think he's trying to tell us something." Yoake said.

"What?" Tybalt inquired.

"I think he might want out. He could be asking for help." Yoake said hopefully.

"He could." Tybalt nodded, sharing her hopefulness.

"I don't think so." Artan crossed his arms skeptically.

"Why not?" Yoake said.

"He's a traitor; once a traitor, always a traitor."

"Come on, Artan, have an open mind."

"He's working for that bastard! How can you so easily forgive him?"

"Because Kyoki is in the same boat. If I say I can't forgive Yeldi, then how could I possibly hope to forgive Kyoki?"

Tybalt added, "And he's my brother."

"I guess."

"Hana would agree with us." Yoake said.

"If you're so sure about that," Artan grouched, still angry about the prospect of trusting Yeldi, "let's go find her." He stared at Yoake for a moment when no one moved, "You don't know where she is do you?" he said, his face deadpan.

"O-of course I do," Yoake sputtered indignantly, "she went back home."

"And where is that?" Artan countered.

"Come on," Yoake grabbed onto his hand and led the two males toward the edge of campus where a gate ran around the perimeter. Just outside, she waved over a taxi and shoved them in. Artan pushed himself close to the far wall, pointedly ignoring the address Yoake gave the driver; he refused to even consider stalking Hana.

"So how far away is it?" he muttered as they drove off. Yoake though for a few moments.

"About an hour, why?" she said.

"I don't like cars," he snapped, "you humans need a better source of transport. Why haven't you figured out jumping yet?"

"Jumping?"

"It's like what I do with my watch to transport you from here to our world," Tybalt cut in, "just over shorter distances." Yoake nodded slowly. The cab pulled up in front of Hana's home just as six o'clock rolled around. Nervously, Yoake walked up to the door, Artan and Tybalt following close behind her. She held Hana's watch close to her chest as a sort of good luck charm and slowly brought her hand up, knocking. Seconds that felt like hours ticked by until-

"I got it, Mom! Oh, what do you want?" Hana starred at Yoake, looking annoyed. Yoake gulped and held the pocket watch out toward her friend.

"No," Hana said flatly, "I already told you I'm through. Kumi is gone and I won't risk having anyone else I love hurt."

"I understand," Yoake said, "but—"

"No 'but's. I'm not going back and that's final."

"Not even if one of the enemy switched sides?" Artan asked. Hana looked over at him, still irritated but intrigued.

"Has Kyoki come back?" she asked.

"No," Yoake answered, "but we think Yeldi is trying to help us. Oh, you should probably know that Yami was Yeldi is disguise. Anyway—"

"He was who?" Hana yelled.

"Not now," Yoake said, "I'll explain later, please just come back. Staying here isn't going to save Kumi. She needs her big sister. She needs you." Yoake held Hana's watch forward to her, a silent, earnest plea in the gesture. Hana stared at the small device and the three outside could easily see the cogs churning in her brain, mulling over all possible scenarios and options.

"Are you sure we can save her?" Hana asked, looking directly into Yoake's eyes. The shorter girl stared back, a determined fire in her brown eyes.

"Yes."

Before she could say another word, Hana had snatched her watch, called to her mother that she was going somewhere important with Yoake, and climbed into the taxi.

"Well," she said, "aren't you coming?" Yoake smiled broadly and leaped in, pulling Tybalt and Artan along with her.

"I'm really getting sick of this pulling." Artan said as he was shoved next to Hana, a slight blush ghosting over his cheeks. Tybalt chucked as Yoake instructed the driver to head to the park where he had first brought them to his world. It was a short drive and soon the three stood at the edge of the familiar stream. Tybalt opened the portal and the four of them crossed over into Cyowan.

"You're back." Alia greeted them.

"We heard what happened." Sakura said. "Is everyone alright?"

"Well, not everyone." Yoake said sadly referring to Kyoki. "But we are regaining our broken pieces."

"That's good to hear." Erasure responded. There was a hint of remorse and shame in his voice.

"It's not your fault." Sakura said, putting a comforting hand on the older man's shoulder. "If anyone is to blame for Saekrin's actions, it's me." She bowed her head, tears stinging the corners of her purple eyes.

"What do you mean?" Hana asked, approaching her teacher comfortingly. She reached out her hand, but Sakura turned and ran in the other direction.

"Sakura!" Tybalt called and chased after her.

"What's with them?" Artan wondered.

"Aimiri look over them." Alia prayed, then said to them, "It is a long story."

"The short version is Saekrin loved Sakura, but she loved—loves—Tybalt." Erasure said. "How long have they been married?"

"A few years." Alia answered. "It was before Saekrin went mad."

"It's what caused him to go mad I think."

"Whoa, back up." Yoake said. "Tybalt and Sakura are married?"

"And expecting their second child." Alia announced proudly.

"WHAT?" all three teens said together.

Alia sighed. "Like I said, it is a long story. Come, let us go to the courtyard. I will explain everything there."

"Sakura!" Tybalt continued to call after his wife. "Sakura, stop!"

But she didn't stop. She just kept running until her legs couldn't go any further. When she did finally stop, she sank to her knees in a waterfall of tears. "Tybalt," she sobbed. "It's my fault he's like this. It's all my fault."

"Saekrin was unstable to begin with," Tybalt said as he wrapped his arms around her. "You can't blame yourself."

"But, Tybalt, those things he did to me; those awful things. I can still—" She shivered in fear as the memory came back to her

"Sh-h." He rested his chin on her head, gently stroking her hair. "It's okay. Come on." He stood up, taking her with him. "Let's go find the others."

In the temple courtyard, the three teens, Alia, and Erasure all sat around a marble table. Alia was silent, she couldn't bare thinking about what her little sister had gone through because of Saekrin, let alone even talking about it. However, she knew that they needed to know.

But before she could say anything, a little girl with golden hair and large green eyes skipped up to them and handed Alia a bouquet of flowers. "For you, Lady Alia." she said sweetly.

"Thank you, my dear." Alia said, patting the girl's head.

The child looked at Yoake and Hana and her eyes became brighter than they already were. "You're the people my mommy told me about." she cheered. "She said some people had come from another world to our world, and she gets to train one of them. Is that you? I bet it is. I'm right aren't I . . ."

"Alright, that's enough, Mineh." Erasure interrupted. "These girls have gone through a lot and are very tired, so they don't need a flighty little child badgering them with questions."

"Oh." she stopped her barrage of inquiries, and brightly said, "Well okay. Bye, Artan." With that, she skipped off to resume the game she had been playing before they arrived.

"She reminds me of Kumi." Hana said, her voice joyful but her shoulders slumped in sorrow.

"That is Tybalt and Sakura's first child, Mineh." Alia explained.

"She's beautiful." Yoake said.

"Yes she is." Alia sighed as she saw her niece playing with a flower she plucked from a nearby garden. "But she is such a lonely child. We keep her and her mother in the temple for their safety."

"Safety?" Yoake asked.

Alia nodded. "We fear that Saekrin may return and take them."

"Why would he want to kidnap them?" Hana asked, confused.

"Because before he left, he raped me." The group turned to see Tybalt and Sakura walking toward them, Sakura still crying.

"What?" Hana yelled.

Sakura nodded. "That's why he thinks Mineh is his."

"I'm confused . . ." Yoake said.

"Let me start from the beginning," Sakura said, taking a seat across from the girls, "It all started the day Tybalt and Saekrin graduated the training academy. There was a big party and my friends pulled me along, hoping to get me to meet a nice boy. I was a shy girl back then. When I arrived, I felt someone staring at me and I turned around to see a boy with long white hair leaning against the wall. As soon as our eyes locked, he looked down and turned red. Next to him was Tybalt. He came over, dragging his shy friend along with him, and introduced them both. All I remember thinking was how handsome Tybalt was . . . and how annoying Saekrin was. He kept trying to talk to me, but I wanted to talk to Tybalt. Eventually, he made some excuse and left. That was the first time I met Saekrin and now that I look back on it, I was rather rude to him . . ." She trailed off, thinking about the event.

"Please keep going." Hana said.

"Right, I'm sorry," Sakura continued, "The next time I saw him was during a unit training session. He was working with Erasure on archery, I didn't know why, but he saw me looking at him and turned red again. He was shaking so much I thought he was going to miss, but then he fired and hit a perfect bull's eye! Of course, I clapped and when he saw me, he smiled and pulled another arrow out. I watched him until Erasure had him switch weapons. Later, just before dinner that day, he and Tybalt decided to have a sparring match. I stopped to watch, partly out of curiosity, but mostly because I wanted to see what kind of power Tybalt had. They fought very hard and were about evenly matched, but then Tybalt knocked him over and won. I clapped and ran over to congratulate Tybalt. Saekrin stayed on the field, looking hurt and angry, but I didn't care; Tybalt had asked me on a date right there. I was so happy."

"Sounds like he got jealous." Yoake muttered.

"You have no idea," Erasure said sadly, "After that he started training like a lunatic. He became obsessed with getting stronger.

I could see how he scanned the crowds during fights, looking for Sakura, and I could see how his eyes would burn with rage whenever she talked to Tybalt. He fought anyone who would take him on and soon he became the top of the army."

"He was very impressive," Sakura said, "I remember thinking that he had come so far from the shy little boy who turned red whenever I looked at him, but I could also tell there was something wrong. I didn't know what it was then, all I could tell was that there was something off about the way he looked at people, like he thought they were nothing but maggots for him to squish under foot."

"Sounds like him . . ." Artan grouched under his breath. Tybalt elbowed him in the ribs, signaling for him to be silent.

"When Tybalt told me that Yeldi had gotten paired with him, I was so excited. Saekrin was very strong and I knew he would be an excellent teacher for Yeldi. It had been a few weeks since I had first seen that strange look in his eyes and since nothing had happened I dropped it, thinking I must have just imagined it. Tybalt and I continued to date, going out at least twice a week when neither of us had missions to carry out, and about three months later, Tybalt popped the question. I immediately said yes and, after kissing him, ran to tell my friends.

On the way back home, I saw Saekrin in the training field working with a long sword. I knew he was Tybalt's best friend and that they had known each other a long time so I walked over to ask him what he thought Tybalt might like as a wedding present. He paused for a minute and put the sword down. Then he turned to face me. For a second, I thought he was going to congratulate us but he took my hand in his and, well, he . . . told me he was in love with me."

"I didn't think he was capable of that particular emotion." Artan said, earning another jab from his teacher.

"It shocked me as well," Sakura continued, "I thanked him for the sentiment but that I already had someone in my life. His face fell a bit and he asked who. That's when I told him about Tybalt and my engagement. He was silent for a few seconds then things went downhill fast. He started shouting about rejection and betrayal; I didn't understand, and then he glared at me. Slowly, he reached for me and pushed me down. I tried to scream but he put a hand over my mouth. I struggled but he was," she stopped, her sobs making it difficult to speak, then, after a few deep breaths, continued, "he was so strong. He pulled my shirt off and threw it away then he put his hand down my pants and, and, and he pulled everything off. For a second, he moved away from me, his hand still on my mouth, and with his free hand, pulled his own pants off. After that—" she broke down into tears, unable to form coherent words anymore. The girls just stared at her in shock, unable to say anything.

"Two days later, he and Yeldi broke into the temple," Alia said, looking sorrowfully at Sakura, who had curled herself against Tybalt's chest, "One week after that, Tybalt and Sakura were married and one year later, Mineh was born."

"Wait," Yoake said, "if Mineh was born one year after the wedding, she couldn't be Saekrin's. He was already gone." The adults stared at her for a moment before Tybalt finally spoke.

"Humans have a nine month pregnancy," he said, "we, however, have approximately one year."

"Does it bother you that Mineh might be Saekrin's child?" Hana asked. Sakura and Tybalt both shook their heads.

"I love her either way," Tybalt said, "If she is mine, then that's wonderful and if she is Saekrin's, her life is still a gift. She did not chose the circumstances of her conception." Sakura nodded in agreement.

"Also," she said, smiling slightly, "she's got Tybalt's eyes."

"Mommy! Daddy!" Mineh's cheerful voice rang out as she pranced up to her parents and jumped into Tybalt's lap.

"Hey, kiddo." He patted his daughter's dainty head. "How've you been?."

"Lonely." the little girl answered. "When can I go play with the other kids?"

"Soon," he answered and, after kissing her head, added, "I hope."

"I hope so, too, daddy." she said, not sensing the concern in his voice. Turning to her mother, she touched her slightly rounded belly. "I can't wait for my baby sister."

"You don't know that it'll be a girl." Sakura chuckled.

"Let her dream." Yoake giggled. "I think every little girl wants a little sister. I would know. When my mom was pregnant with my brother, I hoped he would be a girl."

"You have a baby brother?" Mineh asked.

"I used to." the older girl answered, much to the smaller girl's confusion.

"His life has been claimed by Death." Alia answered.

Mineh's eyes widened and teared up, and she jumped off of Tybalt's lap and hugged Yoake. "That's so sad!"

"It's okay." Yoake said wrapping her arms around the child whose face was buried in her chest. "I'm still sad about it, but I'm okay. Really."

"Are you sure?" Mineh took her face out of Yoake's chest and looked up at her. The older girl's eyes were filled with comfort as she nodded. Mineh smiled and let go. "Okay." With that she bounded back to her parents.

"Death is so mean," she said, climbing into Tybalt's lap, "why does he take nice people away?" She looked to Alia, fully expecting an answer from the high priestess.

"He is not evil," Alia said, "he is natural."

"But why doesn't he take mean people away?" the girl asked, "Why won't he take away the evil man? Then I could go play with the other kids." Tybalt laughed.

"Sometimes he needs help," he said, although the thought of killing the man who had once been his friend still troubled him. Mineh looked up at her father and smiled.

"You're gonna help him, right Daddy?" she asked hopefully. Tybalt nodded and gently placed his daughter on the ground.

"The grown ups have to talk now," he said, "why don't you go play?" Mineh nodded and skipped away.

"She's adorable!" Yoake said. Sakura and Tybalt smiled.

"That's all well and good," Erasure cut in, "but I believe the priority right now should be taking Saekrin down."

Yoake shook her head furiously. "No!" she said, "we have to get Kyoki back first."

"How do you know she even wants to come back?" Hana asked skeptically, "where is she anyway?" She looked around the group, waiting for an answer, but all she received was sad looks, "What?"

"Hana," Tybalt said finally, "Kyoki has joined Saekrin." The girl sat stunned for a moment then-

"WHAT?"

"Hana wait—"

"Wait, nothing! How could she do that? What was she thinking? Well that's it! Wh—"

"HANA!" Yoake grabbed her friend's arm and pulled her down, "Let me explain, okay?" Hana nodded. "She did go but I think she wants out but she doesn't know how to do it."

"What makes you say that?" Artan asked.

"Our last fight," Yoake answered, "Saekrin told her to kill me and she didn't. There were scars all over her back; I could see them behind her corset. He's been abusing her. Also, the only reason she said she was staying was because if she left, Saekrin said he would hurt Kumi! Hana! She's trying to protect Kumi!"

Hana stared at Yoake, shock written across her face. "Really?" she breathed. Yoake nodded then turned to the rest of the group.

"Our first priority has to be finding a way to get Kyoki and Kumi out of there."

Erasure stood slowly, "Well neither of you girls are in any shape to be rescuing anyone," he said, a ghost of a smile on his face, "so we better get you two trained. You've both been slacking off for far too long." Yoake and Hana smiled, jumped up, and immediately followed Erasure onto the training field.

"Wait." Alia said. "Yoake, I need to speak with you, and Erasure, would you take over Hana's training? Sakura is in no condition to be fighting."

"But sister." Sakura protested.

"Don't argue Sakura, we don't want you to injure the baby."

Artan laughed. "Now we just need to make sure Hana stays on our side of the fight." All the adults laughed with him, but Yoake and Hana didn't.

"That's not funny." Yoake said.

"Oh come on. It was just a joke." the green-haired boy said. Yoake and Hana looked at each other and then at Artan. The two then slapped him on the back of the head. "What?" he said.

"It wasn't a good joke." Hana said.

"Whatever," Artan stood up and asked Erasure, "Is it okay if I come watch you practice?"

"Not so fast, kid." Tybalt said. "I think you could benefit from some more training, considering you ran off, and since Yoake's going to be with Lady Alia, I'm free to train you." Artan huffed, but knew it was no use protesting.

"Come on," Erasure said flatly, beckoning Hana over to him. She nodded, waved to Yoake, and ran off after her temporary teacher. With a sigh, Artan followed after her, Tybalt bringing up the rear of the small group. Once they arrived on the field, Erasure told Hana to transform and when she stood ready for battle, he took away her swords, replacing them with a bow and arrow.

"Huh?" Hana said, surprised, "Yoake uses this weapon, not me."

Erasure grunted. "It's part of basic training," he stated, "All of our recruits are trained in the use of all basic weapons: swords, spears, archery, and the like. Now, do you see that?" He pointed across the field to a small circular target. Hana squinted but finally caught sight of the object.

"You expect me to hit that?" she asked incredulously.

"Honestly no," Erasure answered, making Hana frown, "However, I do expect you to be able to do it before he does." Her trainer pointed to Artan who stood a few feet away with a practice bow of his own.

He turned toward Hana and smirked. "Ready for a little friendly competition?" he asked.

Hana smiled back, looking much more confident than she felt, "Sure." Slowly, she reached down and pulled on the quiver that lay next to her foot, gently sliding the strap over her shoulder. With one semi-fluid motion, she pulled out an arrow and strung the bow.

"What's so funny?" she yelled, glaring daggers at Artan who was nearly doubled over laughing.

"Nothing," he answered, "nothing, it's just, well, you're holding it wrong." Hana looked at her hands but couldn't see what the problem was. With a suppressed sigh, Erasure moved forward and shifted Hana's fingers slightly. "If you kept holding it that way, the arrow wouldn't go anywhere." he explained. Hana stared at him, then at her new hand position, and then back, quickly turning a light shade of pink.

"Stop laughing at me!" she snapped at Artan, "I've never done this before!"

"Alright, Artan, that's enough," Tybalt said half sternly half playfully, "Or do I need to remind you of your first day with a bow?"

Artan's laughter stopped instantly as his head whipped around to stare at his teacher with a "you wouldn't dare" look.

"Shall we get started?" Erasure asked, sounding slightly exasperated. Hana nodded. "Okay then. Hold the bow like this. Aim at the target and fire, understood?" She nodded again. Slowly, she drew the string of her bow back, eyeballing the target and trying to make her hand stay still. Her breath slowed as her concentration grew and with a short exhale, she fired.

"Where'd it go?" Artan asked. Suddenly, a short, shrill thump sounded about ten feet in front of them and all three turned to see the arrow sticking proudly out of the ground.

Artan fell over laughing and even Tybalt couldn't help but smile. Hana sighed sadly, extremely disappointed in herself.

"This is why I don't use this." she said, staring dejectedly at the arrow.

"Don't worry about it," Tybalt said, "You're already way ahead of Chuckles here," he nodded to the still giggling Artan, "he tried to fire it backwards."

"Hey!" Artan yelled, suddenly jumping up, "Don't tell her that!" Hana snickered as the boy's cheeks turned the color of ripe tomatoes. Muttering swears under his breath, Artan picked up his bow, loaded it, and fired, hitting just above the bullseye mark.

"I win." he said flatly. Hana sighed; she wasn't shocked that she had lost, but neither was she very happy.

"Alright!" she said, pulling another arrow out, "By the end of today, I'm going to hit that target."

"That's the spirit," Tybalt said happily. Erasure nodded, picking up another practice bow.

"Hold the weapon like this," he said, stringing his own bow. Hana copied his action, "Now as I'm sure you know, the farther you pull the string back, the farther the arrow will go." Hana nodded, "Okay, the next thing to do is aim. Look down the shaft of the arrow, and line the tip up with the desired target."

Hana did what she was told, but couldn't get her hand to line up. Artan chuckled. "Your hand is all shaky, you need to relax."

"Well that's not exactly easy with you watching me!" she snapped at him. Artan raised an inquisitive eyebrow at her, and she realized what she had implied. Her face turned bright red and she said, "Well, it's hard with anyone watching me! I mean, my stage fright is awful. I freeze up and . . ." She trailed off when Artan went up to her and put his hand over the hand she was holding the bow with and his other hand on her shoulder.

"Relax your shoulders." he said, and she released the tension in her muscles. "Now raise your elbow, just a little." She could feel his warm breath against her cheek as her ears lapped up every word that came from his velvety voice.

"Like this?" she asked.

"Exactly." He stepped away and Hana once more stared at the target. A small wind had picked up, making her slightly more nervous.

"Pay attention to the wind," Artan said, "Use your hair to gauge its strength and speed if you have to." Hana nodded and gently shook a few strands of hair into her face. They swayed for a moment then all moved in the same direction, just barely floating off her face. Again, she locked her eyes onto the target. Slowly, as she drew the string of the bow back, she shifted just a bit to her left to make up for the direction that would be lost due to the wind. With a final deep breath, she loosed the arrow and less than a second later, heard the dull thump as it made contact with the target.

She cheered silently; that in itself was an enormous improvement. Looking over, she saw Erasure going toward the target to check it. He looked back and waved her over. Quickly, she scurried to him, followed closely by Artan and Tybalt who were curious as to where she had hit.

"Damn it," Hana said playfully once she was close enough to see the target clearly. Her arrow had not hit the bullseye, instead landing about three inches to the left.

"Looks like you're not going to be a champion archer anytime soon." Artan teased. Hana punched him lightly in the shoulder.

"Be quiet," she giggled, "I hit it didn't I."

"Yeah I guess you did." Artan said, smiling.

"Thanks for the help," Hana said as she yanked her arrow out.

"Uh, no-no problem," Artan replied, blushing slightly.

Tybalt chuckled: *young love.*

Meanwhile, Alia had taken Yoake into the main temple hall, but remained silent. Yoake also stayed quiet in anticipation of what the middle-aged priestess would say. Finally, Alia stopped and turned to face the girl. "I am disappointed in you, Yoake."

"For what?" Yoake asked, suddenly afraid of Alia's narrowed eyes.

"You may not know this, but I am able to monitor each active watch and its user, and I saw what you attempted."

"I see." Yoake hung her head in shame. She knew that denying her near death wouldn't do any good. "So I guess you want to know why I did it."

"I know why." Alia responded, much more gently. "And I understand, but that is not all I wanted to talk about. I didn't ask you to talk so I could reprimand you, I wanted to ask you about Yeldi."

"Yeldi?"

"Yes." Alia nodded. "I saw him save your life and give you Hana's watch, and I firmly believe that he is ready to receive this." She held out a bronze pocket watch with flames etched into its surface that looked so realistic the watch appeared to be on fire. On the back, in fiery letters was the word Pyro. She beckoned Yoake to take it, but the younger girl was almost afraid to touch it for fear of being burned by the blazing pattern.

"Is that what I think it is?" Yoake asked.

"Yes." Alia nodded. "This is the watch that Yeldi was supposed to receive when he finished his training, but was never able to."

"Because of what he did."

"No, it was not his crime that prevented him, but his lack of proper training." Alia explained. "As you may know, fire is dangerous and hard to control, that is why anyone who is to receive any power related to it must have extra training. Saekrin was already training Yeldi to be a spy, like himself. You see Yeldi has the power to shapeshift, much like Artan but not on as great a scale."

"Yes, I know." Yoake said. "Yeldi had disguised himself as a human and infiltrated my class at school."

"I see. Does Hana know?"

"I told her but she probably doesn't remember. Anyway, you were saying?"

"Right. As a tradition, a young soldier, before the official ceremony to receive their watch, gets to know which one had picked him or her and they get a sample of the watch's power if it deemed its user ready to wield it. Yeldi's watch rejected him. It saw that he was not ready to wield the great power inside it. But I firmly believe that he is ready now."

"Well, he certainly knows how to use fire." Yoake joked, but earned a hard glare from Alia.

"This is not something to be taken lightly." she scolded. "Yoake, I am charging you with the task of giving Yeldi his watch and I pray to the gods that you understand the gravity of the responsibility you have been given."

"I do, I do!" Yoake defended. "But why me?"

"Because Yeldi trusts you. Not only that, but he looks to you for guidance. I think it is because of you that Yeldi is beginning to repent for his crimes."

"Me?" Yoake puzzled, and Alia nodded. "But how will I know when he's ready?"

"The watch will decide and tell you, but I don't think you will need it. you will know on your own." She placed the watch in Yoake hands and put her hand on the girl's head, making Yoake crane her neck in response. "Now go and may the gods watch over you as you carry this burden." She removed her hand and nodded. Yoake nodded back and started in the other direction. Alia watched her go and said quietly, "Only you can do this, do not fail."

Yoake made her way to the training field and saw Hana and Artan sparring in hand-to-hand combat. Alkest, who was standing at his guard's post walked up beside her. "Hey, kiddo."

"Oh hi, . . . Alkest, right?"

"Yep." he nodded, looked at the two on the field, and laughed. Yoake looked at him confusedly. "It's nothing, don't worry about it." he said. "I just find it funny to see them like that. They look just like an old married couple."

Yoake laughed; now that she thought about it, the two did go round and round like two people who had known each other for ages.

"They will end up married someday . . ." Alkest chuckled. Yoake's head snapped up at the idea and suddenly the match stopped.

"What did you say?" Artan yelled, running over to stand in front of the guard, "there is no way I would ever marry that loud, obnoxious, know-it-all, little—" He was suddenly cut off by Hana knocking him squarely on the head.

"One: don't let your guard down," she said, blowing on her fist as if it were a gun she had just fired, "and two: who are you calling a know-it-all?"

"Children, please focus," Erasure sighed, walking over.

"How's it going?" Yoake asked.

"Well, I'm fine," Hana answered, "but I can't say the same for this," she elbowed Artan, who had recovered from the blow to his head, in the ribs.

"Don't you start!" He snapped, "I've kicked your ass in almost every challenge!"

"'Almost' being the operative word." Hana said, chuckling slyly.

"What'd I tell you?" Alkest said, looking at Yoake.

"Now, now," Tybalt said, pulling the two squabbling teens apart, "I think it's time for me to take Yoake and Hana home. The two of you have school tomorrow." Yoake nodded and followed Tybalt off the field. Hana followed behind, but not before sticking her tongue out at Artan one last time for good measure.

Soon, Tybalt had the portal open and the girls jumped though, landing just outside their dorm.

❧

Yeldi sat in a corner of the apartment with Kyoki, waiting for Saekrin to finish speaking. Their master was angry, no he was furious, at the loss of Hana's watch. Kyoki looked over at Yeldi in confusion, wasn't he supposed to have it? She leaned over and wrapped her arms around Kumi protectively. The girl shook like a leaf as the older creature continued to rant. All three had stopped listening long ago, but not out of boredom. They simply couldn't take the insults anymore, no matter what, it seemed as though Saekrin was going to be angry at them.

"I'm sorry I lost the watch, Master," Yeldi said slowly, trying to placate his master. However, Saekrin, far from having his anger subside, was only enraged further. He grabbed Yeldi by his throat and pulled him into the air.

"'Sorry'?" he growled, "You lost one of the watches and that's all you have to say for yourself!" Kyoki gasped as Saekrin threw Yeldi across the room, the boy slamming into the wall with such force that he immediately fell unconscious.

"Yeldi!" she yelled, running over to him.

"Leave him," Saekrin snapped. Kyoki looked from Yeldi to his master and back then took another step toward the injured boy.

"Kyoki!" she turned sharply as the cry of a small child pierced the room. Kumi stared back at her with wide fearful eyes as Saekrin held her, a long claw resting against the girl's throat.

"Sit." Saekrin ordered, drawing the sharp claw closer to Kumi's jugular. Kyoki obeyed and sat beside Yeldi who was beginning to stir.

"Since you both seem to care so much about this worthless little human . . ." Saekrin began, pulling Kumi over to the wall where a long hook stuck out of the plaster. Yeldi sat up, rubbing his head; years of his master's abuse had given him a very short recovery time. As he scanned the room, he saw Saekrin tie Kumi's hands and hook her to the wall.

"No!" he gasped. Saekrin simply turned to the two teens and smirked darkly.

"Yes," he said, "Obviously the two of you can stand physical torture but can this delicate little girl?" Kyoki was confused and looked to Yeldi for some kind of explanation, but he had buried his face in his hands.

"Watch." Saekrin ordered flatly, "The longer you don't, the longer the girl gets to hang here." Quickly, Yeldi looked up and nudged Kyoki to bring her focus back to Kumi.

"What's going on?" she asked.

Yeldi shook his head, "Just, just watch. It'll go faster, for you and for Kumi." Kyoki begged him with her eyes to continue but he remained silent. Slowly, fearfully, she looked at Kumi and saw that Saerkin had pulled her shirt and shorts off, retieing them around her chest and waist so that the most skin possible was exposed.

"Don't worry, little one," he whispered, "I wouldn't humiliate you *that* much." Kumi didn't understand but she began to cry anyway, terror quickly overwhelming her.

"What are you going to do to her?" Kyoki demanded. Saekrin smiled at her.

"Would you really like to know?" he asked, his tone almost playful, "Alright then, I'll show you."

He looked Kumi over, like a wolf trying to find the weakest point of its prey. Suddenly, his hand shot out, slashing Kumi's face. She cried out in pain, more and more tears streaming down her face.

"Oh dear . . ." Saekrin mused, "Is that really all it takes to make you cry? Humans are such frail creatures." He laughed and slashed at her again; this time creating four parallel cuts on her stomach. Blood ran down her body, the rag tied around her waist quickly soaking it in.

"Stop!" Kyoki cried, her own tears beginning to roll down her cheeks.

"No, no," Saekrin chuckled, "We're only just getting started." He moved to a shelf just a few feet from the hook, where Yeldi knew his master kept the various devices he had collected over the years. After a few moments of sadistically gleeful thought, Saekrin picked up a rectangular device with two forked points at each end and a leather strap around the middle.

"Look up, my dear," he said as he wrapped the strap around Kumi's neck, forcing the points into her chin and chest. The girl was cute; she reminded him of his daughter, Mineh. Yes, she was *his*.

Saekrin shook his head; he couldn't afford to think about that, it would only make him angry and he needed to be calm. This was about punishing his useless bastard of a slave and the traitor girl, nothing more.

Kumi's eyes widened in horror as her captor smirked. Why was he being so mean? She closed her eyes tightly as Saekrin raised a clawed hand, trying desperately to brace herself but it was useless. A scream tore from her as the long claws slashed her chest. Again and again, the creature brought his cruel hand down, creating more and more deep cuts in the small girl before him.

"Stop!" Kyoki yelled from behind him, "She's just a child! She can't take this!"

Saekrin turned to her, smirking, "I think she can," he said, "and besides, the two of you are to blame for her pain." With that, he turned back to Kumi and let loose another barrage of attacks. This girl was going to be his sacrifice, not only to teach his slaves, but to show

Tybalt, *his friend*, what he could do. Another sadistic smirk graced his lips as he thought about Sakura; he would have her, yes, and soon, but suddenly another pained scream brought him back to the present.

Tears mixed with blood as both streamed down Kumi's face, running down the fork which cut deeper and deeper into her the more she screamed and cried in pain.

"P-please—" she begged but another slash cut her off.

"Quiet!" Saekrin shouted, bringing his hand down on her cheek this time. Kumi's mouth closed but only for a moment as Saekrin's claws made another assault on her exposed, torn flesh. Both she and her captor were covered in her blood and she could feel herself growing dizzy. A final, gut wrenching scream burst from her as Saekrin slashed at her with his harshest attack yet. Blackness clouded her vision and, as the blood dripped down her chest and soaked into the cloth around her waist, she fell unconscious.

Saekrin stepped back as soon as he saw that his victim had passed out and smiled.

"I hope the two of you have learned something," he said, turned, and walked off, locking his door behind him.

Kyoki and Yeldi watched him go and once he was in his room, ran over to help Kumi down. "There's a first aid kit in the kitchen," Yeldi said as he undid the tie around her wrists. Kyoki nodded and ran to retrieve it. Soon she returned and handed Yeldi some wound cleaning supplies and bandages. Gently, he set to work tending to the girl while Kyoki watched, feeling very much like a fifth wheel. She stared at Yeldi and Kumi and instantly came to a decision. No matter what, the three of them were going to get away, and they were going to get away tonight.

❧

"It feels good to be back," Hana said, "I'll ask my mom to send my stuff ASAP."

Yoake smiled. "It's good to have you back."

"Now all we have to do is get Kyoki back." Hana said, stretching.

"That may be easier said than done." Yoake commented as she tossed a spare pair of pajamas to Hana, who gave her a quizzical look. "Since you don't have your own."

"I'll wash them and return them when I get my PJ's."

"I'm sure you will." Yoake laughed and sat on her bed. "Hey. Do you remember what I told you about Yami, before dragging you off to Cyowan?"

"I remember you mentioning something, but I don't remember what it was. Why, what about him?"

"Yami was Yeldi is disguise."

"Wait, what?" Hana looked at her with shock and confusion.

"Yeah I know, I was surprised too. And Mr. Satoru is actually Saekirn."

"Well I guess that makes sense, but Yami? How could he and Yeldi have been the same person? They're so different."

"I know. I couldn't believe it."

"So did you have to fight him?"

"No. I would have rather fought him than Kyoki."

"What about Kyoki?"

"She showed up and after he left she told me that Saekrin ordered her to kill me."

"What?" Hana exclaimed, "She tried to kill you!"

"But she didn't! She said she didn't want to but—"

"She's gone, Yoake! Why can't you accept that?"

"Because she told me she didn't want to! She said that if she didn't kill me, then Saekrin would hurt Kumi! She was trying to protect Kumi!" Hana stared at Yoake in shock.

"She, she was?" Hana said slowly, "Really?"

"Yes," Yoake answered, "And no matter what, we are going to get her back. She's our friend and we are not going to give up on her!"

"Really?" the girls turned to see Kyoki standing in the doorway of the dorm, smiling sheepishly at them, "I didn't think you guys would care so much." Yoake and Hana stared at the girl in shock, their brains slowly processing what their eyes were seeing. Suddenly-

"KYOKI!" Yoake yelled, tackling the girl to the ground, "What are you doing here?" She jumped up and backed away for a moment, "You're not here to kill us, are you?" Kyoki shook her head.

"No," she said, "I, I left him. I'm never going back, ever." Yoake smiled broadly and tackled her again, but Hana stood back.

"Where is my sister?" she asked, "I know Saekrin took her. Where is she?" Kyoki stood, pushing Yoake off, and turned to face Hana.

"Don't worry," she said, smiling.

"Big Sister?" Hana turned toward the door, tears instantly clouding her vision.

"Kumi!" she yelled, running forward and picking her sister up. She swung her around, hugging her tightly.

"Are you okay? Did he hurt you? Oh my God! I've been so worried about you!" Just then a rapping on the window caught their attention and Yoake opened it to let Tybalt in. He smiled.

"I see there's a reunion going on," he laughed, "No one told me." Kyoki pushed Yoake away and walked back to the door.

"Come on in," she said, "It's okay." The group turned to the door again to see Yeldi standing there, looking at the ground and shifting his weight from foot to foot nervously.

"H-hi," he said. Before the girls could move, Tybalt stepped forward and silently pulled his brother into a tight hug.

"Finally," he breathed, "tell me that you've finally come home, my dear brother." Yeldi nodded into Tybalt's shirt.

"I-I couldn't do it anymore," he whispered, "I-I—" sobs took over, stopping his words in his throat.

"What changed?" Hana asked skeptically, protectively pulling Kumi a bit closer. A squeak drew the group's attention and they all turned to see Kumi holding her stomach. Hana immediately pulled her sister's shirt up and everyone gasped as scars and deep looking cuts were revealed. Instantly, Hana's eyes widened and her breathing became shallow.

Yoake could see her getting angrier and angrier. "Hana wait—"

"WHAT DID YOU DO?" Hana yelled, advancing on Yeldi, "TELL ME RIGHT NOW! WHAT DID YOU DO TO HER?" Yeldi jumped back and tried to explain, stuttering out half sentences, but Hana cut him off.

"Don't speak, you bastard! What happened to my little sister?" She grabbed her two and a half inch thick history notebook and brought it down on the boy's head.

"Tell me!" she shrieked, beating him again and again as he tried to defend himself, "Tell me!" Yeldi screamed in pain and fear, desperately trying to keep the book from connecting with his head.

"Stop!" he cried, "Stop it please! I'm sorry! I'm sorry, Master!" As soon as the words left his mouth, Hana stopped and stared at him in complete shock. Once he noticed that the book was no longer attacking him, Yeldi slinked off to the corner of the room and curled into a ball.

"Yeldi?" Yoake said slowly, moving to stand before the trembling boy, "Yeldi?"

"I'm sorry, Master," he said, eyes wide and shaking, "I'm sorry. P-please stop. I'll do better I promise. Please, Master . . ." His words descended into nonsense as fear took over. Slowly, Yoake squatted down in front of him and reached forward, placing a hand on his shoulder. He flinched and renewed his frantic apologies.

"I, I didn't mean to hurt him that bad," Hana said.

"Yeldi?" Yoake said, "It's okay. No one's going to hurt you anymore." Slowly, cautiously, he looked up.

"Really?" he asked desperately.

"Yes," Tybalt answered. Yoake smiled and held out her hand, gently coaxing him to stand.

"You're safe here. He's not going to come. We'll protect you. No one is going to hurt you."

"Speak for yourself," Hana said, brandishing the book again. Yeldi yelped and pushed himself back into the corner. Kyoki elbowed Hana in the ribs.

"I'm sorry, Yeldi," Hana said, "Really. I just, I don't want to see my sister hurt. I know you didn't do it." Yeldi looked at her in surprise, then smiled slowly, an expression that made him look very much like Yami. Gently, Tybalt took hold of his brother again and pulled him in close.

"I'm glad you're back." He turned to the girls, "Now that we're all together—"

"Let's kick Saekrin's ass!" Kyoki yelled.

"Um . . ." they turned to look at Kumi who had spoken, "What's going on?"

Yoake blinked as she watched the girl looked from Yeldi to her sister to Kyoki to Tybalt and back. Hana sighed; they'd known the question would come up at some point but they still hadn't come up with what they were going to say.

"Well," Kyoki said, breaking the awkward silence that had descended on the group, "You see . . . Saekrin, the man-thing that . . . hurt you, he's trying to steal these," she held up her watch, "from people in order to get really powerful." Kumi nodded slowly but continued to stare, silently asking the older girl to continue.

"And we have to stop him," Yoake cut in when she saw the Kyoki was a bit lost, "He's stealing things that belong to other people and hurting them."

"So he's a bad guy," Kumi asked, "like on TV?"

"Sort of," Hana answered, "but he's worse. He won't stop just because the police show up and he won't go easy on children. You've seen that and I'm so sorry that you did, but we're going to protect you and stop him, okay?" Kumi nodded. She still didn't quite understand but she trusted her older sister. Slowly, she turned to Tybalt.

"Who's that?" she asked.

"He's our trainer," Yoake said, "He's watching over us and teaching us how use our powers to beat the bad guy." Kumi's eyes widened and she ran over to him.

"You gotta be a good babysitter and take care of my big sister, got it?" she said, displaying the pride and authority that only small children can.

"I understand," Tybalt said, saluting to the little girl.

"Whoa," said a voice from the door. The girls turned to see Artan standing there, "did I miss something?" Yoake smiled and pulled him inside and explained what had happened in his absence.

"Good to have you back, Kyoki," he said, then glared at Yeldi, "You I could have lived without." Yeldi nodded and backed away from the group again, although this time he continued to stand while in the corner.

"Artan!" Yoake exclaimed, moving to stand beside Yeldi, "Don't be so mean."

"I'm not being mean," Artan replied matter of factly, "I'm just saying that I don't trust him. I don't care if he's had some sudden change of heart. He's still a traitor and he's going to have to work very, very hard if he wants even a molecule's worth of trust from me, got it?" He turned to glare at Yeldi again. The boy nodded quickly.

"I understand." he said softly.

"Good," Tybalt said, "Now that that's settled, we should go back to Cyowan."

"Why?" Hana asked, "We just got back. Shouldn't I take Kumi home?"

Tybalt shook his head. "First of all, I meant we should go back tomorrow, after school, and second, Kumi should come with us. I understand that your parents are probably worried sick but she isn't safe there. Saekrin found her once and will be able to take her again. We should bring her back to the temple. She'll be safe there."

"And she can play with Mineh!" Yoake chimed in happily.

"Mineh?" Kyoki asked, tilting her head.

"Tybalt and Sakura's daughter," Hana explained.

"What?" Kyoki yelled, "they're married? And they have a kid?" She ran over to Tybalt and shook his hand. "I don't know whether to congratulate you or smack you for not telling us sooner so I think I'll do both. Congratulations!" With that, she gave him a short smack on the shoulder and sat down.

"You, you got married?" Yeldi asked slowly. Tybalt nodded. Looking down, Yeldi moved a bit closer to his brother, "I'm s-sorry I didn't come to the wedding."

Tybalt smiled and hugged his brother again, "It's alright, Yeldi," he said, "the important thing is that you're here now and we can be a family again. Besides," he pulled back, jokingly clapping a hand on his younger brother's head, "now you can finally meet your niece." The smallest hint of a grin tugged at the corner of Yeldi's mouth as he moved to stand in the corner again.

"You know you don't have to stand there all the time," Yoake said, "Come on and sit here." She patted the spot beside her on her bed, beckoning him over. Slowly, cautiously, Yeldi complied and sat beside her, a deep blush ghosting over his cheeks.

"So does this mean he's coming to school with us?" Artan said, still glaring daggers at Yeldi.

"I believe it does." Yoake smiled, "don't worry we'll find you some clothes. You can borrow Artan's." she said, noticing the possible objection forming in Yeldi's lips. He nodded.

"Don't give people my clothes!" Artan exclaimed angrily, jumping up, "I'm not having that traitor anywhere near my things!"

"Quiet!" Hana snapped at him, "he needs clothes. You have clothes. Now shut up and pretend like you can get along with him." Artan opened his mouth to protest again but the look in Hana's eyes made him close it and sit down.

143

"Come on, boys," Tybalt said, standing, "Let's let the girls get reacquainted and we can talk about this more later." Yeldi stood without a word and followed his older brother out the door, Artan grudgingly in tow.

The next morning, Yoake was the first to open her eyes. Sleepily, she looked over at the other two girls and smiled. They were finally all back together again. She lay on her back for a few more minutes, thinking about how hopeless their struggle had once seemed, but now, with Kyoki and Hana back and Yeldi with them, it seemed as though nothing could stop them. With a contented sigh, she swung her legs over the edge of the bed and began to dress. A half hour later, the three walked toward the school.

"I never thought I'd miss this place," Kyoki said half jokingly half sadly.

"Well it's good to have you back." Yoake said.

"But I'll bet your teachers have a lot of work for you to make up." Hana teased. Kyoki stuck out her tongue at her as the three parted ways.

"Morning, Yeld-Yami," Yoake said as she sat down behind him. He turned and smiled at her, looking just as he had the day they had met; it was hard to tell that he was otherworldly at all in his human form. At least Saekrin had taught him something useful. Sadly, as soon as he caught sight of Artan's glare, he gasped and went back to frantically copying down some notes Tybalt had given him earlier.

Yoake elbowed Artan, "Stop that," she whispered. Artan just huffed and turned in the other direction.

"Good morning, class." said Mr. Satoru as he walked in. His countenance showed that he was very angry, and Yoake couldn't help but smile when his eyes locked with hers as she sat calmly in her seat, shock evident on his pale face. It was indeed a good morning for her.

After the final bell rang, releasing them from class, Mr. Satoru stopped Yoake, Artan, and Yeldi. "I see the three of you are doing . . . well." he said through gritted teeth.

"Be careful, Saekrin." Yoake warned. "With all three of us and Tybalt, Kyoki, and Hana close by it wouldn't be a good idea to attack us."

"I understand that, and fortunately for you, I have no intention of starting a fight here, my dear." the older man said.

"Don't call her that!" Yeldi shouted, earning a piercing glare from the older creature. Instantly, he flinched and scooted a few paces away, his hands moving in front of his chest and face protectively.

Saekrin smirked. "It seems my slave is still afraid of me," he said mockingly, "I guess some things don't change overnight." He chuckled to himself, then twitched for a moment as if someone had said something rude to him, but it was over so fast, it was as though nothing had happened.

"He's not your slave anymore!" Yoake snapped, "Don't you ever call him that degrading name again." Saekrin smirked again and brushed past them, placing a hand on Yeldi's head as he went, roughly ruffling the boy's hair.

"He may not be by my side anymore," the sadistic man hissed amusedly, "but he is still very much mine." With that, he was gone.

The teens glared at the spot where he had been only moments before.

"Bastard," Artan growled.

Yoake nodded in agreement. "Don't worry, Yeldi," she said, turning to him, "We'll—" she stopped suddenly when she saw the boy. He stood frozen with a look of pure terror in his wide eyes. His breaths came in short, shallow gasps and even as she waved her hand in front of him, calling his name gently, it was as though he couldn't see her.

"M-master," he stammered quietly, "M-master is angry, very very angry."

"Yeldi, calm down." Yoake pleaded, trying to pacify him.

Finally, he regained his senses and looked at the ground in shame. "I really am hopeless." he said.

"No." she put a hand on his shoulder. "You're not hopeless, you just need a little time, that's all. After all, they say only time can heal the deepest wounds."

"I gotta say," Artan added, "I wasn't expecting you to snap at that bastard."

"Right, that in itself is a sign you're improving." Yoake agreed.

"Really?" Yeldi looked at the two of them in surprise.

"Yes, really. Now come on, let's go back to the dorm."

When they reached the dorms Hana, Kyoki, and Tybalt were already waiting for them. "Well it's about time." Kyoki huffed. "What took you guys so long?"

"'Mr. Satoru' stopped us as we were leaving." Artan said.

"Damn it!" Kyoki growled, "I wish I could have been there. I've got a score to settle with that bastard." Hana and Tybalt looked at Yeldi who had moved to sit down in the corner he had staked out for himself, pulling out some homework.

"How did he hold up?" Tybalt whispered.

"He tried to defend me but—"

"Really?" Hana gasped, "that was fast."

"But then it was like he back tracked. He got really scared and froze up; he looked like he was going to pass out. Saekrin really terrifies him." Yoake sighed as she finished, "It really is going to take a long time before he makes any significant progress . . ." Tybalt nodded and went to sit next to his brother, who looked rather frustrated with this algebra work.

"So what now?" Artan asked.

"We should head back to Cyowan," Tybalt answered, "The girls need more training and Kumi needs a safe place to stay." Yeldi's head shot up at the prospect of going back to his home world and he began to shake slightly.

"Don't worry," his brother said gently, "It'll be fine. Everyone is really worried about you." Yeldi nodded slowly and after a another minute stopped shaking. Standing, Tybalt moved to the door.

"Let's get moving," he said then left, the children following along behind him.

As soon as they landed in the temple, they were greeted by a very excited Mineh who ran over and hugged her father. After hugging each girl and Artan she looked at Yeldi.

"What's your name?" she asked.

"Yeldi?" Sakura said slowly as she walked over to greet them, "Is it really you?" The boy nodded and was almost immediately crushed in the hug he received from his sister in law.

"You're Uncle Yeldi?" Mineh asked, looking him over curiously. Suddenly a smile broke out across her face and she hugged him, slipping in next to her mother.

"Hi!" she giggled as she let go, "I'm Mineh." Yeldi waved nervously, shifting from foot to foot.

"Mineh," Hana said. The girl turned to look at her, "this is my sister Kumi. She's going to stay with you for a little while." Mineh looked over to see Kumi hiding behind her older sister's leg and walked over.

"Hi," she said, holding out her hand, "I'm Mineh. Wanna play?" Kumi looked back at the strange looking girl before her, frightened, and then looked up to see Hana nodding encouragingly at her and held her own hand out; if Big Sister trusted this girl then she must be okay.

"I'm Kumi," she said. Mineh jumped and clapped.

"Let's go play!" she exclaimed, "I can show you all over and we can play tag or wumpleball or . . ." her voice faded off into the distance as the two girls ran off, giggling like the children they were. Just then another voice called to the group.

"Hello, Yeldi," he looked up to see Alia standing a few feet away. Instantly, he bowed to the high priestess but she motioned for him to stand, "Come, my dear boy, there is no need to be so formal." Gently, she embraced him.

"Why are you all being so welcoming?" he asked, shaking in Alia's arms.

"Because we have all been so worried about you." she answered and stepped back. "We know what you have suffered at Saekrin's hands and understand your inability to leave until now. But now that you have freed yourself you are ready. Yoake." She looked at the girl who looked back quizzingly, but then realized what the priestess meant.

"Here." she took the copper watch out of her pocket and presented it to Yeldi. "I think you really are ready. Take it."

"Is that?"

Yoake nodded as he stared at it in wonder but was hesitant to take it out of her hand. A smile escaped her lips and she placed the watch in the reluctant boy's hands. His fingers tingled when they felt the warm copper against his skin.

"Is this really for me?" he asked. Alia nodded.

"You are ready now, young one." she answered. Yeldi shook his head in protest and tried to push the watch back toward Yoake.

"But, but, but," he stammered, trying to find a reason for his action, "I've done so much damage. I can't take this." Yoake giggled and gently forced Yeldi to take it.

"We trust you, Yeldi," she said, "We know you can do it." He stared at her with wide eyes but brought the watch to his chest, hugging it gently.

"I know what we should do!" Kyoki yelled suddenly, destroying the mood as she wrapped her arm around Yeldi's shoulders, "Let's get to some training. See what that watch of yours can do!" Yeldi nodded slowly, shocked a bit by the girl's sudden outburst.

"Umm . . . okay," he said and followed (was dragged by) Kyoki onto the training field. As soon as they stepped onto the field, Kyoki opened her watch, black clouds and skulls floating around her as she transformed.

"Well look who showed up." She turned to see Erasure walking over to her and began to fidget nervously.

"So have you decided how you want to pursue your goals?" he asked. She nodded and he smiled broadly.

"Then give me that," he said, swiping her scythe from her hands, "and go give me twenty laps. Move!" Immediately, Kyoki ran off to begin her assigned exercise, smiling all the while.

"Hello, Yeldi," Erasure said to boy. He jumped in fright, too lost in his own thoughts to notice the older man.

"H-hi," he stammered as Erasure held out his hand.

"It's nice to have you back," he gripped Yeldi's hand firmly, shaking it, "Now open that little watch of yours and let's see what you've got." Yeldi nodded and nervously opened his watch. Hana and Yoake watched intently, along with Kyoki who abruptly stopped in her run to look back at the scene.

From inside the watch came a tower of fire that wrapped itself around Yeldi's body, swirling like a serpent. It moved upward and fanned out like two great phoenix wings before thinning out and finally shortening. When it had condensed, they could see a long glowing red and orange whip in Yeldi's hand. He stared at the weapon for a few moments, eyes growing wider and wider with fear. Suddenly, he let go of the whip and ran off the field.

"Yeldi!" Yoake yelled, running after him as the rest of the group watched in confusion, all except Kyoki who knew the kind of things Yeldi had seen a weapon like that do.

"Yeldi," Yoake said as she finally caught up to him, placing a hand on his shoulder so he would stop, "What's wrong? It's a great weapon." She could feel him shaking under her touch and trying to answer.

"M-master liked-d to u-use w-w-whips. They were h-his f-favorite." he stammered, nearly collapsing at the pain filled memories the weapon brought. Yoake watched him, wrapping her arms around him comfortingly.

"It's alright," she said softly, "I know you can do this. You will learn how to use your own whip to help people instead of beat them into submission. Your power will protect those around you and," she pulled back so she could look him straight in the eye, "your whip will one day overpower Saekrin." He stared at her with wide, confused eyes, then the smallest hints of a smile tugged at the corner of his mouth and he nodded.

"Good," Yoake said, grinning, "Let's get back to the others. I'm sure they're worried."

Once they made it back to the training field, Yeldi immediately began to apologize for his actions and promised to get better faster.

"There's no need to rush." Hana said.

"She's right," Tybalt added, "rushing may even cause more problems." Yeldi hung his head.

"I'm sorry." he muttered. Yoake nearly rolled her eyes, still smiling. *This could take awhile.*

"Don't worry about it!" Kyoki said, "You're doin' great!" She clapped him on his shoulder playfully. Yeldi gasped pain and his hand shot to his shoulder, holding it protectively.

"What happened?" Yoake asked, moving to stand beside him. She reached forward and gently moved his hand to reveal a large, painful looking scar just under his shirt.

"Why did you guys stop?" Tybalt asked as he walked over. Just then he caught sight of what they were all staring at, "What did he do?"

"Nothing!" Yeldi answered, trying to pull his shirt back over the scar, but Tybalt stopped him.

"Tell me," he demanded, "Now."

"N-nothing," Yeldi said earnestly, "It was an accident."

"Like hell it was!" Kyoki said, "Yeldi, we both know that bastard doesn't do that kind of thing by 'accident.'" She waved her fingers in the air in small quotation mark gestures.

"No, really," Yeldi protested, "He didn't mean to."

"Why don't you tell us what you mean." Yoake said softly.

Yeldi sighed; he could tell that they weren't going to drop the matter until he told them so . . . "Well, it was a few weeks after we came to your world and Master had been acting strange . . ."

Yeldi sat against the far corner of the apartment. Saekrin had been in his room for a long time and he was starting to get worried. Usually, he would have given his slave something to do by now. Worry finally overtaking him, Yeldi stood and walked to the door.

"—ot worried. Go away." he heard his master say from inside. Slowly, he pushed the door open; what he saw made his breath catch in his throat.

Saekrin stood pacing in the middle of the room, clothing hanging off his body, torn in several places. Papers and books lay strewn across the room as if a large storm had recently blown through. His bed was as disheveled as he was and several watches lay open on his desk, one hanging off the small reading lamp.

"Just stop. I know—yes yes but—will the both of you—argh!" Yeldi looked to see his master holding his head as if he were in pain, frantically brushing his loose hair back with the other.

"Master . . ." he said slowly, walking in, but Saekrin ignored him, continuing to converse with himself.

"Leave me al—I'm not going to. Yes. No." Yeldi moved closer, trying to figure out who his master was talking to.

"Would the both of you stop fighting? You're distracting and I can't—of course I understand. What? No! She's not—" Suddenly, Saekrin tripped on his bed sheet and crashed to the floor, but didn't stop talking. Just as Yeldi was about to rush over, the older creature was up again. He held out his arm, and with one claw, began to make small marks in the pale flesh.

"One, two, six, twenty? I don't know! Why would I count? It's not—of course he is, but—" He looked around the room, eyes sweeping over Yeldi for a second, but it was as though he couldn't see the boy, and he simply went back to speaking.

"No I can't—but—stop it! Useful, that's why. No! Now stop saying that! I am not! NO!" Yeldi could see that his master was getting more and more

frantic, kicking paper and throwing various item across the room only to pick them up again. He drew his hand down his face, his claws breaking the skin and drawing blood. For a moment he simply stared at it. "How nice. Yes, I see—NO! What did I just say? Leave me alone! I'm not going to!"

Yeldi ran forward and tried to grab onto Saekrin, to make him stop yelling and pacing and throwing things, but suddenly a blinding pain erupted from his shoulder. He turned to see his master's claws wedged into his body, but still Saerkin looked as though he wasn't there. With much more force than necessary, Saekrin ripped his claws from Yeldi's shoulder and went back to pacing . . .

"After that, I put some bandages on it and left him alone," Yeldi finished, "I don't know what happened. It was like he was trapped in his head or something."

"Sounds like he really is nuts." Kyoki said.

"Yes," the group turned to see Alia walking over to them, "I was wondering if it had begun yet."

"What?" Hana asked.

Alia sighed, "Let me explain. The watches, as a defense against exactly what Saekrin is trying to do, will override the psyche of a collector."

"English please." Kyoki said.

"Have you ever heard the expression 'going mad with power'?" Alia asked. The girls nodded, "Well, that is very literally what is happening. The watches themselves are against the collecting of enormous amounts of power so will slowly destroy the mind of the person doing the collecting."

"So basically Saekrin's going looney?" Kyoki asked.

"A drastic oversimplification but yes," Alia answered, "Madness will destroy him from the inside out unless he stops or is stopped."

"Master is going crazy." Yeldi muttered to himself. He sounded almost sad, but before anyone could ask why, Yoake spoke.

"We keep telling you that you don't have to call him that anymore," she said.

"Sorry . . ."

"No need to apologize. Baby steps. You know what they say: old habits die hard, but don't worry we'll help you no matter what."

"Th-thank you," he stammered. "I really don't deserve this."

"I'll say." Artan mumbled, receiving a jab in the ribs from Hana.

"All right, should we get down to training?" Yoake said, and Yeldi nodded nervously.

"Yoake, why don't you train Yeldi." Tybalt suggested.

"Me?"

"Sure, why not? You seem to be the best choice, am I right?"

The others nodded in agreement and Yoake blushed. "Okay." she said. Yeldi smiled at the idea and looked at her pleadingly.

"Alright!" she said, hoping she sounded confident. She was excited but also nervous that she wouldn't be the teacher Yeldi needed. Taking the boy's hand gently, she led him to another part of the field.

"Open your watch again," she said. He nodded slowly and, with obvious apprehension, opened the copper watch. Again, fire burst forth and formed itself into a whip. He stared at the weapon for a few moments, shaking slightly, but after a few deep breaths, calmed enough to hold it.

Yoake smiled at him, "Good job," she said, "Now I'm going to go over there," she pointed to a spot on the field about twenty feet away, "and fire a few wooden arrows at you. I know you're good at dodging from all our fights but you need to learn to defend yourself using your new weapon." Yeldi nodded again and patiently waited for her to get ready. Quickly, Yoake transformed and pulled out a wooden bow and quiver from the pile of weapons on the field.

"Ready?" she asked as she strung her bow.

"Y-yes," Yeldi said. He held the whip up and tried to let it unravel just as he'd seen Saekrin do. He hated trying to imitate his master—former master-but he was the only person the boy had ever seen use a whip.

"Okay, here it comes!" Yoake called as she loosed an arrow toward him. As it drew closer, Yeldi tried to crack the whip and slap the arrow away but he was too slow and instead resorted to dodging the attack.

"Sorry," he said as soon as he landed. Yoake shook her head.

"No need to be sorry," she said, "let's just try again." Yeldi nodded and moved back to his original position. He stood with the whip out, determined to at least try to use the weapon this time.

"Yeldi," the two turned to see Erasure walking over to them, "It is obvious that you are a good dodger. Try to use the whip as an extension of your dodging ability. The whip is an extension of the arm and thus can be used as a defensive weapon. When the arrow comes within range, just before the time you would normally try to jump or somehow move out of the way, crack the whip toward it, understand?" Yeldi nodded and Yoake made a mental note to try and get him to speak a bit more. *He's probably just really nervous* she thought.

"Thanks, Erasure," she said happily.

"Hey!" the shout came from across the field and Yoake immediately recognized the voice as Kyoki's, "Come on! I'm all done with the laps! Let's go!" Erasure sighed and with a look of slight exasperation, walked back over to his student.

"Let's try Erasure's advice." Yoake said, moving back. She strung her bow and, after making sure the black haired boy was ready, she fired. The arrow flew straight for him and for a moment, Yoake thought he was going to dodge again, but instead he cracked the whip in the air. The flaming weapon missed the arrow itself but it did reach close enough to set it on fire, almost instantly turning it to ash.

He stared at the falling black dust with wide eyes, shocked that he'd actually managed to do something correctly. Yoake smiled at him. "That was great! You just need to work on your aim." Her encouragement was met with a simple nod of the head. "Alright! Let just keep doing this and if you don't improve we'll see what you're doing that's throwing you off. After maybe an hour of repeating the drill over and over, Yeldi kept getting closer and closer to hitting the arrows themselves rather than the space around them.

"How are you kids doing?" Tybalt asked as he walked over. Yoake smiled and looked to Yeldi who was panting.

"Why am I so tired?" he asked his brother. Tybalt sighed, still smiling.

"Using your own watch takes energy from within your body," he explained, "after working like this for hours, especially while keeping the flames going, is going to take a toll on your stamina. Don't worry, all it takes is training to give yourself more. But I think we should stop for today; you kids still have school tomorrow." Yoake nodded and soon they stood with Kyoki, Hana, and Artan outside the training grounds. Tybalt opened his watch and the familiar portal that always brought them home opened. Quickly, they jumped through and landed next to the side wall of their dorm, away from possible prying eyes.

"I'll see you later," Tybalt said.

"W-where are you going?" Yeldi asked, sad that his brother was going to leave him alone with a boy who obviously didn't trust him.

"I have some work to do," he said and with that he was gone. Yeldi shifted nervously and looked to Yoake for some kind of direction. She smiled at him and he blushed; she could tell it would take a great deal of time for his psyche to repair itself. All she could do now was help him and comfort him.

"Go back to the boy's dorm," she said softly, "we'll see you guys tomorrow." Artan grunted and dragged Yeldi off by his collar, muttering under his breath. Hana sighed.

"He really hates him," she said as the girls walked into their room. Kyoki nodded.

"I kind of understand why. I mean, Saekrin did kill Artan's father and Yeldi helped him, but I don't think he deserves to bear the brunt of Artan's anger. I swear if I find one more scratch on that boy than there was when Artan dragged him off, I will personally rip that little punk's head from his shoulders." Yoake chuckled nervously; Kyoki always had an . . . interesting way of expressing herself.

"I think we should get to bed," she said, pulling out some pajamas. Kyoki shook her head.

"You guys have fun. I've got a crap-ton of homework to make up." With a sigh, she sat on her bed and pulled over her calculus textbook. Hana bid the other two girls good night and crawled under her covers. With a "good luck" to Kyoki, Yoake shifted into her bed and was soon asleep.

The next morning, the girls met Artan and Yeldi outside of their dorm and walked to school.

"How did you sleep, Yeldi?" Yoake asked. The boy blushed, hearing Artan huff angrily from beside him. Hana elbowed the slightly older boy in the ribs and he turned his glare to her, but her own fierce eyes made him look down.

The rest of the walk was quiet and soon Artan, Yoake, and Yeldi walked into class. To their surprise, Saekrin didn't say a word to them all day, except when absolutely necessary in his role as their teacher.

As they walked back to their dorm after school, they tried to figure out what was going on.

"I wonder why he didn't say anything . . ." Yoake mused. Artan shrugged and continued reading the book he was carrying.

"Pay attention!" Hana said, snatching the book away. The boy growled but sighed.

"I don't know," he said, "Maybe he just had nothing to say. I mean, with Kyoki and Yeldi leaving and taking his hostage with them, he's probably had to rethink his whole plan." He looked over to Yeldi for some kind of confirmation. Despite his dislike of the younger boy, Artan had to admit that when it came to their enemy, Yeldi knew a great deal more than anyone else, except perhaps Tybalt.

"Ma-Saekrin-he," Yeldi looked down for a moment, trying to put the thoughts in his head together, "he didn't seem angry anymore . . ." was all the boy could say before the group was interrupted by a low hiss. Yeldi froze instantly, eyes wide and darting in every direction.

"What's wrong?" Yoake asked.

"He-he's here." Yeldi choked out. Instantly, Kyoki began to scan the area, hand moving to her watch.

"Afternoon, children," called a dark, smooth voice. The group looked up to see Saekrin sitting on the top of their dorm. He held a long wooden pole in his hands and at the top, they could see the blade of a diamond ax ornately carved with an emerald snake circling the top of the pole, its mouth open and fangs bared.

"Saekrin!" Yoake yelled, "What do you want?" The creature smirked.

"What do I want?" he asked mockingly, "The same thing I wanted yesterday: your death. The same thing I wanted last week and last month: your watches. I would think you would have figured that by now. Humans really are stupid."

"Shut up, you bastard!" Kyoki yelled, opening her watch. Instantly, she transformed in a black cloud of ghosts and landed beside her friends, who had also changed. The girls looked to see Artan standing beside them dressed in a deep blue tunic, aquamarine shoulder, wrist, and shin guards. A long katana the same color as his tunic rested in his hands, up and ready for battle. Beside him, Yeldi stood in a loose orange half shirt, crimson skort and black metal netting underneath it all. His forearms were covered by plate armor and his whip sat in his hand, flames dancing along the length.

"Looks like you've grown a bit, boy." Saekrin chuckled, looking at Yeldi.

"Don't mock him!" Yoake shouted. The creature on the roof shrugged nonchalantly and stood.

"I really hate unnecessary fighting," he mused, "but it seemes like this will have to be done." He raised his pole ax and swung it forward, but nothing seemed to happen.

"What was tha—?" Hana began but was cut off as she and her companions were thrown back by a sudden blast of air. Yeldi stood and tried to raise his whip, but before he could crack it, Saekrin sent another blast toward him. The boy nearly screamed as Saekrin's face appeared just inches from his own, the man's air extinguishing the whip in the process.

"You're still weak," he hissed, "and you always will be." Yeldi's eyes widened in fear and he could feel his knees shaking, soon buckling under him.

"Leave him alone!" Hana shouted, "VINE WEB!" Green vines shot toward Saekin but he jumped out of the way, cutting several of the strands with his blade.

"Don't let your guard down, you ass!" Kyoki chuckled, suddenly appearing behind him, "REAPER'S BLADE!" Black clouds fused themselves to her blade as she swung it down. Saekrin smirked and twisted his pole, deflecting her attack and sending her back. He landed gracefully but was suddenly hit by a blast of shining purple water, as a simoltaneous cry of "ROYAL BLAST" and "HYDRO-CANNON" echoed out. He turned and spun his ax, sending some of the water flying off as he summoned a swirling current of air. Soaking wet but otherwise unharmed, he smirked sadistically at Yoake and Artan.

"Silent wind tunnel," he whispered. The two still standing strained to hear what their enemy had said, but just as the words sunk in, they were caught in a miniature tornado. Silent screams echoed inside the blast as sharp currents of air cut and slashed at them. Saekrin chuckled to himself and walked over to Yeldi, who sat frozen in place as his former teacher stalked closer and closer to him.

"I'm going to make you regret your betrayal, boy." Saekrin hissed into Yeldi's ear, making him shake like a leaf in a hurricane. Suddenly, a large black wolf leaped toward Saekrin, but he turned just in time to knock it away.

"Let them go, Saekrin," Tybalt said, standing on the other side of the battleground, "Leave." The white haired man laughed and looked around.

"You really should do a better job of training your charges," he said, "they're all rather pathetic." The wolf stood next to Tybalt, baring its fangs at Saekrin, just waiting for its master to give the attack signal.

"Leave, traitor," Tybalt hissed. A small breeze blew past them, rustling the trees quietly. Saekrin shrugged and turned to leave.

"Before I go," he said, tilting his head back toward his former friend, "I just have one question. How is Sakura?"

Tybalt snarled and the wolf charged, but just as it was about to bite, the wind picked up and Saekrin disappeared.

The man growled in frustration, but a groan from Yoake brought him back to the present. Immediately, he ran over to her.

"Are you alright?" he asked, concerned. Yoake nodded and looked to Hana, who gave the same answer.

"Guys!" Kyoki's voice called to them. The group turned to see her kneeling in front of a trembling, terror filled Yeldi, "Come here! Something's really wrong!"

Tybalt was the first to reach his brother, followed closely by Artan and the other two girls. He kneeled down, nudging Kyoki out of the way to get a better look at Yeldi. The boy was staring at the ground, shaking, with his mouth open in a silent scream.

"Yeldi . . ." he said slowly, reaching for him, but the younger jerked away. Yoake leaned down and gently called to him.

"Yeldi," she whispered, trying to coax him back to reality, "Yeldi, he's gone now. It's okay." Slowly, he looked up at her, small tears shining in his eyes.

"I'm sorry," he breathed, "I'm sorry. I couldn't—I couldn't . . ." his words melted into nonsense as the tears started to fall.

Yoake sat down beside him and pulled the sobbing boy into a gentle embrace. "Sh-h." she soothed. "It's okay. You don't need to be ashamed or sorry. No one here will judge you for being afraid." Though still shaking, Yeldi wrapped his arms around her, returning her hug. "There. Doesn't that feel better." she said calmly, and he nodded. "Good, now come on."

"So was that his normal one or the one that can change?" Hana asked once they were back in the dorm. All had returned to normal, or in the case of Artan and Yeldi, to their human forms.

"What are you talking about?" Kyoki said, giving Hana a confused look. The other girl sighed.

"Don't you ever pay attention?" she asked, "Tybalt told us a long time ago that Saekrin was the first in two thousand years with the ability to control more than one watch as his own. He also said that one watch was a basic one power weapon, but the other would change power to be whatever Saekrin wanted. So what I want to know is which one was that?"

Tybalt looked up from his work bandaging Yoake's cuts and shook his head.

"He never told anyone. It was a game he liked to play, to get people to try and guess which was which, but he never told us if we were right."

"But you fought together!" Kyoki interjected.

"Yes," Tybalt replied, "but as you know he spent most of his time as a spy behind enemy lines so we never found out which watch was which." Kyoki sighed.

"Then how are we going to figure this out?" Yoake asked. Artan grunted and pushed himself off the wall he had been leaning against, moving to stand in front of Yeldi, who had once again found his favorite corner. Although, this time he was standing rather than sitting.

"Well?" Artan snapped, suddenly slamming one hand onto the wall beside Yeldi's head, making the boy jump in fear, "Which is it?" he asked, "You should know. You spent enough time with him. Which was the one he used on us?" He glared at Yeldi, fully expecting an answer but the boy remained frozen.

"You're useless," Artan spat and walked back to his previous spot. Yoake immediately rushed over to Yeldi, glaring daggers at Artan.

"Don't be scared," she said as she placed a hand on Yeldi's shoulder, "He won't hurt you." She turned to stare at Artan again.

"That-that one," Yeldi muttered.

"What?" Hana asked, "speak up. We can't hear you."

"That one," Yeldi said again, "The one he used today, that's the one that changes."

"Well then I guess it'll be easier to beat him now that we know that." Yoake said, trying to encourage the trembling boy.

"So what's his other watch?" Hana asked.

"That is his hypnotism watch."

"Hypnotism?" Hana and Yoake said together.

"Oh yeah, I remember you telling us that." the younger said.

"It's a snake, a cobra I think." Kyoki added. "It's not a pretty sight when he uses that one." They all looked at her, surprised by her serious tone. "When he opens the watch this huge snake slithers out of it and it'll look around like it's searching for something to kill. If you guys thought Saekrin himself was scary, you haven't seen anything." Yeldi nodded in agreement and shivered at the memory.

"Is that the watch he used on Kimi?" Hana asked.

"The little girl from the store? Yeah." Yeldi answered. "And sorry about that."

"What little girl?" Artan asked.

"Her name was Kimi and she accidentally ended up as a hostage during one of our early fights," Hana explained, "She saw us fight Yeldi and when we had him captured, Saekrin showed up. After cutting Yeldi loose, he walked over to her and erased her memories."

"So he just f-s up people's minds." he said.

"He did it one other time right?" Kyoki asked, "With Wynona." Yoake and Hana nodded.

"One of the girls in our class," Hana explained. Artan grunted and sighed.

"Great," he grouched, "so he can just grab a hold of the brain of every Tom, Dick, and Harry that walks by. Wonderful."

"It's not quite that simple," Tybalt said, "Just like any power granted by the watches, his hypnotism takes energy. The longer someone is kept under the spell the more energy the hypnotist needs to keep control."

"But that bastard's probably got enough power to keep someone under his thumb for months." Artan sighed.

"Stop being so negative!" Kyoki snapped, knocking him on the head with one of her thinner textbooks.

"Hey!" he yelped, rubbing his sore cranium, "I'm not negative. I'm a realist."

"And I'm not optimistic, I'm a romantic." Yoake countered with a raised eyebrow, waiting for his response of 'touchet', but he just glared at her.

"Hey," Kyoki said thoughtfully, "Wasn't Artan a victim of the hypnotism?"

"Wait, what?" Artan asked angrily.

"Yeah I think Saekrin used his power to—mmmf!" She was cut off when Yoake and Hana quickly put their hands over her mouth.

"What was she going to say?" Artan snapped harshly.

"Oh nothing!" Hana said nervously. "She's just blathering." The silenced teen mumbled angrily against their hands.

"Yeah you know Kyoki, she just talks to hear herself talk." Yoake added, laughing nervously. Artan growled but sat down.

"So what are we going to do now?" he asked, looking squarely at Tybalt.

"Yeah, babysitter man," Kyoki said, finally wrenching herself free of her friend's grip.

"First," Tybalt said flatly, "I am not your babysitter and second, we are going to come up with a strategy. No matter how much of a traitor he is, Saekrin was right when he said you guys needed more training. I only saw the tail end of the fight and you were starting to do it a bit on your own, but you need to work together and play off each other's attacks. Larger, more powerful combinations can be formed that way and we need all the power we can get if you want to have any chance of defeating him."

Hana nodded and walked over to her desk, pulling out a piece of paper.

"What is that for?" Yeldi asked nervously shifting to stand beside her, but a low growl from Artan made him jump back.

"Artan, don't do that," Hana snapped, "He can stand where he wants and Yeldi, this is so we can write down every attack we can think of and see what goes with what or what could go with what."

"Good idea," Yoake said and the group set to work. After about two hours they had several charts and lists scattered all over the room in a strange organizational system.

"All done!" Kyoki said happily, stretching. Yeldi nodded, smiling. Even Artan couldn't help but let a sigh of relief pass his lips.

"Come on, Yeldi," he said as he stood, "Let's get back to our dorm. We still have class tomorrow." The younger boy nodded and followed Artan out the door, Tybalt exiting from his normal spot: the window.

"Aww . . ." Kyoki said.

"What?" Yoake asked, confused.

"They're gone," the older girl answered, "now I have to do my homework." Hana laughed at her friend's childish behavior and bid both other girls good night. Yoake changed and lay down, staring at the ceiling. She soon fell asleep listening to the soft music of the air conditioning and Kyoki's curses.

The next day, Yoake sat down behind Yeldi as always but Saekrin never arrived, instead a sub took over for the day.

"I wonder where he is . . ." she said during lunch.

"To hell if I know," Artan replied, "maybe he's got some new trick he wants to test out before he hits us with it." He looked over to Yeldi to see if he had any insights, but the boy shook his head.

"I don't know everything about Master-Saekrin, Saekrin," he corrected himself quickly, turning slightly pink, "He didn't tell me a lot about what was going on in his head, just orders." Yoake nodded.

"I bet he's getting a new hostage," Kyoki growled, "he seems to like those."

Hana sighed. "Either way," she said, "we should prepare for the worst and get those new combinations we came up with down fast." The rest of the group nodded and went back to their meals.

The rest of the day proceeded without incident, as did the next, and the next. As they walked back to the dorms from school four days later, they decided to walk through the park, stopping to get some work done in the cool spring air.

"Argh!" Kyoki growled.

"What's wrong?" Yoake asked, looking up from her history work.

"I'm so bored!" the older girl whined, "Where is that bastard? I mean we come up with all these kick ass moves and he just never shows up!"

"Chill." Artan said flatly, "The longer he stays away, the better."

"Not necessarily," Hana pointed out, "When we fight, we know exactly where he is and what he is doing, but right now . . . we don't. I'm starting to get worried."

"Aww . . . it sounds like the children missed me." the group looked up to see Saekrin sitting just above them in the tree they were sitting under, poleaxe in hand. Immediately, they jumped up and pulled out their watches, transforming.

"We're ready for you this time!" Kyoki laughed.

Saekrin smirked. "Really?" he asked sarcastically, "Alright then," he stood and jumped down, "let's get started." Suddenly, he swung his ax, sending an enormous bolt of lightning crashing toward them.

"What the hell?" Kyoki yelled as she leapt out of the way. Saekrin laughed.

"Calm down," Hana said, landing next to her, "Just do what we talked about. Ready?" Kyoki nodded and raised her scythe, black clouds beginning to swirl and gather around it. She looked to Hana who had already begun to swing her daggers, green leaves and multi colored blossoms fusing with Kyoki's clouds to form grey, sickly versions of themselves.

"POISON BLOOM!" they yelled together, sending the horde of venomous flora toward Saekrin. He dodged but not before one of the flowers slashed his leg, making him wince. It was a small cut, but enough to cause problems if left alone.

"Got'cha!" Kyoki yelled happily, clapping.

"So you have . . ." Saekrin mused, smirking, "but I have you as well." Just then another bolt slammed down from the sky, sending Kyoki and Hana flying into the air. They fell to the ground with two loud thumps and were instantly knocked out.

"Two down," Saekrin muttered, more to himself than Artan, Yoake, or Yeldi, "Yes . . . five to three then, hmm . . . yes, what? No, not now. Later . . ." His words descended into nonsense and Artan looked at Yoake.

"Our turn," he said, "right now, while he's talking to his own dementia."

"Right." She pulled out a yellow arrow as Artan shifted his katana, bringing it up to attack. The tip glowed blue, liquid light moving up and down the blade.

"Okay!" Yoake yelled, pulling the arrow back, "GO!"

She let the arrow loose, aiming straight for Saekrin. Artan, moved after it, suddenly catching the tip of the arrow with his sword. The whole blade glowed with white light and as a loud cry of "AURORA WAVE" rang out.

Saekrin laughed and turned toward Artan, blocking his sword with his pole ax. With malicious smirk, he sent a jolt of electricity through the boy and knocked him back and into Yoake, electrocuting them both.

A cold chuckle hit Yeldi's ears as his former master turned to him. "I told you I'd make you regret betraying me, boy." he said.

Just then another voice called. "Leave him alone, Saekin," The creature turned to see Tybalt and his black wolf standing about thirty feet away.

"So the babysitter and his puppy have come to save the day again," he said, "how cute." Suddenly, he disappeared. Tybalt's eyes widened as he felt a presence appear behind him and turned just in time to half dodge Saekrin's attack. He could see sparks dancing along the length of the ax and knew that one hit would probably knock him out cold. "We haven't gotten a chance to spar in so long," Saekrin said, advancing on Tybalt, "Let's play."

Yeldi watched in horror as Saekrin and his brother fought. He could see Tybalt trying desperately to deflect the other man's attacks, but it was becoming more and more obvious that he was out of practice. He pulled out a short sword from his watch and tried to push Saekrin's ax away, but with limited success. Dodging, punching, kicking, Yeldi saw Tybalt get one hit in after another, but those hits were answered with four or five counters. The sword and ax clashed together sending up showers of sparks as the two men continued to fight, completely oblivious to their silent, scared observer. Yeldi gasped as Saekrin brought his ax up, slashing Tybalt's chest and sending him to the ground in a spray of blood.

He stood over his victim, smirking triumphantly, and once again raised his ax, sending it toward Tybalt's chest and-

Clang!

Tybalt looked up to see Yeldi standing over him, one of Hana's daggers in his hand. Saekrin looked down at his former slave with shock written across his face. Never had he seen such determined fire in the young eyes. He jumped, smirking, and landed a few feet away. As he came down, he wobbled slightly as his left leg touched the ground. He looked down to see the poisoned cut beginning to fester. With a sigh, he turned back to Yeldi.

"You really are very entertaining, boy," Saekrin laughed, glancing down for a second at his leg, "but I think for now I should add this poison to my little . . . collection." With that, he disappeared in a blast of lightning.

Once he was sure Saekrin was gone, Yeldi dropped Hana's dagger and turned to his brother. Tybalt lay on the ground in a pool of his own blood. The red liquid trickled out of his chest in a steady flow that was interrupted occasionally by his coughing. Yeldi was frantic, knowing that if he didn't hurry, Tybalt was sure to die. His first thought was to use his fire to sear the wound closed but he quickly shook his head, trying to dismiss the thought. It would only put Tybalt in more pain. Besides, Hana was a healer, she could help. Sadly, when he turned to call for her, he saw that she was still unconscious. *"Damn"* Yeldi thought. He was running out of time and options. Tybalt needed healing but the only one who could help was incapacitated. He couldn't go look for someone else. By the time he'd get back with help, it would be too late, and who would believe his story explaining how it happened?

Tybalt's coughs became weaker and less frequent, putting Yeldi beyond frantic; beyond panic even. He had only recently been reunited with his brother and wasn't about to lose him so soon. With the clock ticking, Yeldi's mind went back to its first idea. On the one hand, Tybalt was unconscious and would feel nothing, also it would stop the bleeding and burns are easier to heal than cuts, or so he hoped. On the other hand, being easier to heal didn't make burns any less painful, in fact Yeldi knew from experience that burns were much more painful than cuts, due to—*"The reason doesn't matter, idiot!"* he thought to himself. He shook his head in order to maintain his focus. *"I have to, there's no other choice."*

Taking his whip, he placed it along the slash, but hesitated. *"I can't, it'll only hurt him even more! But if I don't he'll die!"* two voices in his head conflicted, but he had made his decision and was going to go through with it. Eyes full of tears, he said out loud, but quietly, "Please forgive me, brother." and activated the flames. He felt Tybalt's body tense at the flames' touch, but no cry of pain came from his mouth.

It was a deep wound and was taking a long time to heal, but what was worse was that Artan had seen what he was doing. "Traitor!" the older boy cried and charged at Yeldi.

Yeldi stopped his work and stood to face him, "No! It's not what you think! I was—"

"You were burning Tybalt! Your brother!" he screamed as he tackled Yeldi.

"I was trying to heal him!" Yeldi defended as he struggled against Artan's assault.

"By burning him?"

"By closing the wound!" Yeldi cried and Artan stopped abruptly. The two sat up and Yeldi continued, "Hana was, is, unconscious and trying to wake her up would have taken too long, so would going to get help, but he would've been dead before I got back. And no one would have believed me if I told them that he was slashed at by someone who used to be his friend but is now evil and trying to gain ultimate power."

Artan reluctantly stood up and said, "Fine, but I've still got my eye on you."

Yeldi stood too and, with a strangely determined look in his eyes said, rather bluntly, "I don't care what you think, Artan, all I care about is keeping my brother alive." With that, he went back and resumed his "healing".

Artan was shocked beyond words. He stared at Yeldi with his jaw at his chest. There sat a kid who had betrayed his people, who was beaten into submission and taught to fear everyone around him, but here he was trying to help. Even after he came back, he was still careful to not make someone even the least bit upset, for fear of being beaten. The look Artan had seen in that boy's eyes was totally different from any look he'd seen before. That look told Artan that Yeldi cared more about healing his brother than he did about proving his loyalty. Artan had never had any siblings so he didn't understand what that feeling was like. He had no concept of how brothers, or any siblings, felt to each other, but he assumed it was like a bond between comrades, only much stronger. As suspicious of Yeldi as Artan was, he couldn't help but feel a little bad for doubting him, maybe the kid could change after all.

A groan from a few feet away suddenly drew his attention. He turned to see Hana struggling to sit up and ran over.

"Urgh, my head." the girl said, rubbing her temples.

"I'm glad to see you're up," Artan said, "and I'm sorry we can't let you rest longer but Tybalt needs your help." He pointed to where Yeldi was still trying to sear the wounds shut. Hana's eyes widened as she took in the sight of blood and immediately she ran over, pushing Yeldi out of the way gently.

"What happened?" she asked frantically, already beginning to heal the older male.

"Saekrin got him," Yeldi answered sadly. Hana nodded shortly then went back to her work. Slowly, agonizingly slowly, the wounds closed and some of the burns began to heal, but she quickly began to pant in exhaustion.

"What's wrong?" Yoake said, suddenly appearing beside her.

"I-I don't have enough strength to fully revive him," Hana replied, "We need to get him back to Cyowan. I bet Sakura and Alia will know what to do." Yeldi nodded but didn't know how to get there.

"We can use his watch." Yoake suggested, "That's how he got us there before."

"Right." the group turned to see Artan helping Kyoki up. Slowly, she staggered to her feet and wobbled over, dropping to her knees as soon as she reached them. Instantly, she began rifling through Tybalt's clothes in search of his watch, which she found still clutched in his hand. She looked up at the others, the silent question of "any ideas?" written clearly across her face.

"Just try opening it." Hana said, "Maybe that wolf can help us." Kyoki nodded and quickly opened the watch. Almost immediately, the familiar large black wolf appeared, landing beside Tybalt.

On seeing its master's condition, it began to growl at them.

"We didn't do it!" Kyoki snapped, "Saekrin did! We need to get him back to Cyowan can you help us?" The wolf glared at her for a moment but seemed to believe her. It sat down and howled, a haunting sound that made the wind rise and a large pool of light appear just below them. Yeldi grabbed onto his brother as the group was transported back to the temple.

"Lady Alia!" Artan called once they landed in the courtyard just outside of the marble structure. Quickly, the woman ran out, followed by Sakura and Erasure.

"Tybalt!" Sakura yelled, dashing over to him and helping Yeldi carry him toward the barracks.

"What happened?" Erasure asked, "You all look like you've been through hell." Yoake quickly told him all that had happened in the park and Artan filled in with Yeldi's attempted healing. Erasure nodded as they spoke, leading them into the barracks' infirmary.

Inside, they found Yeldi pacing back and forth nervously, anxiously, as he waited for Sakura and his brother.

"All of you should come with me," Alia said, nearly making them all jump, "We must see if you have any wounds as well." The group followed her into rooms, one for the girls, the other for the boys.

"I'm fine!" Kyoki protested as a nurse tried to get her to remove her corset.

"Come on, Kyoki," Hana said with a sigh, already standing in a hospital gown, "They just want to make sure we're all okay." With a sigh, Kyoki allowed her outfit to be removed, but a sudden gasp from the nurse made her concerned.

"What?" she asked, trying to turn around to see what the nurse was so shocked about. Kyoki knew she had scars but they must've healed by now, or at least almost healed, what could have made the other woman gasp like that?

"That sick twisted traitor . . ." the nurse breathed.

"Good lord . . ." Yoake said, coming to stand beside her.

"What does it say?" Hana asked.

"What does what say?" Kyoki demanded, tired of being the only one left in the dark. The nurse walked her over to a mirror and slowly let her turn around.

"I don't get it," Kyoki said, "It's just a bunch of lines and squiggles. Does it say something?" The nurse nodded and leaned over, whispering the word into the girl's ear.

"WHAT THE HELL!" Kyoki yelled. Immediately, Artan and Yeldi ran inside, concerned by the sudden scream.

"What's going—?" Artan started, but stopped suddenly as he caught sight of Kyoki's back, "that bastard . . ."

"YOU BETTER BELIEVE HE'S A BASTARD!" Kyoki ranted, throwing her arms up and pacing the length of the room. "I can't believe him! He's going to pay! If it's the last thing I ever to I will make sure he rots in HELL!"

"Kyoki—" Yoake began but the upperclassman cut her off.

"I've got an idea," she said, chuckling darkly, "I'll catch him, tie him up—onto the ceiling I think—like a pig, like the stupid bastard of a pig he is. Then you know what I'll do?" she turned to give the rest of the group a smile that sent shivers up their spines, "I'll take a taser and then I'll put it against his skin and I'll WATCH HIM DANCE! I can't believe he, he" Her words descended into manic cackles that quickly turned to tears as she sat down in the corner of the room, back pressed against the cold stone.

"Kyoki . . ." Yoake said, moving to sit next to her. She held her hand out and placed it on the other girl's shoulder but she pushed it away. Hana sat down in front of her but kept her distance. Artan stayed by the door, knowing that nothing he said would make it any better. On the opposite side of Yoake, Yeldi sat down and watched Kyoki cry. He remembered the same tears running down his own cheeks the first time Saekrin had burned him and he also knew that words of comfort were meaningless.

Yoake looked over at him for some kind of direction, but he just shook his head.

Slowly, the tears dried and Kyoki looked up. "I will get him back for this." she said solemnly, turning to Yeldi. He nodded in understanding and helped her stand.

"We, umm," Yoake said, "We should finish the check up."

"And then see how Tybalt is doing." Hana added, receiving a nod from the others in the room.

Artan looked at Yeldi who had a look of worry and anticipation on his face since the moment they arrived. "Hey, Yeldi, can I talk to you for a second?" he asked.

The other boy's head snapped up at the mention of his name. His eyes darted from each of the girls to Artan nervously, and slightly frightened. Hana and Yoake narrowed their eyes at the red-haired warrior. Artan put his hands up in defense and said, "I'm not going to kill him, I promise."

Yoake nodded and looked at Yeldi who, though reluctantly, followed Artan to the hall.

"Be sure to come back to get your wounds checked, both of you." Hana called after them.

As soon as they were alone Yeldi, trying to maintain his composure, asked Artan, 'So what's up?"

"I'm sorry." the older boy answered simply.

"Sorry? For what?"

"For attacking you earlier. I didn't know you were trying to help Tybalt."

"It's okay, I guess, you were just following your instinct, that's all." Yeldi shrugged, smiling in a friendly manner that surprised Artan.

"Even still I should let you get even." Artan said. "So I want you to hit me."

"But I don't—"

"Come on, I don't mind, and it'll put my mind at rest." Artan turned to Yeldi in order to give him a good shot. "Go on, take a good whack and make sure it leaves a mark tomorrow."

Yeldi looked at him confusedly. He had never hit someone outside of a fight before, but here Artan was *telling* Yeldi to hit him. Normally, he was the one getting hit, but now . . . Yeldi lifted his balled fist and looked Artan straight in the eye, but something just wouldn't let him hit the other boy. But Yeldi's mind had already made this decision, so he curled back and struck Artan right in the stomach.

The force knocked Artan to his knees. "Damn . . ." he stuttered out. "That hurt."

"Ah! Was it too much? I didn't mean to hurt you that badly!" Yeldi rambled, trying to apologize for an act he hadn't wanted to commit in the first place.

"No. It's fine. I deserved it" Artan slowly rose to his feet and looked Yeldi in the eye. The shaggy-haired boy was shocked to see a friendly look on his face. "You've got a good arm, we should spar some time. That'll give us a chance to knock the crap out of each other."

Yeldi couldn't help but smile. It felt wonderful to have finally gained his peer's trust. "I look forward to it . . . I think."

Artan laughed. "Come on. The girls are probably wondering if I've actually kept my promise and not killed you."

"Where have you guys been?" Hana asked once they walked back into the room. She and the other girls were fully dressed and had been waiting for the boys to return.

"We were just working some stuff out," Artan answered, "Right?" He elbowed Yeldi in the ribs playfully. The younger nodded.

"So are you guys going to be okay?" he asked, looking mostly at Kyoki.

"Right as rhinos!" the girl giggled, thumping her chest proudly. Yoake laughed. Just then, Sakura walked over.

"How's Tybalt?" Yoake asked, voicing the question on everyone's lips. The woman sighed, but smiled.

"Lady Alia says he is going to be fine, but he won't be able to fight for some time. The wounds were very deep." She turned to Yeldi, "Your idea to sear them was good. Without your help, he may not have made it." Yeldi smiled awkwardly and thanked her.

"Can we see him?" Hana asked, "or is he asleep?"

"No, he's awake," Sakura said, "follow me." The group walked down the hall to a small white room with a bed. Tybalt sat up as soon as they entered and nodded as a greeting.

"How're you feeling?" Yoake asked. Tybalt smiled.

"I feel fine," he answered, "He got me pretty good, but I'll live."

"Children," they turned to see Erasure step into the room, "I need you to come with me." They shrugged in confusion but followed the old warrior out into the hallway.

"What's up?" Kyoki asked.

"Tybalt has informed me that the five of you have been working on combination attacks." they nodded, "I would like to show you a more powerful version." He walked toward the training field but continued to talk.

"What you have been doing is a technique that we teach our own soldiers. Each warrior is placed in a team of about five or six, which makes you the perfect size, and, just as you have been, is trained separately and then together. They create combinations of attacks that allow them to exert more power. Once they are able to execute these, the teams are taught how to do what is called a Team Strike. As the name implies, it is a larger version of a combination attack, utilizing the powers of all members of a team. The downside to this is that it takes a vast amount of energy to pull off so is only used as a last resort. When you learn this, you must keep that in mind, understood?"

The group nodded as they stepped out onto the field. Groups of teams already stood waiting for the day's lessons to begin.

"You have all just been wounded," Erasure said, "so I do NOT," he glanced at Kyoki, "want you to try this for at least a week. However, you should see how it works."

Back in the clinic room Mineh and Kumi skipped in. "Hi, mommy. Hi," Upon seeing her father, Mineh burst into tears. "Daddy! You're hurt!" she cried as he picked her up into his lap.

"It's okay, sweetie." he said kissing her forehead. "I'll be fine."

"Was it the snake-man?" Kumi asked and Tybalt nodded. In a way very much like Kyoki, the little earth girl pumped her fist and said, "My big sisters will help you."

Tybalt just chuckled in amusement at the little girl. "They already have." he said.

"Kumi, Mineh" Sakura said, "will you two please give us a moment."

"Okay, mommy." Mineh jumped off Tybalt's lap and grabbed Kumi's hand. "Let's go see what the big kids are doing."

"I bet I can find them faster than you." Kumi said and sped off.

"Hey, wait up!" Mineh quickly followed suit.

"Be careful, girls!" Tybalt called after them and looked at his wife, searching for the same amusement in her face, but it wasn't there. Instead, she looked at him teary-eyed. "Sakura—"

"What were you thinking?" Sakura yelled, capturing him in a hug. "You know you can't fight him head on like that!"

"Your faith in my fighting skills is overwhelming, love." Tybalt said, soothingly sarcastic.

"Tybalt, this is no time to joke." Sakura said into his chest. "I almost lost you again today. Do you have any idea how that feels?"

"I'm a lot stronger than I was last time." Tybalt protested.

"That's not the point! You can't go making reckless decisions like that. The next time you do, it could be the last."

"I know, I know." Tybalt kissed his wife's head and stroked her hair. "but I have a duty to protect those girls."

"Tybalt!" she cried.

"But I can't protect them if I'm dead. I promise I'll be careful."

"Don't scare me like that." Sakura said. "I know you need to look after them and Alia put them in your care, but don't forget you're a father too."

"I don't dare forget that." Tybalt said. "You and Mineh are my reason for fighting, no, you're my reason for staying alive."

❧

Out by the training field, Kyoki was getting impatient. She stared at the teams, eyes bouncing from one to the next. One stood apart from the others, four in a circle and one in the middle. Each one had transformed and closed their eyes, weapons pointing to the girl in the center. She was about two inches taller than Kyoki, with pale purple hair and wielding a bright red sickle.

"Are they going to do anything?" she asked. Erasure pressed a finger to his lips, signaling for her to be quiet. With a sigh, Kyoki joined the others to watch. Suddenly, the ground shook and bright, multi-colored lights appeared around each of the four in the circle. The girls stared in shock as the lights spiraled upward, mixing in the air as the group raised their weapons high. They directed the lights together, mixing them further as their mouths moved in silent chants. Vaguely, they could hear the words.

"Immortal gods, take this power and bestow it on the one in whom we place our trust." The lights moved down as a final blinding white radiance surrounded the middle girl, engulfing her in a blazing stream. Slowly, the lights melted with her skin and weapon as her teammates fell to their knees in exhaustion; their energy gone and now shining in their friend's skin.

Suddenly, her eyes opened and she jumped toward the stone target on the other side of the field; her movements almost too fast to see. The girls gasped as a crash sounded, bouncing off the walls of the barracks. The attacker landed behind the golem with a soft whoosh of air. For a few seconds, nothing happened, but then the stone began to rumble and a large diagonal crack appeared. Slowly, the stone fell

172

apart, spiderweb cracks spreading all over, and suddenly, with a loud boom, the stone exploded.

"Holy crap!" Kyoki gasped, jumping back along with the rest of the group.

"Are we going to do that?" Yoake asked. Erasure nodded.

"The five of you will be able to do that and will practice once your wounds have healed." he said, "If you tried to do it now, there is a very high chance that you would die."

"Cool," Artan said, "the idea we get to do it, not dying." he clarified after receiving several confused looks.

"I think we should go back inside," Hana said, "If that's all you wanted to show us." she looked to Erasure.

"That is all," he said, "I wanted you children to have this in your head for later fights, but I must tell you that the energy output for this kind of attack is very high. You already know that combination attacks put a greater strain on the body from your last fight. These Team Strikes rely on the same principle."

"We understand," Yoake said and followed the others back inside.

"That's so cool!" Kyoki exclaimed once they were back in the hospital room the girls were sharing.

"Right," Yoake said, then she turned to Artan and Yeldi, "Hey, have you guys ever done combination attacks before? I mean before our last fight." Artan shook his head but Yeldi nodded.

"I did it once with . . ." he paused and the girls could see he was trying to make sure he said the right word next, "Saekrin. It hurt." He looked at the ground and Yoake suddenly felt very guilty for asking.

"Well, I think we're going to kick his sadistic ass!" Kyoki said, using all the tact of a drunk rhinoceros.

"Calm down," Hana sighed, "like Erasure said, we need to heal first so you guys," she turned to the two boys, "go to your room and get some sleep." They nodded and Artan grabbed onto Yeldi's arm, dragging him off, "and we," Hana continued, turning back to her two roommates, "need to go to bed."

"Well aren't you bossy all of a sudden," Kyoki said playfully, sticking out her tongue, "okay, Mom, I'm going." She crawled under the covers. Yoake laughed and bid Hana good night as the other sighed again.

"But mommy, I don't want to go to bed." Mineh whined. "I want to practice so I can be just like Kumi's big sisters."

"All little girls have to go to bed; even big girls go to bed." Sakura said as she tucked Mineh in and kissed her forehead. "Don't worry you know that you'll be a big sister soon."

"Yeah!" the child cheered touching her mother's slightly swollen stomach. "Good night, little sister or brother."

"Well isn't that adorable." said a voice from behind them. Sakura felt chills run down her spine when she heard it. She did not turn to see who the voice's owner was, she already knew. That low velvety voice still haunted her dreams; she would never forget it.

"Mommy?" Mineh looked at her quizzingly, but her mother was frozen with fear; her only movement uncontrollable shaking.

"H-how—" was all she managed to stutter out.

"Don't worry, *my love*," he hissed the title out mockingly, "I'm not actually here. This is a projection, if you will, from my temporary home on Earth." Saekrin chuckled. "But that doesn't mean I'm not tangible." He ran his finger down her back, bringing goosebumps to the surface, "I just wanted to see my daughter is all."

"Mommy, he's your daddy?" Mineh asked, but Sakura remained frozen, too afraid to speak.

"No, child," Saekrin chuckled at her naivety. "I am not Sakura's daddy; I'm yours."

"My daddy?"

"Yes."

"No." Mineh shook her head. "You're not my daddy, Tybalt is my daddy, he doesn't look scary like you."

At the mention of Tybalt's name, Saekrin glared at Mineh, his cold eyes boring holes into her own frightened ones. But then his gaze softened and, though talking to the little girl, he looked at Sakura's stunned face as he began stroking the terrified woman's hair. "No, he is not your father, he never was. He is a thief who stole you and your mother from me." Suddenly, he grabbed a fistful of Sakura's hair and yanked her head back. "He took what was—and still is—rightfully mine."

"Stop it!" Mineh cried, seeing the tears forming in her mother's eyes. "You're hurting my Mommy!"

"So it would seem, but she deserves it for betraying me for that scoundrel." He growled and threw her onto Mineh's little bed. "And, not only have you married that bastard, Sakura, now you're going to give him a child."

"I already have given him a child." Sakura retorted.

"She is MY child!"

"No! She is Tybalt's child."

"I refuse to believe that lie!"

"Stop yelling!" Mineh yelled, putting her head in her hands.

"Mineh!" Sakura cried, moving to sooth her daughter, but Saekrin slapped her hand away.

"She does not deserve a *filthy whore* like you for a mother."

"And neither does she deserve a *sadistic madman* like you for a father."

"I will make you regret those words." he said through gritted teeth as he grabbed her stomach, threatening to dig his claws into her flesh.

"No don't—"

"You belong to me, and no one else. Mineh is *my* child and I will make sure he can't claim you." With those words, he squeezed harder.

"No don't!" Mineh cried. "You'll hurt my brother or sister."

"No, I won't hurt it," Saekrin chuckled, "I'll kill it."

"NO!"

"Saekrin!" came a voice from the doorway. The three in the room looked up to see Tybalt with a very serious look on his face. "Let her go!" The white haired creature smirked and squeezed a bit harder, making Sakura cry out in pain.

Tybalt growled, "I said let her go." He moved forward to help his wife but the pain from his wound made him stop and lean against the doorframe.

Saekrin outright laughed. "You're such a party-pooper," he said mockingly, "no cake for you . . . and besides, you're in no condition to fight me." To emphasize his point, he suddenly appeared in front of him and grabbed his former friend by the throat, throwing him across the room. Tybalt slammed into the wall and fell unconscious.

"Daddy!" Mineh yelled, trying to run over to him, but Sakura held her back. Saekrin turned and walked back over to the bed. Gently, he lifted the small girl out of her mother's embrace. Mineh shook in his arms and tried to escape, but in vain.

"Don't worry, little one," he said softly, "I'm not going to hurt you." The girl stared at him with eyes wide as saucers, her breathing shallow and erratic. After a few minutes of running his fingers through her hair, he set Mineh down next to her mother. Immediately, Sakura embraced her, placing herself between the deranged man and her daughter. Saekrin chuckled and leaned down, placing a soft kiss on Sakura's forehead.

"I'm going to leave now, sweetheart, but fear not, I **will** come back for you." With that, he was gone, leaving a terrified woman and child in his wake.

"Summer time!" Kyoki yelled, running toward the ocean. The girls had been discharged from the hospital three weeks ago and the school year had ended two weeks later. Saekrin had been surprisingly absent and in the back of their minds they wondered where he was, but as soon as Kyoki had suggested a vacation to the beach, the danger had been temporarily forgotten.

"Hurry up!" she called, spinning around to face her companions. She wore a black and red bakini top with a skort-like bottom. The outfit revealed her scars but she had long since decided she didn't care and spun on her heel in excitement.

"Slow down!" Hana called back, "You know we'd be faster if you took some of this stuff." With a sigh, she set the two coolers she had been carrying down.

"It's fine," Tybalt said as he pitched a large umbrella behind her, "You kids go play. I can finish this."

"You sure?" Yoake asked.

"We can handle it." Yeldi said. He glanced up at her then instantly looked down again, a blush ghosting over his cheeks as he took in the sight of her outfit. Her bathing suit was bakini style but she wore a long loose skirt around her waist, tied at her left hip. Both were blue with green highlights.

"If you're sure . . ." she said. He nodded and she ran off after Kyoki and Hana.

"What're you so embarrassed about?" Artan asked, setting the towels down like a blanket. Yeldi blinked, cheeks darkening even more. Artan shrugged and looked over at the girls.

"Earth girls wear strange things . . ." Yeldi said as he sat down next to him.

"Really?" Artan asked, "I think they look good." His eyes followed Hana as she ran after a large beach-ball.

"You like her." Yeldi said matter-of-factly.

Artan blinked and shook his head. "W-what? No I don't. I—" He was cut off by Tybalt's laughter, "What's so funny?" he snapped, blushing slightly.

"Oh nothing . . ." Tybalt giggled.

Artan huffed in annoyance but continued to watch the girls play. Suddenly, Yeldi stood and walked over to them.

"In coming!" Kyoki yelled, tossing the ball over to him. Yeldi gasped and reached up just in time to grab the large ball.

"Nice catch." Yoake said smiling. Yeldi smiled back, but just as he was about to throw the ball back, it was stolen from him.

"Why should you have all the fun?" Artan said, clapping him on the shoulder. He held the ball under his other arm.

"I have an idea," Hana said, running over once she saw the game of catch coming to a close, "there are some nets over there, let's play volleyball."

"Yeah!" Kyoki said, "Girls versus losers!"

"What's valley-ball?" Yeldi asked.

"Hey, Tybalt!" Hana called. The man looked up from the book he was reading, "We need one more! Come play!" With a shrug, he stood and walked over.

"Okay," Kyoki said once they all stood beside the net, holding the volleyball under her arm, "guys go over there," she pointed to one side of the court, "and we'll go here. Now all you have to do is stay on your own side and try to hit the ball back over the net so the opposite team doesn't hit it. If it hits the ground, the other team gets a point, understood?" She looked at the boys expectantly. Slowly, Yeldi raised a shaky hand.

"I—I don't get it." he said sadly, "How do you get points?"

"Let me try," Yoake said, "Kyoki was right that if it touches the ground the other team gets a point. For example, if you hit it and it hits the ground on our side, you get a point, but if we hit it and it hits the ground on your side, we get a point, better?" The boy nodded.

"Good," Hana said, "now let the games begin!"

After four games, two to the girls, one draw, and one to the boys, they decided to teach Artan and Yeldi to build sandcastles.

"So you just pack it together?" Yeldi asked, picking up a handful of sand. The grains ran through his fingers as he stared at it, wondering how such brittle material could become a stable structure.

"What a waste of perfectly good throwing material . . ." Artan mused, picking up a handful. He stared at it for a few second, then a mischievous grin spread across his face and he threw it.

"What the hell?" Kyoki yelled, trying to dust the sand out of her hair, "You jerk! Now I'll be picking that out of my hair for three days." He laughed then suddenly began to choke as a large handful of sand caught him in the mouth. "Payback's a bitch!" she yelled, dancing in victory.

"Fine!" Artan yelled back, picking up another projectile. He threw it hard at Kyoki who ducked. His eyes widened in horror as the sand smacked against the side of Hana's head.

"I was planning on not getting involved in your stupid game," she said bluntly as she reached down, filling her hand with wet sand, "but if you insist." She threw the ball back at Artan, but it missed.

Tybalt sighed as he went back to his book, moving slightly to the left to dodge the incoming ball. "Don't hurt anyone, kids," he said without looking up.

"Yeah, yeah," Kyoki called back, tossing another wet sand ball at Hana.

Yoake sighed, smiling, and took Yeldi by the hand, leading him away from the "battle." They settled by a patch of moist sand and Yoake picked up a nearby bucket. She filled it with sand, packing it in tightly, then flipped it over. Slowly, she pulled the bucket off, leaving a half standing structure. Yeldi looked at it and smiled.

"Can I try?" he asked.

"Sure," Yoake handed him the bucket, "We're going to make this together, silly." Yeldi's smile widened and he scooped up the sand, mimicking Yoake's previous movements, and made another small tower. As soon as it was standing, Yoake pushed sand between them, creating a small wall. She looked up at him and laughed.

Suddenly, Yeldi threw the bucket behind her head. She turned to see it come to the ground in a shower of sand.

"Sorry!" Kyoki yelled. With a smile and a sigh, Yoake went back to the small castle. As the hours ticked by, the structure grew larger, spreading out into a small fortress surrounded by a city and then even roads and a small garrison outside the city wall.

"I think we're done." Yoake said with a grin.

"Already?" Yeldi said, slightly disappointed.

"Yeah, I know, but don't worry, we can always build another one. Look it's getting late." She pointed to the setting sun and Yeldi sighed; he knew she was right.

"Hey nice job, guys." Artan said, leaning over Yeldi's shoulder. He squeaked in surprise, but quickly regained his composure.

"Come on, kids!" Tybalt called, umbrella in hand. With a sigh, Yeldi stood and helped Yoake up, following Artan, Hana, and Kyoki toward Tybalt.

"You girls look absolutely *delicious* in your bathing suits." said a voice. A few weeks ago, it would have surprised them, but they had become accustomed to the chilling sound.

"First," Kyoki said, "eww, you are such a CREEPER! And second, this was such a good day until you showed up."

"Your point?" Saekrin replied, shrugging.

"You picked a bad place to fight us, you ass," Artan said, "if you haven't noticed, we're surrounded by water. This is my territory."

Again, Saekrin shrugged. "I was bored." he said mockingly. Artan growled and immediately transformed.

"That's it!" he snarled, "You're going down today!"

"Right!" Kyoki said, standing beside him, ready for battle. Saekrin spun his pole ax and stepped closer. The others growled and transformed.

"Ah Tybalt," he said, smirking at the other man, "How have you been feeling?" Suddenly, he vanished and reappeared in front of him. Tybalt growled in pain as Saekrin grabbed onto his neck, his other hand digging claws into the partially healed wound on Tybalt's side.

"Tybalt!" the children yelled, but a sudden wall of ice appeared, separating the two men from Tybalt's charges.

"We wouldn't want them interrupting us again," Saekrin hissed, smirking maliciously. Tybalt growled, slipping his hand into his pocket. Immediately, the large black wolf appeared, clamping its teeth onto Saekrin's arm. The white haired man hissed in pain and jumped away, landing about eight feet from Tybalt. Snarling, the dog glared at its master's enemy, eagerly waiting for the order to tear him to pieces. Outside the ice, Tybalt could hear the children pounding and trying to break through.

Saekrin tilted his head back to glance at them. "How annoying . . ." he muttered then turned his attention back to Tybalt, "The last time we met," he said, "I was hoping for a match but we were, shall we say, interrupted . . . by my," he chuckled for a moment, glancing back at Yeldi, "bitch."

Tybalt snarled, "He is no longer yours!" he shouted, making Saekrin chuckle.

"I suppose not," he said, "but the weak always remain so, just, like, you."

The dog leaped forward, instantly picking up on Tybalt's anger. It lunged for Saekrin and was instantly impaled by the pole ax. Tybalt's eyes widened in alarm as Saekrin threw the dog off of his weapon as if it were nothing but an annoying piece of garbage.

"Now, now," he said, "Let's not have our pets fight. As you said," he turned to look at Yeldi who was too focused on trying to melt the ice to notice, "my pet is no longer with me."

"Fine then," Tybalt said, pulling out his short sword, "We'll do this the old fashioned way." With that, he rushed toward Saekrin, blade out and ready to slice the man in two. Saekrin chuckled and held up his pole to defend but Tybalt suddenly jerked to the right, slamming the butt of his blade into Saekrin's side. Quickly, he flipped the blade and brought it down toward his opponent's shoulder but this time Saekrin blocked it, crashing his pole into Tybalt's stomach and sending him flying backward into the ice wall which had become a large dome.

Blood forced its way out of Tybalt's mouth as he coughed and slowly pushed himself up. Saekrin laughed.

"You can't beat me," he said, pointing the blade of his ax directly at Tybalt's throat, "I should kill you. I should make your students scream, make your *little brother* watch the last of his family fall but . . ." he pulled the ax away, making Tybalt tense and clutch is weapon tighter, "why should I waste my time. You are not a threat and you never were." He turned and walked toward the other side of the ice where the young fighers were still pounding, "However," he continued as he passed the halfway point, "them I think I will kill."

A roar filled the dome as Tybalt lept forward. "I won't let you touch them!" He swung his blade toward Saekrin but the sadist simply turned.

"What?" Tybalt exclaimed. He tried to pull his sword out of Saekrin's iron grip but the other man wouldn't budge.

Saekrin sighed. "I was going to let you witness this, or at least leave you conscious," he said, tossing Tybalt's weapon away, "but I guess I'll just have to put you down." His hand latched onto Tybalt's throat again and the teacher could feel Saekrin's black claws digging into him. Suddenly, he felt them twitch and a pain like nothing he had ever experienced coursed through him. It felt as though his veins were ablaze, as if every muscle and fiber was being torn apart. He tried to move but he couldn't. His limbs jerked and spasmed frantically, as if electricty had been suddenly jolted into him. Spinning eyes locked with coldly amused grey ones as he tried to hold onto his senses. Saekrin smirked and his fingers twitched again. The last thing Tybalt heard before his vision turned to black was Yeldi's scream.

The teens watched in horror as Tybalt was overpowered by Saekrin. Enraged, Kyoki lunged forward, eyes ablaze in anger. Saekrin, amused by the display, lowered the ice wall and switched his watch's power, simply blasting her with a bolt of lightening that sent her flying.

"Kyoki!" they all cried as the girl hit the sand with a muffled thud.

"Guys, form three!" Yoake ordered. The others nodded and moved to attack together.

"Now, now." Saekrin crooned. "It's no fun if you gang up like that." He switched his power again, this time to fire, and sent a stream of flames in the direction of the botanic barricade Hana created around her. It was set ablaze, and surrounded her in scorching flames.

"Hana!" Artan ran to her, collecting water from the ocean in an attempt to quench the fire.

"Ah, ah, ah." Saekrin wagged a finger at them and converted his ax back to lightning. With that, he sent a powerful bolt in Artan's direction. The boy tried to block it but ended up electrocuted when water and lightning collided.

Yeldi and Yoake watched in horror as their friends dropped like flies. "Stand back, he's mine." Yoake said and charged at him.

"No, Yoake don't!" Yeldi called, but it was too late.

She strung her bow and was about to fire when Saekrin disappeared and reappeared directly behind her. He grabbed her hair, making her stop running, and forced her to her knees. "Now, doesn't that feel more appropriate?" he said sadistically.

"Go to hell." she hissed back.

"There's no reason to be like that, my dear." He looked down at her back and clicked his tongue as if scolding a child. "It seems I don't give Yeldi enough credit, he did a wonderful job on your back, or is that from your little . . . accident when you were a child."

"How do you know about that?" she demanded.

"I have my sources." He yanked on her hair, pulling her to her feet, and, turning her around, pulled her body close to his own. He ran his finger along her cheek while she squirmed uncomfortably against his cold skin. "You know, you remind me so much of my dear love Sakura."

"Is that a compliment, or an attempt to creep me out?" Yoake retorted.

"Take it as you wish." he answered and ran his claw down her spine, digging it into the scar that had formed from the incision Yeldi had made only a few weeks prior.

Yeldi watch on in horror as Saekrin removed his hand from Yoake's back and reached into his pocket. The younger boy was paralyzed from fear; he knew what Saekrin was planning.

Another watch peeked out of his pocket and opened. Yoake watched a translucent snake slither out of it and shivered as it coiled itself around her. "I wish I had been there to see you on your knees in utter pain," he leaned in and whispered in her ear, "covered in delicious red blood, your face twisted as you writhed from the weapon on your back."

"That's not what happened," Yoake said, disturbed by his twisted fantasy.

"Oh? All the same, I would love to see you like that. Would you put on a nice show for me?"

"Like hell I would."

"You're right, so why don't I just resurface the memory for you."

The snake's eyes glowed red and Yoake felt flames shoot through her back like they had when she got the wound. She screamed in pain and writhed against Saekrin's iron grip. He dropped her and let her fall to the ground, where she continued her "performance".

"Yoake!" Yeldi cried and charged, suddenly filled with energy. He looked at Saekrin and no longer saw an oppressor, but an enemy that had to be defeated. Narrowed eyes bore into Saekrin's back as Yeldi focused on his target.

Saekrin turned around to see what Yeldi was doing. *"Well, it appears that I need to re-implant fear of me into his mind. He could become a real threat if he freed himself from the memories."* Saekrin thought to himself, then said out loud, "I think I have enough energy to switch one more time." With that, he switched his weapon to water and easily put out Yeldi's flames. A simple kick was all he needed to bring the boy to his knees. "You're still weak, just like your pathetic brother and your little weakling friends. I could have brought you to new levels of power you never could have dreamed of."

"You're wrong." Yeldi choked, earning another kick to the stomach. "All you did was beat me, it's your fault my watch rejected me."

"Hmm, true, but that was so you didn't become more powerful than me." Saekrin explained. "You have a lot of potential, boy, and all things considered, I'm willing to forgive your little treachery if you come back."

"I would rather die."

"Then so be it."

"Hey!" said a voice. The two turned to see Artan standing with the breaking waves behind him. "I wasn't done with you yet."

"I'll deal with you later." Saekrin growled at Yeldi, then directed his attention to the other boy. "I would love to play. I don't have enough energy to change, so water on water it is."

"You sure that's a good idea? No one beats me when it comes to my own element." Artan answered.

"We'll see."

With Saekrin distracted, Yeldi staggered to his feet and hobbled over to where Yoake lay. "Yoake, are you alright?" He knew she could hear him, because the snake wrapped around her wouldn't let her slip into unconsciousness so she could suffer every second of the torture. He was well aware of what it did; he had been its victim many times before.

Artan smirked and sent a spiral of water toward Saekrin, forcing the older creature to dodge, but not before the sharp wave slashed his leg, opening the old wound. He flinched but landed smoothly, blood dripping down his leg.

"Lucky shot," he snapped.

Artan laughed, "you keep telling yourself that, you bastard." Saekrin snarled at the boy and lunged forward, swinging his pole ax and sending a large wave back. Artan chuckled and spun his katana, creating a barrier and allowing the attack to run smoothly off the sides. He stuck out his tongue at Saekrin, a smirk spread across his face.

"You're slow, old man," he said and raised his sword. The blade began to glow a bright blue, water from the ocean beside them forming a shell around it. He lunged forward toward his enemy with every intention of cutting his arm off, but again Saekrin managed to move aside. With a growl, Artan spun on his heel and slashed Saekrin's shoulder, drawing blood.

He smiled in triumph but was quickly knocked away by the pole still clutched tightly in Saekrin's hand. Artan flew, spinning in the air to land on his feet and one hand. He stood and pressed his fingers into the wet ground, closing his eyes. Quickly, water rose from the sand and encircled his arm and soon his whole body, rising and swerving like liquid whips.

"My turn," Artan hissed. He leapt forward again, this time crashing into Saekrin and sending them both back, landing in the salty waves. He pressed his sword against the older man's throat.

"Today you die." he growled but Saekrin simply smirked back. Suddenly, Artan felt something twist around his leg and found the blade of Saekrin's ax glowing a dark blue, the water beside him forming a rope. Before he could react, he was thrown off, coming to the ground in a spray of seawater. Slowly, both fighters stood, panting, and rushed at each other. The clang of metal on metal echoed off the sand as they brought their weapons down, each trying to cut his opponent. Soon, they stood, weapons pressed against each other and pushing back and forth.

"Just give up." Artan said. He could see the way Saekrin was panting and knew he was tiring, "You've used up too much energy and I'm going to kill you. Accept it." Saekrin said nothing but the amused glint in his eye told Artan that the white haired man was silently mocking him. With a strangled snarl, he shoved Saekrin away, jumping a few yards back.

"I'm done with this!" he yelled, his whole body glowing, "I'm going to make you pay for what you did to my world, to this world, and especially what you did to my father! TSUNAMI TYPHOON!"

He held his blade high as the waves around him began to swirl and grow, spinning faster and faster until they looked like a watery tornado. The water climbed higher then separated to form a massive, rippling wave. Artan smirked as he held his attack at bay for a moment, savoring the slightly wide eyes of his adversary. Satisfied, he slammed his sword down, sending the wall of water hurtling toward Saekrin.

With nowhere to dodge, the man was caught in the wave and tossed around within, the water leaving deep cuts in his skin as the salt burned. The wave flew toward the shore, Artan directing its movements closer and closer to a large collection of rocks that jutted out of the water. A near sadistic smirk spread across his face as the wave broke, leaving Saekrin laying bruised, cut and bloody on one of the rocks.

Artan stalked forward with every intention of finishing the job, but before he could make it, Saekrin hissed and disappeared. The boy growled, angry at himself for letting his enemy, that murderer, escape, but turned to go help his fallen friends.

Once its master disappeared the snake wrapped around Yoake followed suit and released its captive. "How is she?" Artan asked as he ran to her and Yeldi.

"She'll live." Yeldi answered.

"What about you?"

"It's just a bruise, I'll be okay."

"That's good to hear." Artan patted Yeldi's shoulder and said, "I'll go help the others."

"Okay." was all Yeldi responded with, and went back to tending to the now unconscious girl in his arms. He wrapped his arms more tightly around her, tears of guilt creeping out of his eyes. "It's my fault." he sobbed. "It's all my fault."

"Dude, no it's not." Artan said.

"I'm the one who gave her that injury, so yes it is."

"What do you mean?"

"Saekrin can . . ." he trailed off for a moment, trying to gather his thoughts, "You know he can hypnotize people, right?" Artan nodded, "But he's different than the hypnotists on Earth. Yoake told me once that here, you have to be willing to be hypnotized for it to work, but with him it's different. He steals control, not just of your mind, but your body too. It's like he forces your soul out and makes the shell that was you a puppet, one where he controls the strings. That snake," Yeldi shuddered, painful memories suddenly being forced to the surface, "it's a physical manifestation of his power. He, he changes how it works. I'm the one who gave Yoake the burn!"

"I still don't understand." Artan said sadly.

"He took control of Yoake's body, just her body, and forced his way into the scars on her back. He made the nerves send signals of pain, lots of pain. It's like he shocked them and made her feel like the scars were fresh, like she was being burned all over again. He can control anyone he wants, any mind he wants, any body he wants." Artan gulped.

"So he could, you know, in theory, just stop someone's heart . . ." he said slowly.

"It's not a theory," Yeldi said. Artan could see tears poking at the corners of the boy's eyes, as if he had seen Saekrin do just that. "But he doesn't like it," Yeldi continued, "He likes to watch people die slowly."

"Sadistic bastard." he muttered.

"That's putting it mildly." Yeldi responded.

Suddenly Kyoki's voice rang out, weak and worn yet fiery and confident. "That's it, Saekrin, I'm gonna . . . Oh he's gone." Turning around, the two boys saw that she had jumped up, completely consciousness.

"Kyoki!" Yeldi called to her, "Go help Hana."

"Uh . . . okay." she answered, slightly confused. It was then she saw that her friends were unconscious and went to help the one that wasn't already being tended to.

"I'll get Tybalt." Artan said, making his way over to his old teacher.

"Good idea." Yeldi nodded.

Then Yoake began to stir. "What . . . Yeldi?"

"Yeah." said the boy who held her in his arms.

A weak smile crept across her face. "Thanks." was all she said before going back to sleep.

Yeldi looked at her sleeping face, and smiled. She looked so peaceful. Yeldi couldn't help but brush a finger down the outline of her face and bent down laying a small kiss on her forehead. "It's alright, Yoake, you can rest easy, I've got you."

"Uh, guys," Kyoki called, "I hate to interrupt whatever 'moment' you're having, but I think we should get the three who are down to Cyowan." Artan and Yeldi nodded and Artan went over to Tybalt's watch, leaning down beside it.

The black wolf flew slowly out and once again opened a portal. With a bit of effort, the conscious helped their fallen friends inside and soon landed inside the barracks.

"Tybalt!" Alia said, running over, "I told you not to fight! What were you thinking?" The man looked up at her through tired, half apologetic eyes, one beginning to swell. Alia grabbed hold of him and, with Artan's help, pulled him inside, saying something that sounded like "not letting you out of my sight again."

Yeldi and Kyoki followed them and soon their passengers were taken by a pair of nurses. They stood waiting for about two hours, unsure of what to do.

"What do you think?" Kyoki asked finally, "I mean, how is this going to play out?" Yeldi shrugged and sat down.

"He's hurt and angry. I c-can't see it ending well," he growled slightly at the end and Kyoki couldn't tell whether it was because he was upset at the prospect of an upcoming fight or because his old stutter had slipped back.

"Hey, you alright?" Kyoki asked, punching his arm.

"Ow! Yeah I'm fine." Yeldi said, rubbing the stop she punched.

"Oh. Good, for a second I thought you'd gone back to your nervous old self . . . you know the one that—"

"Yeah I got it."

"Oh . . . okay. Well I'm going to see if I can get in some training." Kyoki said.

"You're not going to see Yoake and Hana?"

"I know them, they'll be fine."

". . . okay, if you're sure."

Kyoki nodded to Yeldi and walked off. Even when she was out of sight her voice rang through the building, "So which one of you thinks you can take me on?"

Yeldi shook his head in exasperation, "She'll never learn."

❧

Yoake was running through an endless expanse of darkness. She didn't know why she was running, she just knew that she was. For some reason, she felt a strange presence chasing behind her. She wondered if it was why she was running, but didn't think so, because if it was, she would have turned to face it. Instead, it felt as though the presence was running with her, as though they were both running from something. She looked back to see if the presence had a shape, and, much to her surprise, it suddenly concentrated itself into Yeldi's figure. It seemed to be running with her, but it had an orange-ish glow to it, and didn't have feet, just a trail of light that streamed behind it. It was like Yeldi was a ghost. "Yoake?" he said.

"Yeldi?"

"Why are you running?"

"I-I don't know." she answered with a shaky voice. "I can't figure out why I'm running, I just am. It's like I'm running from something, but I don't know what?"

"I'm running away too." the ghost—Yeldi said, and held out its shimmering hand. "Run with me. I'll protect you, no matter what."

The light from Yeldi was warm and welcoming. Yoake reached out to take hold of the hand, but suddenly, a black smoke cut through Yeldi's shining figure. The apparition screamed in pain as the darkness drove itself through his body. Then the dark matter wrapped itself around Yoake, pulling her away from the disappearing light as it completely engulfed her body. Just before her vision darkened again she saw the last of the light vanish.

"NO!" Yoake shrieked, bolting up. Her breathing was heavy and quick, her forehead covered in sweat. Further inspection of her surroundings showed that she was in a Cyowan hospital room. There was no darkness, no smoke, and no ghost—Yeldi being torn apart. "A dream?" Yoake thought out loud, still panting. "What else could it have been?"

"Yoake!" then the real Yeldi came in. "I heard a scream and . . . are you okay?"

"Yeah I'm fine. It was just a bad dream."

"Oh okay." he said slowly, although there was hesitation in his voice. They sat in silence for a few minutes until-

"So . . . where is everyone?" Yoake asked.

"Hana woke up about fifteen minutes ago, Kyoki has been challenging anyone who will take her on, Artan is the current challenger, and Tybalt is still out." Yoake nodded.

"Umm . . ." Yeldi muttered, "if you're feeling up to it, I was wondering if you wanted to go outside and watch the fights." He looked at the ground, a blush dusting across his face.

Yoake smiled and pushed herself out of bed, stumbling slightly as she put weight on her feet for the first time in-, "How long was I out?" she asked as Yeldi caught her.

"About three days." the boy answered, helping her stand. Yoake looked at him incredulously for a moment then laughed.

"Well I guess it's no wonder I can't quite walk straight," she giggled, turning to the door. Yeldi followed her out to the field, but they had to stop every few minutes to let Yoake rest; her body was nowhere near fully recovered.

"Are you sure you're okay to do this?" Yeldi asked. The girl answered with a smile and a quick nod of determination, settling onto a low wooden bench about twelve yards from the battle. She looked over to see Kyoki and Artan fighting, each using training weapons, and Erasure calling out to them that if they "didn't learn to fight *without* magic, they'd never do any better *with* it."

Yeldi watched them for a few minutes then turned his face to the ground.

"Something wrong?" Yoake asked, seeing the almost forlorn look on his face. The boy jerked his head up and looked at her.

"N-no!" he said quickly, blushing.

Yoake just giggled, "Okay" and turned back to the match.

Yeldi continued to stare at the ground. He finally had the opportunity. It was just the two of them . . . along with the rest of the onlookers. Okay, maybe it wasn't the best place, but he had to do something soon, or he may not have the chance to. "H-hey, Yoake." he stuttered, his face even redder than before. Her head turned to look at him, making his heart beat even faster. He took a deep breath to calm himself down and forced himself to talk. "There's something I've been meaning to—"

"Heads up!" came Artan's voice as his practice katana came flying straight for their heads.

"I win." Kyoki declared proudly.

"As if I'll let you off that easy!" Artan challenged back, grabbing another practice sword, and the fight resumed.

"Maybe this isn't the best place to talk." Yoake said.

"Yeah," Yeldi said and slouched in disappointment, but then perked back up and said, "I know a perfect place."

"Okay." She took his outstretched hand and he lead her back into the temple.

"Where are we going?" Yoake asked as they continued to climb a long set of swirrling stairs within the massive structure. Yeldi opened his mouth, closed it again, then opened it.

"It's a, a surprise," he said, looking down. Yoake shrugged and followed him ever higher until they reached a plain door at the top of the staircase. Quickly, Yeldi pushed it open and led Yoake outside.

At first, all she could see was the blinding light of the sun, but soon her vision adjusted and the white marble of the temple came into view directly under her feet. She looked around and saw curving domes and spires.

"Where are we?" she breathed, already fairly sure, but she needed to hear it.

"The temple roof," Yeldi said, taking her hand and leading her to the side of a gently sloping dome, "Tybalt and I used to come up here sometimes to talk. He told me once that he and-," the boy paused for a moment, cringing slightly, "Saekrin used to come here when they were young to hide from Erasure."

Yoake laughed at bit, but it was forced, the air around them suddenly very tense. "It's pretty," she said, looking out at the training field and landscape beyond. She could see mountains, and a large waterfall in the distance, the topmost peaks surrounded by beautiful red clouds, "I can see why you like it here."

"Yeah I always came up here to think. Especially when . . ." His voice trailed off and he stared at the ground.

"When what?" Yoake asked comfortingly.

Yeldi sat down on the marble-like stone of the roof. "When our mom died."

"Oh." was all that Yoake could say. There was a moment of silence, then Yoake sat down next to him and said, "What was she like?"

Yeldi thought for a moment then looked up at her and said, "A lot like you."

Yoake recoiled a bit, a blush gracing her cheeks. "H—how so?"

"She was fierce, kind, smart," He smirked, "persistent. Remember when you talked to me that one time, when I had possessed Artan? You had that really determined look in your eye and I said you looked like 'her'."

"Yeah, were you talking about your mother?"

Yeldi nodded.

"Well thanks, I think." Yoake said, making Yeldi smile. "So you loved your mother?"

"Yeah, she always kept my hopes up that someday . . . nevermind."

"What?"

"Well, let's just say that my father greatly influenced who I am today."

"What do you mean?"

"My dad favored Tybalt over me."

"Oh." was all that Yoake could say.

"I guess it's sort of understandable. I mean Tybalt is so much older than me and my birth was kind of a surprise, so much so that he didn't think I was his son. I was also premature by two months so I was sick when I was born. He always called me the 'sickly bastard child' and similar names. Mom always said that he would someday accept me, but he never did."

"Yeldi, I'm so sorry." Yoake said. "Did Tybalt know about it?"

"Dad kept us separate, and Tybalt was already in training when I was born so he didn't really see much of me. It wasn't until I started

191

my own training that I finally got to have somewhat of a relationship with my brother. Even then, Saekrin . . ."

"Yeah, I get it."

"I never blamed Tybalt for how my dad treated me, he didn't know, and he was a great brother whenever we were together. So when Saekrin ordered me to kill him I—"

"Wait a second!" Yoake gasped, stopping him. "Saekrin ordered you to kill Tybalt?"

"Yeah. It was when we were robbing the temple. I wasn't originally completely on Saekrin's side—I was so confused and I just wanted to crawl in a corner and never come out—but, but I had been with him so long that," the boy paused for a moment, trying to calm himself down. With a shuddering breath he continued, "when he gave the order I was so terrified of what he would do to me if I disobeyed that I turned on my own brother and tried to kill him."

"What happened?"

"I almost did. I imagine Alia and Sakura healed him because the wound I made didn't kill him immediately, but it was enough to kill him slowly, like Saekrin wanted."

"Of course he did."

"From then on, I just did what I was told without question. What was the point of resisting anymore? I had tried to kill the one person who I felt close to; I had betrayed my entire world and, even worse, tried to kill my brother. I had practically sold my soul to him."

"So that's what you meant when you said that . . ."

"Yeah. But one time I went against him." he said quietly with a hint of pride in his voice. "I took three watches and sent them to your world."

"You sent the watches here?"

"Yes." he smiled a bit, pride shining in his eyes, "I was hoping that they would choose some powerful soldiers as their holders. I never imagined they would choose three high school girls."

"Your faith in us is amazing." Yoake retorted bluntly.

"Yoake, I'm glad they chose you three. I wouldn't have it any other way."

"Thank you." Yoake leaned over and kissed him on the cheek, making him blush furiously. "So you wanted to tell me something?"

"W-what?" Yeldi stuttered, stunned by her action.

"You brought me up here to tell me something."

"Huh? Oh right. Well, Yoake, I uh . . . I l-l-l"

Before he could finish the sentence, alarms started going off. "What's going—"

"Kids!" Tybalt's voice rang out from their watches. "Get to the clinic. We have an emergency!" The two glanced at each other and immediately sped down to see what was going on.

"What is it?" Yoake asked as she and Yeldi reached the hospital rooms. Kyoki and Hana greeted them along with Artan who looked frazzled.

"Alkest came in looking like someone had torn him apart," the boy said, "he was running and bleeding and—"

"Come in here," Tybalt stuck his head out from inside the nearest room and instantly the children walked inside.

The room was as white as all the others in the hospital, but they paid no attention to it, instead focusing on the being lying on the bed. He was bloody and cut in several places, blood dripping down his arms, legs, and face. His left arm stuck out at an odd angle along with his right foot. The armor on his body was dented, his tunic torn, and whole clumps of hair were gone. From the remains, it looked as though someone had forcibly ripped them out. Alkest tried to push himself up, but Alia gently eased him down again as Sakura continued to heal him. Erasure stood off to the side, a dark look spread across his face.

"I have to go back!" Alkest said, "I have to fight!"

"Lie still," she said, "You're in no condition to get up." Sadly, the man ignored her and tried again.

"Alkest, sit down," Tybalt said, his voice gentle yet incredibly firm. With a sigh, he obeyed and slowly stopped his struggles.

"What's going on?" Kyoki asked, stunned.

"Tell them what you said when you came in." Tybalt said. The children looked over at Alkest and waited anxiously for an explanation.

"He's back," the man coughed, "Saekrin has come back to Cyowan."

"WHAT?" they yelled, shocked.

"How? When?" Hana asked frantically, "What happened?"

"I," Alkest paused, wincing as Sakura eased one of his ribs back into place, "I was on patrol, watching the borders, and suddenly there was this-ow! watch it!" he growled in pain as another bone was fixed. After a few deep breaths, he continued. "There was a huge cloud of smoke . . .

"What the hell?" Alkest thought. The smoke, more like a dust cloud, was getting closer and some men had gone out to find its source but they hadn't returned. Suddenly, a chorus of screams rose into the air, a terrible sound, like the cries of the damned. Slowly, slowly, a figure came into view, the wind whipping its long robes around it as it walked.

"Who's there?" Alkest growled, raising his weapon, "Identify yourself." The figure began to chuckle darkly.

"Is that any way to greet an old comrade?" The dust was suddenly, harshly whipped away to reveal the pale, smirking face of Saekrin.

"What are you doing here?" Alkest snarled. Saekrin sighed and looked up at the sky, obviously distracted by something.

"Yes, yes . . ." the white haired man muttered, "I heard you the first time. I suppose," his eyes glanced at Alkest for a moment then turned back to the clouds, "No, no, it's best to leave it alone for now, but—no—I see . . . hmm."

To say the guard was confused would have been an understatement, perplexed would also. He was downright stunned. For a moment, he said nothing but then growled.

"What the hell do you—" he was suddenly cut off by a kick to his chest that sent him to the ground. He tried to stand but Saekrin had his foot pressed against his captive's chest, pushing down on his ribcage.

"It's rude to interrupt people when they're talking . . ." Saekrin mused, like he was only half talking to Alkest.

"Get out of here!" Alkest snarled. Saekrin's attention abruptly changed, switching to the pinned soldier.

"What did I just say?" he sighed. He leaned down and slowly drew his claw along Alkest's jaw, leaving a jagged, bloody cut, "I suppose I'll have to teach you some manners." he said. Suddenly, he grabbed Alkest by the collar and threw him against the wall. Looking up at the sky again, he whispered, "Welcome home."

"After that, he started attacking me—by the gods he's gotten so much more powerful-and I couldn't do anything!" Alkest pounded his fist into the bed below him, growling in frustration. "It was a few minutes after he started attacking me, other guards showed up but he," Alkest paused for a moment, "he killed them and, after he was satisfied with the amount of blood he'd shed, he grabbed me and told me to tell you all he is waiting for you. That sadistic *monster*."

A noise from the side of the room drew the groups attention and before they could say anything, Erasure started toward the door, muttering something that sounded like "I have to stop my pupil."

"Erasure wait!" Tybalt exclaimed, "we have to—" He was abruptly interrupted by a loud cough. They all turned back to see Alkest doubled over, clutching his stomach in pain. Blood dripped from his mouth along with a sickly white foam. He coughed again, sending a pink spray onto the bed.

"Can," was all he managed to say before dry heaving and Sakura immediately fetched a trash can. As soon as it was in his hands, Alkest vomited into it. He panted heavily but lay down again.

"Are you okay?" Kyoki asked, moving closer, but Alia stopped her.

"You girls should be getting ready for the fight. Sakura and I will take care of him, right, Sakura?" Alia said, but the other woman was already gone.

"Sakura!" Tybalt yelled, running after his wife, followed by the children. "Sakura where are you going?" The woman stopped abruptly but didn't turn around.

"Where do you think I'm going?" she said, "I have to fight. I can't just sit by anymore and watch you get hurt. I-I have to do something!" Tybalt stepped forward and reached for her but she moved away from him.

"Don't try to stop me," she continued, "It's my fault this happened and I have to make it right."

Snarling, Tybalt lashed out and pulled her close to himself, his hand clutching her wrist in an iron grip, "Don't you ever say that again," he growled, not angry at her but her words, "Whatever has happened to him was not your fault, it was not Erasure's fault, it was no one's fault but his own and I can't stand to see the people I love beat themselves up over this." Sakura opened her mouth to protest but Tybalt stopped her, "No," he said, "listen to me. I want to stop him, I want to see him punished for what he has done, even if he is my friend, and, if possible, I want to bring him back to the man he was, but I don't know if it's even possible anymore. Sakura, he is not the boy you saw at the party anymore. He is a deranged, sadistic, power hungry madman who will have no qualms about killing and using and abusing anyone, anyone he can, to get what he wants. If you go fight him, what do you expect to happen?"

Sakura looked slightly taken aback at the question. "I—" she stammered, "I don't, I don't know. I just—"

"Think about what would happen if you fought him." Tybalt said.

"But I can't just sit here!" Sakura yelled back, "I have to protect Mineh and Kumi and, and everyone!"

"You haven't actively fought in years," Tybalt countered, trying desperately to keep his voice calm and level, "You haven't seen what he can do. He's so much stronger than when he was here and he's also much, much more irrational and unstable. You studied the watches, you were a historian and a weaponologist before you joined the army; you should know what collecting does to a person's brain! He will kill you, if you try to fight and he'll do it in the most painful, creative way he can think of! The best way for you to protect Mineh is to stay here! Keep her safe here! I know you want to fight; to right the wrongs you think you committed, but I can't let you go out there!"

"And what about you?" Sakura snapped back, "You're still injured. You're in no condition to go out there either. Do you think I'm going to watch you walk out of here again, wondering if this time he's going to decide he's bored and kill you?! No! Everytime you leave, everytime you go out, I don't know if you're going to come home again! I-I just can't do it anymore!" She broke down into tears, collapsing in her husband's arms.

"Sakura," he said, stroking her hair gently, "I understand your feelings, believe me I do, but the best way for you to help, to protect Mineh and our baby, is to stay here. I know he will try to hurt the baby again if you go. Please stay here with Alia. Besides," he tilted her face up to look into her eyes, "You're a healer and there *will* be casualties. We need you here to help them."

Sakura stared at her husband, who was smiling at her comfortingly, and nodded. "Alright," she said, "I understand." then her eyes hardened, "You and the kids had better come back to me or I swear I will march right into Tarel and drag you back here myself, got it?"

Tybalt held up his hands in surrender, laughing nervously at the determined fire in his wife's eyes. "I understand," he said. As he and Sakura walked back inside, they passed the two boys and three very confused girls.

"What did Sakura mean by 'Tarel'?" Kyoki asked. Hana shrugged. "Maybe it's like their version of Hell." she suggested.

"Let's go talk to Alia," Yoake said, "I bet she'd know and besides, we should probably get to know more about the culture here since we're probably going to be staying a while." The other two nodded in agreement and they made their way back to Alkest's room in search of the high priestess.

"She," Alkest coughed for a few seconds before continuing, "she left a few minutes ago, said something about going to pray." Yoake thanked him and led Kyoki and Hana back toward the temple.

Once they arrived, they could see Alia at the front of the marble room, on her knees, and waited for her to stand.

"Is something wrong, girls?" she asked, turning to face them.

"No," Hana replied, "we were just curious about something we heard."

"What was it?" the priestess asked, motioning for them to have a seat on a set of steps in a small alcove at the side of the room.

"Sakura said that if Tybalt didn't come back from this fight, she would go into 'Tarel' and drag him back," Yoake said, "What did she mean?"

Alia sighed and looked around the room, pausing to gaze at each statue, before answering, "Tarel," she said, "is somewhat similar to your world's version of Hell, only we do not believe that only the wicked enter. It is a place for all the deceased." She stood, beckoning them to follow her. They walked over to one of the statues. It showed a man who looked about twenty three or twenty five years old, his hair falling in gentle whisps that brushed against his shoulders and ghosted over his eyes. In his hand, he held a long staff with short spikes protruding from either side and a large, double blade topping it, almost like a symmetrical scythe. Around him, skull-like clouds floated, carved from the marble. A few bodies lay near him, looking up, almost as if they were begging for his attention. The clothes carved on his body were almost like a combination of armor and victorian era style: a patterned button-up vest, cravat, and long pants. Plate armor rested on his shoulders with small tassles hanging in the front and a two toothed skull dipping over each arm. Chains poured from their mouths, eyes seeming to watch all. A tunic fell just past his waist where two criss-crossing belts sat. Shin guards adorned his legs, covering his feet as well. As a finishing touch, a long coat hung down, brushing just past his knees. His carved eyes stared down at the girls with apathy, disdain, bitterness, and the smallest traces of sadness. He looked very tired and incredibly powerful.

"This," Sakura said, after bowing to the statue, "is Oares, the lord of the dead. He rules over Tarel and comes to collect the souls of those who have died."

"He looks like he doesn't care anymore." Kyoki said, earning a jab in the ribs from Hana.

"Don't be disrespectful," she hissed, glancing to Alia who was watching the statue solemnly, as if contemplating Kyoki's words.

"He is . . . very sad," she said slowly. She turned to face the girls who had looks of confusion on their faces, "my watch," she explained, "the first watch, given to the first high priest by the gods, allowed me to communicate with them. Lord Oares is lonely and constantly surrounded by the dead. He does not interact with the other gods often, they shun him because he brings misfortune. Sadly, many here do not give him the reverence he deserves. They fear him and desperately try to avoid him. He has grown bitter toward other living creatures and will only come if he is needed. I have spoken with him only a few times but I can see the loneliness in his heart. His sister is the only deity who voluntarily comes close to him and he has told her repeatedly of his hatred for her. She is deeply troubled by this and wishes her brother would open his frozen heart."

"Sister?" Yoake asked. Alia nodded and led them over to the other side of the temple, stopping in front of a female statue.

"Lord Oares wished for his likeness to be as far from his sister's as possible." Alia explained. The girls looked up to see a young girl smiling happily back at them. She wore a long, flowing dress with a woven belt wrapping around her waist and appeared to be dancing, a flute slung at her hip. Her bright eyes were full of joy and even the stone seemed to sparkle with it. In her arms, she held a newborn baby, who looked as if it was giggling happily as it stared up at her.

The goddess's hair flowed out behind her in one long wave, floating along, with beads and ribbons woven in.

Kyoki looked back at the previous statue, "These two are related?" she asked.

Alia nodded, "This," she said, "is Lady Phana, goddess of life, and yes she is the sister of Lord Oares. She is a kind, gentle soul who enjoys bringing smiles to people's faces. However, her heart aches for her brother. They are twins, but she is older, another source of the strain on their relationship."

"Do you talk to her a lot?" Hana asked. Alia nodded.

"Yes, before Saekrin stole my watch, Lady Phana and I had many conversations together. She is very excited about the arrival of Tybalt and Sakura's baby." The priestess smiled and then turned, leading the girls out of the temple and pointing to other statues as they went.

"This," she pointed to a statue of a mature woman in a long, slitted, greecian dress with medium length hair and caring eyes, "is Lady Aimiri, the goddess of family. She is the younger sister of Lord Oares and Lady Phana."

"She looks older." Yoake said, confused.

"The gods take whatever form pleases them most," the priestess said, smiling and leading them on, "Over here are the elemental siblings: Lord Neyus, the god of the ground," she nodded toward an eighteen year old looking young man wearing a long overcoat, banded sandels, loose belt, and tunic, sitting atop a large rock. He sported short, choppy hair and was gazing lovingly at a rose-like flower that he held gently in his hand.

"He's cute," Kyoki giggled and Hana rolled her eyes.

"Gods are not 'cute'," she said flatly, her eyes scanning the other statues before resting on the one beside Neyus, "except him." She moved to stand in front of a statue of a man in his early twenties with sweeping hair that fell to his shoulder blades. His eyes were sharp but kind, an untamed wildness about them. He was shirtless, showing off a toned chest, with a domed shoulder guard on his left. An intricate, thick belt hung low on his strong hips, holding up a pair of loose pants. He wore no shoes, instead his feet brushed against what looked like coral as he leaned casually against a large wave.

"That is Lord Keidon, god of the sea and the middle of the three element siblings. Lord Neyus is the youngest. Don't worry," Alia said, "Lord Keidon is rather popular with the women." Hana blushed.

"Who is this?" Yoake asked, pointing to the third statue in the line, just to the left of Keidon. It depicted a young girl, fourteen at the most, sitting on a soft looking cloud, looking down at them with a gentle gaze. She wore nothing but a loose, billowing, short, long sleeve dress. Her hair, much like Phana's, had ribbons woven in, but no beads.

"This is Lady Nuos, goddess of the sky. She is the eldest of the three. A gentle girl, until she gets angry, then the storms arise." Alia smiled, "All three siblings are generally on good terms with each other, although Lord Neyus and Lord Keidon sometimes fight for territory. They, like the other gods, tend to shy away from Lord Oares. Lady Nuos and Lady Phana are good friends and often came to speak to me." The priestess sighed, "However, I always had to lock the doors when Lords Neyus and Keidon arrived. Many of our women are a bit smitten with them. Sadly, this is just another point that further irritates Lord Oares."

"He sounds like one big, bitter inferiority complex," Kyoki said and this time it was Yoake who elbowed her. Alia sighed.

"He has heard such comments, and much worse, before, mostly from Lord Keidon. Those two don't mix well. They get into arguments often, most of which cause great tsunamis and vast numbers of dead sea creatures. The most common insults seem to be along the lines of 'water-logged flounder' and 'necrophiliac killer'."

"Ouch," Kyoki said, wincing slightly.

"Which one?" Yoake asked.

"Necrophiliac."

"What's that?"

Kyoki sighed; Yoake's innocence was one of the things she loved about the girl, "A necrophiliac is someone who is sexually attracted to corpses." Yoake looked stunned for a moment then started to twitch slightly.

"Hey . . ." Hana said, trying very hard to change the subject. She looked down to the far end of the temple where Alia had been praying when they had walked in. On the raised dais stood two statues. The first was an elderly, yet strong looking man wearing a long toga-like robe with a pocket watch resting in his hand. Beside him stood a woman of about the same age wearing a similar outfit, her long hair tied at the end in a very loose, low ponytail. Both were smiling, their eyes seeming to watch all the other statues in the room. "Who are they?"

"Lord Crorn and Lady Shiuna, the god of time and lady of fate. They are the original two deities and the parents of the others. It was them specifically who gave the first priest his watch." The girls looked up at the couple, feeling a sense of awe and wonder growing inside them.

"Girls," Alia called from the door, "we should go back to the barracks and prepare for the coming fight." With a quick nod and one last look around the temple, they followed the high priestess out.

❧❦❧

As soon as they left, a low rumble sounded through the temple.

"So what do you think of them?" Neyus asked, suddenly appearing beside his statue. He brushed a few strands of brown hair behind his ear as he looked around the room, waiting for an answer.

"I like 'em!" Neyus glanced over to see Nuos sitting beside her sculpture, kicking her feet back and forth, "I think they're great."

"The rational one seems to like me," Keidon said. He ran a hand through dark blue hair and settled into a seated position in front of his likeness, smirking. "What'd you think, Phana?"

The goddess shifted slightly but smiled. "I find them interesting and I very much hope they will be the ones to end this madness."

"As long as they don't destroy my territory too much," Neyus said, shrugging.

"You could use less!" Keidon called with a smirk.

"Say that again!" Neyus snarled, standing.

"I said you should have less rubble," Keidon answered, "It's taking up too much space and on top of that it's ugly."

"And you think that water no one can drink is better?" the ground lord hissed, "Sure, let's all drown because Keidon got selfish! And—"

"Do you ever just shut up?" muttered a rough, low voice from across the temple. The group turned to see Oares standing beside the door and instantly tensed.

"Hi . . ." Nuos greeted nervously.

"Good bye," Neyus said and disappeared.

"Brother!" Phana yelled happily, running toward the raven haired man. She wrapped her arms around him, hugging tightly.

"Let go," Oares said flatly, crimson eyes staring down at his sister. Reluctantly, Phana released him.

"Do you like the girls?" she asked, trying to ease the tension. She could feel the glare Keidon was sending over and Nuos shaking slightly.

"I don't care," Oares said, moving away from her to stand against the wall farthest from the others, "All this battle means is more work for me."

"Believe me," Keidon said, smirking, "no one wants you around so just go play with that cult of yours and leave." Oares glanced over at his younger brother blankly and sighed.

"First of all," he said, his voice a flat, bored monotone, "respect your elders, you wet upstart kid, second, that cult has nothing to do with me. They just use me as an excuse to go after others, and third, I have much more to do with what is to come then you. So why don't you just shut your mouth and go back to tending to your seaweed garden."

Keidon growled and his hand began to glow blue, a nebulus of energy and water swirling together. Still expressionless, Oares raised his staff, the blade slowly encasing itself in black clouds.

"Are you sure you want to take me on?" he asked, "No doubt you remember what happened last time." Oares flicked his wrist and sent a blast of dark light straight toward his brother. Keidon barely had time to block before the light shifted, pinning him like a chain against his statue. With a growl, he shot a jet of water back toward the death god, but it was blocked.

"Oares! Stop!" Phana yelled, grabbing onto her twin's arm. Nuos ran to Keidon and placed her hands on his, stopping his next attack.

Oares snorted, but lowered his weapon. "Weak flounder," he hissed.

"Necrophiliac!" Keidon yelled and suddenly Oares turned.

"What?" he snarled, his voice deathly calm.

Keidon smirked. "Necrophiliac. We all know you are. That's why you stay down in that dark pit of yours, isn't it? Are they fun? Do they make you scream in pleasure? Does it make you hard just thinking about all that rotting flesh and—"

"ENOUGH!" boomed a voice from the front of the temple. The gods turned to face Crorn glaring at them, "That's enough children. These girls are here to help this world and we will help them as well. You all will have to get along. Is that clear?" The younger deities nodded and with a short glare at Keidon, Oares disappeared.

"The rest of you should depart as well," Shiuana said, standing beside her husband, "We will watch over them." They nodded and soon the temple was left empty and quiet.

***

Yoake sat in Alkest's room with the other girls. The guard was barely alive, just hanging onto the thinnest thread of life. Beside his bed was a bucket that was full with the pink foam he had coughed up. The silence in the room was deafening, but Kyoki'd had enough. "I wonder what Saekrin did to him to make him so sick." she mused, partially trying to make conversation and partially out of true curiosity.

"I don't know." Sakura said. "But I can't take it out of his body. There's no hope of saving him."

The news silenced everyone again, until Yeldi spoke up, "I know." Everyone looked at him in curiously. "Saekrin collects poisons and venom from any source he can, and he coats his weapons with it, to make them lethal to anyone they touch."

"So why didn't it kill Tybalt?" Yoake asked.

Yeldi just shrugged. "Maybe it's because I seared the wound closed and that burned the venom."

"It seems likely." Sakura pondered. "So you think that it's the venom that's killing Alkest?" Yeldi nodded.

"Then you should know how to stop it," Artan said, glaring at Yeldi, "You saw the bastard collect the stuff, you should know how to make the antidote." Yeldi shook his head.

"He, he never taught me how to make it stop," he stammered, looking down, disappointed in himself for not being a help to them, "He just made me drink it."

"What?" Yoake asked, stunned, "He poisoned you!"

"It was," he began, "It was just a little bit. He didn't want me to die, just to feel pain. I was his, to use an Earth expression, guinea pig."

Artan sighed, "Anything else?" Yeldi thought for a moment then nodded slowly.

"He drank the poisons sometimes too," he said, "He wanted to make himself venomous and immune to them."

"I don't think that's how it works," Hana commented, "I mean, sure, he'd get immune, but I doubt he's actually poisonous."

"But why would he do it if it doesn't work?" Kyoki asked, confused.

"Delusional probably," Hana said shrugging, "When did he start?"

"Umm . . . a few weeks before he started having arguments with himself." Yeldi answered, "He had been drinking the poisons before that, but that's when he started thinking he could make himself poisonous."

"Great," Artan groaned, rolling his eyes, "He's having hallucinations and he's delusional. Wonderful."

"He's even crazier than we thought . . ." Sakura said, half to herself, half to the kids. Just then Tybalt stuck his head in the room.

"Girls," he said, "boys, we need to go. Erasure hasn't come back yet and we can't communicate with him. We should go. Come on." The children nodded and, despite Sakura's worried look, followed Tybalt toward the battlefield.

❧

"Saekrin." Erasure said, glaring at his smirking former student, "This ends now." The younger creature just laughed, the deranged sound grating against his teacher's ears.

"Really?" he asked, twirling his pole ax between his fingers, "Because I was hoping to drag this out a bit. It's been *so* long since I had a good bout with you." Erasure growled and tightened his grip on his large longsword. He could tell something was very wrong with his ex-student. Saekrin was disheveled, so much so that all of it couldn't have come from a fight. He had always been put together and on top of everything. Now, he looked like he'd just rolled out of bed. His hair was tied back as usual, but loose with some strands falling in front of his shoulders and still others sticking up at odd angles. Dark circles lined his eyes and Erasure noticed that his left hand kept twitching erratically. The man's eyes held a crazed look that hadn't been there before. Erasure knew what was happening to him; the madness was getting worse.

"Fun as it is to have you staring at me," Saekrin chuckled, a sound that suddenly turned to a strange high pitched giggle, "I really do have things to take care of . . . so go away." Erasure raised and eyebrow. Hadn't he just said he wanted to "drag this out"?

Before he could respond, Erasure saw a blast of fire coming toward him. He jumped out of the way, but not before the flames grazed his arm. With a soft thump, he landed, shifting slightly. Quickly, he looked up just in time so see Saekrin coming after him, ax up and ready to cleave his former teacher in half. Erasure raised his sword to block.

A loud clang echoed in the air as the weapons met. Erasure stared at the deranged creature before him, pushing with every ounce of strength he had against the burning pole.

"Have you been sleeping?" he asked before he could stop himself; Saekrin had been his student and some part of Erasure still cared for him.

Saekrin laughed, "Of course, mother. Two, three hours at most. It's not like I need more." He shoved his ax against Erasure's sword, suddenly changing it to lightning. Erasure screamed in pain as electricity surged through him. Saekrin smirked and swung his foot around, sending the older creature flying.

Erasure landed hard, feeling his spine cry out in protest. He was getting too old for this. Slowly, he stood and readied himself. There was no way he was going to let Saekrin get any closer to Sakura and Mineh.

"You want more?" Saekrin asked. Suddenly, he growled and started running his fingers through his hair roughly, completely oblivious to the cuts his claws were making. "Yes, yes, I'm working on it. Leave me alone. I know that! He has to go—but—I said I now-know-know that. Just go away! Later, later . . ." Slowly, he seemed to calm down and looked back toward Erasure. A smirk spread across his face that quickly turned into a sadistic, insane grin. "Now where were we?"

"Saekrin, listen to yourself." the older man said calmly. "I wish you would let us help you."

"I don't need your help—but maybe—shut up! I don't need you, old man!" Saekrin growled.

"I think you do."

"You never helped me! All you did was put me through pointless drills that had nothing to do with fighting. And now that I am more powerful I have surpassed you!" Saekrin raised his weapon and struck Erasure on the side of the head before the old man could react. He was knocked to the ground a few feet away. Before Erasure could get back to his feet, Saekrin pressed a foot to his chest, pinning him to the ground. Erasure tried to push him off but Saekrin just looked at him with a sadistic grin on his face. The old man closed his eyes as his former student raised his weapon and said, "Good bye, master"

Just as Saekrin brought his weapon down, Tybalt ran over, teens in tow. The dusty-blond haired man's eyes widened as Saekrin's ax dug itself deep into Erasure's chest.

Kyoki, it seemed, was the most shocked. Her teacher was dead, and she suddenly felt tears forming in the corner of her eyes. "No!" she screamed and charged at the snake-man. "You bastard!" She transformed in mid-charge, and began blindly attacking Saekrin with kicks, punches, and slashes from her scythe.

"You know," Saekrin said as he easily dodged each and every attempted blow, "I feel like we've done this before. I believe there is a term for it on Earth. What's it called?"

"I. DON'T. GIVE. A. FREAKING. DAMN!" Kyoki shrieked. "I'M GOING TO KILL YOU!"

"I would love to see you try." Saekrin chuckled, grabbing onto the scythe in mid swing and yanking it out of her hands, but that didn't deter her. She still kept punching and kicking. He grabbed both her fists and forced her to her knees. "Now where is all that tough talk? You're weak."

"Kyoki!" Yoake and Hana cried as Saekrin pushed her down and electrocuted her helpless form.

"Well that was fun . . ." Saekrin muttered to himself, smirking. Yoake just stared at her unconscious friend in horror. She looked to Hana, who nodded, and seconds later all four teens stood transformed.

"You twisted bastard," Artan growled. Saekrin just shrugged at the insult and turned to Tybalt.

"Shouldn't you be protecting your wife?" he asked mockingly, "I mean, it's not like you're very useful here." With a strange, demented giggle, he held up Tybalt's watch.

"Where the hell did you get that?" the wounded man yelled angrily.

"Took it," Saekrin replied flatly, as if the answer was obvious. The teens stared at Tybalt who looked like he was about to strangle his former friend with his bare hands.

"Tybalt," Hana said, her tone soft but rational and forceful, "I don't want to have to say this, but he's right. Go back and help take care of the wounded at the hospital. We can handle this." For a moment, it looked as though Tybalt was going to ignore her, but with a sigh that turned to a snarl of frustration, he nodded and started for the hospital.

Saekrin watched him go, debating whether or not to go after him, but decided against it. There were people right in front of him to fight. "Shall we have some fun?" he asked.

"Fun?" Yoake snapped, "Fun? Is this some kind of game to you? Are the lives of the people you've killed and broken just toys?" She could feel tears stinging her eyes as she yelled, thinking of Kyok, Kumi, Sakura, and Artan's father, but most of all Yeldi. He had suffered the most by this *monster's* hands. "Well?"

Saekrin shrugged, "It's not like I have anything better to do." he said, chuckling darkly at the pained, enraged look in Yoake's eyes. Suddenly, a large spiral of thorned vines and boiling water slammed into him, sending him flying backward, a loud cry of "SCALDING THORN," following. He landed with a loud crash, a large cloud of dust flying into the air.

"Pay attention, jackass," Artan laughed. Hana stood beside him, daggers up and ready. Slowly, Saekrin stood, humming a strange tune. They could see burns and cuts covering his body, dripping blood.

"Well that was fun," he said, smiling. It would have been a warm expression if not for the deranged glint in his eyes, "but I think now it's my turn."

Before Artan could react, a sheet of ice crashed into him, instantly freezing his sword and sending him barreling straight into Hana. Both landed in a heap about six yards away, their arms and legs trapped in thick blocks of ice.

"Hang on!" Yeldi called, running over, his whip ablaze with dancing flames. He settled next to the two, forcing the fire to melt the ice as quickly as possible, but it was taking too long. His eyes flicked back and forth over the ice pieces and he tried to push as much energy as he could into the fire.

Suddenly, a scream drew his attention. Quickly, he turned as saw Saekrin fighting against Yoake, the girl losing more and more ground with every blow. Pole ax crashed into bow again and again and Yeldi could see tiny drops of liquid dripping off the end of the ax. With a smirk, Saekrin spun the pole down, knocking Yoake's legs out from under her. The pole crackled with dark energy, black clouds swirling around it as he stood over her.

"You've been a very difficult creature to kill," Saekrin said, smirking, "but now I think it is time for you to die." He raised his ax and she closed her eyes, waiting for the blow she knew was coming, but it never did.

Slowly, she opened her eyes to see Yeldi standing in front of her, falling as blood rushed out of a large gash in his throat. "Yeldi . . ." It took her a moment to realize what had happened, until Yeldi collapsed into her arms. She looked down at his bloody form and gasped in horror at what had happened. "YELDI!" Her scream echoed in her ears and she grabbed her bow, stringing it with a deep red arrow. Growling, she launched it toward Saekrin. It slammed into his chest and sent him flying. For a moment, it looked as though he was going to counter, but as he tried to stand, he found that his body was too broken, several bones jutting out at odd angles and the cuts had released to much blood. As he disappeared, Yoake ran over to Yeldi, pulling him up and running back toward the hospital.

❦

"How is he?" Yoake asked frantically, grabbing onto Sakura's sleeve as she exited Yeldi's room. The others were sleeping in separate rooms and Tybalt had nearly run out of the hospital when Yoake had brought his baby brother back. Sakura had been forced to sedate him, saying that he would be of no use if he tried to fight in a blind rage. With a sigh, he had agreed and since then had been by Yeldi's side.

"He has slipped into a coma," Sakura answered, "I was able heal the gash in his neck but his blood shows that whatever cut him was covered in venom. Actually, I'm shocked he's still alive."

"It's probably because Saekrin force fed him poison," Yoake mused sadly, "he's probably got some immunity to it." Sakura nodded slowly.

There was a tense silence in the room. Yoake sat down next to him and took hold of his limp hand, tears beginning to trickle out of her eyes. "Don't die, please." she sobbed. "Yeldi, please, I beg of you, come back to me!"

Her heart nearly skipped a beat when his fingers gently wrapped around her hand. "Y-Yoake?" he breathed weakly.

"Easy, don't strain yourself." she said.

"Yoake," he muttered quietly.

"What is it?" she asked frantically, leaning closer so she could hear him, but he didn't say anything else. As he slowly leaned up and lightly kissed her lips, Yoake felt her heart almost stop. "Yeldi . . ." she said when he laid back down.

"I . . . love . . . you."

Yoake's body shook. "Yeldi," she said, the tears coming down in rivers on her cheeks, "I love you too, I do. Yeldi, you can't leave me!"

"Yoake?" said a tiny voice. She and Sakura looked at the door to see Mineh standing in the threshold. "What kind of love is it?"

"Mineh," Sakura said, grabbing the small girl's attention, and lead her out of the room so Yoake didn't have to hear. "It is love that daddy and I feel, and . . ." She almost didn't want to voice her thought, "the love that Saekrin felt for me."

"The scary man that hurts people?"

"It was love that made him scary." her mother explained. "He loved me but I loved—love—daddy, so he hurts people because he was jealous."

"So is love bad?"

"No, not at all. Love is wonderful, it's the people who are bad."

"Was Uncle Yeldi bad?"

"No, he was just confused."

"And he's gone?"

"He will be soon."

Mineh's eyes filled with tears at the thought. "But he can't! He loves Yoake like daddy loves you!"

"I know."

"Why is he gone?"

"Because the scary man hurt him. Lord Oares will arrive soon to take him."

"No!" Mineh yelled. "He won't, I'll help Uncle Yeldi."

"Mineh, there's nothing we can do." Sakura tried to protest, but the little girl was already running down the hall.

When she reached the room, Yoake had already left, at her friends' urging, to get some rest before the next battle. Mineh pulled a chair up to the side of the bed and crawled onto it. She resorted to staying there until Oares showed up.

❧

Artan found Hana in her room. "Hey." he said.

"Hey." was all she responded with.

"You got a moment?"

"No." Hana sat down on her bed, motioning for him to do the same.

Artan sat next to her and began, "So this next battle will probably be the last one."

"Probably."

"And I started to think that we've been pretty lucky up until now and one of us may not survive."

"Artan, don't say—" she started, but he put a finger on her lips to stop her.

"Let me finish. I was planning on saying this after this was all over but what happened with Yoake and Yeldi got me thinking that I may not get the chance to." He turned his body to face her and took her hands. "Hana, I love you."

Hana stared at him in shock, surprise, and happiness. She tackled him in a hug and said, "I love you too."

Artan wrapped his arms around her delicate frame and said the only thing he could think of, "I'm glad." He pulled back and, after the two engaged in a light, chaste kiss, continued, "We should go get ready." With a quick nod, Hana stood up and started out the room, her new love following at her heels.

In her room, Kyoki stood beside the window, looking out over the barracks. She could see the temple off to the east and sighed, pushing herself up. Saekrin had caused so much pain. She remembered hearing about him all those months ago and thinking about how much she wanted to beat him, but it had been an impersonal anger, like the kind people feel when they hear of an atrocity in another country, it was removed from her. She shook her head, that feeling had left long ago. Now, she had seen first hand what he could do.

"I guess this is going to be it," she muttered, her hand unconsciously brushing the scar Saekrin had carved into her. She went to her bed and picked up her scythe. It felt light in her hands as she twirled it, swinging it a bit for practice, and she couldn't help but think of her teacher. "*Late* teacher," she reminded herself with a sigh, setting the weapon down.

She had liked Erasure a lot, much more than any of her school teachers. In class, it had always felt as though they were just repeating whatever the book said, but Erasure had been different. He had been in battles, had seen generations of soldiers come and go, had even trained their enemy. But she never held that against him.

"It's not like he could have known what would happen," she mused, laying back onto the bed. She shifted slightly as the mattress pressed against the scars, making her wince in pain. What had she been thinking? How could she have ever trusted him? Saekrin had tortured Yeldi for years, why had she expected him to be any different with her? He had kidnapped Kumi and used her as a hostage and punching bag. He was just a monster. But she had helped him . . . did that make her a monster too? She hadn't done a thing when he had tortured Kumi, not a damn thing.

"Useless," she growled, smacking herself in the shoulder. Glaring at the ceiling, she saw Yeldi fighting alongside them, the scars in his mind and on his body burning him every time he locked eyes with his former master. She saw Kumi chained to the wall, bleeding and crying, and slowly she sat up, "Never again," she said, standing and grabbing her scythe, "I'm never going to be useless again." With a determined fire burning in her eyes, she marched out of her room in search of her friends.

Yoake stood on the temple roof. She was in full armor, a small upgrade provided by the amory. It consisted of her normal transformation attire, with the addition of, chainmail-like leggings and sleeves, a neck guard, and, to literally top it all off, a lightweight helmet to protect her head not only from injury, but also invasion by Saekrin's hypnotism. She stared out at Cyowan and silently prayed. Her parents were Christian, her mother Catholic if she recalled correctly, and had taught Yoake how to pray to God. Unfortunately, since her parents died, she hadn't spoken to God once, save for her outburst a few weeks earlier. She didn't know how effective it would be, but she had to try. Making a sign of the Cross for the first time in twelve years, she said silently, *"God, I know it's been awhile so I understand if you won't listen, and I don't even know if you can hear me on another planet, but I have to say this. I beg of you not to take Yeldi away. We need him, he could be the key to beating Saekrin . . . I need him, I love him. I know he doesn't know about you, but he is a good pious person in his own religion. Please, don't make him another one of Saekrin's victims, he has suffered enough at the monster's hands. Please, please, I beg of you, even if you don't have authority here, send one of his own gods to save him."* By then, tears had started trickling out of her eyes, but when she finished her prayer she once again had two steady rivers flowing down her cheeks.

"Hey, Yoake!" came a voice suddenly.

Yoake looked to see Hana and Kyoki, also in their armor, standing behind her. She quickly crossed herself again, to end the prayer, and turned to her friends. "Hey, guys." she greeted as they walked to stand on either side of her.

"Tybalt said you'd be up here." Hana smiled.

"Whatcha' doing?" Kyoki asked.

"Praying." Yoake answered. "My parents were Christian, but I haven't prayed since the funeral." She smirked slightly. "What a time to renew my relationship, eh?"

"You praying for Yeldi?" Hana inquired, and the other girl nodded. The three of the looked out at Cyowan, Yoake standing in the center, with Kyoki and Hana on either side. They stood in silence, the only sound was the breeze that gently blew around them, contemplating the battle to come.

Then Yoake thought of something that made her smile slightly. "You know something guys? Kyoki's family adopted me officially today and today's the twelfth anniversary of my family's death."

"So we became official sisters one year after your family died?" Kyoki observed.

"Yeah, and now I'll lose the boy I love." Yoake answered.

"Don't think like that." Hana said. "Think of it as the day he'll finally be at peace."

All Yoake could do was nod, and Kyoki took her hand saying, "But we're still here."

Hana took her other hand, "Through thick and thin."

Yoake smiled, "Unbreakable."

"Together," they said in unison. Then they exchanged amused looks and laughed at themselves.

"Wow, we are so cheezy." Kyoki said.

"It shows how much we know and love each other." Hana shrugged.

"Very true." Yoake nodded. With that, the three made their way to the barracks to get ready for the battle.

Back in Yeldi's room, Mineh had nearly fallen asleep. It was dark when she heard a voice say, "Why are you here?"

Mineh's head snapped up in attention and she saw a man that looked like the statue of the sad man in the temple. "Are you Lord Oares?" she asked.

"Yes." He nodded. She jumped out of the chair and ran in between him and Yeldi. "What are you doing, little girl?"

"I'm helping Uncle Yeldi." she declared in the most threatening way she could.

"That is not your place, besides a puny little child like you has no chance of beating a god." he said, totally deadpan, but she didn't move, although she was slightly annoyed at being called "puny". He walked toward the bed, but each time he tried to step around the tiny barrier in his way, she stepped in front of him. "Will you calm down?" he finally growled, face still blank. "It's his time, I came early to avoid a 'family meeting'."

"Are you going to take Uncle Yeldi or not?" Mineh demanded, glaring up at the god before her. Oares sighed, raising his weapon, and, before Mineh could react, he brought it down onto her head, instantly knocking the girl unconscious. Gently, he caught her before she hit the ground and set her into a chair next to the bed.

"Oares," the female voice behind him was sharp yet gentle, "What did you do to that girl?"

"Leave, Phana," the death lord grouched, "She will be fine in about an hour." He turned to look at Yeldi and placed a hand on the dying boy's head.

"Oares," Phana repeated, pulling his hand away from Yeldi, "You cannot take him."

"And why not?" Oares asked flatly, "He has already crossed into my territory. He is mine."

Phana shook her head. "He belongs to another," she said.

At those words, Oares angrily jerked his hand out of his sister's grasp. "If you give me one more speech about the connection between love and life, I swear I will rip your tongue out." The threat was as flat and emotionless as the rest of his words, but there was a hint of desperation in his voice, "What makes this boy so special? I've ripped apart millions of couples, why does he get the dubious honor of having you defend him?"

"Because there are things he still has to do." Phana answered.

Oares raised an eyebrow slowly then huffed. "Really?" he said, leaning against the wall beside the bed, "Is that the best you can come up with? That's really pathetic."

Phana moved so she was standing directly in front of her twin, her eyes pleading with him to understand. "Why are you so determined to take him?" she asked.

"Why are you so determined to keep him?" Oares spat back, eyes darting to the comatose boy for a moment.

"Because he's a good person!" Phana yelled, grabbing onto her brother's shoulders, "He has been traumatized so much; he deserves some happiness before you take him!" She pulled back a bit, panting, and suddenly noticed Oares shaking. Slowly, she stepped away, afraid of what he was going to do.

"You're such an ungrateful bitch," Oares said, eyes locked on the ground. Slowly, he looked up, glaring daggers at his sister and laughing mirthlessly.

"W-what?" Phana asked.

"You heard me, *sister*," Oares growled, looking slightly deranged, "Have you noticed how these," his eyes swept over Mineh and Yeldi in disgust, "creatures . . . treat you? They love you. They adore you. You have everything; their worship, their praise, their love." He was advancing on his sister now, trapping her against the wall, "Look at me, *my dear sibling*," he laughed, "what do you see? I'll tell you. All you see is a broken puppy, someone who needs to be fixed and brought home and hugged and then everything will be better. Well it won't. You wanted to know why I'm so determined to steal this boy away from his friends and his family, well didn't you?" He was so close to her and so angry, Phana couldn't do much more than nod. She had never seen her brother like this. He was normally so composed, aloof, distant, never had she seen him explode like this and it scared her.

"Brother . . ." she whispered.

"Quiet, bitch," he snapped, slamming his fist into the wall right beside her head and leaving a cracking hole, "I'm going to take him because I have nothing."

"What are you talking about?" Phana said, shoving him away, "You have so much; a family who cares about you, a—"

"THE DEAD ARE ALL I HAVE!" Oares shouted, "and you will NOT take what is rightfully mine away from me!" He turned and walked back over to the bed.

"So you're going to hurt those children just to spite the world?" Phana yelled, rushing forward and grabbing her brother's hand again.

He laughed, then suddenly stopped, his usual blank expression settling back onto his pale features, "Yes, yes I am."

Phana stared in shock at him, "I-I won't let you, brother," she said, placing herself between him and Yeldi.

Oares sighed. "Fine then," he muttered, raising his weapon, "I guess I'll just have to go through you." The two locked eyes, sparks cracking in the air between them, as they glared at each other. In her sleep, Mineh stirred, unconsciously sensing the coming fight between two deities.

❦

"Let's go kick some ass," Kyoki said as she pulled on the new corset the armory had made for her. It was very similar to the old one except it now included a deep red breastplate and layer plating on the sides. She hoped she sounded more confident than she felt. Despite the fact that they had fought Saekrin before and won, the idea that he was becoming more and more of a lunatic scared her. It made his moves difficult to anticipate. With a huff and a few jabs at the air, she picked up her scythe.

"Ready?" Yoake asked, looking toward Hana. The older girl nodded, sheathing her daggers into the belt at her hip.

"You?" she asked. Yoake smiled and put her quiver on along with her bow. Just as they were about to walk out, Sakura arrived.

"Hi," Hana said, waving, then she noticed the look on her teacher's face, "is something wrong?"

For a few moments, the woman said nothing, then, "Alkest is dead."

The girls stared at her then lowered their heads. Sakura turned and led them down the hall back to the deceased soldier's room. Inside, they could see Alia performing some kind of ritual over Alkest's body. Silently, they watched as the priestess moved around the bed, whispering words they couldn't hear, and finally pulled the white sheet over the soldier's eyes. As she walked out, they moved out of the way and followed her down the hall. For a moment, Yoake looked down one of the hallways toward Yeldi's room. She desperately wanted to go in, or at least look inside to make sure he was ok. Sadly, before she could, the wailing of alarms rang through the hospital.

"Attention!" yelled a voice from the speakers above them, "Attention all units! He's here! I repeat: he's here! Get your weapons, all able-bodied soldiers!"

"Looks like it's showtime." Kyoki said smiling. Just then, Artan ran over, katana in hand, and rushed past them.

"Hurry up," he called over his shoulder. Kyoki was the first to go, followed by Hana, but Yoake lingered. She knew she should follow the others, but first she wanted to say something, anything, to Yeldi.

"I'll watch over him," Alia said, placing a hand on the girl's shoulder, "I promise. For now, it is your duty to fight." Yoake nodded in understanding and rushed after her friends.

The front of the hospital grounds and barracks had become a battleground. To the west, she saw soldiers pouring out and into battle, charging towards the main fight. She could see battalions of fighting, centered in a large group around something, but she couldn't make out what. Suddenly, flames shot out of the group, sending at least twelve flying into the air, scorched and likely dead. In the middle of the blaze stood Saekrin, a near giddy smirk plastered on his bloody face. To the north end of the field stood a sight that made Yoake freeze in fear. A giant snake, nearly as tall as the temple itself, was pulverizing soldiers, knocking them away from its master and sometimes eating them. Wave after wave of fighter went down in a haze of blood.

"Where—?" Yoake asked, looking around frantically for her friends.

"Finally decided to show up?" Kyoki said jokingly, suddenly appearing beside her.

"What is that?" Yoake asked, pointing toward the snake.

"Dunno, don't care, but we gotta take it out. Artan and Hana are already close but sent me back to get you. Now let's go, slow poke."

Yoake ran after her friend, following her closer and closer to the snake. As she drew nearer, she could see the true size of the massive animal. It was at least as tall as the temple, with shining, dark green scales covering its entire body. Piercing golden eyes stared down as it continued to slaughter the attacking soldiers. Its long fangs suddenly reached down and picked three fighters out of the melee, crushing them to death in its mouth. Yoake gasped; she could have sworn she saw it smile at the dying screams.

"Come on!" Kyoki said, rushing into the fray. Yoake stood back, unsure of how to help, but knowing she had to fight. She could see Hana and Artan already in the middle of the battle, both bleeding and panting. They looked to each other, then ran in again.

Kyoki screamed as she was thrown from the back of the snake, landing with a loud crash on the ground. Quickly, she stood and ran back in, scythe up and swinging. Yoake could tell they were getting nowhere, but she loosed an arrow anyway, the green weapon bouncing off the snake's scales. She tried again but the result was the same; this random attacking was getting them nowhere and if she didn't know better, she would've said it was amusing the snake. With a frustrated sigh, she pulled her watch over.

"Guys," she called into it. For a moment there was nothing, then Hana's voice floated through.

"What?" she growled, "I'm kind of busy here!"

"This is going nowhere!" Yoake said, "Come meet me by that low building to the southeast. We can talk together there and come up with a plan."

"Right." Hanan replied and the watch went silent.

"How the hell are we supposed to take that thing down?" Artan asked. He stood next to Hana on top of one of the few low buildings that had yet to be destroyed. The girl shook her head.

"I would say fire," she said, "but . . ." She trailed off, purposely avoiding talking about their fallen teammate.

"We could burn it another way," Kyoki suggested.

"How?" Artan looked at her, confused.

She looked over at him and smiled, "Yoake's arrows. They're a long range weapon, which means she won't have to get in close. As you can see," she gestured to the continuing slaughter, "close is not good, so if we . . ." she pulled the others in close and began to whisper her plan. Once she finished, the group again faced the snake.

"And all this time I thought you were just the dumb muscle of the team." Artan said. Kyoki giggled and whacked him on the head with her scythe, "Ow!"

"Enough playing around," Hana said, glaring, "let's move out!" The others nodded and, as Yoake ran off to go take her place on a large pile of debris at the east corner of the battle, the other three ran toward the snake.

"Ready?" Hana called to Kyoki as they rushed into the midst of the battle. The older girl nodded and jumped, swinging her scythe down toward the beast.

"DEATH'S HEAD!" she yelled, a giant vampire skull forming around her blade. Hana crossed her swords in front of her, creating an x of thorny vines that wrapped around their target, and looked to Kyoki. Once she saw that the skull had reached the snake, she pulled her swords up then down hard, forcing the thorns into the scales. The skull broke into millions of smaller versions of itself and latched onto the vines, crawling like ants toward the openings.

The snake hissed in pain and suddenly began to roll, dislodging nearly all of the vines. The few that managed to hang on quickly fell off in the continued struggle.

"Damn it," Kyoki snarled, landing beside Hana. The two watched as Artan sent a blast of boiling water at the snake, but it just rolled off the monster's scales. Turning, the snake glared at the boy and brought its tail up, wrapping it around him.

"No!" Hana yelled and ran toward the captured boy. He struggled against the constricting scales, gasping for air. As soon as she reached him, Hana drove her daggers into the skin, forcing the snake to let go with a loud, angry hiss. She held him close, running back to where Kyoki stood.

"You okay?" she asked. Artan nodded and stood, looking up at the snake.

"We gotta find somewhere this thing doesn't have those damned scales," he said, scanning the beast's entire body.

"I got it!" Hana exclaimed. She pointed to the mouth as they jumped to avoid being eaten alive.

"I'm on it!" Kyoki yelled, bouncing off the nearest slab of concrete and back up to the snake. It tried to follow her, but she kept moving, dodging back and forth and drawing ever closer.

"Kyoki, no!" the other two called, but she could no longer hear them. With one final push, she flew up to the snake's eye level. It glared at her, mouth open, and moved forward, closing its jaw around the smirking girl.

"No!" Hana screamed as the monster's mouth snapped shut. For several moments, nothing happened, Hana and Artan standing frozen in shock, then suddenly—

"Die, you bastard!" Kyoki yelled. Blood rained down as she sliced through the soft tissue of the snake's mouth, cutting the skin of its jaw and upper palette. The monster thrashed and screamed as it bled, trying to knock the girl down, but she was gone before it had the chance. "Now, Yoake!" she called, but the younger girl had already seen her opening and raised her weapon.

A flaming red arrow flew straight toward the snake's screeching mouth and dove inside. Seconds passed with nothing and the others began to think that the beast had simply swallowed it, but then—

BOOM! The snake exploded in a bright haze of fire and black smoke, its head landing right in front of Artan and Hana. They jumped back in shock before realizing that the monster was dead. Off in the distance, Saekrin growled as his pet was killed, slashing the nearest soldier to ribbons.

Anger boiled inside him and he could feel the obsidian watch at his hip break as the snake's head crashed into the ground. With a low snarl, he glanced at the soldiers still trying to surround him and quickly switched his pole ax to fire.

"I'm done playing around with you." he muttered and spun the ax in a wide arc around himself. Fire wrapped around the blade, enlarging it, and, as it spun, slicing soldier after soldier in half, Saekrin laughed. Blood poured out of the bodies that lay scattered around him. He panted for a few moments, but soon settled and looked over to the teens who had been celebrating a small victory but now glared back at him.

Yoake starred in a mixture of shock and absolute horror at the massacre before her. A pile of bodies lay bleeding around Saekrin as he smirked at the, blood dripping from his claws and ax blade. Suddenly, his eyes locked onto hers, grey piercing her to the core, and she began to tremble, knees nearly buckling under her.

"Calm down," Kyoki said, placing a hand on her friend's shoulder. Yoake looked over at her and saw that the older girl was shaking as well, glaring daggers at the creature smirking back at them. Hana watched Saekrin's every move, every twitch, feeling Artan's rage beside her. There was something off about their adversary, something in the way he moved, twitching his hand and muttering to himself.

"Lunatic!" Artan suddenly yelled, "Stop talking to the voices no one else can hear and get ready to die!" Saekrin looked up and laughed, making the boy shake in absolute anger.

"Aren't you missing someone?" Saekrin asked, tilting his head slightly, "Where's the little bastard?"

"Don't call him that, you monster!" Yoake screamed, "You know exactly where he is!"

"I do?" Saekrin said. He looked genuinely confused by her statement.

"He's dying!"

"Really? Interesting . . ."

"What the hell do you mean 'interesting'?" Kyoki cut in, "You're the one who killed him!"

Saekrin stared at her quizzically before realization finally dawned on him. "Oh yes," he said, "I remember . . ."

"That's not the kind of thing you forget!" Hana said.

"He trusted you!" Yoake screamed, stepping forward, "He looked up to you and you destroyed him! You abused him and now, now" she paused, trying to compose herself, "now you've killed him! You don't just forget about him! Do you like playing these games? Pretending you don't know him! Are you trying to mock us, you heartless sadist, or—" she stopped suddenly, the image of Saekrin's confused look flashing through her mind, "or in your selfish madness did you really forget the boy who followed you from world to world, who turned his back on his home and his family for you? Did you really forget Yeldi? Answer me!"

The battlefield was quiet, a silent wind blowing past them as the teens stared first at their friend then at their enemy and back again.

"I really don't know," Saekrin finally chuckled, staring at his bloody, twitching hand, "I stopped trying to perform mental diagnostics on myself long ago. But I remember the boy, weak little runt."

"If he was so weak why did you keep him around?" Hana snapped.

Saekrin shrugged. "He was mildly useful at the time."

"You're lying." Yoake said.

"Oh really?" Saekrin said. "How do you figure?"

"I heard what you said to Yeldi at the beach. I may have been writhing in pain, but I could still hear what was happening around me."

Saekrin narrowed his eyes, becoming severely irritated with the human girl. "What exactly did you hear?"

"You told him he had a lot of potential, and the reason you abused him was so he didn't get more powerful than you." Yoake answered, a smile crossing her face at the sight of Saekrin's annoyance. "So why did you really keep him? Was it the same reason: so he didn't surpass you? It is, isn't it. You saw the power in Yeldi and it scared you. You didn't want your own student to become stronger than you, so you kept him as your little dog. You beat him into submission, implanting fear and self-hate into him so he couldn't see his own potential and rely on you for everything. That's the only reason: you were afraid."

"Shut up, girl!" Saekrin snapped. "I'll crush you like the little insect you are! All of you are nothing but little bugs to be crushed"

"Fine then, have at it." Hana said, playing along with Yoake's notion. "You don't scare us because we know you're nothing but a bully."

"Yeah, you hurt others just to show your power." Kyoki added, stepping forward.

"And you're so involved in putting others down that you don't know how to deal with someone who doesn't obey you." Atran said.

"Since we know this, we know how to beat you." Yoake said.

Saekrin looked at the teens standing before him. They were children, and yet they had the gall to stand up to him. He was supreme, all-powerful, they should have been bowing to him, begging for his mercy, and yet they stood defiantly, challenging him. It infuriated him.

"Much as I love seeing this asshole squirm," Kyoki said as she raised her scythe, dark clouds coating the blade, "I think it's time he disappeared." She rushed forward toward him, scythe up, followed by the other teens. One after another, they slashed at Saekrin, Yoake shooting arrows from the outskirts of the battle.

Kyoki was the first to land a hit, cutting their enemy's leg but not deep enough to slow him down. Quickly, he moved, swinging his pole ax back to block Artan's katana and using the blade to knock Kyoki back. She dodged, dropping low to avoid the sharp metal, and smirked up at him. Suddenly, she slammed her weapon into the ground, releasing the clouds and sending up a haze of black smoke.

Yoake lowered her bow and waited for the smoke to clear. Inside, Kyoki quietly shifted away from Saekrin, moving to stand beside Artan. He looked at her and nodded, water coating his sword. In Kyoki's place, Hana sat waiting for the dust to clear, daggers up and thorns already beginning to form.

As soon as the clouds began to fade, she jumped up, slashing her blades along Saekrin's arms and leaving bloody cuts in her wake. He snarled, spinning his weapon as flames danced along the pole, and brought it crashing down onto Hana's back. The girl screamed in pain as she flew.

"Focus!" Kyoki said, looking at Artan. The boy nodded and, as their enemy watched Hana burn, sent a blast of dark, murky, boiling water toward Saekrin. He turned and, changing his weapon to lightning, cut through the steam, sending sparks back toward Artan and Kyoki. Both teens stopped the attack and jumped out of the way before the electricity could reach them. As he landed, Artan glared at Saekrin who simply smirked back.

Yoake looked over at Hana who was trying to push herself up again, but the burns on her back and knees were too deep and everytime she tried to stand, the wounds sent waves of pain through her body. They locked eyes for a moment, Yoake silently asking if the older girl needed help, but Hana shook her head. She nodded toward the battle where Kyoki and Artan were furiously trying to land a hit on their opponent. Yoake pulled out an orange arrow and fired, green, red, blue, and purple soon following.

Saekrin blocked the first two, then spun away, putting Artan in the line of fire. The red arrow struck him in the side and, as Yoake stood, horrified, Saekrin grabbed the boy by the throat, claws leaving small holes in his neck, and threw him away. Kyoki saw the next arrow and quickly dodged before she was struck. Saekrin turned to go after her but the last arrow hit his leg, causing him to stumble.

He looked down and, with a grimace of pain, yanked it out and threw it down. Blood rushed down his leg but he either didn't notice or didn't care because he ran after Kyoki. Yoake followed the two, hoping to redeem herself.

Kyoki stuck her tongue out as she moved, dodging Saekrin's attacks and trying to land her own. They moved around each other, weapons clashing in showers of sparks. Suddenly, Kyoki jumped back and raised her scythe, spinning it above her head.

"SOUL HURRICANE!" she yelled, dark clouds gathering in the sky. She smirked at the nearly shocked look on her enemy's face and quickly began to spin her weapon. As the scythe moved, so did the clouds, spinning faster and faster above them. Saekrin watched the clouds gather only for a few more seconds before he began to mumble something, lightning wrapping itself around his weapon in a thick layer of electricity. The two glared at each other, Kyoki's clouds spinning around her in a sharp, dark storm. Yoake stood at the side, arrow up and ready, watching. A tense silence descended on them, broken only by the cracking sounds of Saekrin's lightning.

Just then, the two ran toward each other, weapons raised and before Yoake could loose an arrow, their weapons met, sending up an explosion that shook the battlefield and sent up and enormous cloud. Yoake tried to see through the light and smoke, but couldn't find any sign of her friend. Desperately, she continued to scan the field. Finally, as the smoke cleared, she could see two figures facing away from each other.

Saekrin stood on one side, pole still sparking, and Kyoki stood on the other, the remnants of her clouds floating gently around her. Suddenly, Kyoki coughed, blood forcing its way out of her mouth, and, to Yoake's horror, she fell. "Kyoki!" she cried, attracting Saekrin's attention.

"Ah so that's where the sniper's been hiding." Saekrin grinned and raised his weapon. "Now I know where to aim." Electric bolts shot out of the ax, heading straight for Yoake. She jumped out of their path and bounded into another notch to conceal herself. Saekrin snarled in annoyance at losing his target, and randomly shot lightning at piles of rubble, hoping she was behind them. He knew she was hiding somewhere, he just couldn't figure out where. All the same, the surge of power was exhilarating, and he loved seeing the rubble flying in the air as he blasted it. He laughed maniacally and called out to Yoake, "Are you afraid now, little girl? What happened to all your tough talk earlier? Did seeing your friends fall strike fear and terror into your heart? Well, you won't have to worry about that once I rip that sorry excuse for a vital organ out of your chest!"

Yoake tried to ignore his ranting, but couldn't help the feeling that he was right. She was so confident, she felt so brave, but watching Hana, Artan, and Kyoki get cut down so easily sent a ripping terror flooding through her veins. She gripped her bow tightly, trying to control her shaking hands. She could hear him getting closer and closer as the explosions kept getting louder and the ground shook more and more violently. She squeaked in fear as the two ruins on either side of her were blown to bits. *"This is it."* she thought *"I'm sorry, Yeldi, but I couldn't do it. Please forgive me."* She closed her eyes and waited for Saekrin to make the final blow, destroying her and her protection in one fell swoop. But everything was silent, there were no explosions, no laughing, nothing.

A sigh of relief escaped her, but then she felt cold breath against her neck and heard Saekrin's voice whisper, almost seductively, "I found you." She tried to jump away but he grabbed her hair and, just like at the beach, pulled her close to his ice cold chest. Her skin crawled and goosebumps rose as he ran his tongue around her ear and breathed, "My, don't you just act like my love Sakura, you leave the same wonderful sensation on my tastebuds." He chuckled as she squirmed against his grip. "Oh, please, do keep struggling." He flipped her around to face him. "It makes this so much more fun."

She tried to say something defiant, but froze as he bent down and planted his lips on her own. Yoake screamed against his mouth and tried to push him away, but he was too strong. Unwittingly, her scream granted his tongue access into her mouth. Yoake shivered, not just at the touch of his cold skin and even colder lips, but at the thought of what he might do to her. Despite her fear, all her efforts to escape were in vain. He moaned into her mouth, one hand pulling her closer as the other trailed up her thigh. Against her will, she moaned back, but cut herself off as quickly as she could, hoping he hadn't heard her, but he chuckled darkly into her mouth. His hand brushed against her breast as his tongue explored her mouth further.

"Do you enjoy this, insect?" he whispered. For a second, he moved his mouth to her neck, sucking and biting lightly. Yoake tried to say something but before she could get the words out, he was roughly kissing her again. "You make the same noises she did." he said, "I wonder if you feel the same on the inside as well . . ." He shifted his hand lower and brushed it around her thighs, stomach, sides, everywhere but the one spot Yoake was praying he would leave alone. She pushed desperately against him, squirming in his grip. Her mind raced, trying to figure out how far this was going to go. Would he torture her again? Would he rape her like he had Sakura? Slowly, he pulled away, smirking down at her.

"What the hell was that?" Yoake shrieked, as she tried to regain her breath.

"What? You didn't like it? You certainly seemed to." Saekrin said and ran a claw down her face, leaving a small scratch. "I thought would might enjoy it, since I took the liberty of mimicking exactly what Yeldi wanted to do with you." He chuckled at her very apparent anger and pried further. "Though you have a taste on your lips that isn't your own. Did my weakling servant finally find the courage to tell you how he feels—or rather felt—towards you? Did he kiss you as he was dying? I think he did by how recent the foreign taste is on you. How romantic: a love confession on his deathbed. Well, you two can make love once I send you to Tarel with him. Please give Oares my regards, and tell that pathetic weakling what I did, I'm sure he'd get a kick out of it."

"You bastard." Yoake muttered.

"Now, now, there's no call for that kind of language." Saekrin chuckled. He reached down, feeling for the strap that held her armor in place, and slowly pulled it loose. "I promise to be gentle with you," he shifted, placing his mouth against her neck, and bit down lightly. Yoake shivered as his tongue met her skin. She felt like screaming again as he traveled up her neck, but was unable to when he placed a short, slightly rough, kiss on her lips and whispered, "well, maybe not by your standards."

"NO!" She whipped an arrow out of the quiver and forced it into his shoulder.

He pushed her back and yanked the object out of his body looking at the bloody arrow irately. He chuckled as he raised his head and looked at her with murderous glee. "I'm going to make you regret that."

Yoake stared at him. She would never admit it, especially not to the madman in front of her, but she was scared. She had beaten Yeldi on her own, but this was different. For one thing, Saekrin, despite his arrogance and abusiveness, truly was incredibly strong, much stronger than Yeldi had been, and second, all of her friends were down. Frantically, she looked around from something, anything, that might help her fight.

Slowly, he began to advance on her, each step he took making Yoake take one in the opposite direction.

"Where are you going?" Saekrin asked mockingly, his dark clouds wrapping around his pole. "I thought you were going to fight." Yoake gulped, desperately trying to think of something to do. Suddenly, her back hit a large pile of rubble, preventing her from moving any farther away from the lunatic advancing on her. Just then, she heard a voice coming from her watch.

"Yoake," it said, sounding very much like Hana. She looked around and saw the older girl propping herself up against a large piece of concrete. The girl looked like terrible, with burn marks, cuts, and bruises, but still she stood, albeit shakily, "I have an idea. Do you remember that thing Erasure showed us? The team attack?" Yoake nodded quickly, eyes still watching her enemy, "I've already told the others and we want to try it. I think it's the only thing that will work. We'll give our power to you and you go for it, understand?" Yoake could hear her friend panting with the effort of speaking and immediately agreed, knowing Hana was right and that the others were in no shape to fight. She raised her bow, pulling an arrow out of her quiver, as her friends began to speak.

"Immortal gods," Artan began.

"Take this power," Kyoki continued.

"And bestow it on the one," Hana said.

"In whom we place our trust." the three yelled together.

Instantly, bright lights appeared over them, flying into the air and heading straight toward Yoake. For a moment, she savored the shocked and almost alarmed look on Saekrin's face before the power struck her. The sudden jolt nearly made her fall but she stood her ground, knowing that she could not let her friends down. Slowly, she raised her bow and took aim, the arrow glowing with a swirling rainbow of color. "This is for you, Yeldi," she thought and fired.

The arrow flew toward Saekrin, a trail of light blasting apart the ground in its wake. Yoake watched as it drew nearer and nearer, then suddenly she was thrown back as an enormous explosion of burning white light shook the ground. She held her hand up in front of her eyes to block the light and soon felt herself pressed against the pile of rubble, the brightness burning her skin.

When the light faded, she opened her eyes slowly and looked around the field. A large crater sat where Saekrin had once stood, small wisps of smoke flowing out of it and into the air. Shaking slightly, she stood and wobbled over to the hole, peering inside. Nothing was left of Saekrin except smoke. Yoake fell to her knees, panting but relieved. "It's over," she said to herself, "finally."

"Really?" hissed a voice from above her. Yoake looked up to see Saekrin floating above her, using his pole ax like a broom stick, "because I was hoping that your little light show would last longer." He smirked and landed, Yoake staring at him with a look of shock and horror.

"H-how?" she stammered, scooting away from him.

"Wind," he said flatly, "You took so long to power up that I thought I'd experiment." He moved closer to her and reached down, pulling her up by her throat. "Now," he said, "shall we continue?" He dropped her onto the ground and swung his burning weapon.

Yoake screamed as the fire covered blade slashed her skin, tearing the flesh open. She could feel blood running down her body as the blows continued. Suddenly, the fire changed to electricity and then to boiling water. Tears ran down her face as pain overwhelmed her system. She had failed and now she was going to die.

"Good bye, insect," Saekrin chuckled, black clouds once again coating his blade. He raised his weapon high and brought it down as Yoake closed her eyes, bracing herself for death . . . but nothing happened.

Above her, she heard Saekrin gasp and quickly opened her eyes to see Yeldi standing in front of her, blocking his former master's ax with the flaming leather of his whip.

"Yeldi!" Yoake exclaimed. He glanced at her for a moment then pulled his whip back, spinning it and forcing Saekrin to dodge. Yoake jumped up, nearly falling back down in the process, and hugged him. "I thought you were dead!" she yelled, "What happened?"

"I don't know," the boy answered, "Lady Alia said the gods decided to spare me. I guess I'll have to thank them later, but right now," he turned to glare at the stunned Saekrin, "I think we have bigger problems to deal with."

"Right." Yoake nodded and prepared her battle stance, with a new-found courage surging through her. But her body protested. Pain flooded through her, overpowering her new courage. "Ah!" she cringed and fell to her knees.

"Yoake, don't force yourself." Yeldi said as he caught her. "You need to rest. You're too injured to fight."

"I have to help . . ." she choked as he laid her down.

"You have." he propped her head against a rock-pillow, and gave her a chaste kiss. "Now it's my turn to repay you for all the help you have given me."

"Yeldi . . ." she reached up and put a hand on his cheek.

"Rest." He put his hand over her eyes and, after he muttered a small spell, she closed her eyes. "May the gods look over us both." He stood up and stared at Saekrin, his eyes shooting daggers at his former master. "We have a score to settle." he said.

"I suppose we do." Saekrin said. "I need to punish you for your betrayal, and you need to rip me apart for what I did to you and your 'friends'. Is that correct?"

"Sounds about right." Yeldi said as the flames on his whip reformed.

"Well then," Saekrin's pole ax resumed its display of power, "Shall we?" Yeldi nodded and rushed forward, swinging his whip toward his enemy. Saekrin quickly jumped away from the flaming weapon, landing softly a few yards away. Again, Yeldi ran over and again Saekrin simply dodged.

"Fight me!" Yeldi screamed, sending his whip toward Saekrin. The man laughed and swung his pole ax around, catching his former student's whip and wrapping it around his own weapon. With a hard tug, he pulled Yeldi close, ignoring the flames burning his own hand.

"Interesting weapon choice, boy." Saekrin chuckled, looking at the whip almost lovingly, "I wouldn't have thought you would ever go close to one of these voluntarily." Yeldi snarled and pushed more fire out onto the leather, forcing both of them to jump back to avoid being burned. "The whip is such a fierce weapon, yet elegant in its simplicity." Saekrin continued, eyes watching the flames. "It can be used in so many ways . . ."

"My whip is nothing like yours!" Yeldi snapped, charging again. He wrapped the leather around his knuckles, too angry to notice that he wasn't getting burned, and began to punch his former master. Saekrin blocked his attacks, spinning his electrified pole. Yeldi hissed in pain as a few sparks met his skin, but pushed forward. His eyes followed Saekrin's movements and, while some seemed out of place, almost like jerks or twitches, he could see where the ax was moving. It was almost as though the older creature was moving in slow motion.

Smirking to himself, Yeldi dodged another blow and spun, slamming his fist into Saekrin's back and burning his clothing and skin. Saekrin hissed, but turned, a large bolt of lightning following his ax. Yeldi saw it but was in too close to dodge. He screamed as the electricity hit him, writhing as the bolt traveled through his body. His whip uncurled as his wrists jerked in pain. Suddenly, the pain stopped and he was thrown across the field, landing with a hard thump on the ground. Glaring back at Saekrin, he stood, quickly noticing that half of his shirt had been burned away by the lightning, leaving a spider web scar on his arm and shoulder.

"Bastard." he spat, pulling his whip close to himself. He looked down and pulled his hand along the leather, gently removing some fire from it. The flames rested comfortably in his hand as he tossed them back and forth experimentally. Yeldi turned back to his opponent to see that Saekrin was ignoring him, muttering to himself.

"My turn," the boy whispered, forcing the flames in his hand to grow larger, engulfing his whole hand. He looked up at the fireball, then to Saekrin, then back, and smiled, "PHOENIX BOMB!" he shouted, hurling the burning ball toward his target. As it flew closer, it grew, expanding in all directions.

Saekrin looked up from his "conversation," eyes wide, and quickly jumped out of the way, turning in mid-air to see the flames explode against a pile of rubble.

"Got'cha!" Yeldi growled happily. He swung his whip down, wrapping the leather around Saekrin and throwing him into one of the few walls still standing. Without pausing, he raised the older creature up and slammed him into the ground. "I'm. Going. To. Kill. You!" he screamed, crashing the deranged monster into anything his whip would reach. Finally, he threw him into the pit Yoake had created, standing over him, hatred and rage shining in his eyes. Yeldi snarled at him, making the fire on his whip grow and grow, burning Saekrin's flesh as the older creature laughed.

"Then that makes you a murderer like me, boy." he cackled as the flames continued to scorch him. Yeldi shook his head, determined to ignore the deranged demon's words.

"BURNING PYRE!" he yelled, fire rising into the sky, carrying Saekrin with it. He watched as the flames circled his former master, burning away everything. Suddenly, still smirking, Saekrin looked down at the boy, locking eyes with him, and as hard as Yeldi tried he couldn't stop the words from reaching his ears.

"We are the same." Saekrin chuckled, then the flames consumed him.

The words echoed through Yeldi's head as he made his way back to Yoake, feeling the drain on his body from the fight. Stumbling from exhaustion, he nearly fell several times before he reached her, then collapsed.

Yoake woke up in a white hospital bed, bright lights shining down at her. Slowly, she tried to sit up, but a gentle hand on her shoulder eased her back down. Turning, she saw Sakura sitting beside her.

"Where . . . ?" she asked, "What happened?"

"Don't worry," Sakura said, smiling, "It's over now. Just rest. You went through quite a fight."

"Where is everyone?" Yoake asked, worried.

"Kyoki and Artan are helping clear rubble. Those two are tough as nails and jumped out of bed as soon as they woke up. Hana is with Mineh and Kumi and—"

"What about Yeldi?" Yoake said desperately, worried. Sakura smiled.

"He's fine. He used up a lot of power during the battle so he's been sleeping ever since." Yoake smiled. So she hadn't dreamed of him after all. Slowly, she pushed the blankets off and tried to stand.

"I should go see him," she said, "or at least help Kyoki and Artan." Sakura helped her up and the two walked down the hospital hallways. Yoake could see soldiers and their families talking, some with bandages others with missing limbs, and she couldn't help but tear up a bit. How could so much pain be caused by one creature? She looked over again and saw that many of them were smiling and she smiled too. Pain was always overcome by joy.

"Yoake," Sakura said. The girl turned and looked into the room they had stopped beside. On the bed, lay the sleeping Yeldi. He looked absolutely exhausted but content, a small smile on his lips as he dozed on. Yoake smiled brightly at the sight then turned to go outside.

Rubble and crates covered the ground along with puddles of blood and bodies. She looked around for a few seconds, taking in the sight, then walked over to Kyoki and Artan.

"Yo!" Kyoki called, immediately dropping the twisted metal she had been holding, and ran over to tackle her friend, "How are you feeling? Why are you up? Are you okay?"

"K-Kyoki," Yoake choked out, "I c-can't breath." The older girl looked down at her then let go, standing.

"Sorry," she said, rubbing the back of her head sheepishly, "I'm just happy you're okay. Alia says you and Yeldi clobbered the ass. Nice."

"It was really all Yeldi," Yoake said, "I went down just after the union attack."

"Where is he anyway?" Artan asked, walking over after dumping his load onto the growing pile of destroyed buildings.

"Sleeping." Yoake answered.

"Hi guys!" the group looked over to see Hana walking toward them.

"Where are the kids?" Yoake asked.

"Sakura came and took over so I thought I'd help with the clean up. We want to get as much of this cleaned up as possible before the funeral."

"Funeral?" Yoake asked.

"For everyone who died because of Saekrin," Artan explained, "like Erasure and Alkest."

"Oh . . . right," Yoake said, looking down, "When is it?"

"Inside the temple in about three hours," Kyoki answered, "so let's get moving and make this place look as good as possible for 'em." Yoake nodded and they once again set to work.

Two hours later, Tybalt's voice called to them through their watches, signalling for the teens to come to the temple. As they made their way over, they could see a huge crowd going the same way. Once they made it, they took seats in the middle of the large room.

"They really cleaned this place up," Kyoki said, looking around. Yoake turned and saw that the whole temple seemed to have been polished and deep red banners hung from the ceiling. "Why not black?" Kyoki asked, turning to Artan.

"Why would we have black?" he asked in return, "Maroon is the mourning color." Yoake and Hana nodded. Of course the funeral rites would be different than on Earth.

"Hi, guys," whispered a voice from beside them. They turned to see Yeldi standing next to their row. Yoake moved over to make room for him and he sat down.

"How are you feeling?" she asked. He sighed.

"Physically, I'm fine, but I can't shake the feeling that a lot of this is my fault, I mean, I helped him."

"You're not him, Yeldi," Yoake said, placing a comforting hand on his shoulder. She turned to the front of the temple as Alia walked forward, an opal watch slung at her hip. *I guess she got it back* Yoake thought.

As the funeral progressed, Yoake watched friends and family process up and speak about the dead. Some of Erasure's former students spoke and she wondered if Kyoki would join them, but the older girl sat silently, looking straight ahead. Tybalt walked forward and spoke on behalf of Alkest and Artan said a few words for his father.

Once the speeches and eulogies were finished, Alia stood and moved to the front, looking not at the guests, but at a statue. "Lord Oares," she said, "please take these here who have valiantly fallen to protect their home, their friends, and their families. Accept them into Tarel and reward them for all they have done." She closed with a prayer in a language that the girls couldn't understand, then walked silently away.

After the funeral, everyone went into the barracks dining hall which had been decorated in maroon and sat down to a large feast. Suddenly, as they ate, Yeldi looked around. "Where did Mineh go?" he asked.

Yoake turned and scanned the room, "I don't know," she said, "was she at the funeral?"

"Children," they turned to see Sakura walking toward them, "can you help me find Mineh?"

The temple was empty after everyone left to go to the feast. On her way there, she stopped suddenly and turned around, running back to the temple. Slowly, she pushed the door open and walked in, sitting down close to the dead, who lay as if asleep dressed in their armor, and waited.

"Are you here to stop me again?" Mineh turned to see Oares standing beside Erasure and quickly shook her head. Oares said nothing, turning to the corpse beside him, and placed his hand on its head. Mineh watched in wonder as he drew his hand back, pulling a pale blue light out from within the body.

"Wh-what's that?" she asked nervously, curious.

"A soul," Oares said flatly, turning to the light which had formed itself into a pale, floating version of Erasure, "go stand over there until I finish." The ghost nodded and floated to a corner of the temple. "Is there a particular reason you were sitting here?" Oares asked as he moved to the next soldier. Mineh watched, transfixed, as he pulled out another soul, sending it to stand with the first.

"I wanted to say thank you," she said. Oares looked up abruptly, staring at the girl. To anyone who didn't know him, it would have looked as if nothing about his face had changed, but Mineh could instantly see the shock written on his face.

"For what?" the god asked, quickly regaining his general attitude of detachment.

"For not taking Uncle Yeldi away." Mineh said cheerfully.

"Oh." was all he said in return as he continued to extract souls, Mineh watching the whole process. Once he finished, he walked over to the large group and motioned for them to follow.

"Good bye, Lord Oares." Mineh said, smiling as she waved at him. He looked at her for a moment, then disappeared.

Mineh hopped down from her seat and walked off to go find her mother. She had no idea that Alia had seen everything.

❖

"I wonder where she went." Hana said as they searched for Sakura's daughter. They had been looking for nearly a half hour and were starting to get worried.

"I don't know," Artan grouched, "but this is why I will never, ever have kids. They're too much of a hassle."

"Oh come on," Yoake said, "they're cute." Artan huffed but continued to search.

"Hi everyone!" they looked up to see Mineh running over, Alia following close behind. "Mommy! Mommy!" the girl squealed, "guess what Lady Alia said!" Sakura looked over to the high priestess who had a large smile spread across her face.

"What is it?" Sakura asked, looking at the priestess.

"Tell your mother what you were doing in the temple." Alia said to Mineh.

"I said thank you to Lord Oares," the girl giggled.

Sakura gave Alia a quizzical look. "I don't understand," she said.

Alia smiled. "She did not thank the gods like most do," she began, "she saw him, watched him collect the souls, and spoke to him directly. Mineh is to be the next high priestess."

Sakura looked down at Mineh who was smiling brightly, clearly excited, then her eyes moved to Alia.

"Wow," Kyoki said, "that sounds cool."

"It's a very high honor," Yeldi added.

"What's an honor?" Tybalt asked, walking over.

"I'm going to be a priestess, Daddy!" Mineh exclaimed, running to him. He looked at Alia.

"She can see the gods." the woman explained.

Tybalt nodded. "Girls," he turned to Kyoki, Yoake, and Hana, "I believe it is time for you to go back to your own world."

A look of disappointment crossed their faces. "Will we ever see you guys again?" Yoake asked.

"Sure." Yeldi said and wrapped his arm around her. "We'll keep in touch."

"Promise?"

"Promise."

"You'd better." Kyoki said.

"It's not just on them, you know." Hana laughed. "We need to call them too."

"How?" Yoake asked.

Tybalt walked forward and held up his watch, "we'll still be able to talk through these." he said smiling.

"You mean we can keep them?" Kyoki asked excitedly.

"Yes," Alia answered, "You helped save our world. Think of them as a present."

"But don't go becoming superheroes or anything," Artan said, "secret identities would make it hard to find you and just cause a whole host of other problems." They all laughed.

"We won't." Hana said. Tybalt lead the girls to the doors of the barracks and out onto the field. Slowly, he opened his watch and a portal formed on the ground before them. The girls looked into the pool of color, then back at Tybalt and the others, then, with one last farewell wave, jumped in.

They landed with a soft thump inside their dorm room, dressed in their normal clothes with their watches clasped firmly in their hands. Kyoki was the first on her feet and tucked her watch into her pocket as she walked over to the calendar they kept by the door.

"What are you doing?" Yoake asked.

"Just trying to figure out what day it is . . ." the older girl replied, "Ah shit!" she yelled, turning to the next page, "We only have a month of summer left and I still have a ton of crap to do!" Hana and Yoake laughed; after all that had just happened, the problems of normal school seemed like a distant dream and to have suddenly thrown back in their faces made them smile. As Kyoki grumpily flopped down on her bed, grabbing her math book in the process, Hana set to work cleaning her desk. Yoake sat down and pulled out her watch, staring at it and silently promising that she would definitely see Yeldi and the others again soon.

Epilogue

"Hurry up!" Kyoki called, bouncing and waving to the others, as the bandages of her zombie costume flew, "The line for the Drop Tower will be too long!" Hana sighed and put her head in her hands, trying to remember why they had agreed to come to the Halloween carnival in the first place, then she looked down at the stuffed bear in her arms and smiled. She reached down to adjust the obi of her geisha costume slightly. Turning, she saw Artan beside her, completely human in appearance and dressed in a samurai costume, trying to figure out how to eat a candy apple without being covered in caramel. Yoake (a brightly colored witch) and Yeldi (an adorable vampire) were a step or two behind them, the boy looking very red from having lost to Artan.

"Really," Yoake said comfortingly, "It's fine."

"But I really wanted to win that toy for you." Yeldi said quietly. Tybalt was just behind them, watching to make sure nothing happened. He knew the girls would be fine, this was their world after all, but Yeldi and Artan, especially Yeldi, looked a bit overwhelmed by the smells, sights, and sounds of the carnival. With a smile, he looked down at the pirate costume the girls had picked out for him. Suddenly, someone grabbed his hand and started to drag him off.

"Since you people are having a date night or whatever," Kyoki called back as she pulled Tybalt toward the Tower, "I'm temporarily commandeering the supervising adult unit!" Tybalt sighed but allowed the girl to pull him along.

"What's a drop tower?" Yeldi asked.

"It's . . . that." Yoake pointed to the ride, which could be seen above the trees and, as the cart dropped from the top, Yeldi turned pale.

"She-she's going to get on that?"

"Yep," Hana said, "Let's go after them. I'm not going on but I want to see the look on Tybalt's face when he gets off." Artan laughed and, along with Yoake and Yeldi, followed Hana toward the ride. About ten minutes later, Kyoki arrived, giggling and stumbling, with Tybalt right behind her looking as if nothing had happened.

"Did you get on?" Yeldi asked. His brother nodded.

"It was interesting."

"Hey, Lord of Darkness!" Kyoki said, throwing her arm around Yeldi's shoulder, "You wanna go?"

Yeldi shook his head furiously, "N-no." Kyoki shrugged then, with a mischevious shine in her eye, looked at Artan.

"Leave me out of this!" the boy yelled, "I'm not getting on your weird Earth rides. They look like they're gonna fall apart."

"Aww . . . come on, samurai. Dance! live a little!" Kyoki responded.

"Samurai don't dance." Artan said pointedly, crossing his arms.

"Some of them do." Kyoki sang and, grabbing Yoake and Yeldi, ran off toward the next ride. Artan looked at Hana.

"Is she seventeen or seven?" he asked. Hana laughed and followed the other three. Just as they were about to enter the haunted house, a voice called to them.

"I'm glad to see you are all having fun," it said. The group turned to see Alia standing behind them. Shocked, they stared at her. She was dressed in her usual high priestess attire, making a few people turn and call to her, complimenting her choice of costume.

"What are you doing here?" Kyoki asked. Alia smiled.

"I have come with some news for Tybalt," she answered, turning, "the baby is coming."

"Baby . . . ?" Tybalt said, then his eyes lit up, "Baby! Oh gods! The baby! Where is he? She? How is Sakura? Is she alright?" Alia just smiled.

"Congratulations, papa!" Yoake exclaimed, hugging him, "and you too uncle!" she wrapped her arms around Yeldi who looked slightly dazed.

"Well, what are we standing around here for?" Kyoki asked, "let's get going back and see the little one!" Artan nodded in agreement and they followed Alia out of the fair grounds. After quickly jumping through the portal she opened, they landed in the temple and quickly ran to the hospital.

"Sakura!" Tybalt exclaimed, running over to his wife, who was sitting up in her bed and smiling. She looked at him then her face twisted to a look of pain and Alia pushed them away.

"Everyone out," she said, "wait at the end of the hall and leave this to me, Sakura, and Lady Phana." Tybalt tried to protest but with one final shove, Alia had him out the door.

"Come on," Artan said, taking Tybalt by the arm, "let's go wait." With that, he pulled the worried, near frantic Tybalt down the hall.

"You'd think this would get easier the second time . . ." Yoake said to Yeldi. The boy looked to his older brother who was pacing nervously.

"Obviously not," Kyoki said flatly. Artan glanced at the clock above Tybalt's head then turned to Hana.

"How long do babies take?" he asked.

"How would I know?" she replied, "I mean, I learned about how birth works for humans but I have no idea how it works here . . ." The group sat in silence, the only sounds coming from Tybalt's anxious footsteps and muttered, worried questions. After four hours, Kyoki volunteered to go find food and after eight, Hana and Artan had nearly fallen asleep.

"You're going to wear a hole in the floor if you keep doing that." Yoake said to Tybalt who hadn't sat down. Just then, Alia poked her head out of the door and smiled at them.

"Congratulations," she said, "It's a boy."

Seconds later, the group stood around Sakura's bed, staring at the baby. Alia brought Mineh, who had been staying in the temple, over. The girl stared at her new brother in wonder, then turned to the back of the room.

"Hi," she said, walking over. The rest of the group was too transfixed by the baby to notice that Mineh had walked off, all except Alia, who watched with interest as the girl spoke to the death god, "You're not going to take the baby away, right?" Oares nodded.

"Nope," Phana said, throwing an arm around her twin, "I just dragged him along so he can see happiness."

"I've seen it," Oares said flatly, "You don't need to show off how happy you can make people. I'm leaving now."

"Wait!" Mineh exclaimed. She pointed to Yeldi, "You let Uncle Yeldi live, right?" The god nodded slowly, curious as to where the conversation was going, "And that made Daddy, and Mommy, and Big Sisters, and Yoake, and, well, and me very happy. Oh! and the bad man is gone so that means you took him away after he fought Uncle Yeldi, that made lots of people happy!"

Oares just stared at her dumbly, unsure of what to say. Just then, Alia walked over and beckoned the two deities to follow her into the hall. Phana followed along happily and Oares walked out as well, mostly as an excuse just to leave the room.

"She is going to be the next high priestess." the woman said, making Phana smile brightly.

"Awesome!" the goddess exclaimed, "she's so adorable!"

"Whoopee . . ." Oares muttered sarcastically and turned to walk off, but as he moved, Alia saw the ghost of a smile flash across his face.

"He's so cute!" Yoake said excitedly, watching the newborn sleep. He had hair like his father's, and a pair of slightly pointed ears, but had yet to open his eyes.

"What're you gonna call him?" Yoake asked as she touched the baby's soft cheek.

"Tybalt Junior!" Kyoki suggested.

"No." the parents said flatly.

"What about Erasure?" Yeldi said. Everyone looked at him, making him slightly uncomfortable.

"Perfect." Tybalt smiled.

"Erasure it is." Sakura said.

"Alright." Alia stepped up to the bed, with little Mineh in tow. "Mineh, would you like to say the blessing?"

"Really?" Mineh beamed. "I can?"

"Of course. You are the next high priestess."

"Yay!" the small child cheered and put her hand on her little brother's head. "Lady Phana, please bless this child and . . . um . . ." she stopped as she tried to remember the prayer.

"Lord." Alia prompted

"Lord . . . Oh! Lord Oares . . . make . . . um"

"When he passes."

"Right! When he passes into your realm, make his journey . . . far off in time?"

"Good."

"Mother Fate, um . . . keep his life full of happiness."

"Good."

"Um . . . now . . . oh right! I ask all the gods to bless Erasure and . . . uh . . . make him strong, and protect him in his times of need."

"Very good, Mineh." Alia said as the little girl finished.

Yeldi looked at his new nephew with a smile on his face. Yoake tapped him on the shoulder, and when he turned around she planted their lips together. He was a bit startled at first, but closed his eyes and wrapped his arms around her. Hana and Artan smiled at each other and copied their friends.

"Oh would you guys get a room!" Kyoki said.

"Jealous?" Artan teased, breaking the kiss with Hana for a moment, before she pulled him back.

"What? Oh hell no! You guys are making me nauseous." she giggled back, "besides, I get to kiss the cutest person in this room." She leaned down and kissed the baby affectionately, chastely, on the forehead. "I win."

The baby watched them laugh above him and giggled. Although he couldn't understand what was happening, he knew that this was a good place and, as the teens left the room, he looked up at his parents, knowing that the future was bright.